DENIS F. RATCLIFFE
Second Chances

DENIS F. RATCLIFFE
Second Chances

seren

seren is the book imprint of
Poetry Wales Press Ltd
Wyndham Street, Bridgend
Wales

A CIP Record for this book is available from
the British Cataloguing in Publication Data Office

ISBN 1-85411-151-5

*The publisher acknowledges the financial support of the
Arts Council of Wales*

Cover illustration: 'Bombed house and shop' by Will Evans
reproduced courtesy of the Glynn Vivian Art Gallery:
Swansea City Council Leisure Services Department

Printed in Plantin by WBC Book Manufacturers, Bridgend

Foreword

In September 1931 Frank and Doris were married at St Joseph's Catholic Church, Swansea. The bride wore pale blue; there are no photographs of the event. She was twenty years old, her new husband twenty-five.

Four months later their first child was born. To both newly-weds the marriage, unplanned and unprepared, was a deeply shaming affair, chilled by the cold wash of disapproval of the mores of the time: thundering priests and the wickedness of sex, the complete absence of State aid, the lingering social overburden of Victorian values, and not least, the difficult times of the economic depression.

Add to this Frank's family — seven brothers and sisters and a widowed mother who looked to Frank, her eldest son, for support as the only one in employment at a time when her other children were at the most difficult and expensive stage of teenage years. Besides, Frank's mother owned her own house, a rarity at the time, whilst Doris' family lived in rented accommodation on the 'wrong' side of town.

Then there was the society in which they moved and from which they drew their strength. 1880's immigrant Catholic Irish, many of whose matriarchs were only one generation away from the original settlers, and who guarded their religious and social inheritance with the fanaticism of the peasant. Thus the bride's pale blue wedding obeyed the rules of this tight-knit and defensive community, which declared that only virgins wore white. Today's bride, whose brides-maids may well be a selection of her own children, might snort at this intimidation and infringement of 'rights', but in 1931, marriage and pregnancy came in strict order, and woe betide any who breached this divine arrangement, by accident or design.

Frank had matriculated (equivalent to today's 'A' levels) at the age of sixteen in July 1922, and was considered bright enough to enter university the following year, rare enough among the working class of the time. Frank's father died in August 1922. Grants of public money for higher education were virtually unknown, and Frank had no choice but to seek work to support himself and his widowed mother.

His first job was 'picking' at the coal screens in Mountain Colliery, Gorseinon — dirty, noisy and outrageously unhealthy work that must surely have been frightening to a bespectacled teenage boy of academic bent. He never forgot it. When he was moved over the next two years to progressively cleaner and saner work, finally achieving clerk status in the colliery office, he entered a world where attention to detail, careful arithmetic and most important, 'keeping his head down', was all he could ask.

Demoralised by his early experience and avoiding every degree of risk inherent in ambition, he remained a clerk for the rest of his life until he died of cancer at sixty-two.

Doris left school at thirteen in 1923, with little but the basic skills of reading and writing. She stayed at home helping her mother keep house for father and four brothers. Her father died in 1928, and a year later, to help the family budget, she took a job as a waitress in a small Swansea hotel, until shortly before she married.

Photographs of the time show that she was not a beauty. Short and not well proportioned, she was plain featured and wiry haired, with an aggressive thrust to the lower jaw. She knew this, and it was a lifelong burden, often leading to outbursts of misdirected anger after bouts of dwelling on it. By some strange alchemy of reasoning she 'blamed' men who preferred pretty girls, and went in awe of film stars.

Her education had been almost entirely by nuns of the Catholic school, and she was not so much obsessed by religion as thoroughly browbeaten by it. She lived on an island of Catholic mysticism surrounded by a sea of nonconformist realism, and couldn't make head nor tail of the difference; she solved this difficulty by instinct: if you don't understand it, attack it, or at least shout at it — a strategy still used today by politicians.

The most worrying and urgent problem created by a hasty marriage is where to set up home. Quite unable to offer any kind of assistance, both widowed mothers watched helplessly as their newly-wed children rented two rooms in a mean terraced house not far from Frank's place of work. There they found themselves among Welsh-speakers — a tight, closed community whose daily fight against poverty and fear of illness or injury that would bring them final ruin forced them inwards, excluding strangers. Frank wore a suit and a collar and tie to work by this time, and was an object of suspicion to the terrace of miners and steel-workers; and the new-comers were *Catholics*.

And so, far from home and the comfort of family and maternal advice (eight miles was a terrible distance in 1931), surrounded by strangers and new neighbours who were not only suspicious but hostile, a difficult landlady, a severe shortage of money in the most expensive time of their lives, and with a burgeoning pregnancy, Doris did her best to set up home.

In March 1933 a second child was born. Life for Doris in those two small rooms went from difficult to impossible: with no running water, not even a kitchen sink, an outside lavatory a long walk from the first-floor rooms, no pram for the first-born toddler and babe-in-arms, a small stove for cooking, and a husband to care for, things were about to fall apart.

Frank's office and most of its staff was relocated to central Swansea in June 1933, and the young family returned to familiar territory, renting an old terrace house not far from both their parents. There, a third child was born in June 1934.

In 1936 the family moved to a house in a large, grim and dense council housing estate recently completed on a hill overlooking the town. Here, the family settled down to the task of growing up.

What follows is the story of D., Frank and Doris' second child, who grew up in this family.

Chapter One

He didn't hear a sound. Nothing. But he saw the muddy yellow flash and barrelling cloud of dust and fragments, the flailing wires and pipes as the belly of the aircraft exploded. He closed his eyes and ducked, far too late, and he felt his eyes sting and his scalp was peppered with volleying debris. The pieces which struck his dodging head sounded like drumsticks on a dead tree, but he heard nothing outside his skull.

A two-hundred mile an hour hurricane struck him, and he was swung violently around on his bolted-down swivel stool as the hole in the floor of the Lincoln bomber scooped up the air in full flight. He began to fight for breath as the dust and fragmented structural parts of the aircraft swirled around in a choking soup inside the fuselage. He was on his hands and knees, head down, willing himself not to cough, not to draw involuntary gulps of air. Better to swallow the mouthful of grit than to breathe it in.

He was sliding backwards. The floor of the aircraft shook and trembled. He tried to open his eyes, but he saw light with only one, through a thick curtain of tears. The other wouldn't work. He didn't know why. He felt no pain, it just wouldn't work. He dug his fingers into the rails on the floor. Fear penetrated his confusion, deafness and near blindness: if he slid any further he would fall out of the hole in the floor he had glimpsed before the assault on his senses had begun. The plane had been flying at eight thousand feet. There were no windows in the military aircraft, but he had tracked the slow climb on ground search radar ten minutes ago, when they had levelled off and throttled back to cruise. It would be a long way to fall.

The floor tilted, steeper. The rails to which he clung ran the wrong way, along the length of the fuselage instead of across it. He couldn't hold himself and began to slip, tearing his fingertips on the fastening rivets. He began to sob with naked fear. He mustn't fall out of that hole.

Time-stretched slow motion set in. Things happened silently, slowly, invisibly. Two hands caught him at the shoulders of his overalls and hauled him across the floor, then three hands wedged him firmly around a stool fixed to the floor. He clung to it, lying on his side and thrusting his elbows around the pedestal column, pressing it to his chest. He opened his one eye and saw an impression of movement. Must be Squadron Leader Tippett, he thought. He had been in the aft turret with Warrant Officer Leslie, monitoring the radio gear. Perhaps both of them. He was grateful. What the hell was happening. He hoped and prayed there was a plan of action to pull things out of this confusion.

The final violence was fearful. Unable to see or hear, he was dashed forward as the mortally damaged aircraft struck the ground. He felt the bones in his upper arms break where they clung to the seat column. He felt himself thrown through the air. His left knee struck a hard object and threw his leg backwards. As he flailed his arms in self-protection he felt the first white-hot shock of pain.

He had stopped falling. It was cold. He lay on grass, and it was wet. He felt hands move him. He screamed with pain; it came in all colours of the rainbow. Someone pressed his hand to reassure him, and consciousness faded.

And so the cold, damp morning of the twentieth of March 1954 passed, in a field just seven kilometres from the small town of Neuruppin, East Germany. He would be twenty-one years old on the twenty-fifth of the month.

★　★　★

'Just indicate yes or no, old chap.' The smooth cultured tones of a senior officer, gazing in concern at his pain-wracked face, reached him over an orchestra of buzz and whistling in his ears.

'With your head of course, young man.' A second voice, a clone of the first but from a different direction. He turned his head to the second speaker, and was engulfed in a slashing red cloud of agony. He began a shout of pain, and with a huge effort modified it to a manful groan. The sound seemed to come from inside his head, and didn't help him at all. He dare not move anything. The pain was universal, and consumed every limb and most other parts. His own heartbeat became his worst enemy: every pulse sent a fresh shaft of agony through his entire body. In such circumstances, turning his head was a major challenge, and he had been beaten this time. He wouldn't move his head again under any condition. They could shoot him if they wanted. He wouldn't mind. But he wasn't going to use his head for anything, not a nod or a shake.

'Can you hear me, old chap?' came the first voice again. 'Nod if you can.'

'And perhaps you can shake your head just once if you can't,' said the second voice. 'Don't exert yourself.'

He nearly laughed.

'He can't hear you, Squadron Leader.'

'How can you tell that, sir?' The second voice sounded surprised.

'It's here. In his medical record. He's deaf. Temporarily, anyway.'

There was a long silence. D. hoped they had gone away.

'Then why are we here, sir?'

'To ask him questions, dammit.'

'Of course, sir. Yes.'

There was further silence. D. opened his eyes. Or one of them. The other was bandaged over.

He hadn't moved his head again after the last turn, and he found himself gazing at the last speaker. He saw the smile, the impeccable teeth, the sporty moustache. He had no wings over his left breast pocket. Non-flyer, administrative johnny, thought D. He had no medical insignia, either. So what did he want? thought D.

He closed his eye, unable to extract meaning from the words. Even this tiny activity caused him more pain. He tried to level off his breathing to reduce the effect of movement it caused in his body. The outside world gradually ceased to exist as he concentrated more and more on controlling the awful pain. He wondered if he could track the speed and route of the pulses of his heart through his body — which limb flashed agony first, and then next ....

At the foot of the bed stood a nurse. She was older than himself, and he was not surprised at this. Everyone around him seemed older, wiser, cleverer than him. There in the aircraft, and here, in the hospital. Everybody seemed so goddam sure of themselves. They all knew what came next and were prepared for it, but no one warned him or advised him what to do. He was on his own, he felt; an extra, surplus, to be ushered irritably into the nearest vacant corner. In his present state he was an embarrassing nuisance.

'I'm Sister Catch' she said. At least, it sounded like that. D. wondered how it was spelled. An orderly stood behind her, a young man dressed like an attendant at a lunatic asylum, with a long white coat buttoned up one side.

'This is Handel. Handel Stone-Jones.' Was there a flicker of a smile on her lips?

'Handel will look after your daily needs' said Sister Catch. 'If you have any serious problems, just press the buzzer. I'll be in my office.'

She smiled, and he tried to smile in response and gave up just in time as he sensed a fresh round of agony starting at his jaw, which was encased in a framework of steel bars, long butterfly screw rods and metal stays welded into the thick plaster cast across his shoulders. He didn't know where the buzzer was, and couldn't afford to search for it. Why couldn't they give him something for the pain?

Sister Catch moved away in a rustle of starch and cleanliness, her soft-soled shoes squeaking on the shining wood-block floor. He wondered what a 'serious problem' would be, to qualify him for her attendance. She had said it in a tone that implied that he would be breaking tradition if he actually used the buzzer. A sudden thought struck him: it was not expected of him to use it; its use would bypass Handel Stone-Jones, and that would offend him. Risking further pain he managed a small sigh. He could not afford enemies in his present state.

Stone-Jones stood looking at him. The man studied him, more out of curiosity than sympathy or understanding, then picked up the folder of notes left behind by Sister Catch. He moved around the bed, checking off the points of interest as he went. Both legs swathed in thick, soft bandages around metal splints. Left leg under a cage to keep off the weight of the blankets. Left ankle in plaster. Both arms in plaster, the left extending to the fingers. Ribs bandaged from armpits to navel. Neck brace, jaw brace and left shoulder all joined into one unresisting framework of metal and plaster. A black eye and huge fluffy bandage around the head that looked like a cossack's hat, finished off the list. Drips, tubes, feeds and catheters trailing in a bird's nest of confusion.

'You're in an awful state, aren't you' said Stone-Jones encouragingly. 'Never mind. We'll soon have you out of here. We'll get you well, even if we kill you in the process.' He gave a guffaw and slapped the cage over the legs. D. screamed obligingly. Pain ran through his body in red hot waves as Stone-Jones looked at him disdainfully. 'It doesn't hurt that much, surely' he said uncertainly. D. glared at him. Their first contact was not promising. Stone-Jones' accent placed him as a Welsh-speaker, probably from Carmarthen way. D. had not spoken during his six days at the hospital, and no one knew that he too was Welsh, albeit from anglicised Swansea, where hardly anyone spoke Welsh and where the citizens considered their accent and general behaviour more civilised than the 'Valley people', as his mother knew them.

For six weeks D.'s battle against pain continued. Setbacks were regular and frequent. Medical officers in uniform visited him, poking and prodding, muttering to each other in a secret language, scrambled egg on their caps, forepeaks obscuring their faces. The only thing said to him was a detached 'Does that hurt?' and he never had to answer as his anguished cries spoke for him. An hour

11

after their visits, a white-coated medic would arrive, Sister Catch in attendance, and a needle would be thrust into his body somewhere — an arm, sometimes his hand, his neck or his thigh. He awoke later, his condition altered, in more pain, sometimes an extra plaster, sometimes a limb freed from casing and bandage, to be replaced later, with added pain, in a different place, the limb frozen in a different position. He began to feel exhausted, and ceased to take interest in what they were doing to him. He accepted their busy, self-centred officiations as a dog accepted bad treatment from a thoughtless owner. There came the time, in the small hours of yet another sleepless night, when he asked, out loud, 'How the hell did I get here?' and he gazed through the window next to his bed and tried to make sense of the smells of spring, and the owls hooting, and the rustle of new leaves on the trees.

Then one day the tubes were pulled. From his nose, his bladder, his rectum. He wished Sister Catch did not have to remove the catheter to his bladder, humiliatingly taped to his penis with sticking plaster. She apologised, more embarrassed than he, as she gently prised away the tape. He could have eased her trouble by telling her that the skin was no more sensitive to plaster peeling than the inside of the arm, but he didn't. He just wanted the embarrassment over.

At last it was done, and she bundled away the piping and little boxes on wheels and he didn't see her again for three days.

He could use his right hand now despite its painful stiffness. He was looking forward to eating the first food to pass his lips for many weeks. This morning his jaw had been released from its metal clamps. He had been warned that his jaw would be stiff and sore, and it was. He settled for soup finally, giving up on the toast. Stone-Jones sulked at his change of mind, but there was no other choice.

'Letter for you. In Sister's office.' Stone-Jones shot past his bed, officiously consumed by deeds to be done to less demanding but more technically interesting patients in the next enclave. The general hospital layout was designed around a broad corridor, ten feet wide, with small four-bed enclaves to one side, and offices, toilets and special treatment rooms on the other. He had a four-bed unit to himself, though he could hear the chatter and occasional laughter from others along the master corridor. Sometimes the louder laughter was hushed by an orderly. He wondered why, but even not knowing he was grateful. He couldn't believe that with such evil pain in the world there could be room for laughter.

So there was a letter for him. He was foxed by this. What could he do about it? He hardly ever saw anyone but Stone-Jones, and he had disappeared. He hadn't seen Sister Catch for three days. The scrambled egg surgeons he hadn't seen for four days, but he couldn't ask them to pass him a letter anyway. Where was it?

He gave up. Perhaps it was another form. Air Ministry. He'd filled in dozens in the last two weeks. At least Sister Catch had filled them in for him, waving her pen with 'Oh, we'll just say "on duty", all right?' and similar broad answers to questions he didn't understand or even couldn't hear above the pain.

Stone-Jones tramped past again. He swore he could feel Stone-Jones, despite the twelve-inch thick concrete floor of the ultra-modern hospital, as he came on duty in the early morning. He would be awakened from his pain-wracked doze by the vibrating thump of the orderly's boots crossing the threshold of the staff entrance, and his private retreat from the uncaring pretence at a daytime routine would be finished. Temperature-taking, insincere enquiries after his well-being, pulse-taking, and then shaving, washing and towelling, then, his painful parts thoroughly aroused, an hour of purgatory to breakfast.

'Can you read it for me?' croaked D. He hadn't been sat up in his bed yet, and wouldn't be able to hold it properly in his one free hand.

'Sorry, old chap. Busy right now. I'll tell Sister Catch. She'll be here soon.' And Stone-Jones stamped his way into the distance.

He waited until afternoon tea. Stone-Jones tutted irritably at his reminder and hoofed it to Sister Catch's office. He returned and slapped it on the bedside tray.

'You can read it yourself now, can't you? I have to get going.'

The envelope had been opened. No surprise. His previous letters, all two of them, had had to be read to him, and Sister Catch had prepared to read this one to him too. For some reason she hadn't appeared to read him this one, but that didn't matter now.

With some difficulty he manipulated the single sheet inside the envelope to a reading position. The first sentence told him why Sister Catch hadn't been to see him and to read him his letter.

The letter was from his mother. This was the first one she had sent him at the hospital. He had written three to his parents. Or at least Sister Catch had written them. Necessarily a bit stiff. Modestly understating his condition, reserve modifying his plea for comfort at his time of greatest distress. In five weeks he'd had no reply, and in the last letter Sister Catch wrote for him he had insisted on enclosing a self-addressed envelope complete with stamp, in the hope that this would make it easier for either of his parents to write.

And now he lay, awkwardly holding the single page between two skin-peeling fingers as he read the storm of abuse and bad temper shouting at him. The page was one long sentence, without punctuation. A raging outburst of incoherent insults, and he picked out the words 'exaggeration' and further down, 'conceited' and 'you always looked for attention' and more.

She hadn't understood. He had antagonised her with the self-addressed envelope. He should have known better. She was not only not very intelligent but she was defensive about it.

He refolded the sheet of paper and edged it back into the envelope. He laid it on the bedcover and gazed out through the window. It was a flawless late spring afternoon, the heat of the day's warm May sun beginning to tell. He perspired gently, and drifted into a light sleep, tracing an answer to the question he had asked himself often of late — 'What am I doing here?' ....

Chapter Two

Christmas 1939. He was six years old and he dearly wanted a teddy bear. There were hundreds here in front of him in Ben Evans' department store. Brown, black, white and some in between. They had large dark eyes, and every one seemed to be a friend looking for a friend. He looked at them longingly as his want turned into a deep need.

His mother had different ideas. 'You're a boy,' she snapped unsympathetically. 'Boys don't have teddies. They're for girls.' And she pulled him along, away from the bears, whose eyes now seemed sorrowful at his going as tears welled in his own.

He began to cry and his father picked him up to hold him on his arm. 'Over here,' he said. 'See? A smashing car race. With its own track. And two cars.' An attempt to divert his attention from the bears as he strained over his father's shoulder to see the last of them. He finally lost sight of them and resigned himself to his parents' decision. He had never seen anything as wonderful as these shelves full of teddy bears. The clockwork racing cars with their own tracks held no interest for him at all. He had never seen a real racing car, and any other real car was a rare sight. There were none at all in his street apart from Mr Brown the miner's, who worked at night and hid his car under a tarpaulin in his front garden in daytime so that nobody ever saw it.

Then it was done. His father tucked the big cardboard box under his arm and led the way out of the store. There followed the journey across mid-town Swansea, mostly blacked out as a war measure. Ugly grey and black buildings, rocking pavement slabs that shot a fountain of dirty water into the shoes of unwary walkers as they stepped on a yielding corner, the bedding sand long washed out by unending winter rains. The sound of women's voices loudly complaining of the lack of lights, tarty high-heeled shoes an undignified hazard in the uncertain murk.

At intervals they encountered groups of people clustered in a tight knot, blocking the pavement and forcing passers-by into the road. They spoke Welsh, the stop-start undulating accents standing out over the town dwellers' English.

'Silly people. Blocking the pavement like that,' snapped D.'s mother. 'They live next door to each other and just because they're

15

in town on the same day they behave as though they haven't seen each other for years.'

He didn't understand. 'Who are they, Mam?'

'Valley people,' said his mother disapprovingly. 'Welsh, they are.'

'Hold on tight, D,' his father snapped. He could tell that his father was in short temper as he was lifted by one hand over a pool of rainwater collected in a badly cambered pavement edge. He kept his silence as he twirled in the air and landed sideways, stepping desperately to keep his balance. His mother tutted in annoyance. 'Don't you go falling now. I've got enough to do without cleaning you up.'

The rain fell gently as the occasional car washed by, a cloud of water drops thrown up from its rear wheels glittering in the traffic lights.

And finally the bus queue. A groan of suppressed rage from his mother, a grunt from his father as they joined the long line of silent, damp, unhappy people.

'At least three,' said his father with authority. D. thought about this for some time. He wasn't all that good at counting, but he was certain that there were more than three people in front of them.

'Three what, Dad?'

'Busloads,' his father said in a voice which told him that he didn't want to talk. D. couldn't grasp the meaning of three busloads until his mother said, 'We'll be here all night. Do you think we could walk, Frank?'

His father said no. They were some way down the queue already, he said. And it was true. Since they had joined the queue, large numbers of people had fallen in behind them, and they were no longer at the back.

The single-deck buses they waited for stood silent and dark in a parallel side street. D.'s mother complained unhappily as the crews of at least four buses sat together in the leading parked vehicle, the only one visible.

'Can't they see us waiting?' she snapped.

'Timetables, I expect,' said D.'s father in a low, embarrassed voice.

'They don't care,' said D.'s mother loudly, seeking support from the crowd around her. No one joined her and she fell silent. D. sensed his father's irritation, and kept quiet too.

The rain fell and time dragged on. It grew colder as they stood, and people began to shuffle their feet and hunch their shoulders. Occasionally his father changed hands, pushing the large flat box

16

under his other arm and grasping D.'s hand with the other hand. Now and again the traffic fell silent, and the bus crews could be heard, loudly laughing and joshing one another, which enraged his mother.

'Listen to them. Just listen. Enjoying themselves, they are, while we're out here getting soaked, catching our death in this cold.' She glared at the leading bus, tight-lipped. 'They ought to do something about it. I've a good mind to complain.'

They got colder and wetter.

'About time, too. The lazy lot.' From his lowly position stacked among the adults D. sensed the crowd stir. As he peered past his father he saw that the driving lights of the leading bus had been switched on, and he heard the engine start up.

As the bus rounded the corner there were groans of complaint. 'Not ours', rippled through the queue. 'Elphin Crescent', was the resentful mutter. D.'s mother was furious. She complained loudly, and drew much attention from those around her. His father remained silent and offered no support on the grounds that making a fuss would never produce another bus.

There were hundreds of unlucky souls here, waiting in the rain. They would all, eventually, be hauled to the top of the town to the vast spread of cheerless council houses, grim boxes of rendered brick in tight rows packing both sides of winding narrow roads. Architectural variety ventured no further than to alternate blocks of two and three identical dwellings separated by privet hedges. To walk along any street in the endless, shapeless complex was very like treading a large-scale maze, its sameness confusing and wearying.

They got on a bus at last. D. clambering up high metal-edged steps, being pushed forward to the nearest empty seat. The journey was slow. Sometimes the bus climbed the steepest parts of the hill in bottom gear, the bad-tempered conductor staggering as the gear changes jerked the bus and upset his self-printing ticket machine.

It was a short walk from their stop to home. They walked in silence. His mother was in a bad mood, D. felt. His father was angry with her in retaliation. With the instinct of a pet dog he stayed silent.

And finally home. A semi-detached surrounded by a tall privet hedge with a strong, solid iron gate to the street just like every other home in the street.

Inside, there was the front room. The 'parlour' as D.'s mother firmly declared it. Behind, a tiny kitchen, bare unplastered brick walls carelessly painted a colourless green. Two tones of green — dark to the halfway joint and lighter above.

The lavatory had the same daring decorative arrangement, being more or less part of the kitchen, only a rickety door separating the two rooms.

The metal-framed windows dripped condensation, and the ugly anthracite cooking stove bulked large in the small room, throwing out a mild token of its function. A single gas ring stood on top of the stove, its rubber feed pipe dangerously perished by contact with the hot cast iron. D.'s mother cooked chips on the gas ring because the stove was never hot enough. When Uncle Denis visited he would stir the chips to break them up and give them crispy edges, which was great, but D.'s mother got annoyed by it, and ticked off his uncle. Uncle Denis would make a face and put his stirring fork down.

Tonight the house was silent and cold when they entered. His mother began to complain. She would have to get a meal for them all, and nothing was ready. The fire was low, the oven cool, the blackout sheet was not in position, she wanted to go to the toilet, she had to unpack the shopping, to collect his sister next door, take his outdoor clothing off, and on and on ....

When this was all over there was an early bedtime. He was glad. He sensed a looming fight between his parents. His father would not do battle in front of him and his sisters, and his mother took advantage of this. She administered a sly kick to his father's shins and turned to her tasks in sullen, silent rage. His father's face was a mask, tight-lipped and pale; silent, angry.

His father was different from the rest of the fathers in the street. He was tall, thin and wore glasses. He went to work in the daytime and wore a suit. All around the men worked shifts, walked huge distances to and from their work at unearthly hours, and wore thick, dirty clothes which they took off as soon as they came home. There was a coal miner, a steel-furnace hand, a railwayman, a bus driver, a fireman, a hotel cleaner, a man who did things at the Manesmann steel tube works and so on. His father was a clerk who worked in an office, from nine in the morning until six in the evening. And Saturdays from nine to twelve noon. He was always clean and seemed to know everything. He had a slightly roman nose and a small chin, with dark wavy hair, cut short at the sides so that from the back above the collar he was white with a black topping, an unsettling sight after a visit to the barber. This upset his mother, who seemed ashamed of his father's lack of interest in his appearance.

D.'s bed was very old and creaked at every breath. Bedclothes consisted of an undersheet and scraps of old curtains and a shawl over him. In childhood innocence he never challenged this arrangement, though on bitter winter nights as the loose pattern of covers fell apart, he envied his sisters' eiderdown and woollen counterpane. Tonight, it was damp and not too cold. His younger sister would sleep in the double bed in the next bedroom on her own because his elder sister was spending the night with their grandmother. It would be a peaceful night. Normally the first hour of bedtime was spent listening to his sisters fighting for room in the double bed, until his father came upstairs and laid about them, the girls screaming, a blackmail ploy as their mother stood at the foot of the stairs wringing her hands, wailing about the neighbours and what they would think. His father would ignore them all, as he beat the girls in the manly belief of his number one position in the household and his absolute right and duty to impose discipline and order.

In the morning there would be no heating and breakfast was cornflakes lightly dressed in Rees' watery milk. When his elder sister was there he would clutch her hand and set off for school. They would be met by a neighbour's girl at the end of the street, immensely older than they at twelve, who would see them safely through the streets to the Catholic school in town. There, the nuns ruled supreme in the infants' school.

There would be a rustle of nervous dread as Mother Superior made the rounds first thing in the morning. Miss Banbury, their teacher, smiled nervously and placatingly, like a dog rolling on its back in submission to a superior foe, and every child in the class would freeze. Mother Superior liked it. She smiled a thin, mean, Irish smile of deprived womanhood as her eyes glittered in pleasure at the supreme authority of suppression that she enjoyed. These six- and seven-year olds were other women's children, and she felt nothing for them or for their teacher, who did.

There would be a secret, whispered exchange with Miss Banbury, a large flowery woman with children of her own in the upper school. She would nod agreeably as Mother Superior talked, and show exercise books, attendance registers, giant sheets of ruled paper showing records of marks, stars, red ticks and black ticks, occasionally black crosses. The children would never know what these notations meant, and certainly never cared. The only displayed ladder of achievement was the chart, pinned to the wall, of 'Children of Africa', cut into 240 steps at a penny a time, where a child's name written on a flagged pin would climb to the top for a pound. After six months most of the children were stuck at the shillingsworth. Only Patrick Kinsella, whose father was a scrap-iron

19

dealer, strained at the ten-shilling mark. He came most mornings with two pennies, and sat back in his seat to await the official announcement of his personal achievement as he advanced beyond the reach of poorer parents. Most of the children hated him without knowing why.

School was not unpleasant. Indeed, the worst thing about it was the lengthy journey to get there, through hostile streets which seemed to swarm with gangs of hostile ruffians who waged war on passers-through, especially if they were Catholics. Going home it was worse. The infants' school finished the day half an hour before the local senior school, but it took so long to walk home that there was never the chance to escape the attentions of at least two gangs on the way. In fact, mistreatment was quite mild, mostly confined to terrible threats and a fifty yard chase along the street, out of foreign territory.

Today the class spent most of the morning banging tambourines and drums, with some arithmetic in between using cardboard coins. They were left on their own quite often, and that was when the scandal of Mary O'Donoghue happened. She came to school without knickers. Not uncommon at that time, and some children came to school without shoes, even in winter. But Mary O'Donoghue was indiscreet. At seven years old she was the oldest in the class, and as Mother Superior put it, she should have known better. Mary sat down on the floor cross-legged to pound her tambourine, and soon gathered a crowd of curious boys gazing in wonderment at the complete absence of a willie. Mary battered on, unaware of the stir she had created until catastrophe struck in the form of Mother Superior.

'Mary O'Donoghue!' Heads turned at the wild anguish in Mother Superior's voice. 'Stand up at once, you sinful creature!' The boys began to disperse, sensing all was not well. 'Come here, you boys. You, you and you.' She dragged them all, about four or five of them, by the ear to a corner of the classroom. She stood over them, white-faced and shivering with rage. 'You will stay here while I send for Father Murphy,' she shouted. D., among the crowd of boys, wondered who Father Murphy was, but knew it must be serious. The pecking order was well established: teachers at the bottom, the nuns, then Mother Superior, then a priest.

'You come here with me,' she snarled to the unhappy Mary O'Donoghue as she snatched the girl's hand and hauled her out of the class and along the corridor.

That afternoon when school finished each of the boys was handed a note in a sealed envelope. None of them knew what was in it, and Miss Banbury, with an unhappy look, tucked the envelopes into the boys' pockets with firm instructions not to open the envelopes, and to hand them to their fathers.

D.'s mother opened his envelope, and read it with tightening lips. She gazed at D., who sat at the table eating cheese on toast, with loathing.

'Dirty little boy,' she whispered. 'Why did you do it?'

'Do what, Mam?'

'Look up that girl's skirt.' His mother stumbled over a more clear explanation, but this seemed to serve. D. was perplexed. He said nothing because he understood nothing of what his mother said.

'Guilty, aren't you?', she announced dramatically.

'What's that, Mam? Guilty? What's that mean?'

'Just wait till your father comes home,' she said between compressed lips. 'Just wait. You nasty little boy.'

His father read the note when he came home. His mother sat, serious, at the table, while his father ate after reading the note. He seemed annoyed. 'It's nothing,' he said shortly.

'I think it's disgusting,' said his mother. 'That a son of mine ... ' she paused, fashioning the theatre, ' ... should do such a thing.'

'It's nothing,' said his father again. 'It's not worth bothering with. Forget it.'

His mother rose. 'Well. If that's your attitude ... Well!'

D. forgot it too. But the boys were never left unsupervised with the girls again. They were even separated at other lessons, the boys seated farthest away from the door, and the girls let out of the class first at break and at the end of the day.

Christmas came, and went. His father and Uncle Cliff played with his racing cars on the parlour floor and his sisters fought and squabbled in the kitchen. Uncle Cliff was in the R.A.F. and would marry his favourite aunt, Maureen. Auntie Maureen was different to his mother, she didn't snap and shout at him and she seemed to know that he was always hungry. His mother said he was greedy, and to teach him a lesson she gave extra pieces of toast or cake to his sisters. He would come to suppose that appetite should be hidden, and indulgence secret. Besides, Auntie Maureen talked differently. The raw Swansea accent of her birth had been modified by travel and sounded grand, whilst Uncle Cliff wore the officer's uniform of an Observer. He flew in Sunderlands, which were huge flying boats, and D. had difficulty with the image of a boat which flew until Uncle Cliff showed him a photograph of himself with eleven other men standing at a dockside with a huge aircraft floating on the water close behind them.

They had had two turkeys that Christmas. His father had brought them home with a sackful of cigarettes in boxes of hundreds and two hundreds. Gifts from business friends, he said. It would be a long time before D. fully understood.

They ate turkey for the next ten days. It seemed to last for ever. Even his father complained at the nineteenth meal of bread, pickles and cold turkey. There was a sense of relief in the household when the last bones had been picked clean and his father had broken them up to scatter on the garden.

His father was an enthusiastic gardener. The size of their garden compensated for the cramped, simple council house his family struggled to live in. The earth was good, the layout regular, sloping gently away from the house to catch most of the sun in summer. In winter it was a pig. At the end of the garden the ground of the hillside fell away so steeply that only the roofs of the next row of houses were visible, even from their own bedroom windows, and the north-west winds hit the side of their house after a long fetch all the way from the Loughor estuary ten miles away.

Every year the garden produced huge quantities of carrots, potatoes, beans and cabbage. His father grew nothing else. His mother was at best an adequate cook and became very angry if he or his sisters were bold enough to leave anything on the plate. The cabbage was the worst. Soggy, tasteless, if wet cardboard could be discounted as a flavour, and mountains of it many times a week. The only benefit from it was the bonus his father paid him to pick off the caterpillars in the garden — a halfpenny for twenty and a penny for fifty. Even at six years old going on seven it was not difficult to divide a day's catch into twenties to maximise earnings. D. explained the tactic to his elder sister, Jean, but she thought it was dishonest, and eventually split on him to his father, who refused to pay him per catch, instead instituting a system of weekly reckoning. The catch dropped to zero until his father installed a penalty system of extra dish-washing to raise it to a grudging penny's-worth a week at high season.

His father was absent-minded, and a victim of habits. Only that Christmas the family had gone to the pantomime at the Grand Theatre, and some way through his father had leaned towards his mother, muttered something which brought a look of disgust to her face, and edged his way along the row of seats to the nearest aisle. As he stepped into the aisle away from the last seat he genuflected as though in church, and walked away towards the toilets totally unaware of what he had done. His mother, alerted by the first of the sniggers from the surrounding audience, saw him rise to his feet as he completed his act of reverence.

'Oh, my God!' she whispered.

'What is it, Mam?'

'Nothing. Don't look. Just watch the stage,' she snapped.

But D. had seen it. He had wondered where his father was going, but didn't dare ask. Instead, he had watched him, and had seen more than his mother. He wondered what she would say when he came back. Judging from his mother's reaction to even the little she had seen, D. concluded that his father had done something to embarrass her.

His father was ill at ease with his children. They seemed to embarrass him. Throughout his childhood D. would learn little from him — no sport or social activity, not even arithmetic when he later went to grammar school, though his mother would say often enough in years to come that his father was a clever man, and had been prevented from going to university only because his father had died in 1922, leaving no money. D.'s longer-lasting memories would be his father's furious bad temper as he hammered away at a pair of his children's shoes under repair, wasting good drinking time on a Friday evening as he struggled to cut shapes out of sheets of leather, unyielding and a quarter of an inch thick, to fit the soles of small shoes. Shaped leather and rubber soles were sold freely by Woolworth's, to fit any size of shoe, but his father swore by the economies of large pieces, and paid the penalties of unreasoned conviction in sweat and slashed fingers. Not that his cobbling tools were adequate: they were made out of a table knife, specially sharpened to cut the Sunday roast, a hammer, and an iron last with three different-sized iron tongues on short legs. The last was very useful, and served endless purposes, as an anvil, a breaker for large lumps of coal and wood, a step for his mother, who had short legs, to reach the top shelf of the pantry, and as a nail-straightener for his father. These cobbling tools, with the addition of a huge pair of pliers, were his father's entire home maintenance kit. To make matters worse he was left handed, and every stroke of the hammer invited sympathy and sometimes laughter, since no one had ever seen such awkward movements.

Today it was D.'s shoes. For a week now he had had a hole, worn right through the sole. His mother put a small square of cardboard over the hole and teased his foot into the shoe with a warning not

23

to play in any puddles. But inevitably, it rained, and the cardboard patch lasted no further than twenty paces before dissolving into mache, and it became painful to walk on, so he took it out and got his foot wet. It was not easy to decide which was worse, one wet foot or both shoes full of sharp nail ends after his father had replaced the soles. If the nails hurt, his father required proof, which was not easy to show, until one day his thick woollen socks fell apart in the wash. This earned him a clout around the ears from his mother, who accused him of 'doing things' to the socks. At an evening conference with his father, his mother pressing for further discipline, there was reluctant acknowledgement that the damage to the socks had been caused by nails in D.'s shoes. Thereafter, actual flowing of blood was not required to prove that nails intruded into the shoes. Socks were more expensive than pain.

Winter 1940 passed into D.'s birthday at the end of March. It was a sunny day, and in a daydream he gazed at the shadows cast on the shabby two-toned walls as the low sun shone through the high metal-framed windows. He had a new teacher, and was already, at seven years old, in a segregated class of boys only. Miss O'Rourke was speaking to the class about the lesson, English.

'Famous men,' she announced. 'I want you to write about the good deeds of a famous man. I want at least a whole page. In your best writing.'

The boys were nonplussed. They didn't know any famous men. And there weren't any famous women that they didn't know either.

Miss O'Rourke saw their difficulty. 'Have any of you heard of Adolf Hitler?' she asked. Most of the boys said, 'Yes, Miss.'

'Well, write about him. He has done wonders for his country. He has created full employment, saved the poor and built many hospitals and made the country very rich. Now, continue on your own, in your own words.'

They dutifully bent over their exercise books, writing the date and a title. There, most of them stopped, and began looking at one another in a state of block. D. wanted to start with Czechoslovakia, but couldn't spell it, and similarly ground to a halt.

Miss O'Rourke regarded them with tightened lips. She was in no mood to offer hints that might exploit self-expression. Her class was a universally stupid lot.

'Right. You will write down what I say,' she declared and began slowly to dictate her story. Hitler, apparently, was one of her heroes, and for half an hour she trotted out a list of his achievements, her thick Irish accent causing the boys occasional difficulties of spelling.

They learned about autobahns and the importance of punctual trains, of health camps and rallies, clean streets and uniforms as incentives to pride, and the social benefits of concentration camps instead of jails for wrongdoers.

But 1940 wore on to summer and the dreadful events in May and June, and Miss O'Rourke left their school and never came back. The children practised evacuation for air raids and wound their way placidly along the street out of school to the Catholic church, a substantial building on the lines of a cathedral, with flying buttresses and a crypt. The children took shelter in the bricked-up flying buttresses, which would normally have been open cloisters but for the awful view over the slum backyards of industrial built-by-the-mile housing. The air raid precautions were not a total success. Most of the children lived nearby, and ran off home as soon as they could and stayed there, despite warnings from the fearsome headmaster, a small, thin, silent man with protruding eyes, a sharp bony nose, receding chin and thin wooden lips which opened and closed rapidly when he was angry.

The cane was his favourite teaching method and the Head's favourite subject was punctuality — being late for assembly, regardless of cause, was punishable with a cane stroke, delivered with an amazing ferocity across the palm of the hand. One stroke was enough to cripple the hand for a whole morning or afternoon, and it was impossible to use a pen or pencil. Sometimes a wrongdoer could be heard receiving two cane strokes on each hand, and classes along the corridor where the punishment was given would freeze, waiting and then shrinking as the unlucky boy began to whimper and then howl as the caning proceeded. There would be whispered discussion about who the unlucky boy was, and what he had done to earn the punishment, but the unrest would be stifled quickly by a threatening invitation to join the beating. Besides, all the teachers in the boys' school had canes of their own and they were used frequently, without reference to the Head.

As the Germans thundered across north-west France and the British Army scattered to the coast and Dunkirk, things began to change. The war began to get serious. At D.'s grandmother's home, his father talked with Uncle Bernard. Bernard was the tallest in a tall family, and he cultivated a deep voice to harmonise the concept of bigness. Nobody remarked on his voice, and D. assumed that everyone turned a deaf ear to this small vanity. But he was D.'s favourite uncle. He talked to him as an equal, never teased him like his other uncle, Bill, and told him things about life that his own father never did. Bernard was a kind of engineer, and explained to him how iron turned rusty, and how frost formed. He was knowledgeable and wise.

Now he leaned towards the large map of Europe pasted to the wall of the kitchen, over the table. He tapped a spot on the coast of France, coloured pale blue, and said with gravity and certainty, 'If the Germans get as far as this, we've had it. We won't be able to stop them.'

His grandmother looked worried and his father was silent. In the event, they were stopped, or at least they stopped.

The solid steel gates of the houses on the council estate were cut off at the roots and tossed on a lorry which crawled along the street, not stopping as the teams of men using acetylene cutters felled the gates, two more hurling them into heaps amid clouds of dust. Gangs of small boys followed their progress at a respectable distance, and mourned the loss of their casual swings and other games they played around the gates. One of their most precious sanctions against disagreeable neighbours had been to hammer a wedge into the simple catch, to the fury of the owner and a warning to others. Mr Horner, a war service-exempt fireman, had come in for so much attention that he had enclosed his gate catch in a bolted sheet metal gadget that only he could use, much to the distress of his wife, a small, bespectacled, red-haired woman who had panicked and called the police to release her from her front garden when she had first tried to use it. But Mr Horner, a short, squat, grossly muscled, bald man with no eyebrows and prominent eyes, who hated the boys in the street because he was convinced they stole his flowers, and sometimes chased them away with awful threats, had no answer to the boys' revenge. After the gates were taken away, they turned their attention to his hedge, a splendid, and rare, exercise in skill and patience. There was a large road frontage, and Mr Horner had meticulously cut his hedge into smooth, faultlessly accurate semi-circles, rising to peaks crowned with topiaried birds.

It really was a splendid hedge, and deserved a better fate than overtook it. After Mr Horner had confiscated a cricket ball found in his geraniums, the boys declared war on his hedge. Always making certain that the family was not at home, and after a council of war at which volunteers were identified, the birds were cut off, one by one, over a period of weeks. Next, they 'walked' on the hedge, snapping and tearing growth, creating large holes and gaps. By the end of the summer, the hedge was a wreck, and Mr Horner had given up, cutting it to a bare two feet high, and ceremonially burning the cuttings on the pavement outside, an action he regretted when the local council charged him £12 for repairs to the tarmac.

All over the town, non-essential steelwork was cut up and taken away. Miles of railings disappeared around churches and institutions, even private houses. Playing fields and football grounds, railways and factories, parks and farms were thrown open, and the boys in the street sampled a new world where they wandered at will in the long summer evenings. But they didn't vandalise or steal. They simply explored, and quickly and peacefully retreated at the all-too-frequent sound of a shouted: 'Hey, you boys! Clear off before I call the cops!'

Late in the summer they began to see German aircraft, generally in twos and threes, and air raid precautions and warnings were taken seriously. New uniforms appeared on the streets, and neighbourhood husbands and fathers, even some of the older boys, disappeared into the army. Everyone pasted their windows with a criss-cross pattern of sticky brown paper tape and constructed blackouts of old blankets and scrap wood. D.'s father sweated and swore as he hammered together his blackouts, which never fitted properly, and sometimes fell away from the window in the small hours of the morning, sending his mother in a panic-stricken scamper towards the air raid shelter.

The air raid shelter was a solid affair of thick gauge corrugated and shaped steel sheets. These were bolted together with heavy angle iron, and the whole structure half buried in the ground, the excavated soil packed around and over the half remaining above ground level. It looked and felt safe, with the added protection of a single straight sheet leant against the door. There was an ugly drop from the entrance into the shelter, which was equipped with four bunks, solid affairs of hardwood and metal strapping. D.'s family was lucky. Next door their shelter was much smaller and couldn't accommodate bunks. This was because the family consisted of only two adults and one child, but D.'s family was two adults and three children and this earned them two corrugated sheets extra.

Only a few miles away on Fairwood Common, an airfield was built, and the Gower road was closed to form part of it. As the air war hotted up the fighter aircraft used the field more often, and brought the war even closer as they roared in heavy numbers over the sprawling council housing estate which lay in their flight path to the coast. D.'s mother complained bitterly. 'Why don't they fly out over the other way?' she demanded. 'Over Gower. Where there aren't so many people. All that noise. With us honest people trying to get on with our lives. Why don't they leave us in peace?' But in reality D. could see that his mother was very frightened, and she trembled visibly and sometimes had to sit down to save her shivering, weakened knees.

On the street the boys were enthralled by the new low-flying planes. D. had to watch them from his back garden, because his mother wouldn't allow him to play with 'proddy woddies' or Protestants, since he was a Catholic, and 'might stray'. He could still hear them though, shouting in the street, and would often creep outside the garden to join them. Later, after the bombing, his mother relaxed the discrimination and he would join the boys sometimes, but he never really felt part of them. In fact, the boys his mother encouraged him to play with were unrelenting bullies, even though they were Catholics, and became his bêtes noires. They were all older than he, rough, crude, and disliked by the other boys in the street closer to his own age.

The summer wore on, and food became a problem for D. Rationing was becoming strict, and his mother watched him carefully. Her face would twist with anger if she saw him glancing at his sisters' plates at mealtimes.

'Measuring it out, are you? Be careful you don't miss anything. Somebody might be getting more than you. You can do the washing-up for being so greedy.'

In town, their favourite school-side cafe was wrecked overnight. Jesse De Coco was Italian, and sold splendid halfpenny ice-cream cones to the children, and they sometimes crept into his cafe seating to eat their lunchtime sandwiches in the warmth and comfort of his plywood fretworked seats. He threw D. and his sister out last time, not surprisingly, since they had bought nothing, not even a cup of tea. Their mother had been indignant, and told them to do it again, but they didn't and ate their sandwiches sitting on the wall of the park, easy now since the rails had gone. Besides, it was summer.

But Italy had joined the war with the Germans, and the younger men of the town had smashed De Coco's plate-glass windows, and when the police had taken De Coco away to internment, the men had taken axes to his cafe furniture, though curiously no one had interfered with his espresso machine or his stock of food and jars of sweets. For weeks, the children of the school gazed at the jars, persuading each other that if they got hold of one then it wouldn't be stealing, since they had been owned by an *Italian*. Some of the older boys brought lengths of stiff wire to poke through a small gap in the broken window, trying to hook a cake or liquorice stick from the open boxes next to the cash till, and this was played much like a fairground game, where the odds on winning a prize were impossible. None of the boys got anything.

Then the window was boarded up and they forgot about it and a week later Jesse De Coco was back, with business as usual. Only he never sold halfpenny cones again. The cheapest was a penny, and they still bought as many as before.

Mr Churchill made speeches over the radio, and they all listened carefully. Most of the people in the street didn't understand what he said. They wanted to know where the Germans were, and what they were doing. They needed practical advice on what to do if they met a German, gun in hand, at the corner of the street; what to do if they saw a bomb falling towards them or their house. The rhetoric of 'blood, tears, toil and sweat', delivered in the commanding tones of a member of the ruling class, unnerved and alarmed them more than it encouraged.

They discussed it the following day, small knots of neighbours gathered at strategic points, attracting others like a local gravity centre, the remaining men talking quietly, shaking their heads in solemn gloom, the women loud, some shrill in nervous fear, D.'s mother among them. She blamed men. 'Always fighting. It's we women who suffer. They don't care. If they did some honest work they wouldn't have time to go out shooting innocent women and children.' This silenced the women for a time, but they had all seen in recent years the cinema newsreels showing ecstatic German crowds cheering their Fuhrer, and at least half the crowds were made up of excited women clamouring even to see the great man as he swept by in a cloud of black uniforms. Embarrassed by her unthinking outburst, the women moved on to more essential matters — how to feed their families on the dwindling official rations, and for those whose men had gone away to fight, how they were to afford even to buy the rationed food on the miserly army allowances.

As the butter allowance fell to two ounces, so his mother's vigilance over the family food stocks increased. Things were declared stolen. A slice of bread had been cut off the loaf. The cheese had been picked at. There was an onion missing from the pickle jar. All fingers pointed at D. What he did not realise was that he had earned himself the name of thief from an incident at Christmas. Then, someone had crept down to the pantry and eaten half of a chocolate Swiss roll. On top of the roll was a tiny plaster robin which gave the roll a festive tone, and his younger sister had brought this to his bedroom, showed it to him, and then dropped it in his chamber pot. His mother had found it there, scuttled to the pantry and made the horrifying discovery of a mutilated Christmas goodie. She made the connections, and despite D.'s pleas of innocence, he was soundly beaten. He acquired a reputation for daring theft, particularly of foodstuffs. He would never lose that taint, and as the alleged thefts of food were itemised, so he received punishment with increasing frequency.

He protested innocence loudly through his tears, and suspected his younger sister, Dot, who watched his humiliation with vindictive, glittering eyes, a half-smile on her lips. She knew he couldn't win. He knew she couldn't lose.

Gas masks were issued, and they had some fun in the 'parlour' trying them on, trying to frighten each other pretending to be black-nosed pigs, but the smell of the new rubber enclosing their faces was sickening, and the game didn't last. They were required to carry them everywhere, but the fragile cardboard containers and slender string serving as a shoulder strap quickly frayed, so they left them at home. Besides, the Germans wouldn't bomb schools, would they?

His father joined the Home Guard. The Battle of Britain raged, though they scarcely knew it. There were practice air raid warnings, which everyone quickly learned to ignore, though D. was impressed by the howling sirens which filled the sky at odd times in the day. Some of the less literate neighbours called them 'sireens', which pronunciation earned his mother's long-lasting contempt. She came home one day triumphantly bearing the news that Mrs Horner, the fireman's wife, had pronounced 'certificate' as 'cistificate', and, 'Guess what? She said "sireens". "Sireens!" I ask you. "Sireens!" What next!'

His father was silent. Only that morning he had gently told her that 'coupons' was not pronounced 'cowpans' as she and some of the neighbours did.

The summer holidays were soon gone. They had visited Gower for only one week that year, staying in a wooden bungalow tucked away into the corner of a field which topped the cliff over-looking Limeslade Bay. D.'s parents were grumpy, and shouted at each other, his mother complaining that it was no holiday for her, since she still had to make the beds, do the cooking and so on. The bungalow was owned by their local milkman, who let them have the place at decent rates, since his father took his holidays only in September, in the belief that at his office he was essential to the good order and running of the business during the high season when everybody else was on holiday. That's what he told D.'s mother. In fact he was bottom of the holiday list, and had last choice of dates. No one else wanted to go on holiday in September.

Autumn came. In October there were reports on the wireless of cities in England being bombed. At the cinema the newsreels showed the smoking ruins of the mornings after, and people became apprehensive. They consoled themselves by telling each other that they were in Wales, too far away from the Germans, too small for them to bother with.

Christmas 1940 was subdued, though to the children it was still an exciting occasion. Amid the disappointment of sparse Christmas presents from Santa Claus they listened to their father telling them of his Christmases. 'A box of paints', said his father.

'And a brush, if you were lucky', added his mother. She never told them what she had had.

That winter, late in January, the bombing started. Not very frightening at first, the raids developed into three consecutive nights of mind-numbing noise and destruction which wiped out the heart of the town with fearful accuracy. Very few bombs strayed on to residential areas, but even those few wrought great alarm and panic out of all proportion to the damage done. It was an awesome sight, as D. roamed the local streets the mornings after, to see houses bombed flat, to hear neighbours discussing deaths and injuries.

The first of the three nights' alarms came at midnight. Not many people in the neighbourhood took much active notice at first. Then the sound of anti-aircraft gunfire convinced them that there was serious business afoot, and D. and his sisters were roused, rushed downstairs still in pyjamas, clutching a blanket.

Dazed with sleep, they ran down the sloping cinder path to the shelter and clambered over the sharp lip into the damp bowels of the freezing black cavity that gave them safety. There they crouched on the sharp steel slats of the two-tiered bunks, shivering with cold and fear.

The night was a clear moonlight frozen black and white map. A dusting of powdery snow drew outlines of roads and buildings sharply, though this meant little to the bomber crews sitting aloft, who relied on a radio beam system to pinpoint their target and bomb-release point. Such technical impartiality did little to comfort the thousands of souls crouching in dread all over the town, each of them expecting a personal and painful assault from the unseen enemy.

As the bombers drew closer their engines developed a sympathetic resonance, giving the world below a strong three-four waltz time beat, as though from an orchestra of giant muted double basses. The anti-aircraft guns, few enough for the conflict, faded away as the aircraft began to fly overhead and out of elevation range of the clumsy, large-calibre, slow-firing barrels which were reluctant to turn around and shoot bursts over the town.

There followed a strange period of waiting, the whole world slowly yielding to the hypnotising throb of hundreds of engines, like a reluctant patient surrendering to a powerful masseur. They began to relax.

Then the whistling bombs began to fall. Each whistle ended in a thumping roar and in the shelters they twitched and clenched their teeth, and their fingers and toes curled tight. At the height of the raid the bombs were falling so thick and fast that the explosions merged into one huge noise, extinguishing even the warning whistle of approaching death.

As the main stream of bombers did their work and turned for home, stragglers began to arrive, and dropped their bombs anywhere. These were the most fearsome. Not only did the stragglers drag out the raid by hours, but they inflicted real punishment on the packed housing estates surrounding the industrial centres.

After three and a half hours the all-clear sounded. For some reason, the siren of the Cwmfelin steel works always got off first, even though it didn't have a proper siren that wailed up and down the scale as all the other works did. The Cwmfelin siren sounded like a tired fog horn, with a single note broken into three-second burps for a warning, and continuous for the all-clear.

D. heard his mother burst into tears. It was over. They were safe, and as far as he knew, their house was still there.

His father had been outside in the open, on locally-organised air raid rescue duties. He poked his head into the shelter and said reassuringly, 'OK. It's all over now. Let's get to bed.' As D. stirred his father said in surprise, 'What's D. doing here, on his own? On the top bunk?'

His mother sniffled away her tears. 'He's only a boy. He can look after himself. I was looking after the girls on the bottom bunk.'

'It's safer down below,' said his father. 'He should be on the bottom bunk.' He sounded disapproving.

There was no further discussion, and they trooped out of the shelter, frozen, stiff and sweating with nervous exhaustion. As they tumbled wearily into bed D. wondered why his mother had said 'only a boy'. If she had said 'He's a boy, and can look after himself', he would have been proud. But 'only a boy'? He wasn't up to it, and fell asleep.

They stayed at home the next day, listening to visiting adults discussing the bombing. Names were mentioned, in hushed tones. People, places, whole families had 'gone'. Wrecked buildings were described second and third-hand. D.'s father had wanted to go to work but he was persuaded to stay at home like other men in the street, to offer help if needed. He dished out Christmas supplies of whisky, and more neighbours came to talk and to give each other reassurance. Soon the gathering had spilled on to the tiny lawn outside the back door, and someone picked up the bottle of whisky and passed it around. Those without a glass took a swig from the bottle, and someone else called for more liquor. His father obliged, his mother protested, and someone broke into song.

'Run rabbit, run' was in full swing from thirty throats when Father O'Flynn came down the concrete steps. He had come to visit his Catholic parishioners and to offer them what encouragement he could. On the bottom step he paused in astonishment at the sound of carefree carousing. Instead of knocking at the front door he walked slowly around the side of the house to view the party.

D. saw him first. He ran to tell his mother, who had joined in the fun and was drinking from a large glass. She glared at him and promised him all kinds of injury if this was his kind of joke. Unwisely she took the glass with her when she went outside to prove his lies. When she saw Father O'Flynn she gave a squeal, staggered, and dropped her glass in shock. The crowd had moved on to 'The Lambeth Walk', with verses never written by the composer, the women squealing in false protest as the men shamelessly dwelled on the intimate biology of the chorus lines.

As they became aware of the priest in their midst, the singers faltered and slowly hushed. Those inside sensed the change but not the cause, and they piled outside for enlightenment. The crowd stood, silent, glasses in hand, wondering what to do next, regarding the priest not in hostility, nor friendship, but as an alien of uncertain habits. They would take their lead from their host.

D.'s father offered Father O'Flynn a drink. Father O'Flynn refused, politely, and told everyone that he was there to give everyone the comfort of the Church. At this promise of doom and gloom, the party broke up, and everybody had gone within minutes. Nobody wanted that kind of comforting. Dwelling on the mysteries of their eternal souls took a poor second place to the need to block out their night of horror. And perhaps more nights to come. They did not believe in miracles.

D. and his two sisters were ushered out of the house, with instructions to play outside, and their parents took Father O'Flynn into the parlour to talk.

Outside, the children stood on the earth bank at the bottom of the garden, watching the slow, cold drift of the grey-brown mist rising from the smouldering town centre. They didn't fully understand it. It was a long way away. But something had happened last night which had changed things.

'We won't go on holiday in the summer again,' said Jean, his older sister.

'Of course we will. Why not?' said Dot, a year or so younger than D.

'It will all be bombed.'

There was no answer to this. None of them knew a lot about bombs, except that they killed people and wrecked buildings.

Their mother called from the back door. 'Come here, children. Say goodbye to Father O'Flynn.'

They ran up the path and stood obediently in a row. Father O'Flynn smiled in a detached way, muttered something in Latin, shaking a hand over them. D. wanted to ask him what a 'paraclete' was, but thought better of it. Every day at school he would chant, along with the rest of the boys, a catechism that told of a 'paraclete'. He had no idea what this was. When he asked his chums what a paraclete was, they shrugged their shoulders. 'Dunno', would be the reply. He had asked his teacher once, and had earned himself a smart rap across the calves with a cane and a 'Don't be stupid, boy'.

When Father O'Flynn had gone, D.'s mother asked his father 'Will they come again, Frank?' She meant the bombers.

'No. I don't think so,' said his father. 'They don't have enough bombs to keep it up.'

That night they came again. This time there was no hesitation or doubts about taking shelter. Drawing on the previous night's experience, they found time to dress fully, and his mother took a prayerbook with her. This time they were joined by the Michaels, their next door neighbours, whose shelter was only two sheets long, without bunks and too small to lie at full stretch as all the best Ministry of Information advice told them they should do. The Michaels were the only Welsh-speakers in their street, and thus considered 'odd'. Mr Michael ate his peas with his knife, a marvellous achievement that D. tried to copy with conspicuous failure.

They all prayed in Welsh and sang hymns from the local Baptist chapel as the cascade of death exploded all around. More bombs went astray this time, including one that fell into the Michaels' back garden, a scant ten yards from the shelter where they all crouched. There were incendiary bombs too, small blunt-nosed phosphorus ordnance that was rumoured to be able to burn holes through thick steel sheets. Sometime during the raid their father was reported to be blinded, but this was an exaggeration — the glare from an exploding firebomb had temporarily disorientated him, and he was seen in the nick of time as he staggered towards the lip of the crater dug out by the HE bomb that had fallen just a few minutes before in the Michaels' garden.

D.'s mother lay at the bottom of the shelter, wailing and bemoaning her fate with a blinded husband, wisely making no move to leave the relative safety of the shelter to give aid to her spouse.

It was generally agreed that the raid was worse than the previous night. As well as fire bombs, the anti-aircraft guns had continued to fire, even when the debris of bursting shells was bound to fall away over the houses, and this had provided an alarming hail of metal fragments, peppering roofs and roads. Slates were dislodged, and the scraping rattle as they slid down roofs, followed by a short silence then a crash as they struck a concrete pathway or a glass-roofed lean-to, added to the strain. Sometimes the slates were stopped by guttering until it could hold no longer, and collapsed with a frightening clatter. It seemed the whole world was disintegrating around them. And then they heard the siren bomb for the first time. This was truly frightening. One or two German planes flew higher than the rest and dropped small bombs with air-activated sirens attached. These seemed to drop for ever, the sirens getting louder and louder and always in the direction of the listener. The tone of the siren was a lot lower and more musical than the whistling scream of the heavier bombs, and easily distinguishable. To the children, their mother's agonised shout of: 'There's another one!' meant only the emergence of a siren bomb. Paradoxically, before the night was over, they were almost ignoring the real heavyweights and their whistling announcement of death and destruction, and concentrating on being the first to claim a hearing of the smaller, less deadly sirens, though these were quite as capable of demolishing a house and killing everyone in it.

They emerged weary and exhausted from the shelter. The bright, crisp moonlight and frosted snow was a bizarre background to the sound of fire engines and shouts of men in the streets calling for tools, bandages and blankets for the trapped and injured of houses hit in the raid. As they walked up the garden path one side of the house reflected dancing shadows against the yellow glare of a house on fire just down the street. Curiosity numbed by tiredness and cold, they trudged upstairs and fell asleep.

D. didn't know who the Patons were, but they had been hit. One half of a semi-detached house had been destroyed and father, mother and baby killed outright. They had sheltered under the stairs because their steel shelter was too small and cold for the baby. The remaining half was exposed like a doll's house, floor by floor, with all the furniture and belongings on view. D. watched with others as the man of the house tried to recover a pram, parked incongruously at the edge of a sagging floor of the main bedroom. Neighbours shouted advice. 'Use a pole'. 'Throw a rope over the handlebar and pull it'. 'Lower it down' ... and so on. 'The brake is on,' snapped the man. 'I have to get to it to release it.'

Later that day the pram appeared in D.'s house, complete with baby. Reggie Squires was the man's name, and he, his wife and baby stayed with them for a week while the authorities found somewhere for them to live. D.'s elder sister Jean was sent off to her grandmother for the time being to make room.

The bomb that killed the Patons was one of a stick of three. The second one fell just twenty yards away and cut the water main and sewer. Why these should run side by side in a relatively modern housing development was anybody's guess. For weeks the families in the street performed their toilet functions in an old bucket behind the air raid shelters, and clean water came from a bowser truck that called once a day until the pipe was repaired. It was D.'s job to take two buckets, the maximum allowed, fill them and carry them home. On the third day, his mother found a frog in one bucket.

A row with the Army bowser driver followed on the lines of: 'How do "they" expect us to use water with live frogs in it?' and: '"They" ought to do something about it' and: 'We pay our taxes ... ' etc, etc. Uncontrollable sniggers from a group of boys close by resolved the confrontation. The Army driver first twigged the joke, and began to smile at D.'s mother, fuelling her rage. D. also saw it, but did not smile. The bowser driver climbed into his cab, promises of reporting to his seniors ringing in his ears, and drove off.

D. inspected the crater of the bomb that had exploded in the neighbouring garden. He was impressed by the size of the hole, though he was assured by his father that it was a very small bomb. The neighbours' shelter didn't appear to be seriously affected, though anyone in it could have been killed by blast, he was told.

Again, today, leaning from his bedroom window, D. could see the brown-black haze of fires in the docks and town centre area. There was nothing else to show what a terrible night they had spent.

Reggie Squires brought a box of plums in, and gave them to D.'s mother. She took them with ill grace, asking petulantly what she could do with them. They were sour and uneatable. Mrs Squires suggested she should make jam. Reluctantly, because gas supplies were cut off, D.'s mother agreed, borrowed a large aluminium pot, added a little water, and set the plums to stew on the stove, pouring in precious packets of sugar.

In the evening, the gas supplies were restored, and the plums were set up on the gas ring atop the stove, where they bubbled away interestingly. There was no electricity that day, or in the sharp winter night, as they crowded into the kitchen for warmth. One candle was not enough even to play cards, so the adults talked and the children fiddled and got on everyone's nerves until they were packed off to bed early. People had been warned not to light fires in their homes, because this increased the risk of fire if the house was hit by a bomb.

It was cold in bed, and the air was full of nervous expectation. From below D. could hear the muffled voices discussing the war. Was it true, D.'s mother was asking, that the Germans ate the babies of their enemies? No one was sure about this. They certainly were heathens — they had dressed up as nuns and parachuted down behind Dutch lines, where they shot people and then hid their guns under their skirts. They even had bombs disguised as rosary beads tied around their waists. D.'s mother said this was terrible blasphemy, and the Pope should do something about it.

'What religion are they, Frank?' she asked. Perhaps they were Hindu or something. The Pope would be seriously handicapped if they were.

After a pause where D. could detect some embarrassment, his father said that they were the same as in this country. 'A bit of a mixture. Catholics and Protestants.'

'And a lot of neither,' said Reggie Squires.

'Those bomber pilots can't be Catholics,' said his mother, her voice rising in disbelief. 'They can't be. It's a mortal sin to kill people.'

'It's not very nice to frighten them, either,' said Mrs Squires.

'Cliff is a Catholic,' said his father. 'He flies a plane that carries bombs.'

'And a lot of guns,' said Reggie Squires.

'But that's different,' said D.'s mother.

There was a long pause. Cliff was the husband of D.'s favourite aunt.

'They won't come again, will they, Frank?' His mother's voice was fearful. 'They say there's nothing left in town.'

'No,' said his father. They don't have enough planes. Hundreds were shot down yesterday. They found wrecks all over the place. Even if they get up another raid, they'll try somewhere else. Somewhere nearer, and safer to bomb. We're a long way from their airfields.'

Comforted, D. fell asleep. He slept in his parents' bed, head to toe with his sister. His elder sister wasn't here tonight, and there was more room. His parents slept in his bed, and the Squires' slept in his sisters' bed. Complicated and unsettling, but the disturbed nights were taking their toll, and sleep came easily.

They came again that night. There was less warning, and the Cwmfelin hooter was groaning its call as the bombs were falling. On their way to the shelter, D.'s mother, who was in front, asked his father, 'Do you think they can see us, Frank?'

No. Of course not,' said his father. He sounded slightly impatient.

'But they tried to drop a bomb on us last night, though, didn't they? They must have seen us running. There's so much light.'

As they reached the shelter entrance D.'s mother stopped, waiting his father's answer. His younger sister wriggled past and dropped down to the bunk. His father turned away, his shepherding duties done, and ran out to the road with Reggie Squires, ready for rescue work.

Inside the shelter, D.'s mother crouched whimpering on the bunk with his sister. D. lay on a top bunk, face down on the steel slats, above the Michaels' with their baby, and Mrs Squires with hers. He had never felt so lonely.

The night was worse than the previous two combined. The Germans dropped a new kind of bomb, as well as the incendiaries and siren bombs. This was a 'land mine', complete with parachute it was said, though the advantages of this kind were not clear. Anyway, they made a much bigger bang, and there was no whistle.

They were in the shelter for two and a half hours, praying, singing hymns, calling comforting messages to one another. 'That's the main wave gone' or 'They're turning for home now.' They were always false comforts. The bombs continued to whistle and scream, the guns went on firing, slates crashed to the ground, whistles blew, bells rang, men shouted, women and children whimpered, dogs barked and the ground shook.

Then the engines faded, and the sirens struck a clear continuous note and they wept with relief. Numb with cold and fright they clambered out of the shelter, thankful that their house was intact. Inside the kitchen, the plums were still bubbling in the pan over the gas ring. D.'s mother wailed as she examined the pan's contents. The jam had boiled away all this time unattended and had turned to the consistency of rubber. What a waste of sugar, she complained to the world. The incongruous novelty of the gently purring gas flame, undisturbed by the exploding madness of the world outside, escaped her.

Sleep came less easily that night. It was colder than before. R.A.F. planes roamed the air, raising a lurching fear of enemy aircraft returning to make a sneak raid, and there was a growing nervousness that it was only a matter of time before they all came to the same end as the Patons. There didn't seem to be a time limit for the punishment they were taking. It might be better to be sentenced to certain death rather than undergo the never ending threat of a nasty end.

On a short tour the following morning D. found that Reggie Squires' remaining half of the Patons' house had disappeared. By a chance in a million a straggling bomber had released three bombs, exactly as on the second raid the night before last, and they had struck the ground within a few feet of their previous pattern. The water and sewer mains had been cut again. There were other houses too, which had been wrecked. In some of the longer five or six-home blocks there were gaps, neatly cut out sometimes by fire, often by smaller bombs. One of D.'s cousins, he was told, had been killed with all his family. D. remembered his cousin, who had been in his class at school. He had a very pretty older sister.

When he returned home D. found his mother in the kitchen, gibbering insanely over a cup of whisky held by a woman neighbour. She couldn't stand any more of it, she blubbered. Not any more. 'What do they want?' she cried. D. watched impassively. Why was she crying? There was no danger now, at this moment.

'I haven't done anything wrong,' she continued to wail. 'I go to Mass every week. I've never missed. It isn't fair.'

Her knees began to wobble, and she permitted herself to be guided to a nearby chair, where she collapsed over the table, arms outstretched as though to Allah, and sobbed theatrically. The neighbour patted her back sympathetically, but was clearly embarrassed. Nobody in the street had caved in like this. D. became ashamed, and went out of the house to have another look at the bomb crater next door.

He returned to the house to inspect the hole in the ceiling. The base-plate of an anti-aircraft shell had struck the slates near the edge of the roof, barrelled its way through, bounced off the floor boards, hit the ceiling again and come to rest on the bed. Exactly where D.'s head might have been. He looked at the ugly piece of metal, placed by his father on the mantelpiece. Black, with jagged edges on one side where it had disintegrated when it had exploded miles above. His mother had been very annoyed. 'Somebody could have been hurt,' she said. 'You'd think they would aim better than that, wouldn't you? They'll be killing their own, at this rate.'

Later that day two Army engineers called, checking on the utilities supply. The water still fountained from the evil-smelling, mud-filled crater where a dozen men worked feverishly for hours. D.'s mother invited the two men in, and now, completely recovered from her breakdown, flirted with them and made them a cup of tea. This was a golden opportunity to pick up news from the soldiers — what delays on the water and gas supplies, where the bombs had fallen, how many dead, the size of the fires, and so on. She would hold centre stage at a street chat later on.

Uncle Jack came in, quite unexpected. Uncle Jack was a captain in the infantry, a hard man who had risen from the ranks, and his face bore the marks. The engineers in the kitchen leapt to their feet, shocked and fearful — no one would expect a commissioned officer to live here, on this mean council house estate. They stammered apologies, but Uncle Jack smiled and put them at ease. 'It's all right. She's not my wife. She's my sister. And finish your tea, don't waste it.' But the soldiers couldn't get out fast enough, scalding their tongues on the hot, fresh brew, saluted his uncle's piercing blue eyes and James Cagney features and shot away by the back door.

D.'s mother indulged in another, more controlled nervous spasm. Tears and complaints. 'Why can't "they" stop them, Jack? Are we going to lose the war? What will happen to us?'

'Calm down,' said Uncle Jack. 'Not in front of the children.' He nodded to D. 'Can you play outside son, while your mother and I have a chat? There's a good boy.' He was amazingly gentle for a seasoned tough fighter.

D. went outside. Uncle Jack had been wounded at Dunkirk and had a medal. He would have liked to go out on to the street and boast to some of the boys; but he was, after all, only an uncle. It was not his father. His father had a protected job, and some unpleasant remarks about that had already been made by some of the women in the street. A miner, steelworker or fireman with an important war job, yes. But a man who worked in an office?

Rees the milk came as usual in his Wolseley car with the back seats taken out and two churns of milk, delivered by his farmer brother from Carmarthen, sitting in the back. Milk had gone up to threepence a pint since last week, but what would they do without it, asked Rees when the women in the street protested. What would they do, indeed?

Jones the grocer improved his prices too. And there were no sweets for the children at all. They had all gone to the troops, he said. In reality, unless you were a relative or a special friend of Jones the grocer, sweets would wait for a price increase which would follow ration coupons. In January 1941 there would be many months to wait for the ration coupons, which wouldn't guarantee supplies anyway.

Jones the butcher was a sly, treacherous man who charged threepence to keep D.'s mother's turkey in his cold room, but sold wonderful faggots and peas in hot spicy gravy. Six pennyworth was enough, with boiled potatoes, to feed a family of four, but D.'s mother thought it was 'common' to be seen carrying a jug of hot steaming faggots in the street, so they never had any.

Williams the fish was the last shop in the row before the cobbler and Rees the baker. Mr Williams sold excellent fish and chips, and was a cheerful, pleasant man. He said he made a loss on halfpenny bags of chips, but would sell them to the boys anyway.

The main problem with all the shops in the row at the top of the street was the counters. The shop owners varied in their attitudes to children who were on errands for mothers, clutching shopping bags, money, and a scribbled note. Some ignored them, like Rees the chemist and Jones the grocer, and the children would spend half an hour waiting while adults, mainly women, were served first no matter how recently they had come in. Others, like Williams the fish and Rees the baker, would pick them out and often serve them before their turn. But the counters were all too high. A normal seven-year-old could just see over the top standing on tiptoe, not a sustainable position. So, frequently a child would stop at the break in the counter which contained the access flap, because it was only here that a note and the money, as well as the goods, could be exchanged.

Shopping errands were thus not a pleasant task. D. found himself inevitably chosen for the job, because 'he was a boy, and able to carry more'. For years to come, a measure of growth and development was used by the boys in the street. This was judged by the loads carried from the shops and whether the stage had been reached where the boy could get his elbows on the counter top. D. tried every time he went into a shop, and the first time he did it at Jones the grocer without Mr Jones telling him to get his elbows off, he triumphantly boasted to the boys. He was nearly nine then, and they pooh-poohed his claim to status. Most of them had passed the test. Instead, weight gain and hand span from thumb to little finger were taking over as the new standards of approaching manliness.

The Germans went somewhere else that night, but there was a false alarm, and they spent half an hour of biting cold in the shelter, hardly believing their luck as the Cwmfelin hooter moaned the all-clear. There were no bombs, throbbing engines, crashing slates or clenched hands. There were no prayers or hymn singing either, and God seemed a little further away than the night before.

In early March the King and Queen paid the town a visit. Nobody could say why they had come, but the town was flattered and people turned out in their thousands to wave and cheer as the Royals toured the streets in a huge open-topped car. The Queen caught D.'s eye as he stood gazing, mystified at the entourage, and she raised a hand and smiled. Then she passed in regal progress and the crowds moved off. He wondered who she was.

As the hard winter of 1941 drew on, alarms and threats of further raids faded, and by D.'s eighth birthday at the end of March, the only enemy activity had dwindled to single-aircraft daylight raids aimed at vital targets. This collapse of activity seemed to inspire the government to order the evacuation of all schoolchildren to places of safety in the country, and a general order was issued.

Chapter Three

They went by train from Swansea High Street station on a wet, windy morning in early April. Each of them wore a label tied to a coat lapel, and clutched a gas mask in its flimsy card box and a packet of sandwiches wrapped in grease-proof paper inside a used brown paper bag whose corners were twisted into little 'mouse ears' to keep it closed. The rare lucky child had a bag of sweets or an apple. Patrick Kinsella had both. The older girls made loud remarks about his fortune, and one or two even threatened to 'drop him' if he didn't share.

They were organised by school, so that familiar teachers were in charge as they were loaded on to the train. Not many of the children had much idea of what was going on, and there were few tearful farewells.

The train pulled out, and they were excited by the journey and the scenery. Most forgot their sandwiches and other small comforts like favourite dolls, and the journey was not very long anyway. They stopped at Llanelli, about fifteen miles on, and poured on to the platform to surround their teacher groups. After some delay to ensure that none of the children were missing, and after Patrick Kinsella had been persuaded by a conductor and a teacher to come out of the toilet where he had been stuffing himself with sweets, the whole swarm set off on a route march to an assembly hall in town. D.'s elder sister took his hand as they walked, which was comforting, because they all felt the atmosphere of foreign territory.

Their first worries came early. As the endless snake of children wound along the pavements of the town centre, the shoppers and residents of the town came to see. They stood and stared, and made remarks in Welsh.

'They speak Welsh here,' D. said to his sister.

'Yes,' she replied. She said no more, and it was worrying. Their mother had warned them about Welsh-speakers. They were not to be trusted, she had said often enough. D. was not sure what trust was or how it worked, but it was still worrying.

When they arrived at the assembly hall they were told to sit on the floor and eat their sandwiches. The floor was wood block, worn and dusty, and it made awful smears on their clothes, but they were tired after the long trek through the town, and they sat.

Most of them were thirsty, and couldn't face the sandwiches, mainly jam or cheese, squashed, dry and unappetising.

It was mid-afternoon when the future foster parents began to arrive in the hall. After long talks and consultation with lists, names began to be called. Children rose and went to the front of the hall where the teachers stood with the adult strangers. The children were examined, turned around, questioned and assessed by these strangers. Some heads were shaken and the children returned to their places on the floor, puzzled but unconcerned. Most of the strangers were women. D. thought them very old, and they all looked the same. They all wore gold-rimmed glasses, had tight silver hair locked into hard false-looking curls, and were all shaped like barrels under their Sunday-best coats. None of them looked friendly. He looked for what his mother called 'chapel lips', the puckered hardness around the mouth which she said only Welsh-speakers who hated Catholics had. 'You can tell,' she would often say, 'how nice people are, by their lips.' Sometimes she would call them 'Welsh lips', but that had less meaning — he had been born in Gorseinon, not far from Llanelli, and his father's passport declared him Welsh; and Mrs Michael spoke Welsh and she was their next-door neighbour, and very friendly.

D. began to feel very tired. His younger sister was asleep on the floor. When his name was called he rose and went to his aunt, who was one of the teachers.

She smiled at him and said to the woman standing beside her, 'This is Denis.' The woman looked down at him.

'Miss Philips will take you home now. Don't worry. Your sisters will be staying with Mrs Jones, nearby. You'll see each other tomorrow. Off you go now.'

Miss Philips turned away, indicating that he was to follow. He held out his hand, expecting her to take it to lead him away, but she said sharply 'You're a big boy now, you can walk along without holding hands, can't you?' D.'s heart sank. Her accent was heavily Welsh, and not friendly. He looked for 'chapel lips' and there they were — the small furrows along the top lip, compressing the mouth to a disapproving hardness.

A short journey in a local bus, during which he was reminded of how lucky he was that she was paying his fare, and then they were near home. As they stepped off the bus he was assailed by the overpowering stench of the local brewery, Felinfoel Ales. It was everywhere as he trotted alongside his new foster mother up an unmade road to a terraced row of houses, halfway up a hill. The house had a good view of the brewery from the front windows.

Through a half-glazed front door which boasted coloured glass, and he was introduced to Mervyn, Miss Philip's brother. Mervyn was a coal miner, and lived with Miss Philips in the house. He was younger than Miss Philips and unmarried. Miss Philips also had a younger sister, Ceinwen, who was married. When D. was introduced she totally ignored him, continuing her conversation with Mervyn with only a slight pause to look D. up and down and then to turn away.

When Mervyn had gone off to work the night shift and his married sister had gone home later that evening, and when D. was seriously thirsty, and hungry, and very tired, Miss Philips told him he was to take a bath.

His heart sank. He had already sensed that he had no friends in this house. All the talk had been in Welsh, and he had dropped his head in embarrassment at the times when all three stopped talking and stared at him silently: they were so obviously discussing him and examining him as he sat on the hard chair in the kitchen, his feet several inches from the cold, tiled floor.

He wondered if Miss Philips' bathroom was warmer than his at home. Perhaps she might have big towels that were dry and warm.

'Up you get, boy. Make room for the bath.' D. jumped down from the chair and stood aside as Miss Philips moved the chair, then bustled about, finally carrying in a tin bath from the scullery and setting it down in front of the open coal fire.

'Off with your clothes now, boyo. We'll soon have you freshened up then. You have to be clean here in this house, mind you.' So saying she poured in water from a huge black kettle, added cold water, and then measured out, none too carefully, it seemed to D., some yellow liquid from a big glass bottle.

He undressed reluctantly. Miss Philips sat in a chair close by and watched him coldly. He began to feel embarrassed. He had never undressed naked in front of strangers before. Especially a woman. Even at home he undressed, bathed and dried himself on his own now, and he was allowed to bolt the bathroom door because his sisters played tricks on him.

He took off his trousers and stepped quickly into the bath. He never wore underpants because his mother didn't believe in them. 'Toughen you up, it will,' she said when he had complained of the cold in the winter just passed. He sat down in the bath. It contained about two inches of lukewarm yellow water, and he shivered. He was not sure how to proceed. At home the bath would be hot, and the water deep enough to cover his entire body. He looked at Miss Philips questioningly. Soap? Flannel? What should he do now? The answer came soon. His genital area began to sting. Not much at first. Just a tingle when he sat down. It quickly became too much to bear, and he stood up. 'It's hurting,' he said inadequately. 'What?' said Miss Philips.

'What's hurting boy?' She had a sly smile on her lips and D. knew then that she knew what was hurting.

He realised with humiliation that he had an erection, as he stood naked and shivering in front of her. His willie was on fire. It hurt so much that he began to whimper. Miss Philips produced a long-handled wooden spoon and pushed his willie from side to side with it. 'What is this then? What do you call this then? That's a funny thing to have, isn't it?' He put his hands down to cover it, shamed beyond description, and she shouted, 'Take your hands away, you naughty boy!' Her eyes, D. saw, were sharp, dark and bright.

She sat, hunched towards him, and stared, while tears rolled down his cheeks. He was in pain, humiliated, cold, desperately thirsty and hungry, and tired beyond thinking. But Miss Philips wasn't finished. She brought the wooden spoon down, hard, on his erect willie. 'We can't have that,' she hissed. 'You're a naughty boy, aren't you? Very naughty. We'll have to teach you. You're not at home amongst your Catholics now, boyo. Oh, no. Not now. You're with good Welsh people. We'll teach you how to behave.'

The blow to his willie had done nothing to change its condition except to add to the pain, which was becoming unbearable. The erection was nothing to do with his state of mind, but all to do with the stinging yellow disinfectant she had poured into the bath water. He began to cry, openly.

'Oh, it is a baby we are now is it?' taunted Miss Philips. 'We'll soon cure you of that, boyo. Very soon. Now it's off to bed with you. I don't like boys who cry for nothing.'

In his pyjamas, cold and damp with undried bathwater, he ventured, 'Can I have a drink of water, Miss Philips?'

'Drink? Don't they give you anything to drink at home, then?'

She went into the kitchen and came back with a half cup of cold water.

'There you are. That's better than your Swansea water, I bet. That's straight off the mountains, that is.'

He could have drunk a dozen of the same, but didn't dare ask. He handed her the empty cup and stood submissively, waiting for her next move.

'Say thank you,' she snapped. 'That's manners that is. I can see what kind of home you come from, boyo.'

He offered his thanks. He had no thoughts of resentment. He was on his own here, and this fierce woman was in charge.

She showed him to his bedroom. It was large, with a single bed placed near the window at the far end. At least it had proper blankets and looked inviting enough. It was still light enough for him to see the steep garden topped by a line of coal-filled rail trucks. About fifty yards away, they were at the same level as the roof of the house. Perhaps he could explore them tomorrow.

He fell asleep quickly, despite his headache caused by hunger and travel. In the morning he awoke early and made a terrible discovery. He had wet his bed.

It was the first time this had happened to him and he could not explain it. He went through the morning routine of dressing and washing as Miss Philips watched him, and went downstairs to breakfast.

Breakfast was two boiled potatoes and a slice of bread. 'We're rationed too, you know. You can't have a life of luxury here. Everybody must have the same,' said Miss Philips. 'You can have salt on the potatoes if you like,' she said. She watched him as he scoffed his meal hungrily. It was not as appetising as his cornflakes of yesterday morning, but he was desperate for anything.

'They didn't tell me you were a wetter,' she said.

He looked at her, silent.

'Yes. A bedwetter. A dirty little boy who pees in his bed,' she said. 'A bath for you it is, boyo. This evening when you come in from school. No time now because you stayed in your pee bed so long. Off to school now. To your Catholics and your teacher it is you are.'

She handed him his raincoat, and when he had put it on he waited, expecting that she would take him to his new school. He had no idea where to go.

'What are you wanting now?' said Miss Philips sharply.

'I don't know where to go,' said D. in a hesitant voice.

'You go down the hill, past the brewery and turn left. Not on the main road, mind you. Up the side street. A new school there, it is. Now off you go. I have to clean your bed.' She pushed him outside and closed the door behind him.

Outside it was raining. He felt lost. He wasn't sure how to proceed from here, let alone at key points on the way. The brewery, for instance. How big was it? Could you actually turn left around it?

He set off down the unmade street towards the first marker — 'down the hill'. At the bottom he turned left, away from the main road. Sure enough there was a side street. A gentle rise and a narrow road flanked on one side by an endless row of small joined-together houses, and on the other by an equally endless wall of stone topped by wire netting.

There was no one about. Not even an adult going about his business. And no sound of them either. He began to worry that he had got things wrong, and arrived at a different school, because as he came to the end of the wall the buildings he saw were definitely a school. It even said so. Should he go in? Perhaps he was to be the first of the evacuees to get the cane for being late.

As he hesitated at the gate his name was called. His first name. His favourite aunt, Maureen, came to a door to one side of the building and called again.

'This way,' she beckoned, and D. scampered across the yard. 'We thought you were lost.' She was smiling and he felt relief as she walked him along a corridor and into a large classroom filled with children from his Swansea school.

Inside there was confusion. There were four teachers, two men and two women, and only one classroom. A mistake had been made, apparently. There were endless roll calls, boys and girls were divided then joined together again, then they were divided into age groups and joined together again. The noisy shuffling of the scores of children over the dusty wood-boarded floor must have disturbed other classes in the school and the headmistress appeared at the door. Her face was set in annoyance, and D. at the front saw that she had 'chapel lips' and her first words confirmed this as she said, 'What a noise it is you are making here. Duw, Duw, terr-ible it is, my good-ness me.'

This didn't help matters. It was clear that no plan had been made by the Swansea teachers how they would organise the classes, and they were already on the verge of fighting one another.

Mrs Robbins took offence. 'We expected better facilities,' she snapped. 'We can't teach four classes in one room. We must have another room at least. Four would be better.'

Mrs Robbins was Mr Andrews' sister. Mr Andrews was the brutal headmaster of the boys' senior school. Mrs Robbins felt she had the status to flex her muscles. Aunt Maureen who taught the junior boys thought differently. 'We're sorry,' she said, and Mrs Robbins' head turned at this treachery. Her mouth quivered in anger like her brother's, D. noticed.

The children were enthralled. A first-class fight between teachers, under their very noses.

'It will take some time to get organised,' said Aunt Maureen. 'Is there somewhere we could discuss things?' The headmistress glared at Mrs Robbins and held open the door. 'Yes, we can talk out here,' she said. 'Perhaps the gentlemen can join us?' She actually smiled at 'Spud' Murphy, a tall shambling man of great silences and heavy jaw who was ashamed of his Irish accent and didn't know how to change it. But he was gentle, and would leaven the sparks between the women. He joined them, with his colleagues, and the children were left alone.

D. saw his sisters and left his place, a two-seat desk shared by three boys, to talk to them. He was eager to find out where they were staying, what kind of food they had, what their foster parents were like.

'What do you want?' his younger sister spat. D. looked away from her. He couldn't understand her nastiness.

His elder sister said, 'It's awful, isn't it? Why have we come here? The food is terrible, and they speak Welsh all the time.' She was referring to her foster parents, D. realised.

'Do you have to bath?' he asked.

'No,' she said. 'But we have to sleep in a small bed together.' She turned with a look at his younger sister. 'And she keeps fighting. She's awful.'

D.'s heart sank. Perhaps he was lucky to have a bed to himself, and this made his change of circumstances better than his sisters'. There wasn't much to look forward to.

The teachers came back, and eventually lunchtime came. Everyone had sandwiches. Except D. He accepted his exception, since he could do little about it. The teachers didn't eat in front of the class. They just sat there, supervising. D. began to develop a headache from lack of food, and felt ferociously thirsty. His genital area still stung from last night's bath, and as the day wore on he had increasing dread of Miss Philips' promise of another bath tonight.

For the rest of the afternoon the children sat obediently listening to teachers telling them about their conduct 'now that they were guests of kind people who had opened their homes to them'. They must be obedient, keep themselves clean, be polite at all times, and most important, gather at the school here on Sunday to hear Mass. On no account were they to accompany their guardians to chapel. The word 'chapel' took on a sinister meaning as the same message was hammered home, day after day.

After D. got back to his 'billet', the plain wood outer door was closed and locked. What should he do now? He had no contact with

49

anyone else; he didn't know where his sisters were, or the teachers. There wasn't much step to sit on, and that was very wet, so he leaned against the wail, listening to the trickle of rainwater stagger down the iron pipe.

A small fat woman came along the pavement, basket in hand, and stopped as she drew alongside him. She said something in Welsh, but D. didn't understand and just looked at her uncomprehending. She shook her head. 'You're one of those children, are you? Where are you from?'

D. was unsure how to answer. Where he came from was not far away, only half an hour by train. As far as he knew, this little street was part of that same world, though he was beginning to adapt to new ideas on this.

'Mayhill,' he said.

'Mayhill?' Her voice rose as though she had been threatened in some way. 'That's in England then, is it? You're English then, are you? Her lips tightened. 'The coun-cil said we wouldn't have to have the English. Not here.' She paused, as though he should explain the politics to her.

'Mayhill in Swansea,' he said. 'We came from Swansea station.' He hoped this was right. He hoped she wouldn't ask any more questions — she seemed to easily misunderstand his answers.

'How old are you, bach?'

'Eight,' he said.

'Duw, Duw, then don't stand about here in the cold and wet. You go in the back way. Gwladys never locks her back door.' She turned to point down the street. 'Along there, along the path below the railway, and you'll see the back garden gate. Go in there. Don't stay out here, you'll get a chill, you will.'

She walked down the street and D. followed to the corner. She went down the hill, he went up, trying to remember her directions. Eventually he stood outside the back door. It was locked. He began to feel miserable and very much alone. He looked around the small level space outside the back door. The lavatory to one side, and a brick built shed on the other. Then the steps in a steep cleft between high brick walls keeping back the garden piled high to the pathway below the railway line, which stood high above him, a line of dark trucks piled high with coal. He read the signs painted on the sides of the trucks. 'Amalgamated Anthracite Co.,' said one. 'Picton James' another, 'Glasbrook Bros', 'R.T.B.'. They were all different. He wondered who these men were. His father had something to do with coal; he would know.

Suddenly he was overcome by his predicament. Cold, hungry, thirsty, wet, utterly tired, his genitals stinging still, the world full of unfriendly strange adults who didn't even speak his own language, and his legs were beginning to ache from walking and standing. His eyes began to well with tears. He didn't know what to do. But this backyard was the only place in an incomprehensible world where he had a right to be, and his only source of help, so he must stay here.

He turned to the shed door. It was not locked. He went inside and was surprised by the grocer's shop smell. There was little room in the shed, most of it taken up by stacks of cardboard boxes.

He sat on a box and looked around. He read the labels. Soap, sugar, tea and tins of fruit. Boxes of candles and corned beef. Tinned ham and sardines. They were stacked to the roof, which was a long way above him, D. saw. As he looked closer he saw the shed had two floors, each with a separate door. A ladder was the stairway, and the top floor doorway opened on to the garden above.

In boredom he began to count the boxes, and was halfway through when he heard sounds of movement in the house. Miss Philips was home.

He came out of the shed as Miss Philips opened the back door of the house.

'Jesu mawr! And it was burglars I thought I had,' she cried. She sounded upset, and D.'s heart sank. 'You mustn't go in that shed,' she shouted at him. She was unreasonably angry, he thought. What had he done wrong?

'Do you hear me?' she shouted. 'You shouldn't have gone in there. It's none of your business, it is.' He worried about this. The Welsh sentence structure confused him. Was it his business, or was it not?

She soon resolved his problem. 'No supper for you. You're a naughty boy. You'll have a bath and then off to bed with you.'

She held open the back door and pushed him through. He could no longer hold back his tears, though he controlled his crying. Mervyn sat at the table, eating. The room was filled with the delicious flavour of the lamb hot-pot set before him. D. stared at it ravenously.

Mervyn looked up and grunted, and went on eating. 'This boy was in the shed,' said Miss Philips.

Mervyn looked up, and muttered something in Welsh. Miss Philips replied in Welsh. Mervyn's voice rose, as though in warning. Miss Philip's voice began to complain. D. stood, not understanding, waiting for the next move.

'Sit down, boy,' said Mervyn.

D. sat at the table where Mervyn had waved his fork.

Miss Philips went into the kitchen and came back with a small bowl of hot-pot and half a slice of bread. 'Eat it nicely now. None of your Swansea table manners here,' she snapped.

He was willing to be shown what Swansea table manners were — he didn't know he had any. He looked at her enquiringly between mouthfuls until she said, 'And don't you go looking at me like that. You're not at home now, boyo.'

He finished his meal at the same time as Mervyn poured a cup of tea first for himself, and then he made to fill a cup for D.

'No, not for him, it is,' said Miss Philips. 'He'll wet the bed.'

Mervyn hesitated then nodded. He got up from the table and wandered off to the front room with his cup of tea.

D. sat and waited for Miss Philips' next move.

'You'll get your bath as soon as Uncle Mervyn has gone,' she promised.

And so he did. He dreaded another yellow bath. The inside of his legs were raw and had begun to make walking difficult as his trousers chafed the damaged skin.

Again she watched him as he undressed and stepped into the bath. He sat in the two inches of warm water, and tried to hide his penis from her sharp gaze. She made no attempt to help him wash, which he found difficult, with nothing but a huge one-pound bar of carbolic soap and no flannel or brush to raise the water above ankle level. As he twisted and turned he could see that the sides of his bottom were coloured a bright red from yesterday's disinfectant. Tonight there was none.

'Come on, boyo.' She was sitting close enough to the bath to give it a resounding kick without stirring. It gave him a shock, and he jumped.

'Woke you up, did it? I'll wake you up to get you to the pot tonight, I will. Oh! Duw, yes.' Her lips tightened. 'And now get up and wash that thing there. She picked up the wooden spoon and pointed at his willie. 'That's the cause of it all, isn't it?' As he stood she leaned forward and cradled his testicles with the wooden spoon.

'What's this then? What do you call these little things then, eh?' Remembering her anger when he had tried to cover himself last night, he stood there, tears of shame welling, totally unable to know what to do next.

Miss Philips tired of the game. She rose from the chair suddenly, threw him a small towel and snapped at him: 'Get dressed. We won't have you standing around here in that sinful state. Then it's off to bed for you it is.'

His pyjamas were in his bedroom, and tonight she made him run naked up the stairs while she followed closely behind. Once he looked behind at her. Why was she bending so low, climbing the stairs, he wondered. He didn't look again after she shouted at him: 'Look in front silly boy. You'll fall, you will now.'

She watched him as he dressed in his pyjamas and with a warning about using the pot under his bed, went out, closing the door behind her.

It was barely seven o'clock, and some light lingered in the sky. He thought he might sit up to see the coal trucks on the line above the garden. He thought about it, and drifted off into a deep sleep. He dreamed of teddy bears, and his need for a friend.

And so the days ran by, passing into weeks. At school, most of the children arrived without lunchtime sandwiches after the first day, and the teachers organised sandwich lunches for them. His sisters, he learned, were billeted with a Mrs Jones, whose husband was a farm worker. Everyone rose at six in the morning, everyone had to wait until seven, until 'Dai the land' had washed, shaved, had his breakfast, dressed for his messy work, and slammed the door behind him. This hour, his elder sister Jean complained, gave his younger sister Dot great opportunities to quarrel. After two weeks Mrs Jones had arranged for Jean to move out, to a Mrs Evans, a plump, small woman surrounded by cats and with a pig sty in her back garden. Mrs Jones couldn't stand the unending fighting, she told the teachers.

Mrs Evans wouldn't give his sister any food unless she asked for it in Welsh. Jean had tears in her eyes as she told D. She was desperately hungry, she said. He understood that. 'Miss Philips doesn't give me much food either,' he said. He didn't tell her anything else — how could he? He didn't understand what was being done to him.

'Mr Evans brings me food,' she said. 'He's nice. It's not much, but he's nice. She makes me sit on the stairs. All evening, until bedtime. He brings me a slice of bread when Mrs Evans goes out.'

'Where does she go?' he asked.

'Chapel, I think. There's a women's group she belongs to. She goes every night.'

D. was unhappy for his sister. She had been, and still was in many ways, a protective agent for him. He trusted her, while he dreaded his younger sister with her sharp temper, glittering eyes, and her smile which did not go beyond her lips.

At the end of two weeks he had learned that it was pointless trying to get into his billet before five o'clock. Since he finished school at half past three, it left a big gap of unsupervised freedom which he found it difficult to fill at first. 'Uncle' Mervyn slept until five, when he awoke for his meal and left at a quarter to six for the local pub, and thence to his work at the coal mine. The house was always locked up until five o'clock. He never learned where Miss Philips went.

Most of the time he spent wandering among the railway trucks, even walking as far as the bridge at the end of the street, though he lacked the courage to cross it. He was careful not to dirty his clothes, and kept a keen eye open for Miss Philips as she unlocked the back door and crossed the small yard to check on the shed. When he saw her, he would run to the front door, where he had to knock and wait until she opened it to let him in.

He had a bath every night. He got used to her sitting close by, wielding the wooden spoon, sniggering. He no longer had erections as the play proceeded, though he remained mortally embarrassed.

When his mother paid a visit after three weeks he pleaded with her to take him home. She reasoned with him, her chief argument seeming to be that it was the first time in years that she and his father had been able to go out in the evenings together. D. knew she liked dancing.

He cared or understood little of it, and searched desperately for a convincing reason why he should return home. He couldn't bring himself to tell her about bathtime, or the cold, lonely waiting for the door to open at five o'clock every evening. These were vague worries, and he felt they would not impress.

'I don't get much to eat,' he said at last. And this was what concerned him most. The reality of constant hunger, the rumbling tummy, headaches in the afternoon, and the ever-present concern that Miss Philips might decide to give him nothing at all one evening.

'You're always hungry,' said his mother. 'You're greedy. You never know when to stop. Miss Philips is giving you more than you get at home, that I do know. She said so.'

D. wondered briefly how Miss Philips could know what he was used to getting at home. Perhaps his mother had discussed it with her. Perhaps he was greedy after all. He certainly had more to eat at home, and perhaps what Miss Philips gave him was what boys of eight years old really should be eating. His uncertainty grew, and he subsided into acceptance of the adults' knowledge and management. If only he wasn't so hungry all the time.

Two more weeks passed. Classes at school became more organised, and the resident Welsh teachers ignored the evacuees and kept the village children well away from the 'Catholic lot', who far outnumbered them. D. had passed the headmistress one day, near the brewery, and though he had smiled at her and said, 'Good morning, Miss,' she had glared at him and passed by with a snort. So did most of the neighbours in Miss Philips' street. He was not one of them.

Mrs Robbins and his aunt had a difference in front of the class one day. Mrs Robbins said emphatically that Michaelmas Day was another name for Christmas. His aunt disagreed. The class was enthralled. The women glared at each other, his aunt's face full of sullen dislike, Mrs Robbins' lips quivering like her brother's, the headmaster. Tension rose. The children watched and listened. They had never been so quiet.

'Please Miss. Michaelmas is the feast of St Michael. It's a long time before Christmas.'

Patrick Kinsella sat, arm raised, spoiling to be a good boy. D.'s aunt smiled at him. He was in her class.

Mrs Robbins shot him looks of violent ill-will and Kinsella lowered his arm, shrinking in his seat.

'Yes, that's right,' said D.'s aunt. 'Thank you, Patrick. And now we'll get on with our lesson.' This cut Mrs Robbins out from further proceedings, and she flounced out with a glare at Kinsella. Later that week, Kinsella became the first, and only, evacuee at the school to receive the cane for being late for school.

His mother paid another visit. Again D. asked to come home. 'Hungry again, are you?' she said. 'Ew go' bloody worms, ew 'ave,' she snapped. He had not heard his mother speak so roughly before. Raw Swansea accent with temper had betrayed her origins. Then she softened. 'All right. I'll see what your father says. No promises, mind you. And I won't be back for two weeks, I won't. So you be a good boy for Miss Philips. She's looking after you well. Now, no giving her trouble. Jean and Dot aren't complaining.'

He was cheered by this. Translating the code his mother spoke he would be going home. Leaving Miss Philips and his nightly baths and her poking fun at his willie, the potato breakfasts, sandwich lunches at school, and the soup suppers at half past five with nothing else to eat or drink until eight the next morning. But he would have to wait two weeks. That would make seven weeks he had been away from home.

Two weeks later his mother took him home. 'Say goodbye to Miss

Philips,' she said at the inner doorway with the coloured glass. 'And thank her for looking after you so well.'

He thanked Miss Philips, who stared at him impassively through her gold rimmed glasses before she shut the door on them. 'Well,' said his mother. 'That wasn't very nice, was it? She might have waited until we were gone before slamming the door on us.' She hadn't slammed it really, thought D. He wondered why women quarrelled so often. They seemed very bad tempered, with so much to complain about.

Chapter Four

At home, D. hadn't realised how peaceful and worry-free life was without his sisters. Especially his younger sister, Dot, who tormented him constantly. He missed his older sister's protective influence on the journeys to and from school, and in a different way he missed her compulsive bossiness when she divided up and allocated any goodies, all too rare, which found their way to the table.

At school, life was even easier. He found the learning tasks easy, and began to earn himself maximum and near-maximum marks for everything. Occasionally his non-numerical efforts received an 'Ex' which meant excellent, and he was proud to the point of conceit about these, going to his rivals in the class between lessons and, showing them the magic letters written in teacher's red ink, he would pretend not to understand them, asking for translation. His rivals would stare at the 'Ex' with envy, reluctantly mutter the truth, and leave D. smugly happy with his day. There was a limit to the game, sadly, and after the third or fourth time he resorted to asking an explanation of the dullest boy in the class, the rest having ignored him. 'Excalibur', said Matty Dooley uncomprehendingly, and D. gave up in disgust.

His mother was less sympathetic when he told her of his achievements.

'I should think so, too. Your father is a clever man. I didn't marry him for nothing,' she said shortly. 'You'll have to do better than that at senior school.'

Eventually his sisters returned home. The squabbling between them resumed, and loud noisy rows involving both his parents and his sisters became more frequent.

Summer holidays arrived, and on fine Saturdays his father, anxiously consulting the skies for weather signs, would reluctantly agree to take them to the beach. These days out were only partly successful. D.'s mother fussed about the washing-up, cutting sandwiches, getting not only herself but the children 'ready'; if it was dark when they returned then the blackouts must be in position before they left home, towels, swimsuits, salt for the boiled eggs, buckets and spades, plasters for cuts, cream for insect bites, lemonade in case there were no kiosks open at the beach, clean handkerchiefs, spare clothing in case it turned cold: all these things had to be done, she complained. It was only she who attended to these things. Meanwhile D. and his sisters, dressed as though for church, forbidden to play or even speak as the preparations proceeded with rising tension and heightened temper, sat silently in the parlour, trying to look forward to the day out.

Finally, his father turned off the water and gas at the mains and they were on their way.

There followed the trek to the local bus stop and the endless wait for the single-deck bus which seemed to rest forever just in sight half a mile down the hill outside John the Chemist while the crew leisured itself in obedience to the timetable that no one ever saw.

After the bus journey into town there was another long walk to the Mumbles Railway, through streets of bomb-shattered buildings, hollow fire-scarred skeletons teetering on the verge of dangerous collapse. Some streets were cordoned off, others had disappeared altogether under mountains of rubble, and D.'s mother complained loudly about the detours. 'Terrible, innit?' she said repeatedly. ''S not right, it is, making us go all this way around.'

His father would remain silent, embarrassed by her complaints as they passed toiling gangs of soldiers making the buildings safe.

At the Mumbles Pier terminus they piled off with growing excitement, the smell of the nearby sea stirring the holiday spirit. But still their mother worried them, harrying them about their behaviour and 'what would people think' if they ran ahead to the coastal path leading to the beaches.

On the beach the children were constantly reminded of behaviour, and their father wandered off on his own, seeking small freedoms among the rocks where their mother was afraid to go.

Feeding time was a gritty affair. Sandwiches, butter-scarce dry, would have to be vigilantly defended from the intruding sand on which they sat. Not one of the family, however cautious, whatever they ate, would succeed in swallowing a mouthful that had not been interrupted with shock and distaste by the grinding nastiness of grains of wind-washed sand grating between clamping molars. D. and his sisters would gratefully yield to the pleasing alternative of a bottle of lemonade to clear their mouths, even though the simple act of drinking from a bottle was surrounded by difficulties.

'Put your upper lip inside the neck. Not outside. What would people think if they saw you swigging like a labourer.'

D. wasn't sure what a labourer was, but putting his top lip inside the bottle neck made drinking difficult. He had to suck hard instead of allowing the liquid simply to pour into his mouth, and all too soon his turn at the bottle was over. Why didn't they have a cup, he wondered. One would be enough for all of them, in turns.

At the end of the day, tired, irritable, worn down by their mother's constant watchfulness, they would be glad enough to set off for home. Their mother complained, their father was silent, angry, dreaming of tomorrow's night at the Maltster's Arms in Carmarthen Road with his buddies.

Supper was an impatient affair, both parents eager to see the last of their three children off to bed.

The blackout blinds always had to be removed when they got home, because the long summer nights were quite light enough for normal affairs without the aid of electric lighting.

Meanwhile the Germans had turned their attentions to Russia, a huge country of strange habits on the other side of the world. They watched newsreel maps at the cinema which showed the German advance as an enveloping black treacle spreading over the innocent white Russian countryside, with large darting hollow arrows showing how the invader was being attacked and thrown back. Each week, at their visits to the Saturday 'tuppeny rush' of children's matinees, the pool of black treacle grew larger, the hollow arrows more uncertain, until they stopped showing the map. On the wireless, solemn announcers spoke of places that lodged in the memory, like Orel, Smolensk, Kharkov. To D. and other children of his age at play in the street of school, they were only vaguely aware of being involved in something unpleasant, and that the adults were in fear of the enemy, though no one as far as any of them knew had seen the smallest trace of a German, except Uncle Jack, who had been given a medal by the King for shooting hundreds of them.

And so the summer wore on. It was a good summer that year, hot and dry, and the children ranged far from home in the long days, exploring strange streets and sometimes discovering a country lane, where they marvelled at a real cow, fearfully stretching out a hand over the gate to touch its wet black nose when the animal wandered, as cows will do, towards sounds of human activity.

His elder sister was right on one thing: they did not go to Rees the Milk's bungalow that year, or ever again. It had not been bombed, as she had predicted. His father simply could not afford it, even at reduced rates.

In early September they went back to school, and their father took his holidays, digging the garden with great vigour in response to the government's cry to 'Dig for Victory', determined to show the neighbours that even though he was not actually bashing the enemy, he was doing his bit. Every Tuesday and Saturday evening he would put on his Home Guard uniform and set off for Moriah Hall, a disused chapel leaning over a dangerously steep bend of the main road, slick with oil shed by over-strained vehicles grinding upward in bottom gear, to attend training lectures, drill, and to check the stock of explosives kept there.

He had been made quartermaster-sergeant, and kept voluminous records of every fuse and bullet issued to his company. Those he could not account for he brought home, and it took D. only a few days to learn how to load a rifle with live .303 ammunition, cock the weapon and point it in the direction of the enemy, blissfully unaware of the dangers. He even tried to set fire to the long thin sticks of cordite, brown rods of what seemed to be no more than hard rubber. The 3-inch shell fuses foxed him, and after bouncing them on the concrete pathway with no results he lost interest in them and put them back into his father's drawer, a special drawer in the parlour sideboard which contained his father's special things — rulers, blotting paper, pens, pencils, rubbers, thousands of paper-clips, bottles of ink, bicycle clips, old razors, rubber bands, and of course, clips of bullets, fuses, bundles of cordite and grease-proof packets of explosives.

D.'s father had not much dress sense. Though his work demanded a suit and white shirt, which he took seriously as denoted his status, and of which D.'s mother was embarrassingly proud, his gardening clothes transformed him into a tramp, and in his Home Guard uniform he looked, from a distance, like a brown sack of potatoes on two bow-legs. Only his three stripes saved him from the ultimate ridicule of cat-calls by the street's boys as they watched him set off for Moriah Hall. Ironically, if D.'s mother had known anything about army dress regulations, she could have transformed his appearance and sent him out of the house with the same degree of vigilance as she maintained over his clerk's suiting. As it was, D. would watch him stride away up the street, vaguely ashamed of him and his unmilitary appearance, watching him from behind the garden hedge, watching the boys in the street watching his father, dreading the ultimate humiliation of a shouted gibe which would separate him forever from their company.

But it never came. They watched in silence and went about their play after the watchful pause and forgot about it. D. would retreat silently into his own back garden, not willing to press their goodwill or to test their friendship too soon after what seemed to him to be a crisis. After all, he was still an oddity in the street: a Catholic.

He went back to school as the days grew shorter. D.'s mother worried about the supply of coal for the winter, which always arrived on time because D.'s father worked for a company which owned not only coal mines but several small steel works, which brought coal from other mine-owners for the furnaces. It was worth five pounds a ton, D. heard his father say. They had two tons a year, though Mr Brown up the street, who was a miner, had five tons a year free. Mr Brown's coal was tipped in one huge heap on the pavement outside his house, which he had to carry down a steep front garden to his coal shed at the back, bucket by bucket. Even though he was a miner, the task took him days to complete, and while his coal lay in the open on the pavement for the better part of a week, not a grain of it was stolen and no one even thought of making a complaint about the obstruction it caused, even in the hazard of the blackout, which included street lighting.

D.'s father's coal, though less, was delivered in sacks, dumped in the unlighted space under the stairs in flurries of dust that caused his mother to sulk.

Neighbours noted the difference and made sly comments about privilege, and put forward dark prophecies about how 'things would change after the war'.

Christmas that year was more difficult than the previous year. Presents from 'Father Christmas' were smaller, chocolates and cakes were fewer, though the family still enjoyed a huge turkey on Christmas Day and for many days afterwards as usual. There was great fuss over mixing the Christmas pudding, and the ceremony of dropping in sixpence pieces wrapped in grease-proof paper was excitingly the same. This year the sixpences were replaced by silver threepenny pieces. D.'s sister Dot stole one of these, ineptly, before it was wrapped up and dropped in, and the loss was noticed immediately. There were only five of them anyway. D.'s father took over when his mother announced one missing. 'Right!' he declared officiously. 'We'll conduct a search. If it isn't found, the guilty one will be punished.'

This non-sequitur brought a ghost of a smile to his mother's lips.

The threepenny piece was not found. D. was questioned closely, since he now had a pedigree of theft dating from the plundered Christmas chocolate log, but nothing was proved. His mother glared with disbelief as he denied knowledge of the missing coin, but he escaped punishment, despite her muttered threats.

D.'s mother got into a bad mood on Christmas Eve, and it grew into a snappy bad temper by Christmas Day dinner. His father was silent most of the time and stayed in the parlour, reading. Christmas dinner was a trial, his father bossily and officiously carving up the turkey whilst his mother spent most of the meal ticking-off D. and his sisters about table manners. 'Don't hold your fork like that. Like this.' She would demonstrate while the culprit studiously looked away. 'Look at me when I'm talking to you,' she would snap. 'Like this.' The other two children would watch furtively, glad they had not come under attention, fearful of the next rule that would include them.

The meal was miserable, the children constantly nagged for petty infringements of table manners, their father silent as he shovelled forkfuls of food in a way which seemed to D. none too polished anyway. He wondered if his mother would mention this until he saw that his mother took licence with her own plate. She shovelled away like his father.

The Christmas pudding went, accompanied by loud complaints from D.'s mother about the amount of time it took to prepare, and the few minutes it took for everyone to eat it. Next came the chores of clearing the table and washing up. Each of the children was designated a task, carried out under the merciless eye, and tongue, of their mother.

After the chores their father retired to bed to recover from the heavy meal. The children were commanded to play with their toys quietly. Overseen by their mother who sat in an armchair in the room, Dot had less opportunity to wreak her special brand of disruptive mischief on the other two, managing to engineer only two rebukes for them. Both parents found it easier to chastise the victims of her spitefulness rather than her herself, since she would, like Violet Elizabeth Bott, scream and scream at the smallest excuse. She had learned of her mother's fear of 'What the neighbours would think', and squeezed maximum advantage from it. She smiled with pleasure, and a sense of achievement, her eyes glittering with malice at her siblings' distress as they laboured under the injustice of a tongue lashing which she was fully aware was her own due. Snatching a toy not hers, breaking deliberately a vital piece, hiding another treasured item, claiming absurdly a possession clearly not her own, silently and with venom, all actions guaranteed to cause loud protest; these were her weapons to compensate for being the youngest, and number five in the pecking order in a family of five.

As 1942 began, a sixth member of the family made an appearance. His name was Toby. To D. it seemed that Toby was everywhere, his mother referred to him so often, frequently with a puzzling sly smile, and the rest of the time with a contemptuous sneer. When D.'s turn came to fetch a quick supper from Williams the Fish, the shopping list was four chips, two fish and two Tobys. Mr Williams was highly amused by the verbal order, and after a loud laugh quietly explained that the small, wrinkled round cones were rissoles.

Back at home, as he delivered the warm bundles of newspaper-wrapped fish and chips, his mother asked him what he had said to Mr Williams. He told her. 'They're called rissoles, Mam, not Tobys.'

His mother was highly amused. 'Hee, hee, hee,' she went. All the children were puzzled.

'Why are you laughing, Mam?' asked his elder sister. 'Never mind. Ask your father.' She fell into giggles again as she shared out the food on plates and brought knives and forks, salt and O.K. sauce.

By the time their father came home, as punctual as ever at ten minutes past six, they had forgotten about the laughter, and didn't ask him.

As the winter wore on there were only the vaguest of reminders of the ordeals by bombing of a year before. Air raid warnings were a thing of the past, and only the occasional flight of a squadron of fighters from Fairwood airfield on the common to remind them that they were vulnerable.

Other reminders were more subtle. The butter ration fell to two ounces per week per person, like tea and meat.

At this time too, in the winter of early 1942, D. had his first taste of face sores. They were to plague him for many months. At the corners of his mouth, under the lobes of his ears and around his eyes, the sores formed and then cracked, painfully and with immense irritation. At home there were ointments he could sneak into, tenderly and desperately daubing the open cracks to get temporary relief. At school the sores tormented him, and more than one teacher paid him attention as he rubbed his eyes and worked his mouth, distorting his whole face in frustration.

Later that year he was moved to the senior school, two years ahead of his proper time. He found himself in classes with eleven-year-olds at first, then twelve-year-olds, and he still only nine. He didn't question this, and found the level of difficulty in the learning hardly different from his junior school. The only practical difference was that he traded the nuns' oppressive disapproval and universal censure for the rougher, noisier environment of boys much older than himself. His adaptation to the changes was overshadowed by the brutality of the teachers, all men, all with reputations and peculiarities, all armed with thin, cutting bamboo canes. In Standard 6, 'Dwt' Barry, so nicknamed because he was small, was a venomous, Himmler-like figure with a swarthy chin driven to madness by the sight of a boy who, unable to answer a question, looked upwards for guidance. He would slide from his high teacher's desk like a dry, sly snake, cane in hand, and stand beside the trembling boy, hissing quietly 'Stand, boy'. The boy would stand, fully aware of the next stage.

'God is not on your side, boy. There are no answers written on the ceiling.' His voice would rise in rage and excess of power. 'Look to your front. At me. I ask the questions, not the ceiling.' He accompanied these words with slashing strokes of the cane aimed at the bare part of the legs, between stocking tops and trouser edges. It was a wonderment, but he never did cure a whole class for a whole year of looking to the ceiling for guidance.

Spud Murphy of Standard 7 was less poisonous, but terribly threatening as he was a large man, who wore a greasy brown sports jacket with leather elbows and moved as quickly as a boxer. A boy who caught his attention would be genuinely frightened by the speed with which Spud could travel from his desk to his side, the rate actually causing a wind from the displacement of air as he seemed to change places instantaneously. But Spud rarely caned. Instead he sent serious offenders to the headmaster, who unquestioningly punished the boys with merciless vigour.

Mark Walsh governed Standard 8, the most senior class, of fourteen-year-olds. He was as old as all the other teachers put together, utterly humourless, dry, grey, rheumy-eyed and he creaked every time he moved, which was not often. He caned in the classroom as frequently as anyone else, but was so weak that the punishment posed little threat to boys who were determined to offend. Indeed, in the playground at breaks, it was a cause of much humour for a boy to confess to a caning from 'Markie'.

The school had been slightly damaged in the bombing of the year before, and the wood-block flooring in part of the school had been burned. It lent an air of scruffiness to a building that was already overdue for a coat of paint, and seemed to D. to be knee deep in dust, and smelled of decay and outdated purpose. His own father had been taught in this school, by pretty much the same teachers, though he had never spoken about his time there. Curiously, he was on Christian name terms with the teachers, even the awful head-master. None of them seemed to D. to be human enough to have Christian names.

It took D. some days to realise that his elder sister Jean was not waiting for him at the girls' school gate as she usually had done when he had been in the junior school. Now that he was in the seniors he finished lessons at four o'clock, and not at half-past three. His sister was still in junior school, and wouldn't wait half an hour for him. He braved the journey home on his own. He understood instinctively that travelling through gang territories with a girl saved him endless threats and dangers. On his own he was vulnerable.

The Gwili gang was the worst. Gwili Terrace ran parallel to his own street, and was separated from it by very long, steep gardens. The gardens in his street were for the most part neatly kept, with carefully clipped hedges and well-tended vegetable patches and flowers, but the Gwili gardens were a shambles. The weeds grew tall and unmolested among bushes and nettle clumps and were riddled by pathways plundered by the younger children who played games of cowboys and indians amongst them.

The boys seemed somehow to echo this general neglect of values. They were extremely rough, with proud Borstal convictions liberally sprinkled among the older teenagers, mainly for petty theft and public affray. Younger boys were impressed by this evidence of 'toughness' and sought to copy it. Most sensible people, even adults, didn't venture into Gwili Terrace unless they had to live there. They walked around it. Even the girls were formidable, and had been known to set about a defiant child who had strayed into their territory with fists, nails and boots, cheered on, and backed up by, the boys. The girls did it because they couldn't lose: the boys would take over if there was the smallest sign that the girls were being bettered.

So it was with some surprise that D. found himself halfway along Gwili Terrace on his way home one day. Everyone knew about Gwili Terrace. D. did too, and this was his first time on this street, partly explaining why he was there at all.

It seemed peaceful enough to him. No threatening advance of scowling, hostile enemies; no stone-throwing ambushes or stick-wielding chasers. Their reputation was all stories, perhaps.

Then he saw them. A dozen boys, all older than he, gathered in a noisy circle around a centre of some interest on the pavement. They seemed to be prodding something on the ground, using sticks and tentative toes. Loud laughter and shouts of 'Stick it up his arse' reached him.

Perhaps he could pass them by if they were occupied. They might not notice him passing on the far side of the road, which had no pavement anyway, where nobody walked.

As he sidled past the knot of excited boys he paused to see the cause of the excitement. They had cornered a frog. Or more exactly, a toad. They were trying to stuff a hollow straw up its rectum and blow into the straw to inflate the little animal. Overcome by indignation at this senseless torture D. crossed the road, wanting to interfere but unsure how he could achieve anything. Close up, the boys were fiercesome indeed, and warranted their reputation. Clad in assorted clothes of torn jackets mainly too big for them and obviously fathers' hand-me-downs, shattered boots without socks and filthy shirts, they were menacing and uncivilised.

'Please,' said D. to the boy holding the toad. 'I'll give you a halfpenny for it.' The crowd of boys was struck into silence. The boy holding the toad froze. 'What?' he said, unable to understand.

'A halfpenny,' said D. 'For the frog.' The boy stood up, toad in hand. He looked around his colleagues for guidance. They were silent.

The boy finally held out the toad on his hand to D., holding out the other for his money. The halfpenny was D.'s weekly pocket money, and he had received it from his father only that morning. It was all he had. What other way could he rescue the toad?

He took the little animal and handed over the halfpenny. He turned in total silence from the boys, and carried it away with him. As he walked he felt his back tingle. There was nothing to stop them reclaiming his toad by force, keeping the halfpenny and continuing their cruel game. But silence followed him. There was no attempt to interfere with him. Fifty yards on, as he turned off the street to mount the flight of concrete steps connecting his own street with Gwili Terrace, he turned to check on them. If they had remained in the same place he was far enough ahead now to outrun them if they changed their minds.

They were standing in a group, looking at him, silent. There were no shouts, no threats. Just looking at him.

When he got home he released the toad in the front garden, where there was plenty of vegetation and the odd gap under the concrete front steps for the animal to hide.

When he went into the house his mother asked him sharply, 'What were you doing in the front garden? Hiding something, was it?'

'No, Mam. I had a toad. I put it in a safe place.'

'Don't tell lies. It was something else. Something you don't want me to see, isn't it?'

He protested. It was the truth.

'Let's see it then,' said his younger sister. She had been sitting in the shadows in the corner of the kitchen, enjoying his discomfiture.

'It's crawled into the hole now,' he said. 'You can't see it.'

'Of course not,' said his mother. 'Whatever it was hasn't crawled anywhere. It's still there, so go and get it.'

'He's stole something, Mam. That's why he won't show it,' said his sister.

'Have you?' demanded his mother. 'I'll give you a good hiding if you have, mind.' She paused and added theatrically, 'No son of mine is going to be a thief. Oh no. I'll hang him myself first.' She shook a finger close to his face. 'You'll tell everything to your father, as soon as he gets home. D'you hear?' With lips compressed so that her upper lip formed small furrows, she pronounced sentence.

'No tea or supper for you, my boy, until we get to the bottom of this. And you'll get nothing until your father gets home.'

'For telling lies,' his sister taunted.

He glared furiously at her, but before he could deliver a rebuke his mother snapped, 'Get some coal for the fire. Do something right. And don't look at me like that. It's a boy's job. The girls shouldn't have to do that sort of heavy work. You're a boy. At least you seem to be. You've got a toby anyway.'

He looked at her and then at his sister. So that's what the 'Toby' jokes were about. His willie. His sister had a sly smile, gloating.

After he had loaded the stove with coal he went outside to the front garden. He couldn't fully understand what had happened in the kitchen. Rescuing the toad and placing it in a place of safety had led to dark talk of hanging, and losing his tea at least, since his father wouldn't be home much before suppertime.

He found the toad without much trouble. On hands and knees he peered into the gap under the concrete step and there it was, throat pulsing slowly, blinking one golden eye against a thin dead blade of grass bent towards it.

He was deeply startled by his mother's triumphant shout right behind him.

'Aha!' she crowed. 'Back to the scene of the crime, is it? Can't leave it there can you, now that you've been found out.' She had followed him on tiptoe.

Hands on hips, mouth threateningly set, she stood with a baleful glint in the eyes. His sister waited behind her, a smile on her mouth and her eyes aglitter.

'I knew you couldn't be trusted,' said his mother.

'It's the toad,' said D., close to tears of frustration. 'It's in here.' As he spoke he made to grab one of the toad's front legs, but the animal retreated deeper into the hole until nothing short of a crabbing hook could hope to retrieve it. 'It's gone into the hole,' he said lamely. 'I can't get it.'

His mother cuffed him across the head. 'I can't stand liars. Especially weak little boys who don't grow up.' She turned to go back to the kitchen. 'You wait till your father gets home. He's not so soft as I am. He'll teach you. And whatever it is you've got there you have it on the table before you go to bed, or it will be early bed for you, my boy.'

He sat on the concrete step outside the front door, confused beyond his understanding.

He heard the door behind him open. 'And don't go out playing with those Protestant boys, either,' she said. 'I won't have it.'

The door slammed shut. He didn't play with them often, unless he met them on the way back from school. So it didn't make much difference.

He got up and wandered into the back garden. As he passed the back door he looked at the latch, expecting his mother to appear with a new threat. The latch hole was a charred gouger burned by his father with a hot poker. When they had moved into the house all the children were too small to reach the latch, and his father had lowered it. He didn't have any idea how to drill a new hole in the door, and D. could clearly recall his father's officious irritation as he surveyed the problem, until his mother suggested the poker. That's how her father had done such things.

The hole was so big that his mother complained about the draught in cold weather, so it was plugged with bits of newspaper from the inside. The plug prevented the latch from moving, and whoever was outside on a cold windy day had to knock for admittance, hoping that someone would hear. And that wasn't the end of it. The plug often refused to move when teased from the inside. And the only tool that could remove it anyway was a special piece of wire, kept on the floor nearby in total darkness.

On a freezing cold day then, the procedure to enter the house was to knock, wait for an answering shout inside, wait for the wire to be tossed from the nearby lavatory window, then poke away with a running commentary from inside until the plug was cleared. The latch could then be used. Complications arose if someone was in the toilet at the time. There was nothing to do but wait.

Once inside, the plug had to be replaced, a task not entrusted to the children, annoying their parents who complained about 'kids going in and out' having no thought for others, i.e. their parents.

Their mother had been heard to wonder if it was all worth it, but she refused to let them use the front door, which was kept permanently locked 'in case somebody broke in'. Nobody had ever even heard of a break-in over the length and breadth of the huge estate, let alone suffered one.

Today it was late spring and a warm day, and D. was relieved that he would not need to antagonise either his mother or sister to open the door.

In some misery he strolled to the nasturtium bed. The flowers were opening. He plucked one of the cone-shaped blooms, nicked off the end and put it to his lips. He tasted honey, just as one of the boys in the street had said. It was tasty, and he stretched out his hand to pluck another.

The window behind him opened with a clang of the steel frame.

'Leave those flowers alone, you wicked boy! What a destructive nature you got! You naughty boy. Can't trust you with anything, can I?' His mother continued to mutter as she closed the window. She watched him as he stood, nonplussed, undecided, forbidden to play, reluctant to go indoors, every move in the garden watched and circumscribed. In the end he wandered over to the air raid shelter, and sat on the far side of its grass-grown hump, out of sight of the kitchen window.

As he sat contemplating the mountain tops far beyond the roofs of the houses in the next street below, his mother shouted.

'D.!' He raised his head.

'Where are you?' He got up, his spirits falling further. As he showed himself, he saw his mother at the opened kitchen window.

'Yes, Mam?' he replied.

'What are you doing behind there?' she demanded.

'Nothing. I was just sitting down.'

'Well don't sit on damp grass, you silly boy. That will stain your trousers. That means more washing for me. But you don't care do you. You just dirty things, and expect me to get them clean. So come away from there.'

He walked up the sloping path to the house, at a total loss for what he could do next.

'And don't come in here. I don't want you plaguing me. Stay out there.' His mother closed the window firmly. He settled for sitting on the front steps, occasionally bending down to check on his toad, whose gleaming golden eyes and tiny nostrils he could just see in the gloom of the hole under the steps.

When his father came down the steps D. was stiff and cold. The

69

late spring sun had begun to fade and he was on the shadow side of the house anyway.

'What are you doing here?'

His father's gruff question was not encouraging.

'I was just sitting here,' said D., at a loss. He was uncertain about the next few minutes, when his father would be confronted by the long list of misdeeds.

'Hmm.' His father passed him on the steps and went on his way to the back door. He would have his tea next, and D. knew that his mother would not raise any controversial matter with him until he had finished, taken off his collar and tie, put on his slippers and settled himself in the parlour with the day's newspapers — the *Daily Express*, which was interesting, and the *Daily Herald*, which was boring. Usually, D. would wait, eagerly watching his father put aside one of the papers so that he could pick it up to read. Rupert Bear and Beachcomber, who wrote a small piece in naive spelling, which amused him greatly, were his favourites. Tonight he was looking forward to cutting out numbers 42 and 43, the final pair, in a Rupert Bear adventure. He had all the other numbers, glued neatly together in a miniature book, and it would be a disaster if he didn't get the final cartoons.

D. followed his father into the house.

Tension rose as his father neared the end of his meal. D. stood to one side in the kitchen, on hand for the showdown. He did not want to increase his mother's looming anger by being missing at the critical moment.

D.'s younger sister came in, wearing a sly smirk. She wanted to be near the fun. His mother sat opposite his father, darting 'just you wait' glances at D.

The tension increased. It finally became so palpable that his father looked up from his cup of tea and looked around the assembled silent company. 'What's wrong?' he asked.

'D.,' said his mother. 'He's stolen something.' She raised her arms dramatically, and gave a heavy sigh, yielding to the burdens of motherhood. 'I don't know what or who from, but he's hidden it in the front garden somewhere and won't show me.'

His father looked at him. 'Show me,' he said.

'I didn't steal anything Dad. It was a toad. I got it from the Gwili gang. I gave them a ha'penny for it.'

'Where did you get a ha'penny from?' His mother's voice was a snarl of disbelief.

'Pocket money. Dad paid me this morning.'

His father finished his tea and stood up. D. was fearful. His father had a hard hand.

'Come on, then. Show me,' he repeated. 'Let's see this toad.'

D. sighed in relief. At least his father was willing to believe him. Now to produce the evidence.

He led the way to the front steps, his father behind, then his mother, with his younger sister, disappointment in her face, last.

'You have to get down low,' explained D. 'I tried to get it out for Mam, but he went back, down deep. I don't want to hurt it pulling it out.'

His father got down low. D. prayed hard that the animal was still there.

'Yes, I see it. Big one, isn't he?' His father got up. 'Why did you give them money for it, though?'

D. explained that there were a lot of boys, big ones, and they were torturing the toad. His father nodded, turned away and went back into the house.

'Do you believe him, Frank?' D.'s mother was as disappointed as his sister.

'Yes, it's probably true,' said his father. 'Anyway I don't think it's worth bothering with. Not worth a fuss. I'm tired now. I'm going to sit in the parlour.'

When his father had gone indoors, D.'s mother turned to him and hissed. 'You wait my boy. I'll be watching you. You're a thief and a liar, and we both know it. You won't get away with this.'

He regarded her, round-eyed, expecting a blow. She looked so angry. She turned away and went indoors, pushing his sister ahead of her.

He was hungry and thirsty. He had had nothing to eat or drink since school lunchtime, and that had not been very much. He would have to go indoors soon, anyway. The sun had gone down.

For the price of further bullying from his mother he got his supper. His day ended in glowering silences which affected even his father, and he was glad to go to bed at half-past eight. He was tired, and had no difficulty in falling asleep.

The summer holidays came, and like the year before he slipped away with the boys in the street on long exploring walks. He avoided the Hendersons, the only other Catholic boys in the street. They were all older than he, and bullied him. He was glad that their mother forbade them to play with Protestants, so that they remained outsiders. The Protestant boys seemed totally unaware of religion, and regarded him with immense surprise when he crossed himself, as he had been firmly taught to do whenever he passed the Catholic church, on their wanderings.

That summer his Uncle Denis was killed in the war. Uncle Denis had been very good at making crispy chips on the gas ring, and had been given a severe electric shock last Christmas when he tried to fix decoration lights to the ceiling socket.

Uncle Denis was a Merchant Navy seaman, and his ship had been torpedoed only a few miles from the docks at Swansea. His ship had been carrying butter, D.'s mother said. 'That was the price innocent people paid for the Black Market,' said his mother with feeling.

'What's that, Mam?'

'What?'

'The Black Market.'

'I don't know. Everybody's talking about it. It means our boys have to risk their lives for it,' she said.

It made no sense. He would ask his father when his mother wasn't around.

She didn't seem to miss Uncle Denis very much. She showed no apparent affection beyond banning D. from singing 'Red Sails in the Sunset', which was Uncle Denis's favourite song. Uncle Denis faded to a memory of a lively seventeen-year-old with curly hair who played roughly with them on the back lawn. D. remembered when he was smaller, riding on Uncle Denis piggy-back and falling off. His elbow had hurt so much that he went to hospital for an X-ray. He was X-rayed by his Uncle Bill, whose real name was Stanislaus, which he hated so much that he became threatening to any who used it. His elbow had not been damaged, and his mother had turned nasty about it, saying he had been wasting everyone's time 'with his silly crying'.

At around the same time, a second brother of his mother's, Uncle Joe, was taken into care at the town's mental hospital. He was schizophrenic, it was said in hushed tones. In the bombing of last year's winter he had been at home with his mother when the house had been extensively damaged by a near miss, and it was suggested that this experience had been too much for him. Anyway, he was whisked off to the red brick building on an isolated hill outside the town surrounded by stout fencing. D. never saw his Uncle Joe again. His one last guilt-stricken memory had been of he and his younger sister taunting him with the garden fork as he opened the back door to their knock. He was looking after them while their mother was shopping. Even then Uncle Joe had not seemed right in the head.

For many years afterward until he died in his mid-seventies, Uncle

Joe was visited faithfully and regularly by his mother and D.'s mother, every Tuesday afternoon, mostly by a long and tedious bus journey of at least two changes of bus, in all weathers, summer and winter. They brought him Woodbines and a bar of chocolate, his only worldly wants.

Chapter Five

The sharp knife was special. It was, to anyone else, a very ordinary bone-handled table knife, common in millions of household kitchens throughout the land. But this one was different. Its handle was square, the blade sharpened by D.'s father's officious attentions to a sharpness so acute that it removed hair from his arm without him feeling it. This test was carried out every Sunday morning before the knife was handed to D.'s mother with ceremony, visited by the same words, repeated every time with the same satisfied smile of achievement: 'There you are, Doll, shave a baby's bum with it.' D.'s mother would take it carefully and thank him as though he had performed a task which would be completely beyond her. She would use it that morning, preparing vegetables for Sunday lunch, the main meal of the week, while her husband played snooker at the Church Hall after late mass. His snooker was the deciding factor in when they ate, since it was unthinkable to eat Sunday lunch without their father present to carve the joint.

The blade of the knife was eaten away by the sharpening stone so that it curved inwards at the middle, the width less than half of that near the handle. Towards the end it narrowed to a wicked point which sank through a joint of beef as easily as a crisp cabbage.

The children were forbidden to use the sharp knife under any circumstances. Before they took their turns at washing up the dishes, their mother removed it carefully, washed and dried it herself and put it away in the cutlery drawer. Most often, it would not be in the knife box at all, but tucked away out of sight at the back of the drawer. Undoubtedly it was the most real and dangerous thing in the house, far ahead of the fire or the assortment of explosives in their father's drawer.

The wild stab D.'s mother made at his willie with the knife nearly took him by surprise. They were alone in the kitchen. He had returned home after an exhausting day exploring bombed buildings with the boys in the street and was hungry and thirsty, hoping tea would not be far off.

'Hello, Mam. Gosh, I'm hungry. What's for tea?' he said breathlessly as he came in.

His mother turned from the sink where she was preparing a meal. Her face was a mask of fury. D.'s heart sank. She was in a bad mood.

He took a step back from her as the first move to go outside and away from her, but she lunged, knife in hand.

He doubled backwards instinctively, throwing his hands in front of him at the last moment. The knife grated on the bone in the back of his hand, and was instantly agonising, hot, sharp pain stabbing through it. He let out a yelp and turned away to run into the parlour.

'Toby. That's what you'll have for tea,' his mother hissed. Her voice grew louder, filled with hatred and anger. 'Toby. You come near me and I'll have it off. I'll fry the bloody thing and give it to the cat.'

Shaking with uncomprehending fear, shock and no small amount of pain, D. retreated to the far end of the parlour, near the front door, from whence he thought he might get away if she came after him. She didn't. As the threat waned, he examined his hand. There was a semi-circular slice cut into the back of his left hand, bleeding plentifully. He licked it. It stung. He pressed the edges of the cut and the bleeding stopped. Perhaps it was not too serious, he thought.

The plasters were in the bathroom, but to get there he would have to pass through the kitchen, where his mother still cut away at the vegetables in the sink. He could hear her muttering to herself. He looked around. The airing cupboard. That was here in the room. It was where all the clean ironed clothes were kept. Perhaps one of his father's handkerchiefs would serve as a bandage. He had seen that done at the cinema newsreel one week where air raid injured had been bandaged with handkerchiefs and headscarves in an emergency.

He found a handkerchief, after he had opened the cupboard door as silently as he could, not easy when he had to watch behind him instead of looking at the catch. It wasn't too difficult to wrap the thin cotton square around his hand, and he could secure it with his thumb. Holding the injured hand at shoulder height, which was again what he remembered from cinema newsreels, he crept upstairs, avoiding the third step, which creaked.

In his bedroom he sat on his bed, very gently because it was old and creaked a lot. He still trembled, and his face felt cold and was covered in beads of perspiration. He began to feel faint, so he carefully lay down, holding his hand in the air. It throbbed. He looked at the door, which was ajar. It would not close properly because it was a bad fit and fouled the jamb, and his father had no idea what to do about it. In stormy weather and strong winds it swung to and fro with loud squeaking from the hinges, which upset his sisters in the next bedroom who blamed him for it. The remedy was to take several volumes of the set of Dickens stories and stack them against both sides of the open door. Some nights he needed all twelve of the heavy books, so much air entered the house, forced in by the gusts outside. The house was very exposed, a penalty for the wonderful views.

He got up from the bed, and trying not to use his injured hand, placed all the books against the door, which he pushed shut as far as he could. He handled them carefully. They were the only books in the house apart from a thick volume of children's fairy stories, which had been around ever since he could remember. The Dickens books were small print on thin paper, difficult to read, and D. had found that unless he read some every day he soon forgot what it was about and had to go back pages to remind himself, which made one book last a long time. He tried to recall how far he had read of *Little Dorrit*.

He awoke to his younger sister screaming in panic that she couldn't open the bedroom door. The light had faded, and one hand had gone to sleep where he had lain on it. He suddenly realised that he had fallen asleep, and forgetting his injured hand, pushed himself up in bed. His hand hurt, and he remembered. He looked at it. The blood had turned light brown and there wasn't too much of it. The handkerchief was firmly stuck to the skin around the cut, so he left it there, and crossed the room to the door.

He pulled away the books and opened the door to his sister's glaring eyes.

'Stupid,' she spat. 'Your tea's ready. Mam says if you don't come down I can have it. And I'm going to tell her that you put the books there.'

He replaced the books as quickly as he could and went downstairs. His mother paid no attention to him, and ignored his handkerchiefed hand. He was hungry, and at the table she and his sister were already halfway through a fried egg, a sausage and a slice of fried bread.

It tasted miraculously satisfying, but he could have eaten ten of them, one after the other. With his mother watching with menace in her eyes he didn't ask for more.

She poured a mug of tea each for them. He reached for the spoon in the sugar bowl after she and his sister had taken theirs.

'About time you learned to do without sugar,' said his mother. 'It's a waste for you to take sugar in your tea. Rations are small enough as it is. Your father don't take sugar in his tea. It's about time you started to grow up.' He withdrew his hand. He sipped his tea and it tasted awful. His mother watched him.

'You drink it all, my boy,' she said with warning in her voice. 'Tea is too precious to waste on ungrateful people like you. Our boys risk their lives to bring it to you, so finish it.'

He finished it. It wasn't too bad. It must be alright if his father drank tea without sugar.

'Your turn at washing up,' sang his sister. 'I did it yesterday so it's your turn today.'

'That's right,' said his mother. 'You don't get away with it just because you're a boy. You take your turn with the girls. No favouritism here. Good training for you when you grow up. If you ever do.'

The handkerchief came off his hand easily enough in the warm soapy water. It stung a little but didn't bleed any more. When he had finished the dishes he dried his hand and put on a small sticky plaster over the cut. It still throbbed. Perhaps he would have a scar, he thought. He might even claim to have been wounded in the bombing. Pity the bruise around the wound looked so fresh. Still, he didn't mind waiting for it to age until it couldn't be dated.

Later that summer, during their father's holidays in September, the family went cockle-picking at low tide on the beach at Blackpill. Uncle Bernard lived at Blackpill, a small village on the Mumbles Road, where the steam railway from Swansea docks took a sharp turn away from the coast to call at villages inland from the north Gower coast. The railway crossed the road by a high stone bridge, which somehow marked the end of the town and formed the impression of a gateway to the countryside, or to D. and his sisters, holiday country. Beyond the bridge were country lanes, beaches and clear roads without pavements and no lamp posts.

Uncle Bernard's house was a good walk beyond the bridge, so that the trains crossing the bridge could hardly be heard, even at night when the village was very quiet. To the back of the house the Mumbles Train thundered by, quite close to the back garden fence, but the Mumbles Train was special, and its ugly intrusive bulk was treated with a possessive affection by everyone. It was special because it was the only one of its kind in the whole country, they were told. The whole world, perhaps. It ran around the curve of Swansea Bay, most of the way very close to the seaside, its tall, double-deck, bus-like coaches swaying and jerking along five miles of track with intermittent passing places, to serve not only day trippers to the Mumbles beaches of Bracelet Bay, Limeslade and further, but durable commuters to town. It was reliable to the minute, and carried huge numbers of people, especially when two

77

coaches were coupled together to cope with rush-hour workers and peak holiday crowds. It was rare to see anyone left behind at a stop. There were no limits to the number of people standing.

The Mumbles Train was powered by electricity, and took its supply from overhead lines suspended from huge ugly green steel tubes spaced alongside the track, and the overall effect of the system was a massive ugliness, but no one complained. It was special.

At the bottom of Uncle Bernard's garden was a gate that opened directly and dangerously on to the Mumbles Train track. Beyond the track was the beach. To D. this was amazing. To have a back garden gate was interesting enough. To have one that led on to a rail track was intriguing. But a gate that gave uninterrupted access to a sandy beach and the sea was nothing short of a dream.

D. was crestfallen when he visited Uncle Bernard for the first time to be forbidden to use the gate for fear of the trains. He didn't see why he couldn't go to the beach if he kept a sharp lookout for an approaching train. After all, they were very noisy.

The danger of the train was only half the truth, as it turned out. Beyond the track the narrow strip of land before the beach was heavily mined. Though protected by barbed wire, it was easy enough for a stranger to mistake a small gap in the wire for a way through, and for a nine-year-old boy, as both his father and his uncle knew, even the smallest gap was the same as a way through. There were passages through the wire, and these were guarded by soldiers who demanded passes before allowing anyone by. Later the Home Guard took over these duties, and later still as the Germans seemed ever less likely to come, they were abandoned in favour of warning notices. No one ever strayed into the mined strip, though somebody's pet collie had been blown up one night, causing much alarm in the neighbourhood.

D. liked fried cockles and worked prodigiously with the others on the beach, digging with his fingers and scooping them into an enamel bowl, stopping occasionally to wash away the shiny mud and leave the cockles clean and sharp in the bowl. He would be pleased and flattered later to be given a bag to carry some of them home, though his parents would take most of them. At home they would be weighed, in their shells, and everyone would have a guess at how much the boiled and ready-to-eat de-shelled cockles would weigh. His father always won.

They stayed only for the day, and caught the Mumbles Train back to Swansea and the bus up the hill to home and dull reality as the day faded. Sometimes, but not often, if Uncle Bernard and Aunt

Eileen and his parents got carried away in the Woodman's Inn, the pub right opposite Uncle Bernard's house, they stayed until dark.

Aunt Eileen, Uncle Bernard's wife, was a happy woman. She laughed often, though D. seldom understood the jokes she made. Unlike his mother, who had short, thick legs which made her look dumpy and small, Aunt Eileen was tall, slim and good looking. She spoke with a softer accent than his own family because she came from a different part of Wales, and she used words D. had never heard before. But what made her really different and interesting was that she was the only Protestant in the family. Nobody in the immigrant Irish caucus to which D.'s family belonged had ever been anything but Catholic. There were the occasional 'lapsed' members, of whom dark words were spoken in hushed tones; there were some 'saintly' members, who were obsessed zealots and attended mass every day and twice on Sundays and were sniggered at by saner confessors of the faith; there was one who had actually turned to the Church of England, which was almost the same thing as Protestant. But an actual member of a nonconformist church had never entered the family until Aunt Eileen. And she bore the difference with a smile.

Her jokes sometimes made D.'s mother frown, and he wondered if like him she didn't understand them too, and his father would twist his mouth in suppressed laughter. But then his father was clever, and understood most things. But on the journey back home D.'s mother would discuss the evening and analyse Aunt Eileen's sense of humour in tones of disapproval in a low voice which she thought D. could not hear. His father shrugged his shoulders and looked at his shoes. He had enjoyed the day, so it didn't matter now.

Overall, Uncle Bernard and Aunt Eileen seemed to live a wonderfully relaxed life, living so near the sea and the countryside. The afternoon sun shone through the front room windows which had huge panes of glass in wood frames, so unlike his own home with its small mean windows in perspiring metal frames. There was pampas grass in a huge vase in the corner and the furniture was summery wickerwork with rush matting on the yielding wood plank floor. The floors in his own home were painted concrete under their sparse matting. The whole house was light, airy, with sandy pastel colours and many pictures on the walls. The only drawback was that there was no front garden, and the front door opened directly on to the pavement, though nobody ever walked past because the pavement ended a few yards further on. Uncle Bernard even knew a farmer nearby who sold them meat joints off the ration. Fred Barrow had a very broken nose and smelled horribly, but was very friendly and enjoyed taking D. on a tour of his farmyard and buildings where he kept many animals D. had never seen close-up before: pigs, cows, sheep, geese and chickens.

Often, D. would go to Blackpill lane with his parents, leaving his sisters behind. His elder sister would be left at home to 'look after' Dot, his younger sister. But Dot had a difficult personality — D. didn't like her, and she caused him much anguish with spiteful and vindictive behaviour, so it was with a feeling of vindication that he arrived home with his parents to find there had been a battle royal between his sisters. It showed that Dot fought with anyone and everyone, and not just him, so that he couldn't always be held to blame when she began to scream in rage at her inability to overcome him by bullying. Anyway, if anyone fought with Jean it demonstrated a strange nature, because Jean was naturally an easy-going and agreeable girl, and one would have to work hard to offend her.

Once or twice, that September in 1942, the family visited the small, rocky beaches beyond Mumbles, but the weather was bad, D.'s mother complained of the cold, and barbed wire and new concrete pillboxes intruded on the whole area. Besides, all the kiosks which sold ice cream and lemonade were boarded up two years ago, and it seemed that they would never be open again.

The last trip they made that summer was to Pwlldu Bay, much further down the coast, and a long bus ride beyond Mumbles.

They scrambled off the yellow double-deck Swan bus at the last stop near Bishopston Church. The church was a short scramble down a steep slope in a gap between the houses, and then they passed through an arched gateway in an ancient stone wall. Beyond was the church cemetery, where D. and his two sisters tiptoed among the gravestones to decipher the names and dates of the departed, while their parents, slower of foot, caught up with them.

Passing through the churchyard to the cul-de-sac road beyond, D.'s father assembled them to distribute the load he had carried himself on the bus journeys. There was a long walk ahead and he had an eye to partial enjoyment of it, at least.

Then they were off. Their father cut them each a stick from the hedge, and unable to contain themselves with excitement they dashed for the water-washed dry bed of the winter flood river that tumbled from the common above. The bed was littered with stones of all sizes spread in banks of silt, mud and small pools of water, and soon slowed them down. Behind, their parents picked their way carefully, their mother calling out a constant stream of cautions to the children: 'Don't get dirty, don't get wet, don't hurt yourselves on the stones, don't get out of sight, don't tear clothes on the brambles, don't drop your towels ... ' and so endlessly on.

The walk slowed to a steady slog. Bishopston valley was heaven on a fine day in September. To D. and his sisters it was the bees' knees of a holiday outing. There were no fences, no notices or boundaries, no buildings of any kind, no other people, and apart from their mother's constant harrying dos and don'ts, no rules about where they went to see the wonders of real wild nature.

Some way along at a flat dry bank near a narrow cave in the steep valley side, their father called a halt. It was early lunch. He opened the wicker basket and took out a small kettle. D. had never seen it before, though he had explored every nook and cranny of his home and thought he had come to see everything.

Now his father built a fire, gathering sticks from under the giant oak trees scattered around. D. marvelled. A real camp fire in the middle of wild country! It was a real adventure.

His father called to him. 'Come with me, D. We'll get some water.'

Water? D. was puzzled. There was no trace of water around here.

His father walked off towards the split in the rocks, swinging the kettle. D. ran after him. The cave was low and wide. His father bent double and even D. had to bend low to pass under the bulging rock ceiling. It was cold and damp, but water was there, flowing strongly in a sharp bend over clean dark stones. His father plunged the kettle in and filled it. 'Have a drink,' he said to D. D. put his hand in to scoop a mouthful. It was icy cold. The water tasted peaty and wholesome, unlike the tapwater at home. He turned to his father in the gloom.

'It's nice,' he said.

'Best water there is,' said his father. 'Straight off the common. Full of goodness. No pipes or taps. No standing about in reservoirs to foul it.'

The cave was intimidating, and D. was glad to make his way out to the bright sunny warmth outside.

They had lunch with hot tea, sandwiches and clouds of flies, and were glad to finish it. Their mother saved some food for later. They would need it she said. The sea air made everyone hungry. Sea air? The children were not sure about this, since there seemed to be nothing but country around them, huge trees, thick vegetation, brambles and a muddy trail all closed in by steep walls of the valley side. And flies. They were plagued by flies, and their mother complained loudly and at great length. But the thought of joys still ahead spurred them on unheeding.

Now and then they came across remains of farmhouses, walls covered by moss and ivy, some with giant trees growing through their middles, the walls looking like a huge plant pot surrounding the trunks. No timbers from roofs or lintels could be found, so the dates of the old ruins were impossible to guess, though they must have been many hundreds of years old. To stand touching the stones so carefully placed so long ago, and to wonder at the people who had lived and worked there was a romantic experience. D.'s father said that the houses must be at least five hundred years old, and to get to this state of ruin would take at least three hundred years. So the people must have been living in the houses for two hundred years before they gave up. Why? His father didn't know.

They moved on, with lingering last looks at the ruins, hoping to visualise from increasing distance what they could not in touching reach — how it looked when in use so long ago, with whitewashed walls, slate roofs, flowers in the garden, children playing, and animals.

'I wonder how they coped with the flies, Frank?' mused his mother.

His father shrugged and said nothing. Flies might have been the least of their worries, he seemed to say silently.

And still they walked on. Everyone had begun to tire now, and the pathway became increasingly difficult. They climbed around rocky outcrops and swampy pools of mud, and the sun grew hotter and the brambles thornier.

At one of the muddy patches D.'s mother let out a squeal of fright. They all stopped in alarm.

'Cows, Frank! Look.' She pointed at the churned up mud. 'Cows' footprints,' she said fearfully. 'I'm not going any further. I'm going back.' And she started to do that, walking backwards, eyes fixed on the hoof marks in the mud as though a cow might suddenly arise, presumably feet-first, from the mire.

'Don't be silly, Doris,' said D.'s father with impatience. 'There aren't any cows around. Even if there were they wouldn't harm you. Farmers wouldn't let them wander about if they were dangerous to people.' He turned to continue their walk, and called to his children ahead: 'It's okay. There's nothing to be afraid of. Your mother's coming now.'

But she didn't. She walked backwards until she was out of sight and D.'s father dumped his wicker basket in annoyance to go after her. Telling the children to stay where they were he stamped his way across the mud in pursuit.

The children sat down and wondered at their mother's fear. Cows didn't seem nasty. Fred Barrow had cows and they came over to the gate whenever the children stopped. Sometimes the cows would lick their faces with a tremendous wet tongue if they were not quick enough to get out of the way. The animals would always take offered bunches of juicy grass, torn from spots outside the gate that they couldn't reach, very gently — not with teeth like a dog but with the tongue, which couldn't hurt.

The children waited, and were surprised when their parents appeared on the path ahead of them. Apparently their father had had to persuade and lead their mother along a wide detour around the fearful prints in the mud patch. Their mother sat at the edge of the path now, trembling, pale and perspiring. Their father went past them to collect his dumped wicker basket. He was angry.

The river appeared from nowhere, and D. concluded it ran underground to this point, and was the same water that he had collected from the cave with his father. It was gentle, slow moving and clear. It was deep in parts, especially at the bends, and for the first time in his life he saw fish swim freely in their own domain. They were trout, said his father, and very good eating, but impossible to catch. D. looked at their darting shapes with longing, and wished he could take one back to show the boys in the street. They had never even heard of Pwlldu.

A bridge appeared, quite unexpectedly, leading the path over the river. It was concrete with only one iron handrail, and was quite out of place in the wilderness of the valley.

The children walked on to the bridge, leaning on the handrail to gaze at the fish in the water below. It was cooler here, and the air smelled different. Not far away was a building. A large notice on the wall said it was the Beaufort Arms. A pub. Right in the middle of nowhere. To their left rose a steep embracing hill, vegetation stunted by cutting ocean winds, that was the extension of one of the valley walls which had accompanied them all morning.

'This way,' called their father, drawing them away from the bridge and the river, to walk over a gentle path whose grass had been cut with a mower. Another surprise.

They walked past the pub, and on the other side of the path was another building. A house, with a small strip of garden running along the hill bottom and a neat grass area in front. The grassed area had tables and benches set up on it and several people sat drinking tea and eating scones. At the far end of the house there was an enormous glass lean-to conservatory with more tables and chairs.

The conservatory was thickly strewn with pots growing huge geraniums, some over six feet tall, and D.'s father was impressed by them.

'We'll have tea here later on,' said D.'s mother. 'Mr and Mrs Jenkins do a very good pot of tea and scones. And if the weather holds up we can sit on the benches outside. Like a real picnic.' The weather had shown no sign of deteriorating. All morning it had been a breathless hot burden, cooler in the more open spaces at the end of the valley, but unchanging. Perhaps their mother hoped she might be able to say 'I told you so' and unload the unreasonable bundle of woollenware she carried.

As they walked past the house the path broke up into a trail littered with stones. And then, there it was. To D. it seemed that he had opened the centre spread of a picture book of dreams. Their path had entered the beach at one far end, and the whole bay was in front of them at one glance.

At the far end an enclosing arm of cliff, worn to a steep tumbling hillside, ran off into the blue sparkling sea. The side of the hill was covered at its bottom edge by pale sap green grass sprinkled with swathes of colourful flowers; further up mature bracken and ferns were a dark green foam surrounding short, wind-burned clumps of hawthorn. At the very top was flat farmland, and keen eyes could pick out fence posts and other discouraging signs of man-made order.

Between the cliff and where they stood, marvelling, was a curve of narrow beach backed by a bank of rounded limestone rocks. Behind the bank was the valley they had walked all morning. The tide was in, leaving them little room to find a station to park themselves on the sand, so they settled for a quickly-dug platform on the sloping bank of round stones. The sea lapped gently with small waves, and beyond, the surface was flat calm, merging into the azure sky at the horizon.

Everyone changed into beach wear. The water was shockingly cold, pale green, and even when they were up to the armpits in it they could still see their feet clearly. Shoals of small, brilliant green fish swarmed around them, and sometimes a small jellyfish floated by. D. and his sisters got their heads wet and pretended to swim, calling to their parents not so far away to watch them swing their arms out of the water and then cunningly put their fingertips on the sandy bottom to support them and move them forward. Their parents watched them and smiled indulgently. They had played the same game twenty-five years ago.

The afternoon wore on. The sun burned their shoulders and noses, they grew hungry and thirsty and the tide receded, leaving acres of wet sand and hugely interesting pools in the rocks, where they searched out crabs, shrimps, whelks and other sea life.

Shadows lengthened and their day was over. Reluctantly they dressed, sand clinging to their toes and lodged in their ears and hair, and they walked, weary now, to Mrs Jenkins' tea tables. Eating the last of the sandwiches, warm and squashed, D. and his sisters heard their father describe how they would return home. They hadn't given that a thought until now.

'Up that hill,' said their father. 'It's a bit of a scramble up the first bit but it's a lovely walk along the top. Beautiful views. Then a nice walk along a country lane with no hills to climb. Then straight on a bus to town.'

Mrs Jenkins didn't have lemonade. 'It's the war, see. Don't get any now.' So they had tea. D.'s mother complained about the cost. 'A shilling a large pot for five isn't too bad,' his father said impatiently. 'I know. But it wouldn't cost us anything at home,' said his mother. His father looked away and said no more.

The journey back to the bus stop at Pyle Corner was endless and drained the last strength of all of them. There was some relief when father pointed out a 'well', in reality a public cold water tap covered by a stone shroud. Everyone drank their fill, except their father who declined, implying that grown men could tough it out. In reality he badly wanted to pee but couldn't find anywhere to do it without drawing attention to himself.

At the bus stop they leaned against the grassy bank and waited an eternity for the bus, D.'s mother complaining at regular intervals about the wait.

At last the yellow double-decker came. There were no others waiting at the stop, no nervous waiting for others to board. Just straight on to an almost empty bus. D. and both his sisters tripped and stumbled as they climbed the stairs to the top deck, fatigued to dropping point by the day they had had. Their father insisted on the top deck because of the 'views', but really he wanted a smoke. Anyway, his concept of views didn't impress — the trot along the cliffside was so costly in effort that nobody could spare a thought for the miles of sea below them.

As they sat, on the front seats of the upper deck, D. marvelled. For fourpence, they glided along ten feet above ground, with no effort, protected from the wind and dust and able to look around as they liked. What would this place have been like years ago, he wondered. He looked at the houses along their route. Some were very large, with huge front gardens. Some even had ponds in the grounds, and small summerhouses, garages with cars standing outside, huge trees and hedges quite different from the privet of his area. There were even some houses which had telephone wires stretching from poles outside, and once he saw girls about his own age sitting on horses, which stood in a gateway to let the bus pass.

It was a different world. Even D.'s mother understood, repeating 'There's posh, Frank, look,' at endless examples of fine houses and gardens. His father looked, grunted, and seemed glum.

Back home in chilly reality as the day faded with no fires lit and the blackouts in position, the priority was to get D. and his two sisters to bed.

'Right,' said D.'s mother with an air of command. 'You first.' She jerked a thumb at D. 'Use your father's toothbrush. You're ruining mine. I don't know what you're doing to it, but you're not to use it any more.' D. hated his father's toothbrush. Toothpaste was unknown in the house, so the children and their mother used salt to clean their teeth. This left an unpleasant taste difficult to remove even with pints of water to rinse away, but was better than the soot his father used. 'Good for the system,' he would declare with authority and enthusiasm. 'That's all we used when we were children. None of this fancy toothpaste stuff. Never did us any harm.'

His toothbrush was stained black and smelled horribly. D. used it lightly, with water only, ignoring the jam jar of soot on the window sill above the washbasin.

He ran the wet flannel over his face, rinsed his hands and went into the kitchen. He was hungry. Perhaps there would be a small snack before bed.

'I know what you're after, greedy. You've had enough to eat today. Up to bed with you, after you say your prayers.' His mother stood hands on hips, chin forward, a glare in her eyes. She was tired, too, and couldn't wait to be relieved of her brood for the night.

D.'s sisters went into the bathroom together whilst he knelt in the parlour at one of the armchairs to say his night prayers. His sisters had their own toothbrushes, because his mother said that it was more important for the girls to have clean teeth. D. didn't understand why, but he accepted the judgment.

In his bedroom he took a last look at the almost dark mountains. He watched the lit-up single carriage of the railway diesel car enter the Cockett tunnel, and the glowing firebox of a steam-driven lorry labouring up Carmarthen Road. He could hear the awful noise it made from here, through the open window. Its headlights were screened, as every vehicle's was, by a cover with slots cut into it to reduce the light as an air raid precaution.

He fell into bed and was asleep immediately, despite the sticky warmth of the room. The sun shone on his corner-of-the-house bedroom most of the day, and today had been hot.

★　★　★

Back to school, and D. found himself drafted into Standard 6 class, all of whom were at least thirteen years old. He was now in Dwt Barry's class. He was careful to keep his head down at all times, even when the answers were ready. He had no wish to decorate his knees with the painful red and white slashes which half a dozen boys took home every afternoon.

He couldn't remember that he had ever learned very much in Dwt Barry's class. They laboured over arithmetic so simple that D. became bored, and incurred the wrath of his near neighbours who snarled insults at him for finishing the long-multiplication sums so soon. In English lessons he felt compelled to make deliberate mistakes in order to stay at the same level as the rest of the class. This way he avoided attention and praise from the teacher, and at only nine years old he couldn't deal with the other boys' chagrin.

He was never bullied at the school. At nine he was a full two years younger than the boys in the lowest class of the senior school, and he was clearly not serious game. And in a curious way, the oldest Henderson boy, at fourteen, was his indirect protector, since D. could be seen sometimes talking to him at breaktimes. The Henderson boy was a bruiser to be avoided by everyone.

Winter drew on, and with it the maddening sores at the corners of his mouth and earlobes. At home one day he found a small tin container, discarded by his father, which had contained a muscle toner rub. D. washed this out with hot water and transferred to it a fingerful of Germoline. He carried this tin of ointment with him everywhere, daubing his cracking sores with relief whenever he could. It helped, but it did nothing to cure.

His shoes sprang holes again, and when his mother slipped pieces of cardboard over them he replaced the card with small squares of lino, cut from a scrap he had found in a bombed house in the summer. He did this secretly, and it worked better than the cardboard, which broke up so soon in rainy weather.

His mother had not taken a knife to him since the cut of the summer, though she frequently stopped whatever she was doing, glared at him with her face twisted in rage, and mimed a grabbing motion of his willie with her left hand, then bringing her right hand down with a slashing, cutting motion. Sometimes she held a knife in her right hand if she happened to be using one, but often it was the mime of using one.

D. was nonplussed, worried and fearful. What had he done? Why was she doing it? Was there something dreadful about being a boy, with a willie? Or Toby, as it was known in the family. Toby jokes were plentiful, and his mother and his two sisters laughed plentifully, but he could never understand the jokes, with their references to dogs' suppers and fried Tobies with mash.

He wet the bed most nights now, earning himself beatings, short rations and a piece of leather in the bed to protect the mattress. He started to bite his nails, earning his father's disapproval and no small contempt.

It was this Christmas time of 1942 that he discovered the Aladdin's cave in his parents' wardrobe. He wondered, a few days after Christmas, why the large wardrobe in his parents' bedroom was locked. He searched for the key but didn't find it. He had read about 'picking' locks, and here was an opportunity. Using a bent paper clip from his father's drawer, which contained anything and everything he might need for the job, he finally opened the lock. It wasn't too difficult, he thought.

Inside the wardrobe were cigarettes. Not just some of these precious and scarce social comforters: there were thousands of them. Boxes stacked upon boxes, in hundreds and two-hundreds, one or two of them in five-hundreds. There were some with strange names, like Sweet Caporal, Churchman's No 3 and Kensitas.

He counted them. Nine thousand exactly. Where had they all come from, he wondered.

He closed the door and relocked it. That was not so easy as unlocking it, and by the time he had succeeded he had begun to perspire in fear of being discovered. His sisters were downstairs.

There were the interminable and tasteless turkeys too. Four of them this year. One on Christmas Day, and the rest for successive Sundays and Mondays, Tuesdays, and Wednesdays after. His mother kept them at Jones the Meat who put them in his cold room, and charged for it. His mother complained, but how else could the birds keep for up to four weeks, his father said reasonably.

On Thursdays the family ate the last of the bird for that week as a fry-up with potatoes and swedes from their own garden. D. hated it but there was nothing else, and none of the children objected, though they exchanged glances as the meal was put before them, daring each other to be the first to complain.

D.'s mother complained that he was fat. 'You're chubby,' she told him one day. He was silent. What could she mean? He felt permanently hungry, but he was apparently eating too much.

'Look at that belly,' she snapped, prodding his jersey with such force that he recoiled with a gasp. 'I don't know how you do it. None of us is like that. And you get the same as everybody else.'

He could argue with that. Both his sisters had one more sandwich than he for lunch in school. They also had an apple each, while he had just one biscuit. His younger sister also fed herself from the pantry whenever she could. He had seen her.

'No more second helpings for you, my lad. Yew gorroo slim.' Her pronunciation slipped as she grew angry. D. couldn't understand why. He rarely got second helpings. His sisters did, when there were any.

'I'll talk to your father when he comes home. You make sure you're here when I do. Hear me?' She wagged a finger in his face and walked away.

She talked to his father. He hadn't noticed that D. was fat, he said wearily.

'You must do something about it, Frank,' said D.'s mother.

His father sighed, and looked at D.

'Skipping,' he said. 'Handstands. That ought to do for a start.'

He paused, calculating. 'Ten skips with Jean's rope without tripping. And handstands against the wall for the count of three. No, five.'

Thus passing sentence he rose from the table, picked up his newspapers and went into the parlour. D.'s trial was over.

'You heard your father,' his mother smirked in triumph at him. 'Now, get on with it.'

A sudden thought took her. Looking into the parlour she said: 'Frank. Isn't there a time he must do it in? He won't try very hard if you give him weeks to do it. He'll just eat more and not bother.'

His father was silent for a long time.

'Threepence for each task,' he said finally. 'That's sixpence altogether. Can't get fairer than that.' The newspaper rustled and signalled the end of the judgment.

D.'s mother was disappointed. 'If I had my way you'd get no food until you did the skipping and handstands,' she hissed at him. 'Your father's an easy-going man. You're lucky.'

'Go on,' she snapped. 'Start. Don't hang about here, I've got work to do.'

'It's dark,' said D. 'And it's raining.' She couldn't possibly send him outside at this time, surely.

'I don't care if it's thunder and lightning,' his mother snarled. 'Out. Go on. Out. Here.' She picked up his sister's wood-handled skipping rope from under their bench at the table and tossed it to him. 'Now go. Let me hear you jumping.'

She went to the back door, opened it, and stood aside for him to pass. He went out.

Not only was it dark and raining, it was very cold. The wind whistled around the house from all directions, cutting through his sleeves and down his neck and up his short trousers. His mother would still not allow him to wear underpants and the wind penetrated to his waistline unobstructed. Within minutes he began to feel numb and very miserable.

The back door opened, and a shaft of light fell over the steps.

'I can't hear you,' snapped his mother. 'Don't just stand there. Start skipping.'

'I'm cold, said D. tearfully.

'Then start skipping,' his mother's voice rose in anger. 'Keep yourself warm, stupid boy.' She closed the door.

He tried dutifully to skip, but he couldn't see the rope. The wind too took it in hand, and he found the rope was striking him in surprising and unplanned places.

He stamped his feet to keep warm, as his father had taught him last year, and realised that this would sound like skipping to his listening mother. So he stamped away, judging the time thus spent to satisfy the task in hand. He was wrong. A flash of torchlight and his mother's voice, angry, made his stomach lurch.

'Ah! I thought so. Cheating. Typical of you, you stupid boy.'

She walked towards him, the torch blinding him, weak as it was. The family had acquired a small torch since the air raids to light up the shelter interior, but there had been no raids worth sheltering from for a long time, and it was not often used. The batteries were weak from lack of use rather than over-use.

He feared a blow, and raised an arm. 'Get inside, fatty. Straight up to bed. No supper for you.' As he turned to open the door, his mother pushed him in the back. 'Go on. Go on. Inside. And don't try to get your father's sympathy by crying. It won't work. I'll see to that.'

He scrambled inside and made for the bathroom to wash, and

brush his teeth. He heard his mother's voice. 'He's done something to the torch, Frank. He's been using it. The battery's almost flat. Can't see a thing with it.' She was complaining to his father. His father's voice rumbled, indistinct. His mother's voice was clear. 'That's why he's going to bed now.' Her voice was emphatic, challenging.

His father's voice rose in irritation. 'Alright, alright. Let him go to bed then.'

D. was disappointed. He had harboured a lingering hope that his father might intervene and save him from a supperless early bed. He lingered over his wash and teeth brushing, hoping to extend his time downstairs, now that his punishment was decided and he had no more to fear.

His mother came into the bathroom. 'Come on you. Upstairs. And take your pot with you.' He had a chamber pot in his room because he wet the bed, and part of his punishment for this was to empty, clean and take upstairs his own pot.

His bedroom was chillingly cold. For a while he stared out of the window at the view, but there was nothing happening, so he crept under the bits of blanket, curled up for warmth, and eventually, long after his sisters had gone to bed after their supper, fell asleep. He was awakened only once by his sisters fighting and his father angrily slapping them as they screamed.

*   *   *

He was ten years old in March. He had an orange and a threepenny piece for a birthday present. A special treat was roly-poly pudding, which his mother said was properly called spotted Dick. With a great deal of sniggering and giggles which none of the children understood she cut slices from the long roll of sultana-filled suet pudding and loaded their plates, then poured custard over it. It tasted wonderful. Outside, the wind swirled and rushed, and cold rain slashed the window of the kitchen. The stove glowed, the blackout insulated the sharp draughts from the badly-fitting window, and their mother was not complaining about the effort and time she had taken to prepare their evening meal. Things were comfortable, and everybody was happy.

They listened to the news on the wireless at six o'clock. The Russians had won a big victory a month ago at a city called Stalingrad, but had kept this to themselves for some reason. The newsreader said the extent of the German defeat was not known for certain, but was thought to be very great. There was talk of a 'turning point' in the war, at which D.'s mother gave a deep-felt 'Thank God!' and they all looked at her, expecting more. Nothing more came. D. thought that perhaps she knew less of what was going on than he did, because every time he asked a question she got annoyed, and told him to 'ask his father', in a tone of voice which implied that she was too busy on important tasks to answer. But really she didn't know. D. didn't have that much confidence in his father either. He remembered his mother asking him how can an airplane be shot down, when the bullets must bounce off the metal. His father had shrugged, unable to answer, but D. could have told her how the boys in the street had found a way to drive nails through tin sheets. Plane bodies were not as thick.

His father came home at ten past six and they were sent out of the kitchen while he ate his evening meal. The fun was over for the night.

Later, as another treat, they each had a slice of bread and jam. None of them was enthusiastic. There was no mystery about which jam it would be. For two years now they had watched the plum jam in the row of pots on the top shelf of the pantry grow less and less. They never had any other jam on their bread but plum. It was, by common consent, awful. It had to be sliced with a knife and fork like sticky cheese before it was placed on the thin slices of sparsely buttered bread. It was also tasteless, and clung to the roof of the mouth, frequently causing a gagging reflex, which infuriated their mother, who saw this as childish exaggeration.

'Children in Russia would be glad of half of what you're getting,' she snapped.

In fatal innocence D. asked: 'How could you send a slice of bread and jam to Russia, Mam?'

His mother was silent, and glared at him.

'Somebody might eat it on the way,' said his elder sister.

'Perhaps you could shoot it from a big gun,' said D. 'It's hard enough.'

'Ingratitude,' she cried. 'Thankless job looking after you children. Thankless, that's what it is. There's none so ungrateful as your own flesh and blood, that's what I say. None.'

'Now go and brush your teeth. All of you. You first.' She pointed at D. She was angry, and he struggled out of his corner seat at the table to obey. Another early night. But at least he had had plenty to eat.

Later, as their mother saw them off to bed, she looked into D.'s room.

'Stupid boy. I'll cut it off for you. You wait. Tomorrow. When you come home from school. I'll have it off, and give it to next door's dog. You'll see, my boy. Tomorrow.'

She went downstairs. It took him a long time to fall off to sleep.

★ ★ ★

He couldn't help it, he kept saying tearfully. He stood on a chair, naked and shameful, while his mother swabbed the faeces from his legs. She shouted and stormed, paragraphed by expressions of disgust and loathing.

'Why do I have this burden?' she asked the world at large. 'Why should a son of mine shit his trousers? Why is he so stupid? What have I done to deserve this, God? What have I done?'

Tearfully D. stepped down from the chair as his mother told him.

'Now go in there and give yourself another wash. And use plenty of soap. Use cold water, now. I don't want any more stink around here using hot water.'

He went into the bathroom and began to wash himself as he was told. His mother continued to bewail her fate in giving birth to such a monster.

'Your father will hear all about this. Just you wait. Everything, he'll hear. I wouldn't like to be in your shoes when he finds out. He'll give you what for. Just you wait.'

He really couldn't help it, he sobbed to himself. As he got nearer home with his sister Jean whom he had met on the way home from school, he remembered his mother's threat of the night before. I'll cut it off, she had said. His hand still hurt from the cut of months before, and he began to worry.

For no reason, it seemed, and uncontrollably, his bowels opened. There, on the street. Nearby a policeman stood, outside Price the chemist.

'Funny smell,' he said, turning to D. and his sister. D. was consumed by shame and embarrassment. He couldn't move, as the unspeakable happened and a turd slowly slithered down his leg, tumbling to the pavement at his feet as he watched.

He didn't know why it happened, or how. He didn't know what to do about it. But in years to come he would know better than most the truth of the laughing expression: 'he shit himself in fright'.

The policeman turned away and slowly walked off. D. and his sister trudged on, hill after hill, threading their way through mean streets, hostile gang territories and twitching curtains. He grew increasingly fearful as he approached home, a wild mixture of dreads

93

swirling as he paused at the steps of his home. What would his mother do? He felt his trousers. They were a mess. Would she attack him with the knife first? Could he fend it off by appealing to her for help with his trousers? What punishment would he get for doing this awful thing?

In the event his father said nothing. Perhaps his mother hadn't told him. She glared at him for days afterwards, making muttered threats of fitting him with a plug: 'Toby would do, wouldn't he?' she snapped once. 'Cut it off and stick it in your bum, stupid boy.'

Chapter Six

In April they saw their first American soldiers. They were loud, good humoured, and different. For a start they were friendly in an overwhelming way, open and forthright about their boredom, the British coinage, the devastation of the town centre, the wonderful beaches, the dreariness of the town, lack of girls, the constant winter rain and dirty pubs. Then there were their uniforms, a smart cut quite different from the baggy, shapeless British. The cloth was different too: a fine weave that responded well to tailoring, which made every wearer appear as though it had been made just for him.

They were generous, and gave away chewing gum and sweets liberally to the children, offered their toasted and flavoured cigarettes to anyone in the pubs, and passed their own adequate rations of butter and sugar to families which befriended them. Occasionally they got into fights with the resentful British soldiery, and more rarely, with mixed bands of drunken steel-workers and miners whose main grievance was that they couldn't understand Americans and their social outlook: the work-chapel-work ethic and six ten-hour days a week of grinding dirty dangerous labour left no room to consider other ways of life. So they reacted naturally: if you don't understand, fight it, or at the very least, shout at it.

The American Military Police were legendary in their ruthlessness, and broke up disturbances quickly and efficiently. No one ever heard of a civilian being hurt by a M.P's truncheon, though they were used fiercely against their own kind.

There were no acts of violence against the civilians either. No one ever heard of a rape or a beating-up or robbery committed by an American soldier.

D.'s mother disliked them. 'They boast a lot,' she said. 'Everything they've got is bigger and better than ours. And they are vulgar,' she added. Did that mean that they farted out loud at the table, wondered D.? Or even ate peas with their knives like Mr Michael next door? She didn't say any more, but one day as they waited for a bus from town, a group of black soldiers strolled past the queue. They were the first negroes his mother had ever seen, though D. and his sisters had passed many on their way to and from school. She stared at them hard, as though to record the sight to serve old-age memory. Finally she said, almost to herself but loudly enough,

'Just think. Black. All over. Every bit of them is black.' The queuers around shuffled their feet in embarrassment. D. felt his face turn pink. She had made it all too plain what she was thinking. His younger sister snickered. His elder sister exchanged glances with him of shame at their mother's obviousness.

She prodded D. between the shoulder blades. 'What's the matter with you, misery?' she hissed, bending down to his ear. 'You think you're better than everybody, do you? You'll learn, my boy. You'll learn.'

D. didn't understand the words, but felt his mother's anger at herself at having behaved foolishly. He was nearby, so he served her purpose for the moment.

The following Saturday was warm and sunny. D. decided to go for a walk to the brickworks pond. There, he might catch a few stickle-backs, and he took a jar and one of his father's handkerchiefs to catch them. The boys in the street had shown him last year how to do it.

He could see the brickworks pond from his bedroom window. It was a good mile away, beyond the railway and across waste ground where there was a hollow slag tip from a long deceased coal mine. He had sat on the ridge of this tip with the boys from the street, and watched the men gamble. They were working men from the surrounding area, and were fearful of the police discovering their game, so they posted lookouts. Sometimes the men would give the boys a shilling to keep a lookout, and they would sit there, trying to understand the game the men were playing. But all they saw was two half-crowns being thrown high in the air, followed by groans and shouts as the thrower stepped forward to announce heads or tails. Or both. Money would be exchanged, and the coins would be thrown again.

None of the boys was around the street that Saturday, and when D. met Mary Morgan, who lived a few doors away and was the same age, he reluctantly offered to take her. She would take a jar of her own, she said. He shrugged. Any company was better than none.

At the slag heap there were American soldiers gambling with the workmen. There was one black soldier who gave them a long hard stare as they passed the single open end of the hollow heap of spoil. The ridges of the tip were twenty feet high, and hid everything that went on inside except from this one side. It was much like a topless volcano cone with a gap cut into the wall.

They hurried past, wary of the rough shouting men, some of whom drank beer from flagon bottles and who were not too steady on their feet, and were soon out of sight of them.

The brickworks pond was reputed to be bottomless, and certainly looked it. The sides were sheer, of broken unstable earth, and unclimbable except at one point where an agile and determined climber could scramble over the subsiding soil to the water edge. At this point there was a shallow flat bank which allowed stickleback fishers to dip their jars in the water without danger of falling in. The water was shallow here, too, though it faded into green dark depths only a few steps away. It was rumoured that many children had drowned here. D. and Mary stood on the flat bank and gazed at the water with respect. They would not even think of wading in the small area of shallows as some of the more daring boys in the street did. Instead they lay flat, arms over the water as D. laid out his handkerchief, weighted with stones, flat on the clay bottom of the water.

Soon enough, a tiny fish swam over the white square of cloth, and with a whoop D. scooped up the corners to capture it. Shouting excitedly to Mary to fill her jar with water he brought the fish on to the bank, containing its panic-stricken jumps with his hands. Mary held the full jar while he picked up the tiny creature and popped it in. They gazed with triumph as the stickleback swam in circles in the alien vessel, pushing itself against the glass in hopeless attempts to escape to safer waters.

'Wadya got there, buddy?'

They turned, startled and surprised. It was the black American soldier who had looked so hard at them as they had passed the spoil tip.

'A tiddler,' said D. 'Stickleback. Small fish,' he added as explanation. Perhaps they didn't have sticklebacks in America. Or they may call them something else.

'Howdya get down there?' the soldier called.

D. pointed out the barely discernible track running at a steep angle along the earthen cliff.

The soldier scrambled down and stood over them. He was very tall, large, and intimidating. He lips were very thick, D. noticed, and he had wrinkles on his forehead though he was not very old.

He sat down beside them. His presence was overwhelming and completely altered their day. He spoke to them in a soft twang that they had heard only at the cinema, and he used strange expressions, of which his favourite seemed to be 'you all'.

'You all come a long way to fish here at the reservoir?' he asked. He pronounced the word as 'reserve-voy', and D. nearly corrected him. He remained silent. It wouldn't be friendly, he thought.

97

He did tell him it was a brickworks pond. And yes, they had come a long way, he told him proudly. Miles, in fact.

The soldier seemed quite happy with this and smiled. He drew some chewing gum from his pocket and held it up.

'You all see this?' They nodded, interested.

'Well, you all take your shoes and socks off and paddle at the edge here, and you can have it.' He moved to sit next to Mary.

'Not you, belle. You sit next to me.' He pointed to Mary.

D. gazed at the water. It wasn't deep here for some way out. Six inches at most. He looked at the huge packet of chewing gum, and took off his shoes and socks. He sat on the low bank over the water and put his feet in the water. It was cool but not uncomfortable. Behind him he heard Mary giggle, and he turned, suspecting a trick; they might be eating all the chewing gum while he had his back to them. But the packet was still on the grass, untouched.

The he saw what the soldier was doing, why Mary had giggled. He had pushed up her skirt, and his hand was inside the front of her thick navy-blue knickers. D. could see his fingers moving about, and Mary giggled some more.

The soldier looked up and saw him watching.

'You all turn around now. You get bustin' wi' your paddling. You all hear me now?'

He sounded angry, and the frown lines on his forehead were very deep, D. saw.

'I don't think I want to any more,' said D. 'I want to go home now.' He began to feel the first stages of alarm as the soldier rose and came angrily towards him. D. stood, ready to run. The soldier might even throw him in the water, and what would his mother say then?

'Hey, Leroy! You all there, Leroy? Show yourself, you dumb son of a bitch.' Heads appeared over the top of the bank, and several of the black soldier's comrades stood there. They called to him.

'You missed the fun. Joe here took the limeys for everything they had. Cleaned 'em out.'

The black soldier glared at D. and Mary, glanced at the packet of chewing gum, then turned and scrambled up the bank. On his way up the other soldiers joshed him. 'Cookhouse food not good enough for you, Leroy? You gonna catch fish for the cook, then?'

At the top of the bank, Leroy didn't look back. The soldiers disappeared as quickly as they had come, and everything was quiet. Mary suggested they catch some more sticklebacks. D. shrugged his shoulders.

'No. I'm going back home now. I don't feel like staying here any more.' He felt deeply shaken. That soldier had been very threatening.

On the way home they didn't talk very much. Mary taunted him for being a spoilsport and wanting to go home. Besides, she had dived for the chewing gum, which she clutched firmly in her hand. She wouldn't give him any, and taunted him further by only half chewing the tablets before taking them out of her mouth and throwing them at him.

He accelerated his pace up the hills towards home, and she soon trailed behind. Although she continued to hurl insults at him, at least he was out of range of the sticky little bundles of chewed gum. Then he remembered that he had left not only the jam jar with the fish in it, but his father's handkerchief as well. He hesitated, looked back, and decided to go on. Perhaps his father wouldn't notice one handkerchief missing. He had lots, anyway. He got dozens every Christmas. And he certainly wouldn't mention either the jar or the handkerchief to Mary. She would surely tell his sister. He hoped the fish wouldn't die in the jar. Somebody was bound to find it soon.

Back home, their lunch was ready. They ate before their father came home from work at one o'clock. He liked to eat in peace, and spend the rest of the Saturday in the garden. There was cockles, bacon and egg and fried bread. It smelled delicious and tasted just that.

When they were alone eating D.'s sister turned to him and hissed, 'Give me your fried bread, or I'll tell Mam about the handkerchief.' D. was startled. So Mary had realised that he had left the handkerchief behind and she had lost no time in spreading it around.

D. looked at her with an anger he had never felt before, and went on eating, deliberately cutting a piece out of the fried bread, calling her bluff.

'Mam! Mam!' his sister's voice rang out loudly. 'Mam!'

Their mother came into the kitchen. D. stopped eating and stared. Would she tell?

'What do you want?'

His sister gave D. a sly smile.

'Can I have some more sauce, please?' she asked innocently.

Their mother looked at her, hard.

'Of course. You know you don't need to ask. Don't call me again for nothing. I'm busy.' She went out.

'See,' said Dot. 'If you don't give it to me, I'll tell, next time.'

D. picked up what remained of the fried bread and flung it across the table. He half hoped it would fall to the dusty concrete floor but she caught it and began eating it immediately. Perhaps his sister would forget about the handkerchief soon.

But she didn't. Even though she had no more to gain than fleeting self-importance, she told his father. His father gave him a slap and stopped his pocket money for two weeks. For a short while his sister was pleased at his punishment, but sobered up when D. reminded her that she couldn't split on him twice or blackmail him any more. She kicked his ankle, hard. Before the reflex retaliation could develop she screamed, loud and long.

D.'s mother came rushing in. 'What's the matter? What's all that for?'

Dot pointed an accusing finger at D.

'He punched me,' she wailed.

'What for?' demanded his mother turning her furious face on him. Seeing his look of astonishment she modified this to: 'Did you punch her, my boy?' She wagged a forefinger at him. 'You tell me the truth now. None of your lies.'

He shook his head. 'I didn't touch her,' he said, his voice rising in protest. 'She kicked me. Look.' He rolled down his sock to show. There was nothing much to see. It would take a day or two for a bruise to develop. Now there was just a faint red ridge where Dot's shoe toe had connected.

His mother was not minded to play detective and search for detail. Instead she boxed his ears and called him a coward for 'beating up a girl, who was younger than he, as well'. 'Typical male,' she snapped. 'Can't keep your hands to yourself. One day, my boy ... ' she paused dramatically, 'I'll give you a good hiding. You see if I won't.'

His sister smirked at him, her cold, unsmiling blue eyes bright and triumphant. He longed to give her a black eye, but instead wandered off into the garden as soon as his mother had left them.

There wasn't much going on that afternoon. He played a game of football with the boys in the street for a while. The football was a tennis ball, worn shiny by use, and the goalposts two small stones, arbitrarily placed three paces apart in the middle of the road. No vehicles disturbed them. Only Mr Brown the coal miner had a car, and he worked nights.

One by one the football players drifted away to do other things. Mr Horner the fireman stood at his gateway, arms folded, bald head glistening, muscles bulging and features threatening. He was waiting for a wild kick that might send the ball his way. The boys had no doubt that if Mr Horner got his hands on their ball he would destroy it. And possibly inflict some harm on them, too. His hostile presence inevitably depressed their energies, and without admitting the cause, they gradually lost interest in the game. After all, part of the fun was to watch how one of them fared while retrieving the ball from a front garden after an uncontrolled kick.

D. wandered back into his own garden. He knelt down by the front step to check on the toad. It was still there, its heavy throat pulsing slowly, golden eyes regarding him unblinking. D. made no attempt to touch it. There was no point in alarming it, and risking the animal seeking a safer place where it would be lost. As it was, it was D.'s secret.

He strolled down the gentle slope of the cinder path of the back garden. He might look under the cabbages for frogs, he thought. Then he decided to inspect the bomb crater in the garden next door when he heard his mother rattling pots in the kitchen. She wouldn't like him walking among the cabbages, unless he had a jam jar in his hand to pick off caterpillars, and he didn't feel like doing that right now.

The bomb crater was not large, about twenty feet across by six or seven feet deep. Indeed, it was small enough when it had arrived to lead the Army to think that it might be an unexploded bomb, and a small group of complaining soldiers had dug for three days before an officer came by and said casually, 'I don't think you're going to find anything there, you chaps. Better fill it in and report back'. He walked off and the men sat around all afternoon playing cards, smoking and drinking tea brought to them by grateful housewives from neighbouring houses.

No one could tell D. where the earth from the original explosion had gone. Somehow the soldiers had not only made the hole bigger but had lost the earth from their excavation work as well. There was no surrounding ridge like D. had seen at other bomb craters in open spaces: the edge was neat, sharp and circular, like a giant hole in a golf green. He had always understood from his father's complaints that when a hole was dug, there was always earth left over which had to be taken away. Evidently the dug-out bomb crater was a special case, and if the soldiers didn't know how it happened it must be very scientific.

Four years later, at the end of the war, the government offered the air-raid shelters to the public at nominal prices. Mr Michael paid up for his, telling everyone what a good cellar it would make. He would fit it up with shelves, a proper floor, electric light.

He ventured into the shelter for the first time since the soldiers had dug to make sure of the bomb, and found it packed solid to the roof with earth and stones.

He said he would make a fuss, but nothing happened. The earth-packed steel shelter is probably there today.

The crater had been screened off from the Michael's back window by a tall rustic fence, and the roses Mr Michael had planted were now growing thickly all over it, hiding D. as he scrambled through the privet hedge dividing their gardens.

In the absence of natural filling, the crater was being filled with rubbish of all kinds. All the neighbours had been invited to contribute, and in the two years and more that the hole had lain there it was now half-full of every kind of detritus from many streets around. Mattresses, old broken prams, rotten wood, glass, bottles, clothing, pots and pans, even an old gas cooker. It was an immensely interesting pit of curios no ten-year-old could pass by.

Here was an enamel cooking pot, very large, gallon size perhaps. D. picked it up. The enamel coating inside was crazed around a central bulge where the pot had received an impact.

Dropped, thought D. He held it up to the sky searching for holes. It could make a good bowl to keep fish in, he thought.

The pot was heavy, and as he lowered it his hands slipped on the smooth, glassy sides. He gave a yelp of pain as several splinters of enamel penetrated his fingers. He dropped the pot and examined his hand. He had three splinters in his right hand: two at the base of two fingers and one straight down the top of his thumb. The one in his thumb hurt a little, but the other two he hardly noticed. He pulled one out with his teeth. It was quite small and looked like glass. A small spot of blood appeared where it had penetrated, and when he licked this away there was nothing to show where it had been.

He lost interest in the crater and its store of junk. Besides, the old pram had had its wheels removed. Probably that's where Shwni Hughes had got his go-cart from.

He went back through the hedge and up to his house. His sisters were receiving their daily dose of orange juice, and he watched his mother carefully measure out the thick juice from the bottle into a dessertspoon and then mix it with a little water in a glass.

'What are you watching for?' his mother demanded. 'You're not having any of this. The girls need it more than you. There isn't enough to go around, anyway.'

He scratched at the sores at the corners of his mouth. He hadn't tasted the concentrated orange juice, though it had been sitting on the pantry shelf for some days now. There were three bottles, all shaped like the bottles of cough mixture they got from Rees the Chemist, with dull labels printed in blue ink by the Ministry of Food. He concluded that it was a kind of medicine for girls only, since he had been warned as soon as the bottles appeared not to touch them.

The orange juice was followed by a teaspoonful of cod liver oil. He hadn't tasted this either, though judging by the howls of protest from his sisters he felt privileged to be left out.

'You needn't look at this either,' said his mother. 'You're strong enough already. You don't need it.' He didn't disagree.

After the dosing, his mother replaced the bottles on the top shelf, where she thought he couldn't get at them. With a warning glance she closed the pantry door. 'I've marked the bottles, my boy, so I'll know if you've been at them. I know you.'

D. said nothing, as he watched his sisters rush to the taps at the sink to gulp mouthfuls of cold water to wash down the apparently awful effects of the treatment. They were allowed to do this provided they didn't hold the cod liver oil in their mouths to spit it into the sink under cover of washing out their mouths with water.

When their mother had gone out of the kitchen D. asked his elder sister what it was like.

'It's awful,' she said. 'Terrible. It's like dog shit. You're lucky you don't have it. I wish I was a boy.'

His sister coloured as she said the words. D. felt embarrassed. They didn't normally talk to each other like that. 'Shit' was a hard word, heard occasionally by accident spoken by adults and not part of his sister's vocabulary spoken in the house. Their parents would be horrified.

'What's it for?' he asked.

'I dunno. It's supposed to stop you getting colds or something,' she said. 'But I prefer a cold.'

He shrugged, and crossed to the sink to wash his hands. They were very dirty and sticky. He winced as he handled his thumb. The splinter hurt. He would have to try to take it out, he thought. He had often seen his father take out a splinter from his own hands, using a needle or a pin. Perhaps he would do the same.

He failed. The splinter in his middle finger didn't hurt so much so he didn't bother too much with it. But try as he might he could not make any headway with his thumb. Perhaps he would tomorrow, he thought, after letting it settle down.

It did not settle down. After a week the thumb was twice as big as it had been, hot, red and throbbing pain. He showed it to his mother, who told him he shouldn't run around hurting himself. 'Your sisters don't get cut and bruised like you do. You're stupid. Typical male,' she said dismissively.

At night he found sleep difficult. The thumb hurt now like a wound, and woke him up every time he stirred. Sometimes he sat up in the early hours, trying to find a position for his thumb that would allow him to sleep. Even if he found one it was a matter of only minutes rest before having to sit up again to move his hand about.

After ten days he showed it to his father, who tutted in annoyance. 'What did you have to do a silly thing like that for?' he snapped. 'I'll have to take you to the doctor, now. Damned nuisance.'

That same night before the promised visit to the doctor his elder sister brought a chair into his bedroom, sat down and talked to him, reassuring him as he lay in bed, unable to sleep with the pain. The last of the summer light faded and he looked at her, her head on her chest, sleeping as she sat. He felt grateful for her sympathy. His mother said he was stupid, his father thought he was silly, but his sister talked quietly to him as he had told her about the pain.

'I'm alright now,' he said. He touched her arm. She looked up and raised her head. 'You sure?' she asked. 'I'll stay a little more if you like.'

'No. You go to bed now. I'll be alright. It doesn't hurt so much now,' he said.

It did, of course, but it was getting dark. None of the children were allowed to walk about upstairs when it was dark. He didn't want to get her into trouble on his account.

She pulled the chair aside and kissed him on the cheek. 'Goodnight,' she said, and was gone.

He spent a bad night, relieved only by the thought that after his visit to the doctor tomorrow all the pain would be gone, and his pulsing hand returned to normal.

* * *

The doctor's surgery was at the corner of a busy part of Carmarthen Road and a tiny steep street with a gradient so harsh that no car ventured up. Baptist Well Street it was called, though no one knew for sure why. It could be guessed at, but there was no sign that water had ever flowed there, except during a downpour when it must have sluiced off the thirty degree slope like a waterfall.

104

The surgery was dark and dismal, with only two small windows. The floor was covered by dark brown lino, and lined with an assortment of old chairs. Today the chairs were filled by fifteen wheezing fat women, and D. and his father were the only males there. In a system of first-come-first-served the women watched each other carefully, and when each patient came out of the consulting room the waiting room became charged with tension as they checked among themselves who was next.

Dr Harrington was a small, chubby and friendly man. He examined D.'s thumb, tutted in sympathy, and produced a small instrument.

'You won't feel this at all,' said Dr Harrington. D. looked at the wicked hook of bright steel with its needle point. 'We'll have to lance it, Frank,' said Dr Harrington.

Lance it? Knights of old fought with lances, thought D. Was this terrible hook a lance, then?

Dr Harrington held the base of his thumb and lunged with the hook. D. gasped, more in dread than real sensation. The results were startling. As the doctor withdrew the hook, the thumb erupted in a glistening wet mushroom of pus. Green, yellow and white florets of corruption flowered from the hole penetrating the now-dead skin at the top of the thumb. D. felt faint. The doctor quickly moved a metal bowl under his hand. D.'s father grunted in surprise.

'Squeeze it yourself,' said Dr Harrington watching D.'s pale face.

He tried. He failed. The thumb had caused him so much anguish these last few days that he could not bear to arouse fresh pain.

'Look, Frank. I'll put a light bandage on it for now. Just to get home, you understand?' Dr Harrington was sympathetic. 'When you get home, take the bandage off then soak the thumb in warm water to soften things up, and then do some squeezing. There's a lot of muck in there. Let him do it himself or he'll faint on you.'

Dr Harrington wound a bandage lightly around the thumb, taped it and put away his instrument. He looked hard at D.

'You get these sores often?' he asked D.

'Yes. Winter especially.' He touched the corner of his mouth. 'They're getting better now.'

Dr Harrington examined his ear lobes, bade him open his mouth and rocked his teeth with strong fingers.

'Hmm.' He made notes for a minute or so then said, 'Your boy has serious vitamin deficiency, Frank. He should be getting his orange juice and cod-liver oil. Does he take them?'

They both looked at him. His father wouldn't know if he took them, thought D. He didn't concern himself with his children except when their mother used him to discipline them. Which meant to beat them. Otherwise he was detached, distant, unconcerned. He remembered with embarrassment how his father had recoiled when he had squeezed his hand involuntarily on the long trudge home from a visit to his Grandma's. She was his father's mother, and they paid a visit as a whole family once a fortnight. They generally returned home too late for the last bus home, so they walked. It was a long uphill slog, and when he was younger his father would carry him over the steepest parts, and then hold his hand while they walked slowly upward. He was about six then. His father had snatched his hand away and pushed him to the front, curtly ordering to walk ahead and 'make sure you walk fast enough or we'll tread on your heels'.

He looked at Dr Harrington and then his father. Should he tell them what his mother had said about the orange juice and cod-liver oil? His mother would be angry perhaps; his father wouldn't be too pleased either at the idea of being made to look foolish in front of Dr Harrington.

D. nodded, and gave a barely audible 'Yes'. In case he was caught in a lie he added, 'Sometimes'.

Dr Harrington regarded him with disbelief.

'Hmm. See that he takes the stuff regularly, Frank. There will be problems later on if he doesn't. After all, it's free for children now.' He looked directly at D.'s father, perhaps sternly, thought D. 'Lots of young men are dying at sea to get it here, so we ought to show our appreciation, shouldn't we?'

His father glared at D. accusingly. D. felt a sense of hopelessness. He wasn't able to play these adult games, of silences and half-lies, of penetrating disclosure of pretence, ruthless pursuit of answers which pleased them. Besides, his thumb hurt and he was in no small state of shock from the sight, smell and sensation of that bursting suppuration spilling into the bowl. He felt cold beads of sweat on his forehead and cheeks, involuntarily he began to breathe deeply, the men's voices faded, and Dr Harrington caught him just in time as he toppled to the floor.

Their way home did not lie on a bus route, so they walked. Endless steps, steep paths, never-ending winding streets closed in by privet hedging, always upward. Panting and struggling, holding his thumb up at his shoulder as Dr Harrington had advised, D. fought to keep up with his father, who was always ahead and sometimes paused for him to catch up.

'You'll never get to be a man if you can't manage a few steps like this,' said his father disdainfully. They had climbed two hundred and twenty-one steps from Carmarthen Road already. He knew because they had counted them last year, on their way home from Grandma's. He tried harder, but he still couldn't keep up with his father. Perhaps he had longer legs, thought D. That's what his mother said, anyway. His mother had short, fat legs and a long back, as though she were meant to be six inches taller but the bones in her legs had not grown in proportion to the flesh on them. This made her self-conscious, and argumentative when it came to climbing steps. Maybe his father was tough, manly, thought D. He agreed with his father, though, that he had a long way to go to be a man. The road ahead seemed endless and rough. He just didn't know how, yet, but he was trying.

He felt hugely fatigued and tired when he finally got home. He wanted nothing more than to lie down and sleep. His father had other ideas, and wanted to press ahead with soaking the thumb and squeezing it some more. After all, he had given up precious gardening time by taking him to the doctor — he didn't want to do it again if something went wrong by waiting too long. Besides, he had other things to do this evening.

The bowl of warm water was prepared. D. put his thumb in carefully. He didn't look too closely at it. The bandage had come off easily enough, but the lint patch was firmly stuck to the ugly hole made by Dr Harrington's lance, and to remove it now became the first objective.

His father wisely allowed him to do this himself, in his own time. His mother went outside, muttering that she didn't want to see 'that sort of thing'.

The lint patch floated off, and his father urged him to squeeze.

He squeezed. Gently and nervously. His thumb, so much an intimate part of him once, now seemed to be alien, a hostile intrusion which he would rather be without altogether if it was going to give him this much trouble. He vowed silently never to visit the bomb crater again. It didn't hurt, really, as he squeezed. At least his action didn't make the throbbing discomfort any worse. He was fearful of making it worse. He had no idea of what lay ahead if he were to deal out the vigour his father was urging. So he pressed gently, half afraid to look at it while his father, restless with impatience, moved from one side of him to the other.

There was a sudden sensation of release, like a piece of wet soap escaping a clutching hand, and a horrifying skein of pus spewed from the hole in his thumb. It was all white this time, with no coloured bits. D. was relieved that still there was no sign of blood, but the sight of that unbroken thread, nine inches or more long, unnerved him, and he appealed to his father.

'I don't want to squeeze any more, Dad. It hurts.' It didn't really, but he had no reserves of nerve left. He'd had enough.

'Don't be a baby,' his father snapped. 'That's nothing. What will you do if you get a real pain?'

D. felt tears roll down his cheeks. He was stuck here, with the long string of pus falling away from his throbbing thumb into the bowl of water, unable to bring himself to touch his hand any more, fearful that his father would take over and do him unimaginable mischief.

His father burrowed into the cutlery drawer. Where the sharp knife was kept. D.'s eyes widened in horror. His father produced the only pair of scissors they possessed, large and rusting at the hinge, a constant source of complaint from his mother.

'Hold still now, if you don't want to get hurt,' said his father impatiently, and with a swift movement clenched the string of pus and pulled, as though the scissors were a pair of pliers. That did hurt. There was no more foulness left now, and a few spots of pink blood told the end. D. sat down, exhausted, holding his thumb at shoulder height to reduce the throbbing.

His father replaced Dr Harrington's bandage on his thumb. 'Out you go now. Run around and get your circulation going. All that fuss over nothing. I can see it's going to take a long time for you to grow up.'

His father tipped the bowl of water into the sink and washed away the odious contents and dumped it and the scissors in the washing-up bowl alongside the cups and saucers in it. He went into the parlour, to change into his gardening clothes.

D. sat for as long as he dared, judging the moment when his father would emerge in his old clothes. Not a moment too soon he made the back door as he heard his father say, 'What about your skipping and handstands? I haven't seen much practice lately.'

D. said nothing, hoping his father would quickly become pre-occupied with his gardening and not pursue an answer.

His father turned away, shaking his head. D. went to the front garden and sat on the concrete steps. He looked forward to bed time. He had had a rough day, and hadn't slept too well for some nights.

★ ★ ★

A few days later a large boil gathered at the fold of the joint at the back of his knee. It arrived suddenly, during game-play with the boys in the street, and gave him a deep-seated jab of pain when he straightened his leg. He felt the swelling, and thought he had bruised himself and not noticed. It happened sometimes.

The following morning the knee was hot and stiff and much too painful to straighten. He limped to the breakfast table as his mother let out a guffaw. 'Look at the wounded soldier! Limping because he has his thumb in a bandage too long.'

He climbed to his place at table with difficulty, and settled down to eat his cornflakes. His older sister, Jean, looked at him with concern.

'What's wrong, D? Have you hurt yourself?' she asked kindly.

'There's nothing wrong with him,' snapped his mother. 'If there is, it's his own fault. Stupid boy doesn't watch where he's going.'

D. was silent. When their mother had gone out and left them, the children rose from the table and D. asked his sister to look at the back of his knee.

'You've got a huge red lump there,' she said with alarm. 'It's as big as an egg.' She had heard her mother use that expression recently of a neighbour who had the misfortune to have a carbuncle on her shoulder. 'It's like a boil.'

'Or a carbuncle,' said his younger sister with satisfaction.

'What can I do about it?' said D. 'Mam won't help. She just laughs.'

'Wait until Dad gets home,' said Jean. 'He'll know what to do.'

The day passed slowly and painfully and his father was annoyed with him for 'having something new that was wrong with him every time he came home'. But he did take a look at it, and pronounced it as a small boil, harmless, and 'shouldn't need any limping about like you're doing now'.

'Bathe it in hot water,' he said. 'It will burst on its own soon enough.'

A week later it did burst, whilst he was asleep in bed. His mother was upset.

'Just look at that mess.' And it was a mess. The sheet over the piece of leather on his mattress looked as though someone had died on it.

He tried his best to wash the sheet at the corrugated washboard his mother used. He had been sentenced to wash it himself because he 'had been stupid, and should have known when the boil was ready to burst'. He didn't dare point out that she would not allow him to put a protective bandage around it. 'Bad for the circulation,' she had said. 'Let the air get to it.'

He concentrated on the stain, rubbing vigorously with the huge yellow bar of soap his mother had given him. She inspected it at intervals, pointing out spots which still showed, and he had to eliminate these despite his protests that he had 'seen that one last week, before his boil'.

He struggled for an hour longer before she was satisfied. Then he must rinse it and hang it on the line. This took a long time too, but he finally accomplished it.

His mother watched him at the final stages, ready, he suspected, to make him do it again if a corner of the sheet touched the ground as he struggled with the pegs.

'Now you know what it's like, taking care of you ungrateful children,' she said. 'Now you've got some idea of the work you cause perhaps you'll be more careful in future.' She raised the line, fastened it and went indoors. He looked at the sheet, billowing gently over the burgeoning potato stalks, and wondered what he had done wrong. His knee throbbed and he wondered if he could sneak into his parents' bedroom and use his mother's handmirror she kept on the dressing table to see what had happened to the boil.

He looked up. His mother was watching him through the kitchen window. Perhaps later, he thought. He'd go and have a sit down on the wall outside in the street.

In the street the boys were discussing the war. It was late summer now, and it was a long time since they had seen or heard an enemy plane, and their nights went undisturbed. The blackout was still strictly enforced by the Home Guard and A.R.P. men, giving the boys much humour as they pin-pointed the offender the following day. The British had driven the Germans out of North Africa and had captured Pantelleria. There was some argument about where Pantelleria was until Trevor, the quiet elder of two brothers, decided it was somewhere in Italy.

'The war will be over soon,' he said with authority. 'Then everything will be back to normal.'

The boys thought about it. They were chiefly concerned with what 'normal' was. Adults talked among themselves about it, but to the boys it was just talk, of times misted with age.

'Will the street lights go on at night?' asked 'Tiddler' Davies. Tiddler was his own age, but smaller than any of them, despite having a father who was as tall as D.'s father and a mother who was so colossal that the women in the street joked that if she ever fell over in the dark she would have to stay there until the morning for a crane to turn her over.

'Of course,' said Biffo. Freddie Biffen lived opposite D. and had a younger sister who had a voice like the Cwmfelin Works siren. She was sent out to call her brother for mealtimes and could be heard half a mile away in stormy weather.

'That means we can play football in the dark,' said Trevor.

That was an eye-opening prospect. Now, as darkness fell, they were reduced to playing cards in each other's disused air raid shelters, harbouring scarce candle stubs as they gambled half cigarettes and stubbed ends of salvaged ashtray remains from their parents. There was a communal pipe, present at these sessions, into which the broken-up remains of the ashtrays were emptied by the winner and smoked in defiance of nature's urgent reflexes to retch. He who emerged from a dank murky shelter puffing a pipe was hero for that night. Even the girls approved.

About this time D. took up smoking. Everyone did it. The adults claimed it calmed their nerves, and the children simply became addicted. Although cigarettes were not expensive, a regular supply was far beyond the means of the boys, who scrounged and stole what they could at home. For D. this was not difficult. With thousands of cigarettes in his father's wardrobe and the ability to pick the lock, he was assured of unending bounty. Consequently he found it easy to make friends in the street. Especially the Tinder brothers, who never played street games with the other boys because they were Protestants, but were willing to stand around and stop bullying D. as long as there was a chance of free cigarettes.

D. was innocent enough to fail to connect these phenomena until his father's wardrobe ran dry in October, and even his own supplies of smokes ran out. Then he was hurt to find that a card game in someone's shelter had been under way for hours as he roamed the street looking for company, knocking on one door after another to enquire of irritated parents if so-and-so was coming out to play. The Tinders began to bully him again, playing merciless practical jokes, taunting him and provoking him into unfair fights. After Christmas and another full wardrobe the picture would change, though D. was unaware of this, and endured the present as though it would also be the depressing future.

'Let's go to town,' said Trevor. 'Next Saturday. We can scrounge gum off the Yanks.' This seemed a good idea. The American soldiers never came around the housing estate, except on a rare isolated visit to see home one of the local older girls. There wasn't really any reason for them to spend their time on the depressing mean maze of privet-bound streets. So the boys would go to them.

There were endless tales of the Americans' wealth and generosity: chewing gum, bubble-gum, cigarettes, chocolate, even money was said to be handed out with gusto by the soldiers to any who asked. They were especially generous to children, it was rumoured, and even took them for rides in their jeeps. D. thought of the soldier he and Mary had met earlier that summer, and felt a shade of doubt. But he agreed to come.

The American soldiers ignored them. There were hundreds of soldiers in town, wandering bored and aimless through the shattered black remains of the town centre trying to pick up girls, clowning with one another, trying to ignore the taunts of the British servicemen who were trapped into doing the same bored tour, waiting for the pubs to open at six o'clock.

The American soldiers were unfailingly polite. The boys' cries of 'Any gum, chum?' were treated with a smile and silence, and the soldiers walked on.

The boys never tried again. D. felt the same as the other boys felt: demeaning themselves like beggars, and the effort of sinking their pride, had been wholly without reward. They had been drawn, in pursuit of their declared aim, far beyond their normal range of travel, and disconsolately admitting defeat, faced a long hungry trudge home. As they admitted to themselves, tired, thirsty and longing for their afternoon meals, it had been a waste of time. The rumours were false. There was no magic bag of goodies to be had for the asking.

On their way home, through sometimes unfamiliar streets where they argued about direction and the length of their route, they saw many damaged houses. They explored most of them, constantly on the lookout for 'cops', those dreaded guardians of the law whose very appearance was enough to reduce them to anxious silence, breathing a sigh of relief at their passing.

At one of the wrecked houses they found a sheet of metal, flexible thin steel that made a sound like distant thunder when it was vigorously rattled. They took turns at this rattling, trying to outdo each other in generating noise. When it came to D.'s turn, he mismanaged it. Taking a step forward as he vibrated the sheet, the bottom edge sliced through his sock and cut him to the bone at the ankle.

He gasped in shock and dropped the sheet. He sat down quickly to inspect the damage. For no particular reason he always described the pain of cuts and bruises as colours. This was a white pain, the most feared. It meant blood and real damage. A brown pain on the other hand would describe the result of a tripping fall on hard ground, giving a bruise or graze, with little or no blood; a blue pain accompanied a hard knock to the head, when there was little or nothing to show for it.

He didn't want to look too closely. It might be serious. He stood up. Trevor asked him if it hurt.

'No. Not really. Just a cut,' said D. airily.

His shoe filled with blood and caused his sock to slip against the sole of his foot. Walking became less easy. He had a hole in the sole of his shoe, and as the boys walked, he left a trail of offset circular red-brown spots behind. He noticed them before the others and he hoped they wouldn't see them. He was ashamed of the hole in his shoe. He contrived to remain last in the party as they walked along, and this manoeuvre seemed to make the pace slower. He wanted to get home now, this minute. He needed a bandage and comforting advice from his parents.

At home his mother was upset by the state of his sock.

'Just look at it,' she said accusingly. 'You've torn a hole in it. And look at all this blood. That's going to take all day to wash out. Why can't you be more careful, you stupid boy?' With irritation she dumped the guilty sock in the sink and ran the cold tap water over it, arranging the sock gingerly with finger and thumb to minimise contact with it.

'Now go and wash your foot. You'd better do it in the bath. And while you're at it, try and clean your shoe out.'

His ankle ached now, and when he had sat on the edge of the bath to clean it, he ventured to look.

It wasn't a big cut. Just an inch and a half or so long. But it was deep, and he glimpsed a flash of blue-white bone when he flexed his foot. That shook him up a little. He dried his foot and limped into the kitchen to tell his mother.

'I haven't got any bandage to spare. I want to keep it for serious things,' she said. 'If the Germans come back again with their bombs and things I want to be ready for them.'

'But I can see the bone, Mam.'

'Nonsense. You're hysterical. I'll give you a plaster you can put on it.'

'Look,' he said. 'It's all white at the bottom of the cut.'

'Don't show me,' she snapped, turning her head away sharply. 'I don't want to see it. That sort of thing turns me.' She handed him a plaster barely large enough to cover the cut, with eyes averted. 'The girls don't get themselves into trouble,' she said. 'I don't see why you don't take care of yourself like they do.'

It hurt seriously that night, but within days it had healed, and though tender for weeks, it ceased to trouble him seriously.

Within days of cutting his ankle he broke his kneecap.

The Emergency Water Supply tank was a scant hundred yards from his home, erected on the site of a bombed house opposite the unfortunate Patons' and Squires' ruined semi-detached. The tank, built with the usual foresight and planning of the time many months after the bombing ended, was solidly constructed of double thickness bricks recovered and re-used from the destroyed house itself, and was filled with water about five feet deep. No one was sure what the Emergency Water Supply was for — perhaps to put out fires, or, dread the thought, as a domestic supply in case of damaged mains. Anyway, the tank was quickly filled with every kind of rubbish from nearby houses, as well as small boys heaving the remaining bricks of the bombed house into the water in competitions to claim the biggest splash. When the combination of rubbish and bricks and breeding mosquitoes had risen above water level the authorities broke a hole in the side of the tank and drained it. The double strands of barbed wire around the wall top were quickly removed by nearby gardeners anxious to keep small boys out of their gardens and the desolation was complete. The Emergency Water Supply tank was a failure of its time.

It retained one useful function: the curved cement coping gave a wonderful race-track feeling for any boy willing to run fast enough to build up centrifugal force that would enable him to achieve an acute angle from the vertical as he travelled. Two circuits was the record before running out of steam, when the runner had to leave the wall top at a specific and severely limited point to avoid a suicidal landing among piled bricks and concrete surrounding the tank. Failure to leave the wall at this point was unthinkable. No one had failed so far.

D. failed. He had managed one and a half circuits when his step faltered and he found himself inexorably drawn to the outside edge of the wall until a wild desperate leap brought him squarely down on a tangled steel window frame half buried in what was once the chimney. He landed clumsily on his hands and knees, and a searing pain flashed through his knee as it crashed into the corner of an unsympathetic brick. The pain was all colours of the rainbow. Clutching his knee tightly, gasping, not daring to move, he was unable to answer the other boys' anxious 'You all right? Did you hurt yourself?' and the like.

Eventually he got up and hobbled over to the low wall at the edge of the pavement. God! How that knee hurt. He forced himself to look. There wasn't a lot to see, thank goodness. Just an ugly dent in the skin, already coloured purple.

For him the game was over, and he limped painfully up the street homeward, leaving the boys silent and discouraged behind him.

His mother was sceptical. 'It's just a small bruise,' she said after glancing at it. 'Nothing to make a fuss about.'

D. felt carefully along the knee cap. There was a ridge right across it, stabbingly painful in parts. When he flexed his leg in certain ways the pain made him give a loud yelp, quickly muffled at his mother's warning glare.

'And don't you bother your father with that,' she nodded at his knee. 'He's had a hard day's work without being badgered by you.' She busied herself with household chores. 'And don't sit around here all day. Find something to do. If you can't find something useful to do go outside. I don't want you coming in here when I'm busy, just looking for attention after a little bump. You're turning into a real baby.'

Over the weeks the pain subsided gradually, but the ridge across the knee cap remained, and pain gave way to a distressing ache that made sitting difficult unless he could stretch his leg straight at intervals. Sunday Mass was torture. His father allowed him to sit during the not-so-important kneeling bits of the service, but his mother didn't like it, and said so afterwards.

'There's nothing wrong with him, Frank. He's just after attention. He can kneel just as well as the rest of us.'

His father shrugged. 'He'll be alright next week,' he said placatingly.

'Well, if he can sit up for half the Mass the girls should be able to, as well. Their knees are not so strong as boys' knees. It's more of a strain for them.'

His father said nothing. D. felt that he had put his father in a corner by allowing him to sit up and not his sisters. Next Sunday he would have to kneel all the way through or lose his father's sympathy.

He practised kneeling on one knee during the week, setting up some of the Dickens volumes in his bedroom to act as the kneeler at church. By Friday he thought he could do it. He didn't want to let his father down. Thank heavens he had mastered the skipping and handstand tasks given him weeks earlier. His father hadn't paid up yet, even though D. had performed in the back garden in a ceremony witnessed by every member of the family, and despite the discomfort of his thumb which had not healed properly, having a thick shell of dead skin encasing it from nail to first joint. He had succeeded so well at his practising handstands that he could walk on his hands for at least ten paces, but he didn't want to demonstrate this, in case his mother set hand-walking as a further task. If she did, he would be well ahead.

★ ★ ★

The radio announced that Hamburg had been attacked for the third night in succession. Great damage had been caused to the city said the announcer, and huge fires had been seen burning since the first night's bombing. Only twenty two bombers had 'failed to return' over all three nights of the attack, marking a point of significant success in the offensive against the enemy.

It was all very distant and far from their everyday lives. The only connection was the unreal blackout rules, the rationed food and the Pathe newsreels at the tuppenny rush on Saturday afternoons of fuzzy films of a city on fire, others showing British ships putting into port almost cut in half, more film of British soldiers dashing about amidst smoke and dust and ruined buildings somewhere in Italy, the King talking to smiling and head-bobbing aircrews after climbing from their huge bombers following a raid on enemy territory. These were their only contacts with the world of violence being managed by men, far away, out of sight and sound.

Occasionally D.'s father went on manoeuvres with the Home Guard, and returned late on Sunday morning, worn out and muddy, and smelling strongly of beer. D.'s mother strongly disapproved of these military exercises.

'You'll miss Mass again, Frank. That'll be the second time in three months. Why can't they do these manoveer things some other day? Why does it have to be a blessed Sunday?'

'Manoeuvres,' D.'s father corrected her patiently. 'Most of us are working on Saturdays, and we can't afford to lose a day in the week when Sundays are available.'

'You smell of beer, Frank. You've spent most of the day drinking, haven't you?' she accused him one day. 'You can't shoot straight, the condition you're in.' She pursed her lips. D. saw the mean furrows along the top lip. 'Disgraceful,' she said. 'What if Father Egan saw you in that state? On a Sunday? And no Mass, either.' She flounced out of the kitchen where his father sat, wearily drinking a pint mug of tea, the back of his khaki shirt dark with sweat from collar to waist. As she went she uttered black words of warning that, 'We're becoming as bad as the rest of the heathens in this street. We'll all be Protestants by the time this war ends. Mark my words.'

About this time his father developed a large boil on the small of his back. His father complained loudly, packed his dining table chair with cushions and walked with a stoop. After two days of suffering he consulted Dr Harrington. It was too early to lance, the doctor said, and advised him to bathe it in warm water, and it would burst on its own, soon enough.

For a week the household was hushed in reverent awe of their father's pain. The children were insulated from him by their worried mother, who was deeply concerned for his health.

'We're lucky,' she confided to the children in hushed tones as their father groaned in the parlour one evening. 'Your father has a good job, and won't get his pay docked if he has to stay in bed for a day or two. Not like other fathers in the street. Just you remember that.' She wagged a forefinger at them as though this was a warning. 'So don't you go disturbing him now, until he's better.'

This seemed a contradiction, and confused D. and his two sisters, but they obeyed the simple warning as best they could in the confines of the small house.

D.'s mother refused to bathe her husband's boil in hot water. 'I can't stand that sort of thing,' she said, so she called upon a neighbour to do it for her.

Mr Williams was a talker. As he sloshed hot water over his wincing patient's back he talked. And talked. D.'s mother shook her head in disbelief as she sat in the kitchen with the children, listening. Their father said very little. He wasn't allowed to, as Mr Williams proceeded to exploit the gift of speech as though his tongue was powered by electricity.

It was Mr Williams' overflow of verbal liquidity which decided when D.'s father's boil was 'better', that is, no longer needing treatment. The boil had been elevated to the status of 'carbuncle', a condition beyond everyday experience and something that really needed urgent and professional attention, but which, due entirely to his heroic nature, D.'s father had decided to forego, simply suffering the course of nature as a gesture to the 'war effort'. He wouldn't use a doctor's time over something so trivial when others were in hospital suffering from war injuries. In truth, a visit to the doctor would cost money.

He went to work every day, but it was a week before he walked upright. Every morning he fixed a huge padded plaster to his back with the aid of a mirror, monopolising the bathroom while the family waited, talking in hushed tones in the kitchen, until he emerged looking white and shaken to short-temperedly take a swig from his pint mug of cooling tea before dashing off to catch the bus.

'It's better today, Doll,' he said one evening as he sat at his meal. Doll was her pet name. When he was angry at her, everyone knew because her called her Doris, her real name. 'I think I'll do without the plaster tomorrow. Give it a try, anyway,' he added with an air of sacrifice.

'Are you sure, Frank?' She sounded concerned, but to the children her words lacked sincerity, and spoke more of relief that the episode was approaching its end.

'Oh, yes. We all have to make an effort these days. Have to show willing while the war is on.'

D.'s mother was silent. The children were puzzled. They tried to connect their father's carbuncle with the noise and confusion of war, and failed. Perhaps wars caused people to get boils and sores.

★　★　★

D. came in from play at mid-morning to visit the toilet. His mother was at the kitchen sink, peeling vegetables for the midday meal. She glared at him, annoyed that he had intruded on a furious conversation she was having with herself.

'Who are you listening to, nosey?'

D. was silent, not understanding. He often heard his mother having long arguments with someone who was not there. He had never ventured to ask her who it was, and assumed that discussion with invisible people who never answered back was something adults did, anyway.

He went into the toilet, bolted the door and sat on the seat. He noticed that the plug of rolled-up paper filling the old latch hole was gone again. He had put a fresh one in only yesterday. The latch to the toilet door had been lowered, like that on the back door, when they were small. Like the back door, the hole left by removing the latch to a new position had never been properly sealed. He didn't worry too much. His sisters were more concerned by the missing plug than he was.

He stretched out a hand to pull off a sheet from the swatch of cut-up newspapers hanging by a threaded piece of string from a nail hammered into the wall. He paused. He began to hear a collection of sounds that told him someone was standing close to the toilet door. Human sounds. Secretive. The rustling scrape of layers of clothing sliding over each other as the body inside stooped; the click of a knee joint: and his mother's wheezing breathing. He knew his mother's wheeze. At bored winter reading sessions in the parlour when the whole family would sit silently slogging through the few books and newspapers, listening to the wind and slashing rain hit the windows, his mother's wheezing breath was the loudest and most regular sound in the room. Even his father noticed it sometimes, telling her that she sounded 'chesty', but she took offence, so he never took his comment to the level of complaint.

And now D. could hear it, close by, just the other side of the door. She wasn't moving. She wasn't performing any household task that could explain her presence. She continued to wheeze as D. withdrew his hand from the wad of newspapers. What was she doing? Was she spying on him?

'What are you doing, Mam?' he called.

His mother gave a loud embarrassed laugh, and without attempting an excuse she hurried away. The rustling and clicking of her going was many times louder than her arrival.

He stood up immediately, and tearing off a small piece of newspaper, he vigorously stuffed it into the hole. He felt acutely vulnerable as he used the paper for its intended purpose and quickly pulled up his trousers, flushed the toilet and went outside. He rejoined the boys in the street, but had no heart for the games being played. He sat on the wall, wondering what his mother had been doing. Had he himself done anything wrong? Was there something going on in the toilet that she needed to watch?

Eventually the energy and enjoyment of the boys' games drew him in, and he forgot the episode for the moment, running himself breathless in a disordered football game played with a wooden croquet ball. No one knew where the ball had come from, but it served well until it split into small pieces for no apparent reason, and the boys slowly dispersed in search of dinner.

D. went home too, hungry, as the other boys were, and knowing as well as they that it was too early for a meal yet. They would hang around the houses like scrounging pets, hoping for a handout from exasperated mothers who needed room in tiny kitchens to prepare a proper meal.

His mother glanced at him.

'You come in here just to stuff yourself, have you? Can't leave me in peace. Always under my feet, you are. You're worse than a baby.'

D. could see she was working herself up into a rage, and he turned away to go outside. He heard her rustling clothes, and turned just in time to see her point a knife at his genitals. He moved his hands quickly to protect himself, and felt the sharp pain of a cut. She had the sharp knife in her hand.

He ran outside, not stopping until he had reached the end of the cinder path at the bottom of the garden. Beyond was an embankment and then a steep slope away to the houses below. He knew he would have no trouble over these obstacles, but if his mother was still after him she would not follow.

He looked back. No one. She hadn't even followed him out of the house. He looked at his hand. There was an ugly deep slash in the heel of his hand below the little finger. Blood dripped as he assessed the damage.

He didn't want to lick it clean as he would have done with a smaller injury. This one was messy, and revolted him. He felt in need of comforting, and reassurance, but his elder sister wasn't around. Perhaps some of the boys would still be in the street, he thought. At least they could compare cuts, and even offer advice.

He didn't want to go up the path again. It would take him too close to his mother. He would cut along the embankment at the end of the neighbours' garden and then up through the Jameses' garden to the street. The Jameses were rarely at home.

He set off, holding his injured hand at shoulder height as he remembered Dr Harrington's advice for his infected thumb.

Mrs Hughes, next-door-but-one, called to him. She didn't like the boys running along the embankment. He ducked and ran faster behind her raspberry canes, but she was too close, and could cut him off if she wanted. He stopped and stood up.

Her face turned from annoyance to concern as she saw his blood-slicked hand held close to his shoulder.

'What's wrong with your hand, boy? What have you done to it? Let me have a look.'

She stretched out her hand to take his, but D. was reluctant to offer it. He wasn't sure she could do anything about it. Slowly he extended the hand.

'That's a nasty cut,' she said with concern. 'You must go home and get it bandaged, as soon as you can. You don't want to get it infected. Go on, now, as quick as you can.'

She stood, expecting him to do that. He stood, unable to do what she advised. He couldn't tell her that at home, he might well get another serious cut.

'Isn't your mother at home? asked Mrs Hughes. 'Don't you know where she keeps the bandages? Even a big plaster would do.'

He shook his head, unwilling to give her an opening that she might pursue with questioning, adult questions that would eventually squeeze out the truth. It would be shameful if the boys in the street got to know that his mother behaved as she did.

'Come on in,' said Mrs Hughes. 'I'll put something on it until your mother comes home.' She gestured for him to follow, and he walked up the path to the house behind her, guiltily. As she went she told him that he should wash the cut, and use disinfectant, before putting a better bandage around it. He didn't really need persuading, he thought. He already had experience of infection.

She cleaned his hand gently, and put a huge sticking plaster over it. She tutted in sympathy as she worked, and D.'s heart sank when she told him that in her opinion he needed stitches. 'Four or five, I should think,' she said. 'Help it to heal quicker.'

Finally, she was finished. 'There you are. Now don't forget to get it done properly when your mother comes home. You'll probably need to see a doctor. You go home and rest now. That's a bad cut.'

He left her house by the front door, and walked to his own garden. He sat on the concrete steps in front of the house, feeling tired and unhappy. He didn't want to go in. He didn't want to let his mother see the plaster. He wasn't at all sure, either, that he would not be punished if he told anyone else about it. Even if he did tell, it wouldn't heal the cut immediately. It certainly wouldn't undo what she had already done, as though nothing had happened.

His sisters came through the gateless front entrance, hungry for dinner. D. joined them, seeking safety in numbers but holding back, ready to run for it. His mother ignored him.

His hand took a long time to heal. For many days he was unable to join in the street games, and even after several weeks he winced as he handled a cricket bat or swung from a tree branch. The boys were curious at first, but he wouldn't tell them. He thought at first that he would invent a tale of daring, like tackling a German spy, or winning a fight with the Gwili gang, but he calculated that they wouldn't believe him, so he told them he cut himself on a broken jam jar. This was quite believable, because the boys and he had that summer begun a lucrative Saturday morning round of collecting old jam jars. The pickle factory in town paid them a halfpenny for the one pound size and a penny for the two pound. They had built a cart from a tea chest tied with wire to four old pram wheels, and with a long rope attached to the front and two long wooden handles to steer, it was remarkably easy to handle, even fully laden, up the steepest gradients by four or five willing boys. Sometimes there were one or two broken jars, and these had to be picked out of the box carefully to be placed in a dustbin. All the boys' parents disapproved of them collecting jars, and the boys were scrupulous in denying any the excuse of 'carelessness with broken glass' to end the activity. After all, a good day would earn five shillings between them.

They stacked the jars in one of the disused air raid shelters, and once a month they were piled into hessian sacks and hauled off to town. There was no dispute about division of spoils: anyone willing to haul a sackful of jars two miles to the pickle factory was paid for his load. The more he carried, the more he was paid. It was a tough journey for boys all under twelve years old. By comparison, collecting them in the cart was a picnic, and nobody was paid for collecting. The money was in delivery.

Most of the boys had nicks and cuts from all this glass-handling work, borne proudly as the price of riches, and D. secured a welcome notoriety, albeit short-lived, for sustaining the worst injury of any of them yet.

Chapter Seven

In September D.'s father took his holidays, most of which he spent in the garden. Unwillingly he took the family to Bishopston Valley on the usual day-long outing. It rained most of the time, and it was a miserable and uncomfortable day, damp and humid in the sheltered, narrow, tree-filled valley, plagued by flies, unable to light a fire to boil tea, unable to sit outside at Mrs Jenkins' tables to eat sandwiches and, when D.'s mother declared it dangerous to swim in the sea while it was raining, the day was an emphatic failure.

$$\star \quad \star \quad \star$$

And then it was back to school. D. found himself in the top class, Standard 8. Most of the boys here were going on fourteen years old, and with him at only ten and a half, there were no friends to be made in this class. With disappointment he saw that Neville, the youngest of the Henderson brothers, was in the class too. He hoped he would not have to sit next to him at one of the classroom's double desks.

Mark Walsh, or 'Markie' ran the class. He was very old, and yawned very frequently, taking off his glasses to polish them to hide his wide-open mouth and closed eyes. He gave them long written exercises that didn't need any supervision or instruction, and at the end of them they exchanged their sheets of paper and marked them themselves as Markie called out the correct answers from a sheet of paper he hid in his desk. The cane was used so frequently that it was kept on top of the desk, and not put away in the well as the other teachers did. Although Markie didn't hit very hard, he used it remorselessly on those who talked in his class. Poor marks at tests and exercises also earned the cane, and these two faults narrowed the caning field to a consistent unlucky few. There were no excuses, either. Even Gerry O'Halloran, who had a withered arm from polio, had to take his share, for him across the calves of his legs with socks rolled down.

So far, D. was one of the remarkable few who had never been caned, either by teachers in class or by the headmaster. He had also never had to endure the various other forms of physical reminder of the house rules. These reminders were hard, open-handed slaps to the face, hair-twisting, bonking on the top of the head with a slender hardwood chair spat, vigorous teeth-rattling shaking by one shoulder — a Spud Murphy special — and from Dwt Barry a venomous jab with closed fist on a shoulder blade, delivered by surprise.

A week after the start of the new class D. had his first taste of the cane. Not from Markie, but none other than the dread headmaster.

D. hated the school dinners. When he pleaded with his mother to take sandwiches to school, she refused.

'I get enough trouble with your father's food,' she said dismissively. 'Fussing about everything in them. They have to be just so, not too thick, not too thin, with something different in them every day. I'm not having you playing that game with me as well. I've had enough of it.'

So he missed his dinners, even though his mother gave him a shilling on Mondays to pay for them.

On Wednesday his mother asked him what his dinner had been. He couldn't invent a menu. His mind went blank. It didn't take long for her to learn the truth, and she was very angry.

'I can't see why you can't eat the bits you like,' she shouted. 'It can't all be bad.'

'They are,' said D. unhappily. 'They're ugly. Just ugly.' He couldn't think of any other way to describe them.

This amused his mother, whose lips twitched in a small smile.

'Alright,' she said after a silence. 'You come home for dinner. I'm not going to cut sandwiches for you. It's too much for me. So you come straight home from school. No playing on the way, mind you. Straight home.'

D. felt relief and gratitude. The school dinners were truly horrible, so horrible that he would rather go without dinner altogether. Coming home was beyond even his wildest hope, and he could have a cup of tea too.

'The exercise will do you good, I suppose.' His mother's voice held traces of doubt still, and D. crept away lest his very presence might arouse second thoughts on this splendid arrangement for his dinners.

Thursday, the following day, was fine and sunny. D. made the journey home in good time, leaving a good twenty minutes for his meal of egg and chips and a mug of tea before setting off for school again.

On Friday he had scrambled egg on toast with tea. He had arrived home punctual to the minute, and he was able to set off at the same time as the previous day.

The Waun Wen gang brought him to a halt within sight of his school. There were six of them, four on one side of the street and two on the other. D. hadn't expected this. There were very few boys around on the streets at dinner time, and these boys looked old enough to be over fourteen — the usual age for leaving school in this area.

As D. stopped, weighing his chances of getting past unmolested, they stopped joking and clowning amongst themselves and stared at him. He turned to retrace his steps to a side street, a longer way to school, but safer.

The boys began to shout at him. He broke into a run, followed by a terrifying shower of hurtling stones skipping and skidding around him. He heard them shout to each other to cut him off at the next street, and he was forced into another side street, away from school. He was panting for breath now, and fearful of being caught by these boys. He had heard terrible tales of the Waun Wen gang, almost as bad as the Gwili gang, and he would avoid them at all costs. He climbed steep little streets when he should have been going downhill, dashed through driveways and private gardens, and climbed walls in his anxiety to elude them. He was not far from where he had first seen them when he heard the school bell ring for afternoon assembly. He was going to be late.

And he was. As he dashed to the school gates he saw the headmaster, waiting for him and anyone else not registered at assembly.

Silently, his small thin lips moving quickly over each other, the headmaster pointed to the stairs.

'Stand at the desk,' he snapped.

'Sir. I was chased by a gang of boys,' began D.

'The desk, boy. Don't stand there talking to me. I don't want excuses. You're late.'

D. stood at the desk for five minutes, dreading the appearance of the headmaster. When he came along the corridor towards him, in his neat sage-green suit and shiny brown shoes, he signalled with the cane already in his hand for D. to hold up his hand for the cane. He seemed disappointed that D. was the only boy waiting to be punished. He looked as though he had enough energy and malignant purpose to beat half a dozen boys.

D. took a full-blooded swing of the cane on each hand in turn. He hadn't protested or pleaded an excuse again. The headmaster's face wouldn't allow it. Instead he concentrated on suppressing any noise of fear or pain that anyone in the surrounding classrooms might hear. The pain was shocking, especially when the thin bamboo cut into his thumb, still tender from the poisoning of a few weeks before, and with a new skin still growing.

His hands were numb as the headmaster nodded and waved a hand in arrogant dismissal.

Markie looked up from his desk as D. went into the classroom.

'Where have you been?'

'I was late, sir.'

'I hope you got the cane?'

'Yessir.'

'Sit down.'

D. sat, nursing his hands. He eventually looked at them. The palms were an angry red, a white bloodless stripe diagonally across each where the cane had struck. It wasn't just painful punishment: it was real damage to such an important part of him, thought D. The ligaments and tendons all throbbed in protest, and the small bones at the edges of the white mark bore small blue swellings that were specially painful.

He put his hands, palms up, on his knees, and hoped it would not be too long before they stopped hurting.

The next lesson was another 'mark-it-yourself' exercise. One of the boys dealt out sheets of paper to each of the others, and they all took up pencils ready to start. Except D. He found he couldn't bend his fingers to grip the pencil. The centre of his hand seemed to have a wooden plate glued to it. His fingers remained stubbornly separated, refusing commands to close up.

Markie began the exercise. It was a simple arithmetic task, easy enough for most of them. As the teacher spoke the questions D. calculated the answers. He looked at Micky, his desk companion, wondering if he could ask him to write down the answer for him as well as his own.

You, boy. Forgotten how to write? Trying to copy? Perhaps you've got time to spare, eh?'

D. looked up, startled. Markie was looking directly at him.

'Yes. You. Are you pretending to be surprised?'

D. was silent, the shock of rebuke before the class being an entirely new experience for him.

Markie beckoned to him with a withered finger. 'Bring your paper,' he said.

With difficulty D. picked up his paper between forefinger and thumb, and took it to the teacher's desk.

Markie slapped it on his desk top and glared at it.

'I've called out four questions, boy, and you haven't answered a single one. Why?'

D. hesitated.

'Why?' thundered Markie.

'My hand, sir. It's sort of — stiff. I can't hold the pencil, sir.'

He began to tremble. He had never heard Markie speak like this, even to the most troublesome boys in the class.

Markie's hand moved towards the cane, lying beside D.'s clean sheet of paper. He began to feel real fear. He couldn't take more caning on his damaged hands, could he? What could he do to protect them from further injury?

Still sitting, Markie swung around to face D.

'Hold out your hand.'

D. hesitated. Could he have the caning on his legs, like Gerry O'Halloran, he wondered desperately.

'Hand, boy. Now.'

'No, sir. My hand is swollen. I had the cane at dinner time from Mr Andrews. I can't use it.'

Markie's eyes popped, and his glasses slipped down his nose to reveal his watery pale blue eyes. A boy refusing to hold out his hand? Brute force was the only way to deal with this.

With a snarl he lunged with his left hand for D.'s wrist, and with his right he picked up the cane. Beside himself with rage he hoisted D.'s hand to shoulder height, and struck with all his power, not once or twice, but repeatedly, as though he were attacking a dangerous and elusive poisonous insect that threatened to bite him.

D. squirmed and put up a physical struggle to escape, but even for an elderly, short-sighted and tired man like Markie it was all too easy to hold a ten-year-old in check. Blows rained down upon him, a lot of them thankfully landing on his jacket sleeve, but all too many striking painfully on the back of his tightly clenched knuckles. Closing his hands was almost as painful as the blows from the cane, but D. was determined to suffer no more blows to the palms. He must protect them.

White with anger, breathing so hard that white lumps of snot were caught unheeded in the hairs fronting his nose, Markie finally stopped. He flopped back on to his seat from where he had aroused himself in his fury, and suddenly realising his excess, waved D. to return to his seat.

D. walked back slowly, shaking with the shock of it all. Behind him he heard Markie blow his nose in one of his huge linen handkerchiefs. What D. dreaded now was Markie's thinking time. Would he dream up a further punishment now, immediately? Or would he spend the rest of the afternoon thinking about it and call him back as he left at the end of the day to announce a special revenge? He might even send him to the headmaster.

He couldn't hold back the tears. He didn't sob. He just let the tears run. Micky dared not look his way, and could not offer sympathy. The whole class was silent: not a shuffle or a cough, nor even the scrape of a foot accompanying a change of position.

Markie ran his eye over the class for long minutes, testing them, provoking any one of them to give him an excuse to exert his authority. There had never been a boy who had said no. Perhaps he hadn't dealt with this one properly.

'Question five,' said Markie, and the class audibly sighed with relief. For them, things could go back to routine, even if the air was still charged with tension.

D. sat still, nursing his violated hands, making no move to use his pencil. Markie ignored him. At the end of the lesson, when each boy had checked the answers against his own attempt, Markie didn't call out his name.

The afternoon break was signalled by the bell ringing in the corridor, and they all streamed out into the yard. Freed from supervision and out of earshot of teachers, the class of Standard 8 surrounded D. in admiration and praise. He was astonished. He had done nothing heroic. He was just protecting himself. The news spread across the playground as the boys gazed at him unbelieving.

'What, him?'

'Refused the cane? From Markie? You're kidding.'

'He said no? What did Markie say?'

'What's going to happen to him?'

D. was acutely embarrassed. He remained silent, prodding the wall with the toe of his shoe, wanting to wander off to talk to the boys in the lower classes who were his own age. It was several days before things settled down and he felt free to wander the yard unnoticed.

As Christmas approached, there were tests held most days for the simple spelling, writing and arithmetic regime of Mark Walsh's teaching. D. found these easy. Since the fuss over the caning he felt somehow that he had to prove that he was not caning material, that the caning was a rare and irregular event, and that unlike most of the boys who were caned, he was in school to learn. He no longer felt it necessary to hold back.

He came consistently top of the class. Every self-marked paper gave him maximum marks, and even the end of term exam which Markie himself marked, he was one hundred per cent right.

On the last day before the Christmas holidays there was a raffle.

Some benefactor had given the school a bag of flour, a dozen eggs and a box of candied peel. The raffle was free, so every pupil took a ticket to enter. At assembly for afternoon, the headmaster ceremonially and with his usual inscrutable and hostile mien dipped has hand into a box of counterfoils, then held up his hand to show the number, calling it out.

D.'s was the first number called. '536,' said the head, waving the counterfoil slip. It took a moment of disbelief, then D. called out.

'Sir.' He held up his ticket. There was a stir around him.

'Well, come on, boy. Up front here. I'm not going to throw the first prize to you.'

Smiles from all the other teachers in attendance. D. felt a glow as he threaded his way to the front. He had won a dozen eggs. Mam would be pleased. Eggs were strictly rationed, though Mrs Prosser down the street sold them at fivepence each, an extraordinary price, to her neighbours. His mother never got any, because she was unwilling to pay this price, though D. suspected that she wasn't very friendly with Mrs Prosser, who helped run the Presbyterian chapel in town.

His mother didn't show the pleasure he had expected. When he showed her the eggs she frowned. 'I bet they're old,' she said. 'I don't know if I should use them. They're probably all bad.'

Everybody had scrambled eggs on toast that evening. His father was pleased to find two eggs-worth on his plate.

D. brought them home,' said his mother. 'He won them in a school raffle. At least, that's what he says, but I dunno, with him.'

His father gave him a sharp glance, and said nothing. D. felt no more than disappointment. He had felt very excited on his way home from school, having won several shillingsworth and at least two weeks' ration of eggs, and carefully protecting them in their thin wood container, ever watchful for marauding gangs of boys who would take great delight in smashing them. He had thought that everyone in the house, particularly his parents, would be pleased. His elder sister, who walked home with him that day, was full of praise. Perhaps he had misplaced the importance adults placed on such things.

Christmas was the same as last year. The pudding was ceremonially stirred and the silver threepenny pieces wrapped in grease-proof paper then dropped in by each of them, five in all. Amidst short tempers, Christmas dinner was achieved rather than enjoyed. Then father retired to bed for the afternoon, the children played with their sparse Christmas presents, and their mother washed up until tea time.

Tea time was cold turkey. And supper. Like other years they ate turkey well into the New Year, but at least D. could boast about it to the other boys in the street.

That winter for the first time, D. realised that there was an important difference between him and the other boys in the street. The others all went to the same school. His attending a different school meant that he and the boys shared nothing in common for a large part of their day. The boys relived their days when they got together in the evenings, sitting on the low brick wall opposite the lamp post, and D. found he couldn't join in. He didn't know the school teachers, the bullies, or the way that rival gangs behaved, or their lessons — what they learned, their games or their punishments. Their school was a short convenient walk away up the street. He was, apart from the horrible Henderson boys, the only one who went to St Joseph's Catholic school, miles away in the centre of town. He supposed his sisters must feel the same as him, but they never spoke about it.

He felt, not for the first time, left out of things. Separated from boys his own age at his school, he made few friends among the older boys in his class. Separated from the boys in the street by different schools, there was lack of contact and a distance between them. Separated also by religious show, he began to feel self-consciously different as he wound his way past the game-playing boys on Sunday morning on his way to mass, and in the afternoon on his way to and from Sunday School. His greatest misery was the Easter Procession, when the parishioners of Our Lady, Star of the Sea, set out with priests in full robes, altar boys and a shoulder-borne carriage upon which stood a gaudily painted statue of the church's namesake. The bearers walked slowly and in step, like pallbearers, while the rest of the following chanted a mysterious mixture of Greek and Latin intonations which foxed the curious bystanders and participants alike. The procession wound its way through the mean streets of the housing estate, the priest in front swinging his censer filled with burning and smoking incense, other priests attending holding aside gorgeously embroidered robes of gold and white to allow him freedom of movement to swing the gold vessel on its gold chain.

Afterwards the boys in the street, barely grounded in even the most elementary principles of Protestant Christianity, would question him about the meaning of the show. Squirming with embarrassment he would seek to explain it in terms of adult behaviour. He himself most certainly couldn't understand the whole business. He was simply compelled to join it. The boys, to give them credit, never mocked him, and sensing his humiliation, rarely pursued it to the point of demeaning him.

* * *

A few weeks before his eleventh birthday he sat the scholarship examination, a test designed to separate those of academic bent from others slyly described as 'practical' by teachers themselves armed with the distinction of an 'O' level in English History.

He sat the exam in the Grammar School, an intimidating building of solid stone and polished wood. The rooms were clean and shiny and smelled of paper and uniforms. The teachers wore gowns and the headmaster wore a mortarboard. They all looked stern, and said very little as the boys were warned about cheating, then told to start.

He answered questions that seemed a little silly at first, like 'what is one quarter and one half?' but warmed up to the laughable when he came to 'If P comes after Q, write R. If P comes before R, write 4.'

He enjoyed the English essay, and wrote about a storm, his chosen title. When the exam was finished, he went home, to have the rest of the day off school. His mother asked about the exam, and when he described what he had written about she laughed, and told him that he had overdone things, but he knew that it wasn't what he had written, as Markie had told them so often, but it was the way he had written it: plenty of verbs and adjectives, and lots of paragraphs.

His father showed no interest in the exam, and never talked about it. D. soon forgot it too.

Six weeks later the headmaster walked into Markie's class and handed Markie several sheets of paper, nodding at D. as he talked in a whisper to Markie.

D. felt a wave of dread. What now? He had carefully avoided trouble since the contest with Markie, and apart from a slap from another teacher for hanging around a radiator during break on a viciously cold day in February, he hadn't done anything worth the cane, as far as he knew.

The headmaster went out, and Markie pointed a finger at D. and said, 'Stay behind at break. I want to talk to you.'

There was no clock in the classroom, but like a dog which was fed punctually once a day, all the boys had a well-used natural instinct for time. D. shared this instinct, and as ten-thirty grew near, so his fears mounted. By the time the break bell sounded, he had long sat riveted to his seat, caring nothing for the teacher's talking and the boys' responses.

He stayed in his seat as the others filed out.

Markie yawned, cleaned his glasses, then beckoned to D.

'You've passed the scholarship exam. Your new school will be Dynevor. That's the school at the bottom of Mount Pleasant Hill. You start in September.'

He handed D. the papers the headmaster had brought in earlier.

'Take these home and show your parents.'

D. took them, perspiring with relief. He had no real feelings about starting a new school, felt no sense of achievement, and understood only that N. Henderson, who had sat not far away from him at the exam, had not been given similar papers. Perhaps he would not be going with him to the new school. It was a welcome prospect.

Neither of his parents showed great interest in his news. His mother complained about the expense of the school uniform as she read the papers. 'And a satchel,' she said in dismay. 'That's two pounds fifteen shillings.' She read on. 'They even tell you where you must get it all. They know how to make money, don't they.'

Back at school the next day, D.'s sense of escape and relief of the day before, as he looked into the implications of leaving St Joseph's and starting at the big new school with the uniforms and gowned teachers, began to fade. Nothing had changed since yesterday. Only the Henderson boy asked him, nosily, what the papers had been for. When D. told him, Tinder had scowled, called him stupid, and walked away.

★   ★   ★

The weather grew warmer, spring blossomed into summer, and at weekends the boys in the street began their adventurous wanderings. Sometimes they went straight to the beach from school, without towels or special swimming gear. 'Trunks' as their parents called them, were scarce, and although one or two of the boys borrowed their fathers', most of them didn't bother, and swam quite happily in the cold muddy waters of Swansea Bay when the tide was in, and just as readily clowned on the wet sand when the sea had disappeared from sight.

At other times they wandered country lanes, once even venturing to sit atop a dead tree overlooking the airfield at Fairwood until they were chased away by an aggressive army guard who had a gun.

Their favourite day out was undoubtedly to Cadle Mill, just off the main Carmarthen Road out of Swansea, where there was a short stretch of river deep enough to swim in, with trees that had over-hanging branches thick enough to stand on to make spectacular and satisfying dives. Not far away from the river there was a drift mine, Mynydd Newydd, that had a shaft descending at a shallow angle into the hillside. Sitting at the top, they would listen to the strange hollow booming of men and machines busily at work deep inside the hill, and watch the huge steel hawsers run over the grease-laden rollers first one way and then the other, never actually bringing anything to the surface for them to see.

In June, the American soldiers suddenly disappeared. Rumour was thick and fertile, and mostly, mutually contradictory: the soldiers had gone home; they had gone to fight a huge battle at sea with the Germans; the Germans had landed at Cardiff and the Americans had gone off to give them battle, and so on. The residents of Nicander Parade had the best interpretation, because they had the best view: the night before last, June 4th, Swansea bay had been suddenly filled with ships of all shapes and sizes. The Crescent curved a long winding path alongside a steep hill overlooking the town, its docks and the bay. It was a one-sided street, the other side so steep that nothing would ever be built on it, and on that historical night all the residents of the Parade and quite a few from surrounding streets had crowded along the pavement to see the huge gathering of vessels in the fading light. No one had ever seen anything like it. The exercises held in recent months had caused a stir of interest across the town, but this evening was exceptional: large areas of the coastal road were cut off, with no traffic of any kind allowed. The lower part of the town near the docks area was totally inaccessible, and there was the amazing sight of no fewer than six trains, all following each other at dangerously close distances, steaming along the overhead viaduct, the rumbles of grossly laden wagons audible for miles as they rattled slowly over the stone archways. The Victorian builders could never have imagined this traffic.

It was three days before they heard over the radio about 'Operation Overlord'. In the main, the feeling was that the whole business was being pursued by powers beyond their reckoning, distant and mysterious. Nobody in the street that they knew of had ever been to France, though Mr Williams 'the talk' had been to Cardiff for a holiday once, and since his distinguishing talent was speech, everyone knew that.

France was a Catholic country, D.'s mother announced, implying that there was some great redemption to be gained by liberating that country from the pagan Germans, even if that liberation was won by Protestants in the British Army. D. could not understand the undertones of religion in his mother's view of the war, and unwisely he said so.

'Why are the Catholics fighting Protestants, Mam?'

His mother glared at him. 'They're not,' she snapped.

'But you just said ... '

She cut him off. 'Never mind what I just said. Don't you go putting words in my mouth, that's all. Just you be careful.' She turned away to busy herself with chores. 'Trying to make me out a liar,' she muttered to the world in general. 'Nasty boy.' Working herself up to a climax of anger she turned to him and thrusting her face close to his she shouted, 'Out! Get out. Go on. Outside. I'm sick of the sight of you. Just because you've passed your scholarship you think you know it all, don't you, you big head. Go on. Get outside.'

She grabbed his shoulder and hauled him to the back door, opening it and pushing him out in one angry movement.

★   ★   ★

Cinema newsreels and the radio news made it clear that the Allies were well on their way to winning the war. The newsreel maps seen at the cinema showed a curious reversal of the spreading black treacle of corruption indicating the German advance of just three years before. Now, Stalin's 'Order of the Day' triggered liquid spurts of white across the map of beleaguered Russia, denoting grimly-won advances by the Red Army of five, ten, or even twenty kilometres a week.

The Daily Express, the newspaper favoured by his father for its lively reporting and loved by D. for Rupert Bear, carried aerial photographs of Caen, a small French town in Normandy, that had been bombed to small pieces by the R.A.F. The newspaper carried descriptions of the accuracy, weight of bombs and killing power of the aircraft taking part.

After a while the flurry of interest died away, neighbours in the street occasionally complaining that things seemed to be taking an awfully long time, and it would be Christmas before the war was over.

During the school holidays D. and his two sisters were summoned to the local school for a dental examination. Earlier that year the government had set up a system of free dental care for all school-children. The little card dropped through the letterbox was the practical outcome of years of political wrangling, delayed and then precipitated by Hitler's antics and the coalition forced upon warring political parties blackmailing each other as the price of co-operation.

Neither D. nor his sisters had any deep concerns about a visit to the dentist. They had never been to a dentist before. Besides, as far as any of them knew, there was nothing wrong with their teeth; at least, none of them had ever had so much as a twinge.

So it was with mild curiosity and some small resentment at having to don Sunday-best clothes not just at midweek, but in holiday time, that they set off with their mother to the local school. It was Protestant, she said, and heaven knows what might be found there. All kinds of corrupting anti-Catholic messages might be written up in the classrooms for the children to see. After all, St Joseph's school was full of statues and saintly strictures reminding pupils of their religious duties and the strength of their faith, so why shouldn't the Protestant school have similar, but heretical, reminders?

There was nothing remotely religious anywhere in sight when they entered the buildings. Having satisfied herself on this, their mother declared in embarrassingly loud tones, 'There you are, I knew it. There's nothing here at all. They just don't think of God at all. I bet some of these children don't know He exists.'

D. was now eleven years old, and his sisters ten and twelve. He exchanged glances with his elder sister. Neither were fooled by their mother's verbal side-step. They both felt blushes of humiliation as the family walked along the corridor lined with children, a lot of them known to them, most with mothers, all waiting patiently for the same ten o'clock appointment. Only their younger sister seemed unaffected.

Their mother strode up the corridor as Mother Duck would push her way through reeds, cleaving people aside in her path, now and again checking on her brood behind. She was finally stopped by Mrs Jenkins, a large, fat, badly dressed woman from the next street, near, but not quite in, the Gwili gang territory.

'Take your turn, missus. Like everybody else here.'

'What? said D.'s mother, surprised. 'My appointment is for ten o'clock,' she said haughtily.

'So is mine. And everybody else's. You wait your turn.'

Mrs Jenkins took up a more solid position, blocking their mother as D. and his sisters dropped their eyes to the floor, aware of dozens of interested eyes half-expecting the start of a fight.

'Well. I don't know what things are coming to,' said their mother as she turned in defeat to push her three children ahead of her towards the back of the queuing throng. 'They should have said first come first served,' she complained loudly several times as they worked their way back up the corridor. 'If they had said, I'd have got here earlier.' Those at the front of the queue smiled in triumph. Most of the later ones ignored her. Only the people who joined after her made any sounds of agreement, ripples of discontent propagating in waves from D.'s mother as the other mothers and their children slowly shuffled on for the next hour and a half.

The young woman seated at the desk in the corridor wearily asked her name. D.'s mother began to complain about the waiting. The woman looked at her and ignoring her words repeated, 'Name, please.'

She told her. 'And I want you to know that I shall be making a complaint about this waiting. We've been here for hours.'

The woman looked up. 'Do you want to take your children to another dentist? This is free medical care,' she said slowly and carefully. 'If you want to go to a private dentist you'll have to pay.'

There was a long moment of silence. The young woman broke it by asking yet again, 'The names of your children, please?'

Their mother made no more complaints, and the family was shown into a small classroom which served as a waiting room. Inside, there were even more people waiting, and D.'s mother shuddered with annoyance. But here at least there were seats.

When their turn came, the two girls went in first, one by one, accompanied by their mother. After a while they came out, looking slightly dazed, with unsure steps. They came out together and D. had no time to question them before he was ushered into the treatment room.

Before him stood a large, dark-haired woman in a long brown coat. She had a moustache, D. could see, and long black hair climbing out of a mole on her chin. In front of her was a huge swivel chair in red leather. It had no arms, and sloped back sharply. There were two huge cylinders standing behind the chair, and a crane-like pantograph of struts and spring-loaded joints over the chair headrest.

The woman beckoned him, and gestured towards the chair, unsmiling and hostile. His mother gave him a push. 'Go on. You're not going to die,' she hissed. She sat down on a wooden chair to one side of the makeshift dental surgery while D. clambered into the big leather chair.

'Open,' said the large woman bossily. D. opened his mouth. The woman poked about his teeth with a piece of metal, pulling aside his lips with a brutal finger until he thought the skin would split. Thankfully he had no sores at the corners of his mouth since they had healed for the summer.

She took the metal and her finger out of his mouth and he licked his lips. He was surprised to find the skin on them all wrinkled after the fierce stretching.

He turned his head as the woman's right leg began a vigorous pumping action on the gantry stretching over his head. Wheels began to buzz, pulleys whizzed and the leather chair began to vibrate. An awful penetrating whine erupted suddenly from the loose end of the contraption. She gripped the handle in a fat strong hand, and D. was surprised to see that her finger nails were untidily bitten.

'Open,' said the woman again. D. was less willing this time. 'Wider,' she said, irritated. 'This isn't going to hurt you.'

From the first moment of starting her work D. wanted urgently to tell her that she had made a serious mistake. It hurt like nothing else on earth. The pain was engulfing, awful, frightening in its intensity. Any activity which caused such agony couldn't possibly be good for him, even when it was over. But he couldn't even make a gurgle. She had at least three fingers in his mouth, the roaring, whizzing drill took up all the remaining space, and a constant hurricane of chips and tooth-dust swept his tonsils. He did manage a low growl in a desperate reflex, to exclude this violence in his mouth from penetrating any further down his throat, but the woman took no notice.

Perhaps she had come here to kill him, he thought wildly. All the other people in the queue was just a front, as Edward G. Robinson would say. His mother had hired this woman to pose as a dentist and to inflict so much pain on him that he would die. He would rather be shot by a firing squad; people died quickly. Or even blown up, then he would disappear in a cloud of smoke. But this was awful.

She had stopped. He opened his eyes. He hadn't realised his eyes were clamped shut, or that every muscle in his body was rigid and aching with tension. He turned to look at his mother. She was gazing out of the window at a passing double-decker bus.

'Open.' Once more. This time she spooned in a silvery paste, pressing it into his tooth. He hadn't dared explore the site with his tongue while she was busy mixing things at the small wooden table to one side of the chair. He dreaded what he might find. Now little bits of ragged metal fell to the back of his tongue, and as he worked it to keep them in his mouth she snapped, 'Keep that tongue still. I can't work if you wave it about, boy.'

'Behave yourself, D.,' said his mother. 'Don't you go giving the dentist any trouble now, d'you hear me?'

Denied the power of speech, unable to move his head, and with both hands pinioned to his knees by the woman's huge thighs, he

137

was unable to confirm that he had heard his mother, or to agree that he would not give the dentist any 'trouble'. He only wished he could find some way to cause her trouble, but then she might send for one of the teachers to hold him down, or cane him into submission.

She had finished with his mouth now. She tidied the jars and bottles and little knives on the table and seemed to be consulting a small flat box full of rows of short thin drills. He sat up, shaken but relieved that it was all done. Perhaps he could suggest the dentist take the tooth out first, then she could drill it to her heart's content, all day if she wanted, then stuff it with that paste before putting it back again.

His mother stood. 'I'll just go and see how the girls are,' she said. The woman nodded.

'Lie back. Open.' She turned to him as her right leg began to rise and fall, pumping that dreadful machine into life.

It was a different tooth this time. And the next. And the next. By number six he could not stop the tears rolling down his cheeks. He was not crying. To that he would swear. It was just that his eyes were watering so freely that it looked like tears.

When she took her foot off the machine after number six he asked timidly if he could spit out the cheekful of metal gravel he had been tucking away.

The dentist tutted. 'If you have to, I suppose. Here, in this.' She handed him an enamel mug without a handle. Gratefully he shovelled out the debris with the help of a finger. She waited impatiently for him to finish, and when he handed her the mug she nearly threw it to one side on the table.

Number seven. Already she had savaged two teeth each on the bottom and top of the left side, opposite each other, and two on the bottom of the right side. Now it was the turn of the opposite two on the top right. He began to feel pale at the prospect of yet another after this one.

The woman's fingers slipped where she steadied her hand on his cheek while her thumb hauled away at the corner of his mouth. 'Damn,' she muttered. She stepped back. 'You're crying, boy. I can't do my work if your face is wet. Here, wipe things dry.'

She flung him a cloth, and he defended himself, his voice unsteady. 'It's just my eyes watering,' he said.

'I hope so. How are you going to grow up to be a man if you cry over a little pain like this?' She snatched the cloth away from him. 'You'll be wanting gas, like the girls, at this rate. Now be a man, and open your mouth.'

Gas seemed a good idea to D. He wasn't sure what it did, but if it eased this kind of torture he was all for it.

When she had finished number eight, he had had enough. He wouldn't open his mouth for her again. He felt utterly spent. He had no more nervous energy left. His hands were shaking all the way to his shoulders and his whole body was awash with perspiration. And he felt cold. He had had this feeling before, in Dr Harrington's surgery, and he had fainted then, much to his father's annoyance. Now he recalled what they did to people in church when they fainted, as they regularly did at midday mass, which was a long one with full ceremonial and an endless sermon.

The men would carry the sufferer outside and seat him or more usually her in a chair, and force the head down between the knees. This was supposed to increase the blood flow to the brain and aid recovery.

D. did this, leaning forward in the leather chair until his face turned blue. He couldn't breathe properly like this, but he stayed doubled up until the woman told him to get off the chair. When he straightened himself he saw stars, and staggered as he got off the chair, but at least he wasn't going to faint. And better than that, this cold hard woman had finished with him, and there was no more agony. No more hissing, whining drill, no more powdered teeth flying around in his mouth, no more nauseating stench of friction-scorched enamel biting his nostrils.

He walked away from that dreadful chair and out into the normal world.

His mother and his two sisters were smiling at a subsiding joke when he joined them.

'You were a long time,' said his mother accusingly. 'What were you doing? Not giving that nice dentist trouble I hope?'

'No, Mam. Honest. She just took a long time, that's all.'

'Come on then. Let's get home. It's long past dinner time.'

She turned to the girls as they walked along the corridor, past crowds still waiting their turn. 'Do you feel better now? I must say it doesn't seem right if you felt sick after the gas she gave you.'

'It wasn't the gas, really. It was that horrible rubber thing she put over my face. It smelled awful. Like a gas mask.' His elder sister made a 'yuck' sound. 'But what did the dentist do?' she asked. 'I can't feel anything different with my teeth. She didn't take any out.'

'No. Of course not,' said D.'s mother. 'She filled one of your back teeth. Drilled a hole in it and put a kind of metal filling in it. She

139

said your tooth was decayed. The filling will last for years,' she declared with certainty. 'Dot had two teeth filled.'

His younger sister smirked. 'I had eight,' said D. His mother laughed scornfully. 'Don't be silly,' she said. Her voice changed to a warning note. 'And don't tell lies. Typical boy, isn't it. Can't stand the thought of a girl taking more than you. Don't forget that I saw what the dentist did. She did only one.'

They were outside the school now, and the journey home was not long. As they passed the Catholic church they all crossed themselves dutifully, D.'s mother turning a sharp eye on him to ensure he conformed. He felt embarrassed and foolish, but did as he was expected, holding his eyes to the ground as a crowd of passing boys guffawed and cat-called after them.

'Heathens,' snarled his mother. 'God will take His revenge.'

Further along as they walked, she added further evidence of the boys' doomed futures.

'They are the sort whose mothers hang out washing on the line on Sundays,' she said in a tone of quiet triumph.

Back home, the children sat around the table while their mother set about preparing a quick meal. She rummaged around in the pantry, setting out bottles, jars and packets on the draining board, which was her working area.

'Who's been at the orange juice?' She emerged from the pantry, her face twisted in anger, holding a bottle of juice, half full. 'You, isn't it?' she glared at D.

He denied it. He had some, yes. Just a small amount this morning, but he had left the bottle much fuller than she was holding now.

'Don't tell me your lies.' Her voice rose as she crossed the floor to lean over the table and cuff his head. He ducked, and her sweeping hand missed him altogether. This made her very angry, and she screamed at him. 'Come out of there. Now. This minute. I'm going to give you what for. Stealing the girls' orange juice!'

She stood away from the table to allow him to clamber out of his corner seat, her knuckles resting lightly on her hips. As he squeezed behind his elder sister's chair he watched his mother's hands. When she raised her right hand he moved fast and dodged under her flailing arm to the back door. He snapped the latch up and flung open the door, not bothering to pull it to behind him to delay her. He knew that once outside, he could evade her. There were hedges, banks, fences and gradients that he knew intimately and could traverse with agility to escape. Besides, an instinct told him that he could go places where an eleven-year-old boy might bring no more than a shouted warning, but an adult woman would be very unwelcome.

His mother didn't follow him. She didn't call out after him, either. She would be too concerned about what the neighbours might think if she shouted threats at him as he legged it down the garden path and over the bank into Ivor Williams' fenced-off garden.

Reaching a distance he considered safe he stopped, listening, eyes alert. After a while he retraced his steps, stopping at the bank at the bottom of his garden, raising his head slowly to peer through the thick grass at the back of his house. He remained at full alert, ready to flee in case his mother might spring a surprise on him by hiding somewhere he hadn't thought of.

The drifting smell of frying told him that his mother was busy in the kitchen, cooking dinner. He turned away, relaxing, and sat on the warm grass below the bank and out of sight of the back of his house. He would miss his meal now. It would be a long time before he could venture back into his home. He might even have to wait until his father came home. There was just a chance that if his mother went out somewhere he could sneak in and find something to eat in the pantry. There was some American dried egg that wasn't too bad eaten in small amounts, and was very filling. A couple of teaspoons would do. And the dried milk mixed with sugar was good too. Only he had to look out for his younger sister, who would split on him.

★   ★   ★

August was the time when the world of education on the move bought its distinguishing pennantry. Blazers and coloured knee-high socks, coloured peaked caps and ties, cardigans and sweaters edged in school colours, expensive leather satchels embossed with the owner's initials, new sober raincoats which had to be Burberry; and of course new shoes, which must be black no matter which school you went to.

There were two Grammar schools in the town at that time: Dynevor and The Grammar School. The school colours of Dynevor were primarily black, with edgings of red and amber. The Grammar School colours were a loud red with some yellow. D.'s mother thought The Grammar School colours vulgar, and didn't want 'to see a son of mine in that uniform'. Besides, his father had gone to Dynevor as a boy, and it was to Dynevor that D. would go, on both counts his parents agreed.

The list of needs was in the sheets of paper D. had brought home from Markie's class. The list was precise, and named the only clothing store in town where they could expect to be fully equipped. The list even had details of pens and pencils, geometry drawing tools, rulers and rubbers and colours of inks, but D.'s mother said that she could get these sorts of things much cheaper at Woolworth's, and the school outfitters were already making big profits out of the rest of the gear anyway, and wouldn't miss it.

He went shopping with his mother in town on a Saturday morning, the most awful time of the week. Much of the town centre was rubble, stacked high in parts, now being taken over by weeds and thriving buddleia bushes. Criss-crossing the wasteland were pock-marked roads, often without pavements, sometimes roughly patched, thickly strewn with pot holes, and densely packed by crowds of shoppers. D. couldn't guess why most of the people in town that day seemed to be in a part where there was absolutely nothing for them to do.

His mother grew steadily more irritable as the two of them picked their way across town from the bus stop to the school outfitters. She became more and more annoyed at the groups of Welsh-speakers knotted together at random on difficult pavements. By the time they reached the shop she was in a towering rage, her face set and an ugly flush to her cheeks. To D.'s dismay the male shop assistant, elderly and hoping to please, greeted her in Welsh.

'What did you say?' she demanded in a tone that implied he had just made an indecent suggestion.

As D. watched, the man's face fell in disappointment. He sighed and said, 'Is this the young gentleman, madam? And which school is he starting?'

D.'s mother melted under the flattery. With proprietorial pride she simpered, 'Yes. This is my boy. He's going to Dynevor.'

'Clever young fellow,' said the assistant, pleased that he had completely destroyed his customer's defences. She would buy well, now; false pride would very likely force her to spend a lot more than she had intended. He would show her quality first.

D. winced at the man's words, furtively glancing around the crowded shop, praying that none of the dozen or so boys of his own age there would be in his class at his new school. This was going to be embarrassing.

And it was. His mother told the assistant endlessly how clever D. was, how clever his father was, and his uncles and aunts and cousins. He flinched with shame as she smiled at him with pride, ordering his school outfit absent-mindedly, as though she had come into the shop for something else, perhaps to show off her son to a roomful of strangers.

'Don't mind him. He's just self-conscious,' she said as D. reluctantly and unnecessarily tried on new socks for size. She hid her face from the room and twisted in threatening rage at D. and hissed, 'Behave yourself. If you show me up in front of everybody I'll get you when we get home, my boy.'

She turned a sweet smile on the assistant. 'Is that all, now? What about initials on his satchel?'

'Yes, madam, of course.' Initials were a bonus. Most parents did without them, preferring the cheaper security of the owner's name and address written in Indian ink on the inside flap.

The man's hand hovered over the order pad. 'What are they, madam?'

'D.F.R.' said his mother with pride. What was special about his initials, wondered D.

The man repeated them as he wrote. 'Do you know', he said with mock interest, 'that these initials are almost the same as F.D.R.'s?'

D.'s mother looked blank.

'The American president,' said the man. 'Franklin D. Roosevelt.'

'Oh yes. Of course. Well, well. Do you hear that, D.? Initials like the president. I bet there aren't too many like that.'

He was glad when it was all over. In the street, burdened by bags and flat soft packages D.'s mother said, 'What a nice man. Pity the clothes cost so much, or I would do all my shopping there.' She was in good humour.

'Let's have something to eat at the Park,' said his mother. She was positively gay. Perhaps things wouldn't be too bad after all, thought D. He had been dreading the bus queue and his mother's reaction if a bus was not ready and waiting.

The Park was a fish-and-chips cafe really, even though it called itself a restaurant. It sold little else than fish and chips, and the menu card listed only four or five variations on that theme, all strictly controlled on price and quantity by the Ministry of Food. The dining room was in the basement, a small room sprinkled with cast iron pillars and squeezed-in rickety bare tables. Each table had four fragile chairs, some of them of different patterns, and on top of the table there was a jumble of pepper and salt cellars, ketchup and vinegar bottles, ashtrays and a jug with water in it.

The place was crammed. A hot and perspiring waitress stood at the bottom of the stairs directing incoming customers to the few vacant seats in the room, sometimes standing on tiptoe to point out an empty chair. As D. and his mother descended the stairs, the temperature and humidity rose uncomfortably, and his mother began to complain.

'They ought to do something about this heat,' she said loudly enough for the waitress at the bottom of the stairs to hear.

She turned nasty when the waitress asked her to wait.

'I'm not waiting about here,' she said haughtily. 'I've come to have a meal, not wait about.'

'The restaurant is full, madam,' said the waitress patiently.

'I don't care. I'm going in,' said D.'s mother. 'Come on.' She turned to D. and pushed him in front. 'We'll find a table ourselves.'

But the 'restaurant' really was full. There was not even a spare chair, let alone a table at which they could sit. Not only was there nowhere to sit, but there was no way of moving between the chairs and tables either. The seating arrangement was so densely packed that even if the place was empty it would have been difficult to make one's way from one side of the room to the other. Packed as it was now, it was impossible to move in any direction.

'People can't get out,' said D.'s mother. 'That's why it's so full. Once they're in they can't get out again.'

People around them at their tables raised their heads. Some snickered, others leaned across to companions and whispered. D. felt his face hot with embarrassment.

'Well,' snorted his mother in defeat. As a last salvo she said loudly, 'They ought to do something about this. I'm sure more people would come here if it wasn't so crowded. They're only keeping people away like this. Losing good customers.'

She turned, pulling D. after her, and marched up the stairs to the street, muttering about everybody coming to town on Saturday, and why couldn't they do their shopping during the week.

They proceeded along the streets towards the bus stop and home, D. unhappy and trying not to hear his mother's constant complaints, she in an aggressive sulk. Along the way a roadside petrol pump boom swung away from the groping hand of the attendant and struck her across the chest. The pump was on the inside pavement and the hose crossed the pavement to fill tanks of cars parked at the kerb. An accident of this kind was bound to happen, and probably did several times a day.

D.'s mother gasped. Not in pain, because the blow was slight, but in astonished indignation. This sort of thing just did not happen to her. This was an unthinkable affront to public dignity.

144

The attendant grabbed the swinging boom as fast as he could, but it was too late. Despite his apologies D.'s mother went into simulated shock and might have fainted, but the pavement was very dirty.

'Oh! My God! I thought I was being attacked,' she cried. 'What's happening?'

The attendant grasped her arm, wholly at loss what to do next.

'You all right?,' he said helplessly.

People began to stop, and then ask what was wrong. Soon there was a small crowd, and D. found himself on the outside, cut off from sight of his mother, who was making sounds of deep shock in a faint voice.

The crowd soon drifted away when there was no prospect of blood or fainting, leaving D. once more with his mother, who now made a quick recovery as the attendant went about his business of filling the tank of the parked car. The driver looked annoyed.

'Just wait till your father hears about this,' said D.'s mother. 'He'll show 'em. He'll give them a talking-to. Dangerous, hitting people about like that.' They walked on.

'He did say he was sorry, Mam.'

'Shut up.'

He did. He wondered about Woolworth's and the pens and pencils. This was something new — in St Joseph's every boy was given a pencil to write exercises, and it was handed in at the end of the day, a long queue of boys filing past the watchful teacher who counted them into a box which was locked away in his desk overnight. To use your own personal writing tools was excitingly different. Perhaps his father would buy him a new fountain pen for his new school. But he wouldn't mention this now. His mother was in no mood to listen.

The bus queue was dreadfully long, and they waited half an hour before their turn came. It was the usual embarrassing performance — his mother complaining loudly, searching for an audience to join her in her perceived injustice at having to wait because of a timetable. D. was shamed into silence until she dug him in the back demanding, 'What's the matter with you, big head?' which he didn't understand, and to which he could make no reply.

On the bus, he tried to ease the folds of his tight short trousers as he sat, but his mother saw the furtive movement, and snarled, 'Take your hands off Toby, you dirty little boy. I saw you.' She glared at him and he submitted to the discomfort helplessly, unable to assess the seriousness of what he had been doing. Perhaps there was another way of doing it. None of the men around seemed to have the same trouble as he was having right now. The sun glared through the window of the bus, hot and blinding. He closed his eyes. He'd be glad to get home, and then out of the house to play with the boys.

★　★　★

Before the end of August he went to stay for a week with his favourite aunt, Maureen. She had moved to Romford, where she lived with her husband Cliff, who was an R.A.F. navigator flying in Sunderland flying boats out of Poole, in Dorset. Cliff came from Llanelli, ironically close to D.'s evacuation foster home, and his surname was Davies. He spoke Welsh, a fact D.'s mother disapproved of but never openly spoke about, though she had spluttered about 'having a Welsh-speaking Davies' in the family when Maureen had married him in 1941, three years before.

Cliff was on leave after a gruelling tour of duty U-boat hunting off the Azores. He had landed at the islands, and had brought back with him a selection of fruits that were not only rare in wartime Britain, but ones D. had never even heard of. They were mainly citrus fruits, limes, fresh lemons, grapefruit and oranges. They were interesting, but scarcely gave him the excitement he was expected to feel, judging by his aunt's enthusiastic urging to 'try this one, or that one'.

D. stayed for several weeks. He didn't know why. Romford was a noisy place, buzzing with traffic, people and thundering trains all day and most of the night. His aunt and her husband lived in a maisonette, a completely novel form of house to D., who marvelled at living on one floor upstairs. To the side of the house was the River Rom, emerging from an endless series of road and rail bridges to flow briefly alongside Town Council allotments before disappearing again under more bridges.

Behind the maisonette ran the main line trains from Southend on Sea and Colchester into Liverpool Street. They travelled at huge speeds and were often twelve coaches long, more than D. had ever seen before, and made a terrible noise. Playing in the river and hunting for frogs was pleasant enough, but he found sleep difficult because of the incessant traffic, punctuated by the roar of passing trains.

Thirty years later he would see from the window of his speeding train that same maisonette with the shallow river flowing alongside, as he commuted daily from Rayleigh to Liverpool Street.

He sometimes ventured up the street towards the main road, where he would stand at the corner watching the traffic. The roads

146

were covered with a light, golden brown rolled gravel, which to D. was a wonderful contrast to the dull, grey limestoned tarmac of Swansea, and everything smelled different too.

He stopped going to the corner when he was chased away by a group of older girls, who swore horribly at him when he told them his name as they demanded. Then one of them kicked his leg painfully, and he ran.

Uncle Cliff was not a tall man, and he had a small moustache. He was trying to grow handlebars, he said, like the captain of his aircraft. He wore uniform most of the time except indoors, because this was wartime, he said, and officers always had to be in uniform, even when on leave. He was unfailingly kind, which D. found difficult to deal with. He found himself reduced to silence as Uncle Cliff talked to him man-to-man about his interests and home life. It was a kind of closeness that D. did not know at home, and he felt uncomfortable with it. His father would never talk with him like this.

As the days passed D. warmed to Uncle Cliff and looked forward to his returning home in the afternoons. He went out with Aunt Maureen most days, coming home in the afternoon when they would have tea and cakes and talk excitedly of their time in town and bring out the things they had bought. D. joined in the chatter and happiness in a way that was impossible with his own family at home, and he began to feel at ease with himself and glad to be in such happy company.

It was a sad journey back to Swansea. He felt lonely and unhappy, as though an interesting chapter in a book had ended suddenly. He would like to read it again, but the book had gone.

He never saw Uncle Cliff again. No one else did either. He was shot down over the Atlantic one winter day in December 1944, and the crew of the Sunderland disappeared, as had so many pointless thousands before, into the freezing, trackless black depths of the ocean.

Chapter Eight

He started at his new school in September. Decked out in his new school uniform he was escorted on his first few days by Bernard, a sixth-former at the school, who lived not far away. Bernard was very big, and at seventeen, he seemed to D. to be very old for school, but these qualifications were more than enough to protect D. from the brutal initiation ceremonies inflicted on new boys by the older pupils. The worst a new boy faced was a ducking under a cold tap. If he unwisely struggled the water would run down under his collar and soak him to his shoes. There were many eleven-year-olds on that traumatic first day who sat through their first lessons with wet shirts, seats, trousers and water-filled shoes.

D. stuck close to Bernard before the bell went for assembly, and again at breaks in the morning and afternoon. He was glad to be ignored. He wondered, as he watched the first-years being dragged struggling to the cold tap in the yard, why the teachers did not stop it. He asked Bernard.

'We all had it,' said Bernard. 'You ought to, too. It's supposed to show you that you're not so clever, and you're only just starting here.' He paused, considering his words. 'It's the grown-ups who make the rules,' he said finally. 'The older boys try to make their own, just to show the first-years.'

D. didn't follow this. It seemed that older, bigger boys were allowed to bully the younger, smaller boys. That was something St Joseph's hadn't allowed. Bullying there was severely dealt with. He began to feel twinges of regret at leaving his old school.

He chose Latin as his main foreign language, and he was placed in class 2b. He didn't like the 'b', since it seemed to imply second class status, until he learned that 2a took Welsh as the main foreign language. It was a novel experience to find himself in a class of boys of his own age instead of thirteen and fourteen-year-olds. Even so he sensed competitiveness from these boys, who had all passed the scholarship exam. Most of them had pals from their primary school days who had passed the exam, but D. was on his own. He was the only one in his school who had passed out of twelve entrants.

The first day was a disaster. There were thirty-five boys in his class and he was the only one who had no fountain pen, no pencil and no ruler. The Form Master was Mr Cox. D. had seen Mr Cox before. His father owned a shop in Brymelin Street, surely the nastiest, dirtiest, scruffiest street in the whole town, running alongside the church from which his old school took its name. The shop smelled horribly and swarmed with flies and there were holes in the worn wooden floor. D. had gone into the shop once with a St Joseph's classmate friend, and was glad to escape the awful gloom and stench. Mr Cox had served his friend.

Mr Cox bore a discouraging resemblance to Mr Andrews, D.'s old headmaster. He was short, thin and dour. He had a large, thin, straight nose and a receding chin, and his lips quivered when he was angry, which was frequent.

'No pen, boy?'

'No, sir.'

Mr Cox leaned over D., his lips beginning to work. He seemed unable to believe that a boy would dare come to school so ill-equipped.

'Where do you come from?' he said finally.

D. was unsure about this one. A facetious answer based on nature's laws was out of the question, and this left a choice between two: his old school, or the district where he lived. Which one would satisfy him?

He plumped for his old school, mainly because he hoped Mr Cox would be more sympathetic since he himself once lived near there.

'St Joseph's, sir.'

Mr Cox glared. 'Where you live, boy. Where's your home?'

D. felt the first-ever rebellious stirrings of resentment. Alright, so he came from a poor home on a council estate, but it wasn't his fault, was it?

'Mayhill, sir,' he muttered.

'What? I can't hear you.' D. squirmed. Mr Cox wanted his pound of flesh. And thirty-four boys strained to hear it being carved.

'Mayhill, sir,' D. said, louder.

'Hm.' Mr Cox stood for a moment and then, as though to take pity on a boy with such a terrible handicap, moved away.

On that first day it proved not so vital to have a pen or pencil. D. was issued, like the other boys, with a set of blank exercise books, impressively emblazoned with the school crest in gold. They also collected text books, some worn, but most brand new, again impressed with the school crest. They must write their names in these, take note of lesson timetables in the exercise books, the names of the teachers who would take them for different subjects, and sundry school rules which, if strictly observed, would keep them clear of prefects for the first few days.

There was also a lot of tedious philosophising from Mr Cox about hard work and the joys of learning, but D. found this difficult to follow. His main objective now was not to draw attention to himself, after the painful encounter at his first lesson. Looking around at the classful of strangers he wondered what other weaknesses he had that he did not yet know about, but were waiting the ill-found chance to reveal themselves.

Dinner break came. He had his last week's pocket money, a penny, but dinner was sixpence. He tried to lose himself, but first-years were not allowed out of the school. Two prefects stood at the main entrance, the only one D. knew, to stop any who tried. In any case, he didn't know where the dining room was, or who to pay, and it seemed simpler to hide away in the lavatories until dinner time was over.

'Loppy' Lewis took the first lesson after dinner. He had been wounded in the first world war, and held his head at an acute angle over his right shoulder, which earned him his nickname. D. learned later that this same teacher had taught his father twenty-five years before.

D. wasn't too sure what subject Loppy taught. It was now firmly in his mind that every teacher in this school taught his own subject, in contrast to St Joseph's, where one teacher taught everything. Here, teachers visited the classroom or the whole class moved to a teacher, as for physics or chemistry. The topics and subjects were clear, and there were textbooks and exercise books separately for every one; there were none for Loppy, who spent a lot of time telling the class about his impressions of the first car ever to be driven in Swansea and how it seemed a puzzle that it could be steered around corners.

D. drifted off into a daydream. Now Loppy was talking about milk, and how it was sampled for purity and added water.

'How is it sampled? How is it tested?' He was looking at D., who was electrified back to reality.

He looked around wildly. He had no idea how milk was tested for illegally added water. His mother said often enough that Rees the milk watered his to make it go farther, but she never said how she knew.

D. played for time. Why should Loppy pick on him, for heaven's sake?

'Who, sir? Me, sir?'

Loppy bristled. D. could tell that he was annoyed because his lips began to work, as though he was sharpening his teeth behind his closed mouth. He began to walk slowly towards him. He was very old, thought D.

He stood over D. finally, and asked again.

'How do you test milk for added water, boy?'

Desperation wiped away common sense as D. suggested, 'Drink it, sir?'

Loppy's eyes bulged. After a deadly, silent pause, with the class frozen in disbelief, D. realised he had made a mistake.

With a lunge surprising in an elderly disabled man, Loppy brought the flat of his hand venomously and with violent force to the side of D.'s unprepared and unprotected face. His head sang. Stars burst in his eyes and he was deafened. His eyes watered as he righted himself from the seated stagger the fierceness of the blow had inflicted.

He was vaguely aware that Loppy was speaking to him. He could see his lips move but he couldn't hear him. As he stared, so Loppy's voice, growling with rage, gradually became audible.

'I'll ask you again, boy. Where do you come from? Or are you deaf as well as stupid?'

D. was in real fear of another blow. He couldn't take many like that without bursting into tears, the ultimate defeat. If the boys in his old school got into a fight, the boy who cried first was the loser, and he was jeered mercilessly for days. Only the headmaster's caning was unanimously accepted as sufficient reason for crying. For all D. knew, tears after a teacher's slaps might be a jeering weakness here at his new school. He must avoid further punishment.

'Mayhill, sir.'

'Ah! I thought so.'

He didn't elaborate, but the judgment was there, silent, hanging in the air, the rest of the class feeding on it.

D. was in little doubt now that Mayhill was the worst possible place in the world to come from. It seemed to be the root cause of every fault and failing, every mistake he might make; even, perhaps, poor performance at school work. He began to feel that he was different from the rest of the class, a tailender, a prime suspect for any disruption of good order in the class. An outsider, even, ungraciously sharing the privileges of his betters from nicer parts of the town.

The side of his face felt hot and bruised. It tingled, and the eye on that side continued to water. The inner ear ached with a straight-line, white pain, as he would describe it, quite different from the pulsing darts of pain from a wound such as a cut.

Loppy seemed to forget watered milk, and rambled on for an hour about his youth. D. vowed to get a seat at the back of the class. He had opted for a seat in the front row because he was eager to see and hear everything the teachers had to say and do on the blackboard; he hadn't bargained for the hazards of such a seat. At the back he might even read during Loppy's boring lessons.

He had to wait until the following week to get his writing and drawing equipment, because his mother refused to make a special journey into town 'just for a pen or a pencil'. 'Can't you borrow one?' she asked complainingly. 'Surely one of the boys would lend you a pencil for a few minutes?'

He tried to explain that there seemed to be a great deal of writing to do, and most of the boys wanted their pens themselves, but he soon lost his way as his mother scornfully dismissed these facts as 'excuses'. He was confused. Whose excuses? His, or the other boys'? What did she mean by excuses?

He considered stealing one from his father, who had a drawerful of pencils, and more in the top pocket of his jacket that he hung over a chair behind the door of the parlour when he came home in the evening. But he thought his father might notice. He was reluctant to ask, since his father seemed to need them all for his work, and his father's work took precedence over everything that went on in the house.

So he waited, and aroused the fury of a succession of teachers, who all asked where he came from and all said 'Ah!' or 'Hm!' and nodded their heads in understanding and contempt. He tried to borrow a pen or pencil, but the boys looked at him strangely, and refused. He tried to set a seat further back from the front row, so that the teachers would see less easily that he was not writing when the whole class had been instructed so to do, but he failed. Seating territories had hardened from the first few minutes of the first day, and no one wanted to change. It might also be, thought D. bitterly, that none of the boys wanted a Mayhill boy any nearer than they could avoid.

On Friday of that first week the first Assembly was held. The first for the new boys, that is. They joined the rest of the school at the massed gathering of the whole school in Mount Pleasant Chapel, a large building close to the school and approached by a private door from the school.

It was a shock to D. This was the first heathen Protestant place of worship he had ever been in. Nervously aware that he might be struck dead at any moment by a God-sent bolt of lightning as retribution for betraying his Catholic teaching, he looked around as he filed into the severe wooden pews like the rest of his class. There was no altar with its crimson light signifying God was present. No statues, paintings or candles, no hassocks to kneel on, no holy water font for him to dip fingers into and then cross himself as a sign of humility before entering God's house. This was a wholly new and strange experience, through which he must pick his way carefully.

Assembly, it was soon made clear, was the more civilised way of gathering together the whole school to make announcements. The headmaster, garbed in gown and mortarboard, stood in the pulpit, high above the hundreds of boys, to make his announcements on school rules, new teachers, the erosion of standards and the school team's rugby results.

Next he proclaimed an act of worship — not a radical event since they were in chapel, after all.

'All Catholics and Jews should go now, as quickly and quietly as you can.' He stepped down from the pulpit.

This was another shock. D. looked around. No one moved as far as he could see, which wasn't all that far. No other heads in his row were turning, and he was reluctant to display vulgar curiosity by being the only one to turn around.

Here was a huge dilemma: should he sit tight and pretend he was no different from the huge majority which surrounded him, or should he, could he, find the strength to walk out of that place under the gaze of hundreds of eyes? And every teacher grouped at the raised area to the front would see him too. Bryn Cox and Loppy Lewis would nod to themselves in disapproving certainty: he came from Mayhill and was a Catholic. Irish immigrants, probably. The worst kind of boy to have in the school.

D. fought with himself for endless seconds until he sensed a scuffling noise as several boys clambered to the centre aisle from inside seats. This was it, he decided. There were others here who didn't belong, and he could join them. He wouldn't be on his own.

He stood, turned, and made his way along the row. He was careful not to genuflect as he reached the aisle, and simply turned to walk to the back of the chapel and out through the school's private door. He was last in the exodus. There were about two dozen or so boys in front of him, walking. He hoped fervently that not all of them were Jewish or Hindus.

Outside, the boys milled around, the older ones withdrawing to one side to chat and clown among themselves, the first-years standing in embarrassment, waiting for what came next.

They didn't have long to wait. Mr Cox appeared, clearly in a bad mood, and snarled at them. 'Four B all you Catholics. Any others into Three A,' he snapped, and marched off, leaving them behind.

They followed. In Four B classroom, they sat and waited while Mr Cox busied himself with secret teacher's business until he looked up finally, studied them as a warder might study a batch of new prisoners, and said, 'Williams. You're not a Catholic. Why are you here?'

Williams was in the Upper Sixth. There were only seven boys in the Upper Sixth, and all of them were feared prefects. To the lower school they held much the same status as teachers, so it was a surprise to hear Mr Cox speak to Williams like this.

'I changed, sir. Last week. Presbyterian to Roman Catholic.'

'Changed?' Mr Cox was puzzled.

'Yessir. I saw the light.'

'Light? What light? Are you trying to be funny with me?'

'No, Mr Cox.' Williams' voice was firm, with a hint of resentment and possibly warning in it. 'I'm not being funny. My religious beliefs are not an occasion for fun, sir.'

Mr Cox's face purpled, and his small thin lips worked furiously. He was very angry, D. saw, which was not good for any of them except Williams. He was too big for Mr Cox to slap around as he would the rest of them.

Bernard, the other sixth-former and D.'s protector, sniggered.

The whole class held its breath. Williams smiled. Mr Cox trembled with anger. Williams rested his chin on his hands and stared challengingly at him.

'I wonder how many here are really Catholics,' snapped Mr Cox finally. 'I wonder.'

'Why don't you test me, sir? I'll lend you my catechism book. You ask the questions, we'll answer.'

The catechism was Roman Catholicism's secret weapon. It asked rhetorical questions, with stylised set answers, which ranged from: 'Who made you?' to 'Why am I on earth?'. Every Catholic schoolchild must know all these questions and answers off by heart. Woe betide him, or her, if nuns asked the questions and had hesitant answers. To set these questions to a non-believer, let alone the uninstructed, would immediately reveal a fraud.

Mr Cox declined, sourly. Things were already out of hand.

'Check your homework or revise until the rest of the school joins us,' he instructed the boys. He turned to leave the room. 'I shall be a short distance away, so behave yourselves.' He left.

While the younger boys did as they were told, the older ones

154

formed a card school, noisily wagering imaginary thousands in an endless hand of poker. The younger boys were allowed to watch these games and to learn the rules. It was a useful and painless introduction to the adult world.

D. found difficulty settling into his new school. He had no friends and all the other boys seemed to have brought pals with them from their old schools. He was the only Catholic in the class, and this seemed to mark him out. And he came from Mayhill. And he had no fountain pen. And he smoked with the older boys in the lavatories at morning break.

He found difficulties too, coping with the teachers' brutality and their willingness to hit out at any boy who annoyed them. He had never been smacked open-handedly in St Joseph's, but here in Dynevor he was cuffed many times in the first few weeks in a variety of ways: ear twisting by 'Windy' Lewis the physics master, hair twisting by the maths master, the wooden spat of a chair bonked on the top of his head by Sandy Morgan the arts master. And wild, open-handed slaps to the face by Roberts the music. Any one of these assaults was enough to reduce an eleven-year-old to tears, and by the end of the third week D. was no exception. He shed tears more in frustration than weakness of spirit, for the punishment always came as a surprise, incurred by innocence of a particular teacher's personal rules. He began to think that he was being used as an example, or even that he was marked in some way that made him easy prey.

At home his mother objected to him using his bedroom for homework.

'I can't stand someone up there, over my head, working. I don't know what you're doing. You can write whatever it is you want to down here, in the kitchen.'

He couldn't use the parlour either. The kitchen table was free only when his father had finished at seven o'clock, but the kitchen itself was never free. There was always someone there, most often his sisters playing indoors, particularly in wet weather, which was most of the time.

By Christmas he had become adept at making excuses for not completing and handing in homework.

At the end of term examinations he began to feel out of his depth. The results placed him thirty-fourth of thirty-five. The thirty-fifth boy was John Waters, whom no one had seen after the first day.

★ ★ ★

The last physical attack by his mother was surprisingly indiscreet. Usually she waited until there was no one around, but this time the whole family was present. It was Saturday, early afternoon. They had just finished a splendid lunch of bacon, lavabread, cockles, fried egg, mushrooms and tomatoes. Everyone was in a good mood, and the weather was fine, a quiet early April day with the smells of spring all around.

Whilst his father joshed with his sisters still seated at the table, his mother stacked the dirty dishes on the draining board. D. stood near the stove, preparing to go outside, where he might find some of the boys to go for an exploring walk. None of those at the table were looking when his mother picked up a table fork, turned and lunged slyly and silently at him.

Too late D. saw the look on her face as she turned. He had learned not to stay around when he saw that look: her cheeks had an angry, dull red flush, her forehead had a deep single vertical furrow running as far as the bridge of her nose, while her lips, thin and hard, had the shape of a shallow, upturned 'U'. She looked ugly and hateful. Normally he would have fled at the sight, but today he stayed. His father was here, after all.

Only one prong of the fork punctured his scrotum. The other three struck him in the groin. Like a startled cat D. scrambled away from his mother. The way that was quickest was over the top of the table, to his father's astonishment and anger.

'What the hell ... '

D. crouched in his chair in the corner. His mother was restacking the dishes, unconcerned, pretending to share the family's surprise.

'Did you see that?' His father turned in theatrical amazement. 'Running over the table. What do you think this is? An obstacle course? You a bloody rabbit or something?'

D. said nothing.

'Don't you ever do that again, my boy. D'you hear me? I'll give you something to jump about if I see you doing that again. My goodness me.'

His father got up from the table. It would be the garden this afternoon.

D. hurried out of his corner as his sisters rose to leave. He walked inbetween them as they left the house. He needed to see his latest injury. It stung, though walking didn't trouble him. He decided against using the lavatory. He would go to the air raid shelter if the girls were not going there.

In the shelter he took down his trousers to inspect the damage.

The prong of the fork had caught a loose fold of skin and entered one side and come out the other. Two small holes about a quarter of an inch apart. It didn't hurt much. The other prongs had barely broken the skin. It wasn't serious, but he nevertheless was trembling slightly. Then he thought, how do I put a bandage, or a sticky plaster on it? The thought made him smile. What would the boys in the street say? He'd better say nothing.

It healed on its own in a few days, well before his next P.E. period with the grim Mr Burgess. Just as well, thought D. He might want to see the excuse.

★   ★   ★

He was twelve years old now, and beginning to be conscious of girls. He didn't know why his mother was punishing him for mistreating them. He hardly spoke to the girls in the street, and never met any anywhere else.

At school he began to daydream during lessons, paying less and less attention to proceedings. He made a few friends, but he knew these friends were not the kind of boys he ought to be friends with — Douglas stole from Woolworth's during the dinner hour, and Alan stole the brighter boys' homework books to copy from and then threw them away. Jack came to school only two or three days a week, and after the first year he was sent to a special school. Borstal, it was rumoured.

D.'s end of term exam results were terrible. John Waters had been taken off the register, and this left no one at the bottom of the class league table to boost him up, so D. came last out of thirty-four.

His father said nothing. His mother sneered. His younger sister thought it a great joke. Only his elder sister said little.

For the first time in his life D. was conscious of being depressed. He felt there was something wrong in his life; rather, that he was doing everything wrong. That he himself was wrong, somehow. He went to his bedroom early that evening. He stayed there, looking out at the distant mountains, a vague longing in his mind, a need to get away, to leave everything behind, to wander in those vacant hills, free of his taunting mother, his bullying younger sister, his stern, indifferent father, the oppressive, violent schoolteachers, the bully-boy Hendersons who still troubled him, the threatening street gangs.

He went downstairs briefly to brush his teeth and wash before bed. It was still quite early. His mother noticed this and said, 'That's right, dullard. Early bed. Wasting your time in school like that.

When I think of all the money I spent on you to go there, and this is how you thank me. Ungrateful wretch.'

He said nothing as he climbed the stairs, her voice following, 'There's none so ungrateful as your own children. I've always said that. And it's true. Look at you.'

As he fell asleep he thought, in less than a year he had fallen from being the brightest pupil at his old school to being the dullest at his new school. Worse, he didn't really have any idea how to put things right; he just wanted to run away from it all.

⋆ ⋆ ⋆

The war was over, and the bombing, the American soldiers, the roaring fighters taking off from Fairwood, false air raid warnings, the newsreel pictures of doodlebugs, all quickly became memories. The street kerbstones were painted red white and blue, home-made flags and bunting were hung from lamp posts and a grand street party was held. D.'s mother refused to contribute, saying it was a waste of time and good food, so D. and his sisters were chased away when they tried to join in. They were allowed to take part in the bonfire, lit in the middle of the road despite police warnings, but someone lit it too early, when it was still light, and by the time the bonfire should have come into its own in the dark to add a touch of romance to the singing and dancing, it had shrunk to a dull glow in a puddle of melted tarmacadam. Still, the people tried their best, and even if it was not a screaming success, it marked firmly the end of a chapter in their lives. From now on things were going to be different.

It was about this time that D. discovered music. Serious, classical music. At school all the boys had been mercilessly drilled, week after long week, in the subtleties of Handel's *Creation*, an oratorio of immense dullness, unreal words and plodding music. At first they sang in small groups, then they joined the classes of the same year to sing en masse in Mount Pleasant Chapel, accompanied by Roberts the music's wife, who played the piano. It was a colourless, uninteresting struggle, performed under the remorseless, baleful eye of Mr Roberts only as a matter of school discipline. None of the proceedings contained recognisable elements of musical education which might have been aimed at identifying individual talent, except insofar as they served Mr Roberts' purposes in finding the star boy sopranos who would sing his oratorios.

Then, one evening in the early summer holidays, the men and

older boys joined them. Bass, tenor and alto singers gave their best, creating the most staggering effect D. had ever experienced. At one stage he forgot to sing, so busy was he listening to the overwhelming magic of the whole choir blending its separate parts into an incredible tumbling wave of colour and harmony. As D. collected himself and restarted his own contribution he noticed that some notes which he had considered odd and ill-fitting on their own, now blended perfectly with the notes struck by the three tone levels.

He was to remain indebted to Roberts the music for the rest of his life for this insight into music. There were difficulties at home, of course. None of his family would listen to the great composers being played on the radio, and with his mother leading the way both sisters joined in a long-term campaign to prevent him listening too. There was no gramophone at home, but his maternal grandmother had a wind-up job which he played as often as he could when he went to visit her.

He became an addict. At every small opportunity he scanned the radio for music, ignoring the big bands, silly thirties songs and the new 'popular' music, searching for orchestrated melody, the arithmetic of organised sound, the subtle romance of measured artistry in the great composers. In a matter of months he could recognise different composers by style, though not necessarily name the piece, since he had probably never heard it before. The pursuit of music gave him an excitement he had never experienced before, and he attended every practice at school in the evenings, to the sceptical disbelief of his family, especially his mother who said with scorn, 'Just watch. It won't last. It's just like him, all fuss and rush and then it's over. That's men all over.'

He wasn't a man, and he wasn't too concerned if they sneered at him — there were plenty of people at the gym where the choir practised who welcomed him and seemed to share his new interest in music.

After their practice with voices only, the next stage was even more magical. They gathered at the Brangwyn Hall, Swansea's premier concert hall, to practice with the orchestra and soloists.

D. was transported by wonder from the first moment the violins began to play. To listen over a crackling radio was one thing. To be right in the middle of it was totally different, an enchantment that swept him away from the real world.

The concert proper was held in the Hall later that summer. It was a great success. Most of the audience was composed of parents and relatives of those who performed, and D.'s parents were among them. Afterwards they expressed their surprise at the accomplished and tuneful performance, and D. found himself strangely resentful of their approval. Did they think he had been telling lies, or exaggerating, when he had described the music, urging them to attend the concert? His mother had expressed contempt, and his father patronising disbelief, arousing much family laughter as he comically described D. singing away on a concert platform, when D. had brought home tickets pleading with them to buy and attend.

Now that the performance had been so successful he felt that he did not need their approval of his music interest. He boldly declared that he would learn the piano.

'I'm not going to waste any more money on you,' his mother said with finality. 'You've cost me enough already. I can't afford to throw money away on you.'

He hadn't bargained on this. He hadn't realised he would need to pay a special teacher. He had been vaguely thinking of Roberts the music at school. What a fool he was!

He was so dejected that he went to his bedroom and cried, gently and quietly to himself. He hadn't cried for a long time, not since he had caught his fingers in the lawn mower when he had been cleaning the edges of the blades; his younger sister crept up and kicked the machine, rotating the blades and jamming three fingers. His father had had to use a screwdriver to lever back the blades to release his fingers. As he pulled his hand away the pain began, and he had cried, to the delight of his sister and the exasperation of his father.

Eventually D.'s parents gave in, and he was allowed to take piano lessons. He was overjoyed. At last something was going his way. He would start in September, his mother said. They already had a piano in the parlour. His grandmother had given it to them for safe keeping, on a sort of permanent loan. His elder sister practised her lessons three times a week, and D. thought she was quite good. Perhaps after a while they could play together.

He held the promise of more music quietly in his mind for weeks, looking forward to September.

'Mr Andrews,' his mother said, 'Your old headmaster. He'll take you in your piano lessons. I saw him today and he's agreed to take you.'

D.'s jaw dropped in horror. 'Mr Andrews?' he croaked. 'Mam, I can't. Not Mr Andrews. Not him.'

'Why not?' His mother was angry immediately. 'What's wrong with Mr Andrews? He's a headmaster. He must be clever, and he's been teaching the piano for years. Besides, he's one of us. He's a

Catholic. He's not a Protestant with their funny ideas. You'll go to Mr Andrews and like it, my boy. And that's final.'

His father agreed. 'Any more trouble from you and you'll go without any lessons at all,' he said. 'So. It's Mr Andrews or nothing at all.' He folded his newspaper and left the kitchen table, jumbo cup of tea in hand, to sit in the parlour. He left the saucer behind on the table, a sign that the conversation was definitely over — he had a strange way of drinking his tea, pouring it from the cup into the saucer, then raising the saucer to his lips, little finger curled delicately, and drinking in long slurping draughts. If anyone was seated at the table when he performed this ritual, there must be total quiet and no movement. Often the whole family would freeze, even if they were only nearby and not actually seated at the table, as his saucerful of tea was slowly raised, the liquid quivering and swirling as he adjusted the angle to compensate for the changing height. He was left-handed, too, which added to the anxiety of the watchers. It all looked so awkward and unlikely. There would be a palpable sigh of relief when he got his lips to the edge of the saucer and could start drinking.

Nobody would dream of challenging this strange habit, even though when D. had tried it in imitation he had earned himself a cuff across the head from his mother. 'None of those disgusting table manners here. You do what everyone else does. None of my children are going to drink like that.'

'But Dad ... '

'That's different. And don't you answer back or you'll get one.'

His father closed the parlour door behind him to shut himself off from further family matters. D.'s mother shook her finger as she warned, 'Don't mention it again. Your father's decision is final.'

Dejectedly D. accepted it. It was better than nothing. And since D. was no longer in Mr Andrews' school he was not his headmaster any more, and couldn't use the cane on his hands if something went wrong. When he had worked this new relationship out, he persuaded himself that things might not be too difficult after all.

He was wrong.

D.'s perceived new relationship was a delusion. Seated at the keyboard in Mr Andrews' house, not a stone's throw from St Joseph's school, D. found himself treated with the same grimly silent contempt as though nothing had happened in the fifteen months since he had left that school. The headmaster stood, silent and inhuman, his small lips working furiously at every hesitation and uncertain movement of D.'s untutored hands. There were a million questions D. wanted to ask about scales, tones, harmony, instruments, structure and melody, but his tutor's freezing hostility subdued him into perspiring silence.

He tried once more, trudging the long uphill route from his mid-town school after the school day was finished, carrying the music case borrowed from his elder sister. The walk took him three-quarters of an hour, tiring and dusty in the September late afternoon sun. As he stood outside the door of Mr Andrews' house, he was reminded of his foster mother's house in Llanelli. Miss Philips' house was in a terrace, and her front door had coloured glass in it, just like this one.

As at his first visit he knocked on the door and waited. The door opened after a long wait. Mr Andrews stood aside to let him pass, no word of acknowledgement, no change in his expression. D. had a sudden urge to walk away, not out of weakness or fear, but from resentment. He didn't have to take music lessons at all, much less from Mr Andrews. And if he walked away, the headmaster could hardly drag him back, could he?

He wondered why Mr Andrews seemed to have it in for him. He couldn't think why. Was it the one-leg business that was still being held against him? It was a long time ago, now. He remembered reading in the *Daily Express* then, how R.A.F. pilots ate hundredweights of carrots every week so that they could see in the dark; and one of the ways a recruit was selected to be a pilot was his ability to stand on one leg for long periods. D. never understood how standing on one leg helped to fly a warplane, but he thought there was no harm in practising. Next day at school he went everywhere and did everything on one leg. When other boys asked him why, he explained it to them, and although some did not believe him, other *Daily Express* readers did. They hadn't thought of the idea of practising. It seemed a very manly and glamorous thing to do.

By the afternoon break, most of the senior boys were hopping everywhere on one leg. Teachers everywhere could be heard bawling at boys to 'use your other leg, boy' and often, when the offending boy swapped one leg for another, there was the follow-up: 'Both of them, boy'.

In the yard at afternoon break, one-legged events were held. Races and endurance hops across the yard and back, up and down stairs or simply standing facing one another in a circle, no holding the idle leg with hands.

Teachers' faces could be seen at the window of the staff room, Mr Andrews among them, nose twitching and little lips moving. Then he disappeared.

The bell for end of break went early, catching out the smokers in the open-top lavatory. Instead of swarming back to their classrooms, which the boys were preparing to do on one leg, they were kept outside as Mr Andrews stood in the middle of the yard and read the riot act.

'Anyone seen hopping on one leg from now on will get two strokes of the cane,' he shouted. 'Any boy seen in the street as well as in school, hopping, will get three strokes of the cane.'

None of the boys defied this order. There was nothing to be gained. They all filed meekly into their classrooms and soon forgot it.

Not so Mr Andrews. As D. passed him, he pointed a finger.

'You. Stand aside. I want to talk to you.'

D. stood aside, filled with dread. So far he had not been caned.

When the last boy had gone Mr Andrews turned to D.

'You were hopping about this morning when no one else was. This afternoon everyone is at it.' He paused for a long time, possibly hoping D. would blurt out some hidden secret under the silent pressure of threat.

'Well?'

'R.A.F. pilots, sir.'

'R.A.F. pilots? What are you talking about, silly boy?' Mr Andrews' eyes were bulging more than usual thought D. He was getting mad.

'They stand on one leg, sir.'

Mr Andrews stood, eyes popping, nostrils flaring, lips working, silent.

'I read it, sir. In the papers. If they can stand on one leg for a long time they are chosen as pilots in the R.A.F.' D. paused. Mr Andrews was still silent. 'So I was practising, sir. To stand on one leg.'

Mr Andrews stared at him for a long time before he turned away snapping, 'Get back to your class. And no more of this nonsense, upsetting the whole school.'

Mr Andrews had glared at him frequently after that, as though to warn him not to start anything new. Seated at the piano now, D. could feel the same glare, cold and silently aggressive.

He didn't go again. His mother threatened all manner of dark punishments and his father had little but contempt for his lack of determination, as he saw it.

D. simply refused to go. He didn't elaborate. He couldn't. How could he describe Mr Andrews' attitude, his blatant hatred of boys? The overwhelming urge to get away from Mr Andrews' presence?

In the end D.'s mother paid the full fee for the full course. Mr

Andrews charged for all the lessons he hadn't given, and D. had a tiny twinge of conscience when he learned later that the bill was three guineas.

The experience didn't end his deep interest in music, though it slammed the door resoundingly on his ability to learn the technicalities of it. He began to feel that his world was filling up with teachers, the people who knew about everything of worthwhile interest, whose chief interest was in blocking him.

Chapter Nine

Christmas 1945 was the same as the year before and the year before that. The end of the war brought scarcely any change to the lives of D.'s family, or, as far as he could see, anyone else. Food was still severely rationed and he had still to run the gauntlet of his mother's scorn and watchful eye to try and feed his never-ending hunger. Though he was taller now than most of the boys in the street, he weighed far less than most. The boys of twelve and thirteen years old were around eight stones, whilst D. was just seven stones.

He had read in the newspapers that Americans were sending food parcels to Britain because they thought that the British were starving, but he had never heard of anyone who had received a parcel. Perhaps they all went to London, he thought, where there had been so much bombing. He wondered what would be in the food parcels. Pounds and pounds of chewing gum, Ginger had said when they talked about it, but D. thought that wouldn't be sensible.

'Spam and dried egg,' said D. 'That's good food. I could do with some of that myself.'

But they got no answers to their queries of where these parcels could be found, and in the end they put it down to rumour, and gave up.

The new year's winter was mild, and gave them little sport. Spring was early, and as May grew hotter, D. joined groups of boys both from his own school and the Technical College to go swimming at the beach, straight from school. None of the boys worried about swimsuits or towels, though now as puberty approached they were more aware of their state. A cry of 'There's a cop' sent them scampering for cover. Those near the water dashed into the waves and sat down to conceal their offensive parts.

The policeman on the railway embankment behind the beach gave them a long hard stare, then moved off without saying anything. The boys in the water were slow to come out, and those holding trousers in front of them for the policeman's benefit quickly put them on. They realised that this was probably the last year they would have such a carefree time.

They never went back.

For some reason D. had expected the bombed town to be rebuilt the day after the war was over. It seemed reasonable to him to make a quick start, anyway. But as 1946 drew on there was little change apart from the weeds and bushes on the bombed sites getting larger.

At home D.'s mother had eased up on penis jokes and sneers, not out of respect for his feelings but because she had begun to notice that his sisters didn't laugh very heartily any more, and perhaps even appeared to be embarrassed by her comments. D. never protested. He didn't understand why his willie was a matter of such consuming interest to her. There was never so much as a breath of comment on the girls' part.

Instead, there developed an increasing flow of complaining about men in general. His mother held forth on neighbours' husbands who 'drank away their pay', on other men — she had a gift of putting much venom into this word, as though it was the same thing as the pox, or a destructive tidal wave — who beat their wives and sometimes threw their children outside the house 'in all weathers' if they had been 'drinking'.

D. had never seen any of this. He knew most of the households in their part of the street a lot better than his mother, and he had not even suspected that such goings-on were part of their lives. Some of the boys' mothers were fierce, but they had never harmed him. The men, as far as he knew them, were friendly and often chatted with him, and none of them had ever made him feel uneasy at any time, except Mr Horner the bald fireman.

His mother complained about the kitchen sink. It was too low, she said. So, logically, 'Men must have designed this sink. And they put it in,' she snapped after a long dishwashing stint. 'If women did it, they'd do it properly.'

The noise of the wind on a stormy Saturday afternoon came in for complaint too. 'Just listen,' she said to the three children seated at the table, driven indoors by the wild weather. 'All that noise. It's men who built this house. As if they couldn't do something about that noise. They must have known it would blow gales up here on the hill. That's men for you.'

D. wondered how she would fare living in a cave, but said nothing. All three of the children were puzzled by their mother's words.

At school he daydreamed. Whole lessons passed by without him noticing. He rarely completed his homework, and after the first few punishments of fifty lines for not handing in homework, he didn't hand in the lines, either. He collected quite a few cuffs around the head for inattention, and a few more for reasons he didn't understand.

End of year exam results put him a long way last. His younger sister had passed her eleven-plus, and this year her examination results placed her at seventh in her class. She tormented him with this comparison throughout the summer.

The children no longer went to Gower or Bishopston Valley with their parents. They were old enough, said their father, to find their own pleasures, and to amuse themselves for the holidays. His own holiday in September was spent almost entirely in the garden, furiously growing vegetables that none of the family ate, even though food was still rationed. There were just too many cabbages and carrots.

So D. wandered the town and surrounding countryside with the boys from the street. The Hendersons never came because they were still not allowed to play with Protestants, and D. was thankful.

Sometimes in the summer holidays there were raging stone-throwing fights with neighbouring gangs. The Elphin gang disputed territory on the allotments, a small valley forming a cleft of unusually steep land driven into the mass of housing, which had been divided by the council into tenants' plots for growing vegetables. It had, ironically, fallen into disuse in the war, because such a lot of men were called up, and by 1946 it was a barren waste with vestiges of embankments and pathways, with the odd battered remains of a few sheds.

On this land the gangs would slug it out with hails of stones to retain the advantage of the high ground. The valley was too wide for either side to be a threat to the other provided they stayed on their own slopes, and most disputes ended in stalemate, with shouted insults and gibes ringing out across the gap until the language worsened to the point where parents, usually mothers, ordered the boys indoors.

The Gwili gang was the most threatening. They fought on level ground and on the street. The bombed houses provided ample ammunition, particularly pieces of slates, which when thrown with skill were very awkward to avoid because they curved in the air. The slates were also dangerous, and most of the boys bore scars on shins, and some on the face, from a well-thrown piece. The Gwili gang also had boys a lot older than D.'s own gang, and could throw bigger stones much further. The end of the gang fighting came when the Gwili gang broke the rules and began to throw bottles and pieces of metal. Someone called the police, who arrived in force, and frightened everybody with their fierceness. There were no arrests or charges, but plenty of bruises, mostly amongst the Gwili gang.

Now that they were in their teens, most of the boys left the stone fights to the younger boys. The arrival of the police had impressed the older boys that they were no longer children, who could be indulged with a cuff around the ear. Fighting of any kind at their age was serious, and the law would step in, brushing parents aside.

Their wanderings that summer were restricted by their age. Innocent trespass by small boys was a nuisance and easily dealt with by an adult defending his territory. Boys of thirteen and fourteen were seen to be dangerous, and D. and his friends discovered a new hostility even on the open streets and in public places — parks, the beaches and the seafront promenade. The boys were not noisy, they never used bad language in public and generally went about their business without any thought of provoking others, and certainly were not aggressive or threatening in any way. Yet here was a shopkeeper, about to be asked to sell the boys five Woodbines, which after a pocket-scraping whipround was all they could afford, who was suspicious of them. Three of the boys stayed outside, chatting. Two went inside to buy.

'Where you boys from?' The shopkeeper glared at them, hostile, aggressive.

D. looked at him in surprise.

He didn't answer the question. He knew that Mayhill was not a good place to come from, and here they were in a better part of town near the beach. 'We thought we could buy five Woodbines,' he said.

'Get out,' said the shopkeeper. 'We don't want your sort around here. Go on. Out. Before I call the police.' He leaned over them, hands spread on the counter top, his voice rising, his face turning ugly.

D. quailed, and turned to go, but Ginger, who was with him, was over a year older, and made of sterner stuff.

'You can't refuse to sell us something if it's on display,' he said reasonably. He pointed to the green cardboard carton behind the glass of a counter-top cabinet. '500 Woodbines' was printed on the carton, and they could see it was at least half-full.

'I can refuse your sort anything, at any time. Now shove off.' The shopkeeper made to open the counter-top flap, to add physical persuasion to his words. D. and Ginger moved off, slowly and reluctantly. Outside, the other three were unaware of the goings-on, and crowded the other two with hands out for their Woodbines.

'He wouldn't sell us any,' said D. sullenly. 'He called us all sorts of names. Thought we were ruffians.' Ginger said nothing. The boys were silent too. Then Tiddler Davies thumbed his nose at the shopkeeper, who stood inside his shop looking at them through the plate glass window.

The other boys joined Tiddler, and in a short time all five of them were cavorting about in front of the shop window, shouting, taunting, making obscene gestures. Passers-by stared, and the shopkeeper got madder and madder until he came out of his shop waving a sawn-off broom handle.

The boys ran. He didn't follow. He just stood there, stick in hand, watching them. After a few catcalls the boys gave up. They had had some small revenge, but the sense of injustice spoiled their mood as they slowly wandered back home.

That summer D. wore long trousers for the first time. It was long overdue. He was the only one in his class at school still in short trousers, and very nearly the only one in the street gang — the only others were two years younger than him. He soon found out that looking after long trousers took some care. Rain demolished creases, and walking through wet grass or playing with water caused the turn-ups to wilt and unfold. Kneeling too had its problems — he soon had unexplainable holes at the knees which his mother was lightning quick to spot and just as fast to reprimand with a smack around the head.

They went swimming off the beach in Swansea, and hitched lifts to the more distant sands in Gower. They picked cockles off Blackpill beach, accessible now that the mines and barbed wire had been cleared. They played around the giant cubes of concrete lining the shore, and watched the Mumbles train thunder by, swaying and jerking as it went, an ugly double-deck vehicle that dominated the bay with its claim to prime tracts of land skirting the sea, forcing everyone under or over it at widely spaced intervals and cutting off the shore from the town behind.

That summer the cinema newsreels and the radio news carried reports of the Nuremburg trials. Surviving captured Nazi leaders were shown on trial, strangely reduced figures, powerless and human-sized, bearing no resemblance to their fearsome wartime warlord stature.

D. remembered last year, when Himmler, the head of the Gestapo, was shown in a large, full-face photo on the *Daily Express* front page.

'What an evil-looking man,' said D.'s mother, aghast at this first sight of the enemy who had made life so difficult for the past six years. And she was right. There had been an abundance of cartoons in the newspapers and cinema newsreels during the war, and they had was no difficulty in identifying the faces ranged along the hard wooden enclosing benches of the trial court. But D. reflected that a real photo of Himmler during wartime had been wisely concealed — such a face must have struck fear into the hearts of his best friends, let alone his enemies.

Later that summer D. finally overcame his bedwetting. It happened suddenly. Dreaming that he was in the toilet when in fact he was in bed was the core of the problem. He slept too deeply. With a huge effort and the help of a check such as counting the stairs on the way downstairs to the toilet, he discovered the means to distinguish reality from dreaming. He was secretly very pleased. Now the ragging and sniggering from his mother and his younger sister, as well as the impatient contempt of his father, would end.

He was wrong. There was constant reference to 'D.'s wet bed' for years to come, in what might lightly be called 'family humour', which made him miserably embarrassed when it was brought out in other company.

Nail-biting was a different problem. He could not explain it, no matter how deeply he examined himself. So it continued, though he was increasingly self-conscious about its effect on his appearance.

Chapter Ten

Then back to school. He had become blasé by now — no longer wearing school colours except for a tie. He affected not to care, preferring the undistinguishing mufti worn by the boys in his street, though the underlying reason was that his mother refused to buy replacements for his outgrown blazer, pullover, socks and cap. She had no pride in him any more, she told him, and new school gear was a waste of money. He might just as well not be in Grammar school for all the good it was doing, she said. He wished he was not in Grammar school, or any school at all. They were, in his experience, places of tyranny, inexhaustible punishment, humiliation and inevitable failure.

He went to school, as most thirteen-year-olds did, because it seemed the main purpose of life. He had no long term vision of change, or of progress, or even of purpose. Simply to get through a day without a beating was a triumph.

The famously severe winter of 1947 began soon after Christmas 1946. There had been a light snowfall on Christmas Day, adding to the excitement of the season, and spirits were high, though the snow was not enough even to gather a snowball, as the boys found.

At the start of the first week in January the snow began in earnest. After two days there were nine inches of it everywhere. And it was cold. There had been no wind and no drifting, so that even the tiniest bare twig bowed under a pyramid of frozen white crystals. Where did small birds go to rest, wondered D., when everything was covered like this?

Anywhere they could, was the answer he found. In a moment of idle excitement on the second morning of snow, he had cleared the tiled sill of his bedroom window, watching the soft blocks float to the ground below. In the late afternoon, gazing in wonder at the magic landscape, he was suddenly aware of a robin, feathers fluffed against the bitter cold, fat and round as a rusting tennis ball, sitting in the corner of the cleared sill.

They gazed at each other, one in curiosity, the other in wariness. Wisely D. did not open the window. Instead he backed away slowly so as not to frighten the bird. He soon forgot it, and went out into the street to play in the snow — icy slides of undreamed-of lengths, snowball fights, traps of overhanging shelves of snow to lure the girls under, toboggan rides on the old air raid shelter bunks, and even one mad ride down the side of a hill on one of the curved galvanised steel sheets from an air raid shelter. That ride cost one of them a broken arm, but for the rest of them the evening ended in darkness, breathless tiredness, exhaustion and utter contentment at a day well spent.

In the morning the robin was still there. As D. dressed as quickly as he could in the freezing bedroom, he resolved to bring the little creature some breadcrumbs after breakfast. Perhaps he might fancy some cornflakes.

He tidied his bed. His mother insisted on it, now that he was thirteen.

His father had had a pay rise that summer, and D. had got his first blanket. His bedding normally was a loose collection of shawls and pieces of curtain, difficult to keep together in a complete cover all night, which was not too bad in summer but gave him many broken nights in winter. He still did not have sheets as his sisters did, but he had valued his enveloping blanket these last few bitter nights.

Everywhere it was cold. In the kitchen his father bad-temperedly set about lighting the stove whilst D.'s mother complained. 'This is a cold house,' she said. 'I've never been in such a cold house. It's disgraceful. They ought to do something about it. Expecting us to live in such cold houses.'

The children were quiet, cowed by their parents' bad mood. They ate their breakfast of cornflakes and Rees' watered milk in crunching silence.

'And now I suppose you're waiting for tea, is it?' Their mother spoke angrily, resentful. 'I wish I was you. Just sitting there, waiting to be fed. What a life.'

She swung around, cold kettle in hand, on her way to crashing it on the gas ring perched on the stove as she had done so often these uncomfortable early mornings. She glared at D.

'What have you got there?' She was looking at his closed left fist. 'Nothing.'

'Let me see. Open up. I don't trust you.'

There was no way of hiding the half dozen dry cornflakes he clutched in his hand. He opened it to show her.

'What's that for? Found some nasty frogs who like cornflakes, have you? Come on. Tell me. Or is it something else nasty that you've got in your bedroom? Eh?'

She put the kettle down on the cold stove, not the flaring gas ring, and D. saw in despair that she was going to make an issue of it.

'A robin,' he said. 'On my windowsill. It's been there all night. I thought I could give it something to eat.'

'A bird? On the windowsill?' She paused, the kitchen silent. To everyone, even D.'s father kneeling in futile determination at the stove, trying to blow the reluctant damp sticks into flame, it was so obvious she was turning over in her mind how she could disallow this activity. She was in a terrible mood.

'I'm not having any birds shitting on my windowsill,' she said finally. 'They make a mess. Can't get it off. Dirty creatures. Get rid of it. D'you understand me? You get rid of it, or I will.'

Their father turned his head away from the fire and frowned in annoyance. He did not approve of coarse language in front of the children. Very rarely, he signalled extreme anger by a muted 'bloody', but never used anything stronger. The word 'shitting' was out of bounds. He didn't say so directly; instead he took D.'s side against her.

'There's no harm in tending God's creatures,' he said quietly. 'They're having a bad time just now, in this weather.' He disengaged himself from his task at the stove, and turned, placing an elbow on one knee, signalling his intention to join battle.

She backed down. Not directly, but with a snarl. 'Move, Frank. How can I get the children's tea ready if you're in the way? And what's wrong with that fire? We're freezing here. It's about time it was going, isn't it?'

D.'s father wisely recognised victory and said no more. He made a token movement to allow her to place the kettle on the gas ring and then set about puffing life again into the fire.

D. scrambled out of his corner seat, anxious to be out of the kitchen before the reluctant mood of unspoken consent changed. Clutching his fistful of cornflakes he bounded up the stairs to his bedroom, quieting himself before softly opening the door and approaching the window.

The robin was still there. It looked very unhappy, though D. would have been hard put to say how he knew: after all, a robin did not turn blue in the cold.

The metal window frame was iced up and stuck fast. It took several careful minutes to ease it open. The robin, eyes wide and wings half raised, watched him. As D. opened the window, wide enough for his hand to pass, the cold air struck him and made him gasp. It was colder than yesterday, he thought.

He broke up the cornflakes in his left hand and slowly extended it towards the crouching bird. With a startling rush the robin flew on to his hand, clutching D.'s little finger with tiny cold claws, and pecked furiously at the food.

D. was astonished and delighted. Never before had he been so close to one of nature's small creatures. For all his interest in frogs, for instance, he had never seen one snap up a fly as he had read. It was a continuing disappointment to him that whenever he came across a small animal, it behaved as if it believed that D. wanted to eat it, or at the very least do it some serious harm. Many times he had seen these small animals in stages of extreme fear, desperate to escape. It was only recently that he had begun to acknowledge these fears, though disappointedly he regretted his inability to tell them he meant no harm.

Watching the robin picking away on his hand, feeling its claws change their grip as it countered the gusts of cold wind edging around the window, D. suddenly understood the small brain. Everything was concentrated on reaction. There was no considered thought. All life was a matter of food or flight in these conditions.

Pecking furiously, the robin scattered as much food as it ate. D. wandered if robins ate worms. There wouldn't be much chance of finding any in this terrible weather. Perhaps he could persuade the boys in the street to help him find some. Most likely not. Though the boys were not as cruel as the Gwili gang, they were not enthusiastic about nature's small creatures either, which D. found difficult to understand. Perhaps his father would help. He could certainly offer advice, thought D.

His father was not interested. At least he said so. D. instinctively understood: his father saw no gain in prolonging the tensions of breakfast time; if D. wanted to continue his affair with the robin he must do it on his own.

'School for you, my boy.' D. looked up in shock. His mother stood, hands on hips, her face dull red in temper.

'And don't look at me like that, either. You haven't been to school since Monday.' Today was Thursday.

His father spoke. 'All this snow ... ' he began.

'I don't care,' said D.'s mother. 'I'm sick of him hanging around the house all day. Can't get on with my work with him always under my feet. Besides, I just saw other boys going to school, so it won't hurt him.'

D. wondered how his sisters managed to avoid getting under her feet all day. He must ask them.

'What about the girls?' his father asked hesitantly.

'The snow is too deep for the girls. They'd freeze, walking all that way. The buses aren't running.'

'One of my shoes has a hole in the sole,' said D. as a last hope.

He had only one pair of shoes, and there really was a large hole in one of them.

'Trust you,' his mother snarled. Then in triumph she said, 'Wear your father's boots. They're not all that big for you.'

D. took size seven. He knew his father's boots were size eleven. And his father wore his boots only in the garden, and they were old, scuffed and muddy. They were in fact his old Home Guard boots.

'But Mam ... '

'No buts. Get ready. You can wear Jean's scarf. You don't need gloves. You'd lose them anyway. Now get your father's boots out of the cupboard and put them on. I'm staying here until you get ready, so don't think of wasting time.'

And she did stay until he was ready. The boots were so big he stumbled. 'Don't pretend,' snapped his mother. 'They aren't all that big for you.' She glared at him as he buttoned up his overcoat. 'What a baby of a son I've got,' she muttered. 'Afraid to go to school because of a bit of snow.'

Outside, the cold was a shock. After a hundred yards of slipping and sliding inside his boots as well as outside, the cold became a bigger worry than the snow itself. His ears stung, his fingers hurt and his eyelashes gathered frost. He hoped his eyes wouldn't glaze over with ice as he had heard that young German soldiers' had in the winter of 1942 in Russia. Peering through a screen of ice must have been worrying, he thought. Did it irritate like a piece of grit under the eyelid, he wondered.

He caught up with the other boys from the street on their way to school. They went to the Technical College halfway up Mount Pleasant Hill, a long climb from his own school in the centre of town.

He called out to them. They stopped and waited for him to catch up.

Ginger was the first to notice his boots as he drew near.

'Let's stand on D.'s boots,' he chortled. 'We can slide into town all the way on them. Look at them. Fuck me, D., where did you get them sledges?'

D. was not happy with this. 'They're my father's,' he said, irritated. 'My mother made me wear them.'

The boys were silent, affected by his mood of resentment. They walked on together, temporarily depressed by his show of emotion.

It began to snow. Big fat slow flakes settled around them, the sky grew dark and the world went quiet. There was no noise, no wind, no sound of human activity. They hadn't heard a car for days. As far as the boys could see, they were the only moving things in the shadowless white world.

The boys began to fantasize as they trudged on, brushing fat wet flakes off their eyelashes.

'My father said it's the worst winter since Queen Elizabeth's time,' said Ginger.

'How does he know that?' asked Billy.

'He read it, I suppose.'

'My father said that if it doesn't stop snowing soon nobody will be able to go outside. They'll have to stay indoors all the time. And if they drop food to us by parachute we won't be able to find it anyway.'

'We'll all be dead then. From starvation. And when the snow melts there'll be boxes of food all over our back gardens,' said Ginger.

'We'd better start living outside the house then,' said D. 'We can watch the food parcels dropping, and see where they land.'

'How're we going to get them?' asked Richard. 'Under twenty feet of snow?'

'Big tunnels of course,' said Ginger. Without warning he flung himself full length, face down, arms outstretched, on a virgin patch of snow two feet deep. He picked himself up carefully as the others watched in amazement.

'What d'you do that for?' asked Billy.

'See that?' Ginger pointed to a perfect outline of his body held in the snow. 'They'll think somebody fell there, perhaps even died, of cold. Like they do in Russia. They'll be looking everywhere for the body.'

The other three studied the 3-D imprint for a few moments. It was good, they admitted. Even the creases in his clothes showed clearly.

'It'll fill up with snow soon,' said D. The others agreed. Ginger shrugged, and they trudged on.

The character of the snow changed as they slipped and slid along. The soft fat flakes disappeared, and in their place fell a rain of hard round granules which bounced down their necks and into their ears. A keen wind sprang up, and it grew colder. D. wished he had underpants. The wind cut through his trousers as though he was naked below the waist.

The boys were silent now as the going became difficult. All of them felt their hands, feet and ears get painful as the exposure continued. Finally, as they saw the bright red brick walls of the Technical College ahead through the wind-swept murk, Billy said, 'I'm going home. I'm cold. I'm not going any further.'

176

They all stopped, indecisive. They all wanted to go home, but having come this far …

'I've got further than you to go,' said D. He found it hard to speak clearly. It was some time since he had said anything, and he was surprised to find his lips numb, and slow to respond to his wishes.

'You go on if you want to,' said Billy. 'I don't care. I'm cold. I've got German first lesson. Just sitting down. It was terrible on Monday. The heating boiler isn't working.'

'No,' confirmed Richard. 'No coal, they said. Trains can't get through, or something.'

'You'd think they would deliver by lorry,' said Ginger.

'I haven't seen a lorry for days,' said D.

Billy turned and started back. It would be all uphill on the way home, and no opportunities to slide part of the way. The other three watched him go, undecided.

'Perhaps school is closed,' said Richard hopefully. 'Let's go that far, anyway. Just to see.'

It wasn't far. Just a hundred yards or so. At the top of the school steps to the main entrance the sliding gates were closed. The boys didn't need to climb the steps to see that there was no school today. There were no lights on in the building anyway.

'Let's catch Billy up,' said Ginger, eager to be away now that doubts had been resolved.

'What are you going to do, D.?' asked Richard.

D. looked down the hill towards his school. Mount Pleasant was normally a main thoroughfare between town and the hilltop housing developments, but now it was silent and deserted. Only one car was on the road, pointing uphill, parked on the wrong side and under a thick coat of snow. It had been there some time. There were no people in sight. Even the sprawling Grammar School buildings just below the Technical College were deserted. The odds on Dynevor School being open were small.

Uppermost in D.'s mind was the likely expression on his mother's face if he returned home. She would be very angry. He would be more confident of facing her if he knew for certain that his school really was closed.

'I'm going,' said Richard. 'Wait for me,' he called after his brother Ginger, and he set off back home, leaving D. standing in the swirling skeins of freezing snow, indecisive.

D. turned and followed the boys. He had made, with little agony, the most important decision in his young life. For the first time he had consciously disobeyed his parents' instructions. However disagreeable, he had always, with varying degrees of success, carried out his parents' orders to the letter. He believed in his parents. They must know what they were doing. He relied on them for guidance. He had no reason to challenge their wisdom. But now, obedience was impossible. He was not aware of a turning point in his life, but from now on he would find it ever easier to dodge unpleasant duties.

It took them nearly two hours to reach their home street. Teeth chattering, they sucked their fingers to relieve the pain as they struggled up the last slope to the gentler levels at the top of the hill and home. They had been silent most of the way. For a long time each of them had separately longed for the protection and warmth of home: a fire, and a window through which to watch the raw nastiness of this winter instead of being part of it. Their feet were numb to the ankles, toes painful, cheeks and noses blanched with frost. They had tried hunching their shoulders to cover ears and necks until the muscles ached. Each of them in private distress, sought his own solution to the inadequacies of his clothing. The sheer physical effort of raising their feet to clear twenty inches of snow at every step had severely taxed them, winding them and causing rasping breath and painful coughing.

Eyes watering, they parted to their homes with a bare 'See ya', stumbling over the steps with no thought in their heads but rest and relief from the cold.

'Kick your feet on the outside step, stupid boy. Don't you dare tramp your snow in here.'

D.'s mother stood at the stove, warming her hands. His sisters, engrossed in a game of Ludo, sat at the kitchen table.

'Why aren't you at school, eh?'

'It's closed,' said D. He didn't know if it was a lie or not. He coughed, a rasping chesty and painful hawk. 'All the other schools are closed too. I came back with the boys.'

His sisters watched him, silent, their game suspended.

'Take your coat off and shake it outside,' said D.'s mother. 'And close the door while you do it. We don't want to freeze just for you.'

As D. went to take off his coat his mother shouted, 'Outside. Take your coat off outside. Look at the mess you're making in here. Snow melting all over the place. Stupid, thoughtless boy.'

He did as he was told. He was glad there was no dispute about his reason for coming back home.

After the brief warmth of the kitchen, the cold outside as he shook his coat was frightening. He gave his coat an extra-vigorous shaking

178

as he stood on the step. He didn't want to have to do it again if his mother faulted his efforts.

Inside, he hung up his coat on the hooks nailed to the back door. His father never screwed anything if it could be nailed instead. His mother inspected his coat, raising each sleeve to examine it for traces of snow. She dropped them reluctantly and went back to the stove to warm herself.

'And you don't need to feed that bird any more. It flew away,' she said with an air of finality. It sounded as though she had wrung its neck, thought D.

His younger sister sniggered. Jean looked at him with sympathy. So it had not flown away of its own accord, thought D. His mother had taken some action to force it.

'And don't look at me like that either. I can't afford to waste good food on a silly bird. We need all we got in this weather. Jones the bread didn't have anything today. Who knows when we'll get another loaf. You'll be the first to complain if you don't have enough to eat, greedy.'

D. went upstairs to his room. Sure enough, the robin had gone. He heard the rattle of the doorknob at the foot of the stairs.

'You stay up there, now. I don't want you under my feet all day. And no noise.' Pause. 'D'you hear me?'

'Yes, Mam.'

The door closed. D. looked at the crystallised window and the grey sky outside. It was cold here, in his bedroom. All the heat downstairs was trapped by the closed doors.

He went to the window, breathed on it and rubbed with a throbbing hand. His fingers were only now recovering their feeling after the exposure of his morning journey.

The landscape was all but unrecognisable. White and grey extended everywhere. It was snowing furiously, the same hard grains that had begun on his way to school. They clattered against the frigid steel-framed panes in gusting icy waves. D. felt no sense of hostility in the onslaught — just the grim, overwhelming persistence of nature. He was glad to be at home. At least the bricks and mortar would stand up better to the coughing, ice-laden winds than the German bombs of just a few years before. He wondered when he could go downstairs, perhaps to share the warmth of the kitchen stove with his sisters.

The winter went on and on. Chancellor Adenauer, he heard on the radio, had had a confrontation with the British Army, which wanted to cut down several kilometres of mature trees outside Koln for fuel, not for the civilian population, but for the British forces short of coal. The chancellor had won, and the trees remained, gracing roads built in the 1890's for a different world.

All over Europe the news was grim. Unequalled snowfalls and low temperatures were widespread. Food was short, fuel scarce, whole countries had ground to a halt, and people suffered. Only Russia appeared to have escaped the freezing onslaught, but then, no information of any kind was allowed out of that devastated country anyway, so who knew what was going on there.

In Swansea the snow eventually stopped and people began to move about. Neighbours who called on D.'s mother to beg a bucket of coal were turned away, even though they offered to pay silly prices for it.

'I'm sorry, but we got barely enough as it is,' D.'s mother would say. Both neighbour and she knew this was a lie. Everyone was well aware of the ton of anthracite tucked away under the stairs. The whole street had watched the twenty full sacks taken down the steps to their house in November, and who burned a ton in just a month or so?

When the first neighbour had been turned away, D.'s mother told the children, 'Not a word, you understand? Don't you say a word about the coal we've got here. Especially you, blabber.' She glared at D. 'No telling your pals that we got loads of coal. Let them get their own. We got none to give to them Protestants.'

On the street afterwards D. was asked slyly by several of the boys how much coal he had. 'Not a lot,' said D.

'My father said you had lots,' said Billy.

'They're keeping it for themselves,' said Ginger disapprovingly. 'They won't help anybody else who've run short.'

D. was silent. He felt suddenly isolated. Everyone knew his parents had coal, and yet he was denying it. He resented having to lie to his pals. After all, it wasn't he who had decided to keep the coal to himself. The neighbours would have given it back anyway, as soon as Williams the coal's lorry could make deliveries. They lived amongst honest people, generally, who valued give-and-take in emergencies. He had learned that much from his mother, who had gushed her gratitude and praises in the past when she had borrowed sugar, milk or potatoes from neighbours.

The affair drove a wedge between D. and the boys in the street that was never fully closed. Things were not the same again. The boys spoke criticisms of D. and his family in words that were not their own. They were adults' words, parents' phrases. D. could see that, and countered as best he could without quarrelling outright. He had never had a fight with the boys; he had never had to. They had never threatened or bullied him. The only ones who did that were the Hendersons.

The rift between D. and the boys had real consequences. As the winter drew to a close and the days grew longer, there were things to do, games to play, places to visit, especially at weekends. D. was not invited as first choice. If team games were to be played, he was often last to be chosen by the opposing captains; left out altogether if there was an odd number of boys. If they went on walking expeditions on Saturday afternoons he was not told of their plans, and faced an empty, boring street until the boys returned late, to sit around the street lamp yarning and joshing until suppertime. It embarrassed D. to join them, but he forced himself, pretending that he hadn't missed them, and that he had been busy all afternoon. After all, there was little choice: to risk his mother's irritation and inevitable anger if he stayed around the house, or to seek out the bully Hendersons. He might possibly go for a walk on his own, but there were inherent dangers in that. And it was unbearably lonely.

It was to take the rest of the summer to get accepted by the boys again, and then it mostly turned on his standing up, foolishly perhaps, to Dick Reynolds, the demon fast bowler.

Reynolds was seventeen, and the star of the street team which bordered Mayhill Park, a tattered patch of worn-out playing field, provided by a considerate local Council which had also laid a concrete cricket pitch. Reynolds was a fast bowler. Not just a technical distinction to distinguish him from a medium-fast or slow bowler. He was dangerously fast. He slung the ball at the batsman with the blatant intention of killing him. After an insanely long run over the gravel surface of the field he slammed his left foot against the raised ridge of the concrete strip, and with the aid of this mechanical advantage his whole body jack-knifed to the level of his knees, and he released the ball.

In the very nature of his delivery, he had little idea where the ball would go. Fielders close to the wicket raised their hands as the ball hissed through the air, not in trained readiness for an anticipated catch, but to protect themselves from his legendary wildness and frequent painful injury to those nearby.

Most of the balls he bowled roared past the batsman unseen and off target, but at least one every over was dead centre and flung the stumps in all directions with a terrifying crack. The wicketkeeper had only one proper glove, and used a thick piece of plywood, about two feet square, as the other. There had been some protest about this at first until the boys realised that if the wicketkeeper couldn't stop the ball they would lose it altogether as it rocketed out of sight to the boundary and the back gardens of distant houses, despite three long-stops strung out in a line behind the batsman.

On that day, Reynolds' team had scored thirty-two. D. was last man in as his side struggled to twenty-seven. Richard, Ginger, Jamo and Billy, the side's best batsmen, had all been clean bowled by Reynolds for ducks. As D. took up his batting pose — for his lack of skill meant it was no more than that — his own side began to drift off, certain of defeat.

As Reynolds thundered up for his first delivery, D. readied his bat, and started to swing it as the bowler's foot struck the concrete lip of the pitch. Hardly anyone saw the ball in flight, least of all D., but there was a loud click as it snicked the edge of his bat and then scorched away in a shallow arc into the distance.

'Six!' yelled the boys. 'It must be a six!'

'No,' shouted the Reynolds' team. 'It can't be. Nobody saw where it went.'

'That proves it,' said Ginger. 'If it was four we would have seen it hit the ground.'

There was no escape from this logic, and Reynolds took his team off with bad grace to search for the precious ball, amid shouts of glee from the boys. D. was a hero for all of five minutes.

When the five minutes were over, he was one of them again. Not quite the same as he had been before the coal shortage, but good enough.

Back in March, D. had turned fourteen. Most of the other boys were fourteen and fifteen. They regarded non-teenagers with contempt, and refused to include them in activities. They were growing up. Quarrels were few but feelings ran deeper. Girls took up an increasing amount of talking time, as the boys discussed the perplexing mountain of rules they would have to learn if they were to get girlfriends. The rules that parents made were increasingly irksome too, and the boys unanimously agreed that mothers were oppressive and fathers irritable and easy to anger.

At school, D. had learned a few tricks to avoid the more fearsome teachers. The best way to prevent a beating, he found, was not to attend the class. A double period of physics for example, conducted by the hair-twisting 'Windy' Lewis, was dealt with very satisfactorily by a wander around the docks, where he could see all the levers and pulleys he liked, without the troublesome arithmetic of the physics lab. As the summer term drew on he grew bolder and more selective. Maths periods were best spent skulking around the bombed ruins of the town centre, away from the hostility and physical attentions of 'Tojo' Jones, the new teacher. He was nicknamed Tojo by a wit in the sixth form, who saw the likeness of the short legged, pebble-glassed teacher to the infamous Japanese military figure of the war years.

History, or at least the history teacher, bored him to a standstill. Not that he was allowed to move. The smallest gesture of life amongst the desks aroused the immediate hostile attention of Lewis the History, who would pause in mid-sentence to intimidate any bold enough to sharpen a pencil whilst he spoke or drew one of his confusing chain-link diagrams on the blackboard. Star Chambers and Restorations remained phrases in D.'s mind forever associated with the battle against sleep whilst seated at an unyielding wooden desk, fighting the urge to move a leg to relieve pins and needles.

D. crossed history off his list of worthwhile interests, and spent the time on the beach at the Slip, the steel bridge over Oystermouth Road and the two railways of the Mumbles train and the steam train which ran to Gorseinon. There were kiosks at the Slip selling ice-cream and lemonade, and sometimes he could afford a twopenny cornet as he strolled along the water's edge, wondering about life.

Geography, conducted by Mr Davies, who pronounced Great Britain as 'Grit Brittayne', and French, by Mr 'Rubbo' Morgan, D. found enjoyable. Both teachers were enthusiastic, and believed in their subjects, and somehow found no need to defend their interest and dedication.

Playing truant and avoiding the difficult subjects of maths, chemistry and physics caused him no small degree of frustration: he was deeply interested in the real, practical world around him, yet he had given up. He had surrendered every chance of studying it. English, Geography and French were easy. He didn't have to try. He obtained consistently high marks at examinations, even though his submission of homework was rare. But what was the point of doing something he felt he knew already?

Towards the end of term, just before the year-end exams, even English lessons were sealed off. Not by the seasoned violence of the well-known, ready-fisted Praetorian Guard of long service teachers, but a newcomer.

Mr Greenaway was a rarity. Not only was his name unusual because it was not Jones, Evans, Williams, or even Davies, but his accent was non-Welsh. He wore a new suit, too, and had sparkling white teeth and used the word 'please' when instructing his pupils.

Mr Greenaway taught English, and D. settled into his lessons, and began to centre his learning interests around them. Indeed, he began to pull back slowly on other subjects as he lingered in school for his next English lesson.

His recovery fell to pieces one unsuspecting midweek afternoon at 'milktime'.

Every afternoon, every boy who so wanted received a free bottle, one-third of a pint, of milk. This milk had to be brought to every class at the appointed time from the milk room, a small washroom off the main cloakroom supervised by two stout elderly women who set out the crates of bottles ready for collection. D. was a milk monitor, an appointment based entirely on his physique, which was taller and more developed than any boy in his class. A crate of milk needed two boys from the junior classes. D. could manage one on his own.

Not every boy drank the free milk, including D., who thought it tasted awful, so he carried only twenty-four bottles as a rule, and today was no exception.

Ten minutes were allowed by the rules for drinking. An additional part of the milk monitor's duty was to take the full crate around the class of seated boys who took their entitlement, with a straw, while the lesson continued. At a signal from the teacher, the monitor collected the empties which were returned at the break later.

D. placed the crate of full bottles at the front of the classroom, near the teacher's desk, and returned to his seat, hoping he had not missed too much.

'Come and get it.'

D. stared in astonishment. Twenty-four boys hesitated as D. stood up at his desk, ready to haul the crate of bottles around the rows as was the rule. Then the storm broke. All the boys who took milk rose from their seats and dashed to the crate at the front of the room. A scene of wild confusion followed as boys grabbed bottles as though their lives depended on it, fighting each other as though some bottles of milk were better than others, or that one might be left with none.

D. stood at his desk aghast, bundle of straws in hand. And here was Mr Greenaway, literally fighting his way through the maul of scrambling boys, face pink with anger.

Mr Greenaway made no attempt to sort out the scrum around the milk crate. He made straight for D., who stood gazing at the proceedings, feeling slightly foolish.

He caught D. with a slamming open-handed slap to the side of his totally unprotected unprepared face. D. staggered from the blow, dropping the straws, his left ear singing. He suddenly felt angry. What on earth ... ?

'What was that for?' he demanded.

Mr Greenaway had gone back to his desk. 'You were grinning,' he said.

'I was not grinning,' shot back D., his voice rising as he grew angrier.

'Yes, you were.'

'I was not,' snapped D., thoroughly aroused. There was no question of using the respectful 'sir' as he spoke. He didn't even think about it. Here was a man who had just given him a shockingly hard knock to vent his anger at having made a procedural mistake in handling a class of boys. D. happened to be the nearest target.

Mr Greenaway was silent. D. still stood. The class was silent. D. glanced down at the books on his desk and made up his mind. Gathering his books he stepped into the aisle and walked to the door. There was no challenge from Mr Greenaway.

D. walked out of the classroom, angry beyond measure. He was fourteen now, not eleven. He was as tall as Mr Greenaway and he was expected to fight back against older, bigger boys who bullied him. He had just been bullied, but he was not allowed to fight back.

He stamped along the corridor, nowhere near tears, but very angry. He left the school by the teachers' door, barred to all pupils, and gave it a hearty slam as he left. He knew that would bring the headmaster to the window. Let him, thought D. Let him see me. I just don't care any more.

He crossed the road and began the trudge up Mount Pleasant Hill to the Technical College. He would wait there for the boys and go home with them. It was only an hour to wait.

* * *

He never went back to Mr Greenaway's lessons. No questions were asked. English, the only subject which flowed naturally and gave him pleasure, was closed off.

He spent the time throwing stones into the water of the fire-fighting reservoir built into the basement of the Marks & Spencer store in Oxford Street which had been destroyed by fire before the bombing of 1941. Jew-haters were responsible, it was rumoured, and there was great concern amongst the authorities until the town was engulfed by destruction on a scale that set aside the circumstances of the Marks & Spencer fire. Besides, the basement was large and central, and a simple dam wall was all that was needed to turn it into a ten feet deep pool, to fight fires that never came again to a town centre that had already been destroyed.

He got into the reservoir by squeezing through an inadequate wooden fence placed where the main store entrance had once been, facing the street. One day he was stopped halfway through the fence by a middle-aged woman laden with shopping.

'Aren't you supposed to be in school?' she asked. Not aggressive or challenging. She might have been asking him the time of day.

He stopped squeezing himself through the slim wooden slats.

'Yes,' he said, shamefacedly.

'Then what are you going down there for? You won't learn anything down there.'

'The teachers beat me,' said D. surprising himself.

'You should stand up for yourself,' said the woman. 'Have you told your parents?'

'I do stand up for myself,' said D. remembering Mr Greenaway. 'But I think the teachers hand my name around in the staff room, and they all try and have a go at me.'

He was surprised at this. He had never even considered it before. Was it possible, he wondered. Did the teachers come out of the staff room determined to teach this reportedly troublesome boy in 4d a lesson? Did they return to the staff room later to report success to their colleagues?

He stepped through the fence. The woman was no danger to him, as she had at first appeared. He walked away from her with no small embarrassment. She walked off, shaking her head.

He spent the next hour in dismal misery. He really did not know how he should behave, what to do next.

It began to rain. The reservoir was covered by the remnants of the ground floor of the remaining building, supported on pillars which receded into the murky dangerous distance of the deep, pale green water. Seated on the dam wall, unseen by the busy town, he was protected from the rain. He smoked his father's cigarettes to relieve the boredom. He struggled to analyse what was going wrong. He dreaded going home, with his mother waiting to sneer and his younger sister ready to bait and trap him, when his mother was present, into compromising behaviour which would be described as 'typical male', or 'just like a man'.

★ ★ ★

When the rain stopped he left. As he squeezed through the fence and entered the street several people looked at him in curiosity. This concerned him; he didn't want attention of any kind whilst playing truant. It could give him trouble.

At the Technical College, the boys were waiting for him. He was grateful for this. He needed any kind of friendship just now.

The sun was shining now, and it was very warm. For no particular reason they decided to walk home through Nicander Parade, where they would have some inspiring views of Swansea Bay, and talk excitedly of the coming summer holidays, making plans for days out to the beaches or into unexplored countryside.

Outside Mount Pleasant Infirmary which had been a workhouse until a few years before when the Poor Laws of 1834 had been repealed, sat two elderly men. As the boys passed, one of the men gestured. He held a bag of sweets in his hand. He was offering the boys some.

With some embarrassment the boys declined politely. They must get home, they said.

The man with the sweets was disappointed. 'What school do you boys attend?' he asked.

They told him.

The old man nodded, and thought for a while.

'I remember your school being built,' he said, pointing at D. 'It was a long time ago.' He thought a little more and then he said, 'I'm ninety-six, you know. I've been in this place — ' he jerked his thumb at the old workhouse buildings behind him — since I was fifty-two.' He paused again, and thought. The boys began to shuffle, keen to move on.

'That's the same age as my father was when I was born,' said the old man. 'He was a sailor, you see, and they married late in those days, did sailors. No life ashore for them. Not fair on their wives. Or on their children, who never saw them.' He paused for such a long time that Ginger said, 'Nice to meet you ...'

'Do you know,' interrupted the old man, 'that my father served on board a ship that took supplies to Napoleon Bonaparte when he was on St Helena.' He looked at Ginger. 'You've heard of Napoleon, haven't you?'

Ginger nodded. 'My father used to tell us about Napoleon,' went on the old man. 'How he would watch the ship arrive, and stand for hours at his window, watching the crew unload.' He paused and the boys waited. They exchanged glances. Could he be telling the truth, or was he inventing things to impress them?

'He wore a uniform,' said the old man. 'A dark green, with

epaulettes of red and gold, and gold embroidery on the cuffs. Great big badges of silver and gold, with red and white ribbons and sashes. My father said they were very valuable, and Napoleon had two men just to look after them.' He stopped, dug into the bag of sweets in his hand and put one in his mouth.

Richard said, 'We have to go now, or we'll be late for our tea.' He began to move off, and the other boys moved with him.

The old man began to speak again, but the boys had broken away now and there was no going back.

'He bit his nails badly,' said the old man. 'That's how he died, they said. Bits of nails in his stomach. Took a long time to die, he did.'

The boys moved out of earshot, but when they looked back the old man was still talking to them. They were silent, embarrassed, and filled with an emotion strange to them. None of them could name that emotion, but they all understood the old man's loneliness and isolation, and his need to talk to people. They felt sorry for him, and it was a long time before any of them spoke.

'You bite your nails, D.,' said Ginger.

D. said nothing. He did bite his nails, but he was certain he didn't swallow any. At least, he didn't feel any the worse for it.

'D'you think he was kidding us?' Richard spoke for all of them.

'Dunno,' said Billy. 'Ninety-six,' he mused. 'That's very old, isn't it? Perhaps he's daft. Napoleon's been dead a long time anyway. They had sailing ships in those days, didn't they?'

They trudged on, up the increasingly steep hill. Moriah Hall, built at a steep angle against the leaning bulge of rock cresting the hill, lay on their right. D.'s father had taken him once to the hall during the war, when he had been quartermaster sergeant of the local Home Guard. D. had helped him check and count the fuses, grenades, bullets and explosives stored there. Now it was disused, derelict and locked up, with rotting wooden shutters on the windows. It had once been a busy centre of local religious activity, attracting the consciences of a small community clawing a living from the hard hillside of 1875.

Billy picked up a stone and threw it at the chapel.

'Don't do that, Billy. What you do that for?' D. felt a sense of ownership about the old building. After all, he was the only one of them who had actually been inside it.

'So what?' said Billy. This was an Americanism, much in vogue at the time. It was an expression of defiance used in every film they saw at the local cinema, and was used often by the boys in reply to threats from bigger boys — at a safe distance. There were more advanced forms of Americanisms called wisecracks, but they were harder to invent, and anyway, D. thought some of them very childish.

'It's not doing you any harm, is it?' D. countered. He surprised himself. If ever a wisecrack came in time, that was it.

Billy shrugged, and they walked on. They were soon at Nicander Parade, and slowed their pace as they scanned the town and the sea beyond, glittering in the afternoon sun.

'Did you hear about Mary?' said Ginger.

The others looked at him blankly.

'She took her knickers down and showed the Gwili gang her fanny. One of them gave her a penny to do it under the street light by the steps.'

They were silent as they strolled along. None of them was sure that Ginger was telling the truth: as far as their experience went, girls just didn't do that sort of thing. Besides, Mary lived opposite D., and she was very pretty.

'Did she have hair on her fanny?' asked Billy. Pubic hair was an important measure of growing up.

'I dunno,' said Ginger. 'I wasn't there.'

'What else did she do?' asked D. 'I mean, where were the boys? What did they do?'

'Nothing as far as I know,' said Ginger. 'She made them stand on the other side of the street and she stood under the street lamp. She just pulled her knickers down and held her skirt up for them to see.'

'Cor!' said Richard. The others were silent. They could not imagine it.

'What was she doing out so late?' asked D. 'The street lights go on very late now. It must have been gone ten.'

None of the boys were allowed to be out on the streets after ten. Most of the girls in the street were kept indoors after sunset, whatever time that was. Darkness was considered very dangerous for the girls. The boys didn't feel all that sure of themselves, either.

'How should I know.' Ginger was nettled. 'I just told you what I heard, that's all.'

They thought some more about it as they strolled along. What strange and confusing creatures girls were.

'Do you know,' said Billy, 'that if the serial number on your bus ticket adds up to twenty-one, you can show it to a girl on the bus and you can kiss her.'

The other boys found this difficult.

'Why twenty-one?' asked D. after a while. 'I mean, it's no different to any other number, is it? Why not forty, or nineteen?'

'I don't know,' said Billy. 'It's twenty-one, that's all.'

Ginger spoke, with his voice lowered and after looking around carefully in case he was overheard. 'If a girl has a bandage around her left ankle, it means she is having periods.'

He seemed quite certain of this. It was information, not hearsay or rumour. It fell flat because none of the boys had any idea what periods were. They had all heard of them of course, but exactly what happened was a mystery that they were not allowed to investigate, and if girls wanted to advertise it by tying a bandage around their ankles, it did nothing to enlighten them.

'What are you supposed to do?' asked Richard. 'If you see one, I mean.'

Ginger thought. 'You must cross the road,' he said finally. 'Use the other pavement until she's passed.'

The thought that they had probably broken the rules of this custom many times in their ignorance caused them grave concern.

'Do the girls know?' asked Richard, 'that we're supposed to cross the road, I mean?'

'Yes, I suppose so,' said Ginger.

'What if you met one on the pavement by Moriah Hall?' asked D. 'There's only one pavement there. None on the other side.'

There seemed to be no answer to this.

'Stand in a gateway until she passed?' suggested Billy.

'Or turn around and pretend you're walking the same way,' said Richard. 'Let her overtake you, then turn back up the hill.'

'That's daft,' said D. 'I've never seen anybody do anything like that, ever.'

They walked on.

'We've got exams tomorrow,' said Richard. D.'s heart sank. He had exams the next day too. It was the first of the summer end-of-year exams which would go on for the next two weeks or so. He was ill-prepared, and was dreading them. Should he opt out, he wondered. Where would he go? The Marks & Spencer reservoir was getting risky. Perhaps he could hide in the closed-off parts of the school that had been damaged in the bombing of 1941. There had been no attempt to repair or rebuild those parts, and exploration last year had revealed a washroom with toilets, and intriguingly, a window through which he could crawl that brought him into a well underneath the pavement outside. The roof of the well was covered by boards with large gaps between them, which let through sufficient light to read by and was a good alternative place to smoke during breaktime without the perils of the main lavatories, where their activities were frequently broken up by marauding teachers. Perhaps he could persuade Ronnie and Cornelius to join him. That would make him feel better about it.

The boys ambled on. There was no hurry. Only the pressing pangs of hunger would turn them homeward eventually.

They drew level with the 'bowl', a mysterious concrete structure surrounded by ten-feet tall steel railings. The bowl was about twenty feet in diameter and filled with water of unfathomable depth. No one knew what it was for or when it had been built. There was no sign of pipes leading to or away from it, the level of water never varied, there was no animal life in it and no weeds. It was dark, still and dangerous. Boys had been tossing every manner of sinkable rubbish into it for years, and it had swallowed everything without a sign of indigestion. In recent times, one of the protective railings had been forced aside in a shallow bend, enough for a boy to push his way through to the forbidden water beyond.

Let's go and take a look at it,' said Billy. There was only mild enthusiasm. After all, there was nothing there, just water; there weren't even any stones around that they could throw in, and nothing to hand that would float, like a tin can or, best of all, an empty bottle, so that they could compete to sink it.

No sooner had they squeezed through the tall railings than a tall and hostile figure appeared. A boy of sixteen or so, large and aggressive.

'What yah doing in our pool?' he called. The boys froze. Even Ginger, who was fifteen and bigger than any of them, was silent. He, like the others, sensed trouble.

'You got no business in our pool,' the youth continued. 'It's ours. I'll teach you to stay away from it. You just try and get out, that's all. I'll keep you in there all night. I'll punch the first one who tries to get out.'

And he did. After some minutes of pretending they didn't care, Billy fearfully tried to force his way through the gap with the bent railing. He collected a bloody nose, and pulled back into the enclosure, with its narrow grass verge surrounding the concrete lip of the bowl, close to tears. 'You can't do that', he shouted, shocked and trembling. 'We have to go home,' he added, as though the youth should be impressed by this.

The youth laughed. 'Try it,' he scoffed.

With horror they saw two more local youths approach. They were even older and bigger than the first one.

'I know him,' said one, pointing at Ginger. Ginger quailed. He recognised him as someone he had taunted from a safe distance only recently.

'Where they from?' asked the second newcomer.

'Who cares?' Another Americanism, withering disregard in the words.

All three stood, hands in pockets, regarding their captives.

'Let's throw them in,' said the youngest youth.

The two older youths shrugged, silent, and continued to stare at them.

D. suddenly recognised one of them. George Haddon, who had only recently been released from Borstal. What his crime had been D. did not know, but here was an opening for a long shot.

'If you don't let us go I'll bring in the police,' he said.

The youth identified by D. looked suddenly alarmed. Only D. saw this. He was encouraged. He walked purposefully to the gap in the railings, provoking the youngest youth to stride forward aggressively.

'Leave him,' said George Haddon with authority.

The youth turned with disappointment. 'But George ... '

'Just leave him, alright?'

D. squeezed out of the railed bowl and walked carefully past these large threatening young men. After hesitation, the other boys followed, silent, the air crackling with threat and tension. Billy was the last to squirm through the railings.

The boys walked away quickly, not looking back, fearful, and wishing they could move at the speed of light away from the ugly, unknown violence.

They walked through the streets quickly and with few words. They were shaken and humiliated. They never walked home through Nicander Parade again.

* * *

The exams were a disaster. Last year he had been awarded marks in the low thirties for maths, physics and chemistry. This year he gained two marks for maths, none for physics because he didn't attend, and five for chemistry. The marks for maths were earned for putting his name and the date on the exam paper, the teacher said. Where the chemistry marks came from D. couldn't say.

Surprisingly he did well in English. Mr Cox took the exam and had set the paper, and D. came top with over ninety per cent for his marks. Mr Cox was disapproving as he announced the marks to the silent and nervous class. 'Seven per cent marks for English Grammar,' he said coldly, glaring at D. Following the ninety per cent for literature, there seemed to be a lesson here, thought D. Mr Cox shifted his buttocks on the high, hard, wooden teacher's seat.

'There is a difference between expression of English and understanding of it,' he said cuttingly. 'Boys who think they can get away with a few flowery phrases and ignore analysis are in for a rude shock.'

Parsing, identifying subjects, objects, adverbs and nouns. Ablatives, nominatives and datives. These were analysis. This was what Mr Cox and, for all that D. knew, Mr Greenaway, were keen on. Perhaps it made their easy subject appear more scientific, thought D. If English was made difficult, it would make its teachers appear more clever.

Dolefully he carried home his report, bound in the official and impressive green folder embossed with the school crest and motto in gold, telling a tale of 'Could do better' and 'Spends too much time daydreaming'. The teachers didn't pull punches. It was true that when he was in class, which by now was probably less than half the time, he did daydream. He often found himself staring fixedly at the floor in front of his desk, dreaming of a Canadian forest where he could lose himself, and be free of the barbed, vulgar antagonism of his mother and his younger sister, the violence and contempt of his teachers, and the ever-present threats of bigger boys.

He had read about the logging camps of Canada in the *Daily Express*. Canada was looking for immigrants, particularly young men, to expand its industry. The forests offered interesting possibilities, with wide-open spaces, hunting, shooting and fishing, living in log huts, and lots of friendly faces. It did get very cold though, and D. thought he might well try somewhere else first when he left school.

On the afternoon of the last day of the school year he attended the final lesson. Roberts the music was holding the final soprano and alto rehearsal for the summer concert, and D. was an alto since April when his voice had broken. Mr Roberts was in a bad mood. He smelled of beer, his tie was stained with dropped food and his wife, who played the piano as accompaniment in these later rehearsals, glared at him every time he stopped proceedings to correct a perceived fault in the boys' performance.

'Right, now,' said Mr Roberts for the tenth time. 'Let's get this right. The sopranos are coming in too soon. I keep telling you. This time wait until Mr Evans' bell end rises before coming in.'

A small snicker came from the back row. Mr Evans was the trumpet player, a friend of Roberts the music who had kindly given up an afternoon to help rehearsals. As a cue to the younger boy sopranos, he was to lift his instrument to his lips as a signal to them to start singing.

The snicker grew into a widespread giggle. One foolish alto laughed out loud. Several of the older, more scatologically knowledgeable boys trembled with suppressed mirth behind raised hands.

Mr Roberts glared.

'What on earth is the matter with you boys?'

Mrs Roberts stood up at the piano, snarled something at her beery husband and walked out of the room.

Mr Roberts failed to recover full control, and the rehearsal was abandoned and they all went home early.

★ ★ ★

The summer of 1947 did not compensate for the hard winter. It rained a lot, and although the post-war depression was over, there was still an air of hopelessness hanging over the town. The pot holes in the roads grew larger, shattered pavements disintegrated further, buddleias, nettles and giant hogweed flourished among the wreckage of the bomb sites, and many shopfronts were still plywood blanks. There was a general air of patchwork and makeshift repair, and it had gone on too long. Even the smallest sign of recovery was nowhere to be seen, everywhere settling into depressing decay while the Town Council argued the details of reconstruction.

Later that summer there was an eruption of council house building, well away from the established estates, but with the same hopeless visual offence, every street a despairing pack-of-cards sameness, every garden and boundary hedged with relentless privet, every front garden bounding the road sealed off from the pavement by cheap simulated-stone concrete blocks. Gates were made of fragile 'utility' steel tube of breathtaking thinness, carelessly welded, roughly painted, and hung by men who shrugged their shoulders, so that few would ever close properly before they fell to rusting bits in a few short years.

The houses were of two kinds: prefabs and steel. Prefabs were everything the name implied. Factory-produced of temporary war-discovered materials, they were suitable only for the shiftless burden of working class unable to discriminate between a real home and a tent. The steel houses were two-storeyed. Again a product of production-line building, they boasted a wonderful curlicue of wrought-iron (actually twisted steel bar) and cheap wood thrusters around the front door that gave a short-lived impression of advanced design thinking, a ploy to lead the eye away from the extraordinary, nasty elevation of pleated steel sheets and vulgar roughcast. A roof of asbestos sheets completed the dismal picture. Imagine row upon row of these things, sitting upon each other up the side of a sharp hill, half a mile long as you passed on the skirting road below. Inexplicably, the single-storey prefabs were sited along the lower slopes of the hill, with the two-storeyed steel houses looming over them, ranking themselves over the skyline in ugly defiance of every instinct of taste and proportion.

On their slow, wandering outings to Mumbles, D. and the boys passed the new housing development at West Cross, not far from Blackpill where D.'s Uncle Bernard and Auntie Eileen lived. The boys stopped to watch the army of workmen and machines tearing up the quiet fields laid over the steep rounded hill. Ancient hedges were being scraped up into mountains of shattered scrub and then set on fire; small streams were forced into concrete tubes and buried out of sight, and giant terraces were being carved across the swell of the hill as platforms for roads and houses.

'It'll be a nice place to live, down here near the beach,' said Ginger wistfully.

'It's not much of a beach,' said Billy. And it wasn't really. Just a short band of sand and then miles of flat, mud-slicked deposits of clay and grit dumped by the river Tawe in the bay. It was impossible to swim there unless the tide was full in and even then the water was a nasty brown murk of floating poisons. The boys had tried walking to the water's edge once when the tide was out, and then they had plodded out to sea for half an hour and never got deeper than knee high. It had taken so much time to walk out and the going was so unpleasant that they didn't try again.

'I wonder what kind of houses they will build,' said D. 'It must be nice living in your own house,' he went on. 'You can sell it and go somewhere else if you don't like it.' D. had in mind that he would dearly like to be able to say that he lived somewhere else than his present home when he was asked that ever-present question 'Where do you come from?' It would be interesting to see the reaction if he were able truthfully to say 'West Cross', the posh end of town.

'Rich people,' said Ginger. 'Only rich people can do that.'

They watched a little longer and then moved off. They still had a long way to go, and already Richard was complaining of thirst.

At Oystermouth they were chased away from the only cafe open that Saturday morning. The proprietor behind the counter eyed them up and down as they entered one behind the other, slightly overawed by the wickerwork furnishings and the glass and chrome decorations.

'What ya boys want here?' he snapped aggressively.

'Just a drink,' said D. who was first. 'We thought lemonade ... '

'Get out,' said the fat Italian owner. 'We donna want your kind here. Only gentlemen served in this cafe.' He took off his apron and raised the counter flap meaningfully.

The boys protested, more to each other than against this unexpected rule, but they turned and went out. The customers seated at the tables, all adults, gazed at them silently.

'Where can we get a drink from?' asked Billy. 'I don't know anywhere around here.'

'The pier is the only place,' said Richard. 'I don't know if any of the kiosks are open, though. The pier is still closed.'

And it was. Although it had been closed off in the invasion scare of June 1940, no attempt had been made to restore the large slab cut out of it at that time, and it all seemed too much to repair it. Nor were any of the kiosks around the headland open. The boys trudged along the coast road, eyeing the breaking surf of Bracelet Bay, studying the rocks and cliffside pathways for further investigation, growing despondent as they grew hungrier and thirstier and their distance from home grew.

They eventually found a small kiosk at Limeslade Bay that was selling pots of tea and ice-cream. The woman behind the counter flap glared at them as they approached.

'No teas for you lot,' she said. 'I don't trust your kind with my china. You'll break it. I know you.'

Ginger shrugged. 'How much is the ice-cream?' he asked. They couldn't afford the tea, anyway. It started at one and six for a pot for four people.

'Tuppence for cones. Sixpence for wafers.'

The boys held a conference. None of them had enough to buy a wafer for himself. None of them wanted to spend nearly all his money on a cone, either. In the end they bought two cones, and carried them away to a grassy embankment overlooking the beach, where they would divide them into four by breaking off the bottom halves of the cones and filling them with ice-cream from the top halves.

There was playful joshing and complaint as those who got the bottom half protested at less than half share of the ice-cream, but at the end they had all had a decent lick for only a penny each, and they were quite happy with this.

The sea muttered in the background, the sun was warm and they were tired. They sat on the grass bank and idly considered what to do next.

'Where are you lads from, then, eh?'

The boys spun around. Behind them stood a huge policeman, feet astride, hands behind his back, clearly there to stay until he got answers.

The boys were silent as they scrambled to their feet. No one tangled with a policeman, least of all teenage boys far from home and with not enough money for the bus fare.

'Mayhill,' said Ginger.

'Hmm.' The policeman stood, silent, sizing them up. The boys stood, fearfully, wondering what he would do.

'I thought I didn't recognise any of you,' he said finally. 'Now you boys get off home, before you get up to mischief. If you're here when I come around again, I'll run you in, understand?'

'But we haven't done anything,' said Ginger bravely. The boys looked at him with a mixture of admiration and concern. If he made too much of a fuss, would he land all of them in trouble?

The policeman took a step forward. 'Don't you give me any cheek, boy.' His voice rising, his face coloured and he moved his hands from behind his back to hang, threateningly ready, at his sides.

'Now, off with you. Get going.' He raised his right hand to point generally in the direction of Mayhill, some four miles distant.

The boys got going. After a while they looked back to see what the policeman was doing. He was chatting to the woman at the kiosk, and both of them were looking hard at the boys, nodding and agreeing with each other.

'It's not right,' said Ginger. 'We weren't doing anything. We've got a right to go to the beach if we want to.'

The other boys agreed, and they walked on out of sight.

On their return journey, well into the afternoon, they were so hungry that they pooled their cash to buy a small loaf from a bakery near the General Hospital in St Helen's Road.

'Just one of us had better get it,' said Richard. He didn't need to explain why. Ginger volunteered. The rest were glad: the baker's shop wasn't too far away from the tobacconist who had chased them away not so long ago.

They shared the loaf by tearing it to pieces in a free-for-all. The soggy insides fell to the ground as they fought for the crusty bits and was abandoned until a watching woman called out to them about wasting good food.

'You ought to be ashamed of yourselves,' she shouted. 'Throwing away good bread like that. And making a mess on the road, too.'

'Ah, sharrup,' yelled Ginger, exasperated.

A man appeared at the doorway beside the woman, and the boys ran like hell.

Climbing the hill that led to home, they paused and rested their elbows on a low stone wall overlooking a steep rock slope. Back gardens lay at the foot of the slope, and houses not far away. The boys looked down at the roofs a hundred feet below and mused.

'I wouldn't like to live there,' said Billy. 'Just think. This cliff hanging over you all the time.'

'You could smash things if you threw a stone down there,' said Ginger.

'You wouldn't have to throw it,' said D. 'You could just roll a big boulder. Drop it over the wall.'

'What you want to do that for?' asked Richard. 'You'd get into big trouble if you did that.'

'I know, I know,' said D. impatiently. 'I just said ...'

'Right. Got you now haven't I?' The boys turned, alarmed. An angry man strode the last few closing steps towards them, plainly intent on violence.

The boys scattered, Ginger and Billy dashing back down the hill, the other two haring off up the steep lane away from the wall.

'I know you,' shouted the man. He was fat and short in the leg and wore slippers, and sensibly chose not to chase any of them.

'I know you, and where you live. I know you're the boys who've been throwing stones over the wall. I'm going to get the police now.'

This transparent bluff calmed the boys. They had been severely frightened by his appearance, but now in relief from shock they laughed. He couldn't possibly know them or where they lived. They had never been this way before, and they were still over a mile from home, a lot of streets and boys away.

They were soon reunited, and they continued their plod homeward. They planned their route carefully, avoiding known hostile gang areas, walking fast and silently past street junctions where territories merged, making detours and taking short cuts, always vigilant for possible danger. Only the previous week Tiddler Davies had been soundly beaten and held captive for an hour, threatened, frightened and terrorised by three older boys of the Gwili gang. He had told the boys about it when the gang finally let him go, and they showed their support and friendship by promising terrible revenge, but in the end they didn't do anything. The incident had sharpened their caution though, and they took no risks as they drew near to home.

D.'s mother glared at him as he entered the kitchen. 'I suppose you want feeding now,' she snapped. 'We've all had our tea. Why don't you come home on time?' Her eye fell on his swimming gear — trunks wrapped up in a tightly wound towel and tied with string to loop over a shoulder.

'That's dry,' she accused. 'You haven't been swimming. So where have you been, eh?'

'The tide was out,' said D. He didn't want to, nor could he have fully explained, how the zest of the day had been drawn from them, their enthusiasm drained by a series of disagreeable events.

'You're lying,' said his mother. 'You said you were going to Mumbles. It doesn't matter if the tide is out there. It only goes out a few yards.' She sneered at him. 'Frightened of the water, were you? Too cold for you? Typical boy. The girls would have gone in soon enough. But of course you didn't want girls with you. You wouldn't take them. Always thinking of yourself. Typical. Just like men.'

She cooked him beans on toast. He had to do the toast himself by the opened door of the stove, and keep an eye on the beans heating up on the gas ring.

'Can I have an egg, Mam?' he ventured.

'No. You're too late. Beans on toast is all we had, so why should you get more, greedy? Fill up with bread and butter.'

Silently he toasted his slice of bread, impaled on the end of a piece of soft wire that his father had fashioned into a 'toasting fork'. The wire slowly sagged as he held it to the feeble glow at the firebars, so that it had to be repeatedly reversed to restore its best position. In the end, D. decided to push the prongs right through the bread and rest them on the firebars. That way the bread was steady.

'Don't do that,' his mother snapped and prodded his thigh with her foot. 'You'll spoil the fork. Do it properly.'

He complied, mystified.

'And don't you butter any bread yourself. I'll do it. We're still rationed, in case you've forgotten. Not that you've ever noticed, greedy.'

He ate his beans on toast and felt even hungrier afterwards. He considered bread and butter but rejected the idea. The butter would be so thinly spread that he might not be able to finish it. And that would annoy his mother.

He made himself a cup of tea and drank it outside on the back doorstep.

199

His mother came to the back door. 'What's this?' she snapped. She held his soiled plate which he had left on the table.

'Dirty plate. It wants washing up, donnit? Or is it an octipal delusion?'

Octipal delusion? D. frantically recycled the words, searching for meaning.

'Optical illusion?'

'I know what I'm saying, smart bugger. If only you'd be half as bloody clever at school you'd get somewhere. And don't you dare correct me. I'm your mother.'

He took the plate from her, went inside and washed it. His mother muttered angrily in the background.

D. went out into the soft summer evening and sat on Jamo's wall to talk with the boys. As the light faded, more boys joined them, and some of the girls. When the street lights went on there were about twenty of them, and they made their own fun. They played leap-frog, touch, hide and seek in neighbours' front gardens — avoiding Mr Horner — and step and watch. A lot of the games broke up in confusion as the girls claimed exemption from some of the more exacting rules, and there was fun and laughter and good natured joshing until mothers began to appear at gateways, calling first daughters and then sons, to supper and bed.

There was finally a hard core left, all boys, sitting around their territorial street lamp, smoking tiny bits of shared cigarettes. Quietly they sang harmonised popular songs of the time, learned quickly and easily from cinema and radio, and talked in hushed whispers about girls.

'What about this artificial insemination,' posed Jamo, the oldest boy there.

The others were silent. The thought seemed an assault on their budding masculinity.

'Not all women will want it that way though,' said Ginger.

They pondered, and the implications were beyond them. The boys found girls attractive and mysteriously interesting for what they were — girls. Different, pretty, forbidden, and contemptuous of boys. There were compulsions they did not understand and found difficult to control, and found confidence and reassurance in sharing their puzzlement with each other.

In the end the discussion fizzled out from sheer lack of knowledge and understanding, and they turned to easier things.

'Do you know what my father said to me yesterday?' challenged Ginger.

'Your arse isn't your own. He bought it second-hand in the market when you were a baby,' sniggered Billy, moving away fast.

'Naw, stupid. He said I couldn't guide my doodle straight. There were pee spots on the lavatory floor. But I said it was Richard's pee, not mine.'

The boys laughed. They all knew that Ginger had a huge doodle, because he had showed them once and they had been amazed by the size of it. At a contest that summer amongst the dunes and sandy brush of Brynmill beach he had hung three wet towels on his erect dong, beating all the other boys to a hollow. All they could manage from their erected hangers was one dry towel. If anyone was going to miss the bowl, it would be Ginger.

One by one the boys were called home, and the day faded into the next. The July night sparkled with clean stars and blue-black night between the sparse yellow street lamps, with a warm, scent-laden, gusting breeze holding promise of a good day to follow.

* * *

In September, D.'s father announced importantly that he was to have three days fewer holidays this year. This was because he had taken that number of days off in the winter, during the fierce snowfalls of the long cold snap. 'Have to do the right thing, you see. The office gave me time off when I wanted it, so I have to give it back.'

* * *

When he returned to school at the end of the holidays, D. was kept back a year, and not allowed to go forward to the fifth form. He hardly noticed. By now, school work meant nothing to him. He had no ambition outside school either, which made matters difficult with both his father and mother.

His father was stern, distant and disapproving. His mother sneered and was contemptuous.

'You were in the Fourth form last year,' she said in pretended puzzlement. 'Why are you still in the Fourth this year?'

She waited for an explanation, but D. was unable to give one. He did not, in fact, grasp the significance of it. In later years he might reflect that the teachers kept some kind of faith with him and had given him a second chance. Of course they had no cause to expel him, which was the only way they could officially show him the door — but he was gone fourteen years old, and boys of his age who had

201

not gained the selective luxury of a Grammar school were at work earning their keep. A pupil of such low performance and negligible output must have been frustrating.

By his fifteenth birthday, in the early spring of 1948, D.'s father had put forward the idea of a job in the newly-formed National Coal Board. The Labour government elected in 1945 with such national conviction was sweeping the country with social reform, and every capital-hungry industry was being nationalised. The slogan was public ownership, 'everyone owns it now'. The results were only partly successful, but the changes were earth-shaking. Administration of single, country-wide industries spawned swarming armies of clerks and management structures set in rigid promotion chains, new Ministries and officialism, and breathtaking form-filling. It was a popular conception that the purchasing power of the pound sterling had been replaced by its own weight in authorising signatures.

Chapter Eleven

Early in April D.'s father told the family that they were all to move house.

'Where, Dad?' was the cry. 'Tell us where?' None of them asked what kind of house they might move to. There could be no reduction to their present circumstances that they could imagine.

'West Cross,' he told them, with a secret smile that hinted at special efforts conducted on their behalf in modest silence.

D. thought of the mauling works that he had seen with the boys last summer, and particularly of Ginger's words about the beach nearby.

'When do we go, when do we go?' was the chorus.

'Soon. D. and I will go this afternoon to check up on the house, see that everything is ready, and then we'll be off next week.'

There was excitement and sadness. D. learned that, as far as anyone knew, no one else in the street was moving house with them. He would lose his friends.

That afternoon he set out with his father on a two-bus journey to their new house. As he stepped off the second bus, D. viewed the dismal terraces of prefabs and steel houses, his heart sinking.

'Are we moving into those?' he asked. 'Not those prefabs? They look horrible.'

'His father maintained a secret smile, and ploughed up the hill, passing the prefabs to the two-storeyed metal-clad houses above.

Number 8 was roomy, spacious and airy. The ceilings were higher, the windows larger, the rooms bigger, the doors had handles instead of knobs, there were built-in cupboards in the kitchen and a real gas cooker with four burners, as well as a fire in the living room. There was even a radiator in the dining room, and others in the two main bedrooms. This was different. The walls were of plasterboard, and perilously thin, but, as his father pointed out, nobody walked on walls. Besides, they now had a hallway, to walk past the stairs into the house proper, where there was a space to receive visitors under a rose-coloured light before they were shown into the 'lounge'.

The lounge had a huge window covering most of the wall facing the street, and it stretched almost from floor to ceiling. It was strikingly different from their present house on the hill.

The garden ran away steeply from the house, and was virgin sheep-grazing hillside where no man had turned a spade. D.'s father was a little depressed by this, but soon forgot it in his enthusiasm for the house itself.

D. was dispatched to collect the keys, plugs for the bath and wash basin, and the only doorknob in the house, that from the back door.

D. didn't get them. The Clerk of Works, sitting on a beer crate in a tin shed surrounded by tea-making gear and stacked boxes of sink plugs and doorknobs, told him to clear off.

'How do I know who you are?' snarled the Clerk, his voice rising with accusation. 'You could be anybody. You can't just come up to me and ask for things just like that. I need signatures. Authority.'

D. could have kicked him. He was big enough.

His father was exasperated. 'Can't you do anything right?' he snapped bad-temperedly. 'If you want anything done you have to do it yourself.' He strode off, leaving D. to explore the house.

He felt neutral about it. Whilst the house was definitely an improvement, and the surrounding area hugely more interesting, he would be losing the view from his bedroom window, which gave him so much pleasure. In the new house, the small third bedroom was tiny, and looked on to the street and houses opposite. The large bedroom was at the back, overlooking the sea. That would be his parents' room. His sisters would share an equally large room facing the street, like his.

They returned to the waiting family in Mayhill, his father clutching a newspaper-wrapped bundle of accoutrements released on proper authority by the Clerk of Works at West Cross.

The family moved house a week later. When they took up residence there were no neighbours, and D. felt very superior to the first of those who moved in nearby. Everyone settled in very quickly, and the awful bare-brick kitchen with adjoining lavatory in Mayhill was quickly forgotten. He went exploring, and found not far away real woods, a small forest with no defined pathways, and with a slow-flowing stream, at least a foot deep in parts, flowing through it. There were frogs in it, and in the occasional pools, sticklebacks and silverback beetles. It was heaven. The ferns were head-high, and the bramble thickets were impenetrable, with no sign of human onslaught. There were trees to climb, unwatched by disapproving adults, birds' nests to peer into, dams to build across the stream, strange burrowed holes to speculate on, tunnels in the grass to follow with a pointed forefinger, quick rustling sounds to turn a head to, and tracks with strange pawprints to wonder at.

* * *

Two weeks later he left school to start work at his first job. He never went back to the woods.

* * *

He made a poor start at work. As the office junior his duties consisted mainly of taking messages and distribution of mail, and, in the evenings, packing mail into envelopes, sticking stamps on them and taking them to the the post office. On his first day he hadn't grasped that although everyone else had left for home, he was expected to stay until the product of their labours that day had been sent off. Next day his immediate boss, mentor and teacher, a huge, bulky, clumsy clerk with an awkward German name who spoke fluent Welsh, bawled him out for 'dereliction of duty'. The clerk had been in the Army previously, and it had so impressed and influenced him that he saw everything in terms of duty and rank order. D. was to learn that this man was treacherous, and besotted by 'correctness'. His writing hand was laborious, careful and characterless, and he resorted to printing in capital letters whenever he could, as though joined-up writing had come to him late. Moreover, his lips moved as he wrote.

His name was Stanley, and he refused to answer to 'Stan'. His face was 'un-British', with sallow thick skin pitted with pink scars. He had jowls, though he was only twenty-four, and walked awkwardly as though his huge shoulders gave his ankles trouble.

He was pally with Ken, who was only slightly shorter but had the same bulky shoulders. Ken was twenty-eight, unmarried, and had whiskers so high on his cheeks that they looked like extra eyelashes. He said he had been a rear-gunner on Lancasters in the war, and wore faded green sports jackets to the office with leather bits at the elbows and cuffs like some of the teachers in D.'s school. He had huge dark sweat patches under his armpits and smelled curiously like a wet wickerwork basket. Ken claimed to have taught Stanley 'all he knows', though D. would never learn what this amounted to, since all he ever saw Stanley do was to pack little parcels in the stationery store with sellotape, pencils and canary seed to send off to colliery storekeepers.

There were nearly thirty people in the office at number 45 Wind Street. Most of them were 'out of town' staff who had worked at local coal mine offices before nationalisation. Now they were gathered under one roof to do the same job, and travelled long distances to work. Only a few were Swansea locals, the bulk of the staff being Welsh-speakers from the Carmarthenshire coalfield, mainly around Ammanford.

Apart from Stanley they were very friendly, D. found, much to his surprise. And much to his confusion he found the friendliness difficult to deal with, especially when it came to the girls.

Roughly half the office strength was female. They were all typists or secretaries. The men were clerks of varying grades and degrees, and in charge of everything. The women ranged from their early thirties to late teens, while the men were a lot older and mostly married. Only two of the women were married, and one was the top manager's secretary. She treated D. with silent disdain and never spoke to him directly, but sent Marion, her deputy, with messages now and again.

Meeting Marion was a turning point in his life, though he did not see it like that at the time. She was twenty-one, the daughter of the manager of one of the biggest mines in the area and thus treated with some wariness by everyone in the office. She was bony, small, and her face was shiny with cleanliness from plain soap and water. Her hair was black, straight and short, her hands slim and fragile like her figure, and the only make-up she wore was bright red lipstick on her thin hard lips, ill at ease with her piercing blue eyes.

On his second day at his new job, Marion threw her arms around him in the privacy of the postroom.

D. recoiled in horror. He couldn't say why he experienced fear rather than the sensual excitement plainly expected of him as she pushed her pelvis into his genital area, pressing her small, tight breasts into his chest. He was a good deal taller than her. Even at just gone fifteen he was already five feet ten inches, and she was probably seven or eight inches shorter than that. She stood on tiptoe to press her belly into his, and he was appalled.

It could have been the explosive effect of bright, new, surprised hormones, though he didn't know about these at the time.

He was unhinged with embarrassment, and in panic as he felt an erection gallop out of control, he thrust her roughly away. His face scarlet he stuttered, 'What do you want?'.

She dropped her arms and smiled knowingly. She stepped back and smirked, 'Afraid of girls, are you? Or are you one of "them"?'

He had no idea what she meant by 'one of them', but he was glad enough that she was keeping her distance. He tried to turn away from her, fearful that his erection might show. His mother still did not approve of underpants, which might have helped to conceal his mortification.

She didn't want anything really. She turned and went out of the postroom and he didn't see her again that morning.

Glenys worked in a small office of her own on the second floor of the three-storeyed building. D. wasn't sure whose secretary she was. She was older than most of the other girls, and not very good looking. She used a lot of powder on her face and very little else. She wore very large glasses which emphasised big brown eyes, and she was soft-spoken and smiled a lot.

Glenys kept a lot of files in a row of boxes stacked on a shelf high on the wall, above door height. On the afternoon of his second day she telephoned him at the postroom and asked him to help with the files.

'Use this chair,' she said. 'I want that one, and that ...' She pointed and he did as she bid.

Reaching for the second boxfile he was struck rigid as he felt her hand clutch his buttock.

'Nice bum you've got, D.,' said Glenys softly.

He tried to ignore it, in a panic for the second time that day. What should he do? What would the men in the office do? What did Glenys expect him to do?

Giving his bum a pat with her hand she took the boxfile he handed to her. Blushing furiously he stepped off the chair and hesitated as he wondered what else she might want of him.

'I need these boxfiles quite often, D. They're hard for me to reach up there. You don't mind getting them for me, do you?'

D. shook his head. 'No, I don't mind,' he said, desperately anxious to get away. She smiled at him warmly as he backed out of the room.

Barbara was the daughter of the deputy boss. She was nineteen, the youngest of all the girls in the office, and she bore a remarkable resemblance to one of D.'s pet rabbits. She had a long sloping nose, emphasised by drawn-back blonde hair, which appeared to have a life of its own. D. found that if he watched it carefully when she was not looking at him, her nose twitched.

Barbara also had large pointed breasts, which to D.'s huge embarrassment she would rest on his forearm as she explained where her recently typed letters were to go. He tried backing away, but she followed him, and taking a deep breath which raised up her chest, she would rest them afresh on his arm. He felt the soft weight of them, especially the one that came to rest on his wrist and thumb, and was reminded of his Aunt Eileen who had hauled out an enormous white football from her blouse to breastfeed his new-born cousin at the tea-table. D.'s mother had been appalled, and talked about it in hushed tones to his father even now, five years later.

Barbara's breasts seemed to be everywhere that he moved, and he was reduced to stuttering confusion when he unwisely dropped them off his bent arm and turned to face her. His hands, and the papers he held in them, were instantly enveloped in soft cotton-covered flesh as she pressed forward at him.

He was saved on this occasion by Stanley, who lumbered into the postroom, arms dangling like a chimpanzee, frowning in disapproval at what he saw and beckoning to D. to follow him.

'Switchboard,' said Stanley. 'You must learn how to operate it to relieve Olwen for breaks and for lunchtimes.' He clumped down the brass-tipped staircase to the ground floor, which housed the stationery store where Stanley spent so much time, and the reception office and switchboard.

Olwen was a Swansea woman, in her early thirties and married to a plainclothes detective, a huge man with a rubbery red face who totally ignored D. whenever they met. Olwen was cold, hostile and disapproving. She reminded D. of his mother. The cubicle that housed the switchboard was tiny and cramped, with only the small swivel chair of the operator to sit on.

'I'll leave him with you, Olwen,' said Stanley in a fed-up voice, and went off. D. stood self-consciously as Olwen looked him up and down.

Finally she said, 'Sit here. I'll show you what to do.'

She got up from the swivel chair and squeezed past him. She smelled of cornflakes.

D. sat in front of the switchboard. It was as big as the upright piano at home, with as many bits to poke and press. Olwen stood close and bent over him, explaining the machine.

'It's awkward like this,' she said finally. 'My neck is starting to ache, standing here in this position.' She sat on his knee. She was quite a small woman, and he felt no physical discomfort as he took her weight. She took his right hand and guided it to the various switches and knobs as incoming calls were dealt with. She moved from one knee to two and he was obliged to put his left arm around her waist to steady her as she held his right hand over the plugs.

D. perspired freely, and by the time the lesson was over and she had clambered off his knees, he was in a deep panic. He had learned nothing about the switchboard. His main concern was how to avoid it in future.

'You've done very well,' said Olwen, in a detached voice. She had prominent eyes and a halo of tight, hard-looking blonde curls. She wore no make-up, and her puffy face shone like Marian's. Her eyes were a cold, neutral grey. 'Come down tomorrow at the same time,' she said. 'We'll have another lesson.'

* * *

By Friday the end of his first week D. was a severely disturbed fifteen-year-old. He had developed blushing shyness and a low-voiced stutter. He had grown a deep dread of entering the typing pool, where five girls sat at their machines grinding out the business of the office. It was a large room, only half of it occupied by the girls, the other half by wall-to-wall, floor-to-ceiling shelves of files and the copying machine. Since the office thrived on statistics, returns, analyses and submission of endless facts and figures to Divisional, Group and Head Offices of the structured reporting layers of the nationalised industry, the copying machine was heavily used to produce masses of blank forms, to be sent out to the forty or so collieries in the Area.

It was part of D.'s duties to operate the copier. He hated it as soon as Stanley introduced him to it. For a start, every girl in the room stopped work to watch him. Blushing furiously on his first lesson from Stanley, he tried turning his back on the girls, but he still felt hot, and perspired freely. And the machine was a pig. It was messy and temperamental. Moreover, anyone could use it at any time, and usually left it in a state that was deemed suitable for D. to clean up, much as the chore of washing up the lunchtime dishes might be for the maid.

He never really mastered the machine, though this was more due to his constant anxiety at being in the room with the girls watching him than his lack of skill. He felt a desperate need to get out of the room as soon as he had entered it. He never thought to ask himself why.

He began to develop a slow, unreasoned, unreasonable and confused resentment of the girls who were causing him such anguish and blushing misery.

He finished his first week in a state of exhaustion. As he sat in the Mumbles train on his way home he scarcely considered the turn of events that had taken him from Mayhill roughness to a bright new home by the sea, and from dismal school failure to a job in town. In his pocket was his first pay packet, one pound fifteen shillings and sevenpence, after stoppages of tax. Not much more than his elder sister's first week's wages, which their mother had pinned to the pantry door: it was exactly one pound. Now Jean earned more than two pounds a week.

D.'s mother held her hand out as soon as he got home. Humourlessly she demanded his pay. 'I hope you haven't opened the envelope,' she said. 'I want to see what it is. And to count it.'

He handed it over. He had been warned that morning before leaving for work not to open the pay envelope.

She took it from him, opened it, and counted it carefully, comparing the total with the figures written on the outside. She took some coins and handed them to him.

'That's your allowance,' she said. 'When you get a rise you'll get more. But for now you'll manage on that.'

He looked at the two half-crowns in the palm of his hand. Five shillings. He put them in his pocket and walked outside, saying nothing but furiously working away at mental arithmetic. The train fare to work was eightpence return a day. That was three shillings and fourpence a week. That left one shilling and eightpence a week, or fourpence a day. From that he must buy lunch every day, and he knew that the cheapest lunch around was in Cascarini's, a few doors away from the office, which was beans on toast at one shilling and fourpence. Lots of the Ammanford girls ate this, and claimed the two shillings and sixpence allowance that they were given to compensate them for having to move to Swansea to work.

He bought ten cigarettes instead. They didn't last a full week, but he could raid his father's cigarette case to help out.

He lost weight steadily over the months as he went without food at midday. Aunt Eileen paid a visit once, and as usual greeted him warmly. He blushed and confusedly returned her greeting.

'Doris! He's so thin. What are you feeding him on?' His aunt turned in half rebuke to his mother.

'Oh, don't worry,' said his mother, annoyed. D. felt quite guilty. 'He'll fill out when he gets older. Boys of his age always look thin.'

He had tried to take sandwiches to work, but he was not allowed to use the cheese. 'That's for your father,' he was told. 'And I want to know exactly how much bread is here, so I don't want you helping yourself. Your father would be very angry if there was no bread for his sandwiches.'

Mealtimes in the new house were wonderfully different from the old one. There was a separate dining room, with superb views out to sea across Mumbles Head, and the window of the room was huge, letting in the day directly over the table. Saturday lunches were a treat, all the family squeezed around the oak table, eating a wild mixture of bacon, egg, sausage, cockles, lavabread and tomatoes with lashings of tomato ketchup and sometimes pickled onions. The only sour note was if D.'s mother made hissing remarks about 'people just sitting there, waiting to be fed'.

On Sunday mornings the whole family set out for mass at 9:30 in Nazareth House, which had a small church used by the nuns of the House and, in summer, by holiday visitors to Gower.

Nazareth House was a mixture of orphanage and old people's home. It was run by the Sisters of Nazareth, hard-working nuns who seemed to D. to be in a state of perpetual anxiety and never-ending poverty.

The House stood incongruously isolated on what must have been the last safe piece of ground for building before the bog and brush of Bishopston Common took over. It was about two miles from their house at West Cross, and most of the way was an open road without pavement or protection from weather. It was an uplifting journey on a fine summer morning, but was a pig in winter.

Sunday lunches were a bore. D.'s father became officious and formal, insisting on a ceremonial seating of all the family before he carved the joint importantly and in silence. Grace was said with clasped hands and downcast eyes, and everyone kept still until D.'s father cleared his throat and said gruffly, 'Right. Go ahead, Doll.' Whereupon D.'s mother would start to fill plates.

The lunch was invariably roast beef and vegetables, which D. had come to loathe. The meal was eaten in formal silence, and no one was allowed to finish before anyone else, a tricky thing for D. when he was hungry, which was often.

The ice-cream van came at two o'clock, sounding its chimes to attract attention. As if it was a Pavlovian trigger, D.'s father would shout 'Give the kids some money for ice-cream, Doll. And come in and have it, or it will get cold.' With a wide smile at his own joke, he would reseat himself at the table to await the ice-cream. D. began to dread the sound of the chimes on Sundays as week after week his father cracked the same joke, wore the same smirk, looked around at his family for the same approval. He even began to sing loudly to drown his father's voice, at least from his own ears, until he was told off for 'spoiling his father's joke'.

They no longer had to go to Sunday School in the afternoon. D.'s father still retired to bed after lunch as he had always done, and sometimes enquired, 'You coming, Doll?' with a note of hope in his voice. Every week he asked her. Every week she snapped, 'No. I've got too much to do. You go up on your own.' D. could not understand his father's dejected look at this reply, and it was only many years later that he understood.

The Sunday afternoon sleep was a hangover from the not-so-distant twelve-hour, six-day weeks of the men who had formed the background of his father's young life, shaping habits like drinking tea from his saucer, and keeping chamber pots in the bedrooms of a home that had an indoor lavatory; the sleep was a luxury which would have lasted them through another slogging week of long days and short nights.

Sometimes when the weather was fine that summer of 1948, D. could escape to the beach, and once or twice he walked to Mumbles. But it was no fun. He was lonely. He badly missed the boys from the street, and the boys at school. There were one or two boys his own age around, but despite attempts to strike up a friendship they remained strangers. Disconsolately he watched other groups of young people at play, on the beach or around small boats, sometimes with girls with them laughing and squealing as the boys clowned around.

So he walked around places that a few years before had meant excitement and happy hours of play on a day out with his parents. In those days a trip on the Mumbles train had been an experience in itself, loaded with promise for the rest of the day to come. Now he travelled on it every working day and disliked it: it was slow, and the conductors were impatient, bad tempered and demanding. The ticket inspectors especially were oppressive and bullying and always seemed to be on the train that D. was on. The only pleasant inspector was Harry Secombe's uncle, but then, he had a family connection to honour.

At the beginning of August Nazareth House held a fête and gala in an adjoining sportsfield. It was a jolly occasion, and was one of a long line of successes organised by the Catholic community from all over the town. D.'s father was heavily involved, particularly in the financial reckonings. He was much sought after on the big day, and D. admired his grasp of detail and the matter-of-fact democratic way that he dealt with every emergency and hundreds of queries and requests for help.

Things were different afterwards, at home. D.'s father came home late, exhausted and tetchy, carrying bundles of paperwork and odd packets of money. In a flimsy bag he would have hundreds of pounds in notes, whilst back at Nazareth House were hundreds more in coin, all counted, bagged and recorded. Next day after tea, he took over the dining room table, spread out his ruled and lined sheets of paper and began to cast what he called the trial balance.

It was a nervous time for everybody. No one was allowed into the dining room, no matter what. In the other house the parlour had served as his accounting house, and even the children's bedtime would be held back until their father had finished his book-keeping to his satisfaction. The parlour lay between the kitchen and the stairs to the bedrooms. In the new house there was access to other parts of the house without breaching the room where he worked. Even so, D. and his sisters were cautioned to silence.

Late in the evening D.'s father would emerge, quiet satisfaction on his face. He had balanced the books.

'Cuppa tea, Doll.'

'Finished?' D.'s mother asked, an adoring look in her eyes. Her husband was a clever man.

'Yep.' He would go on to explain the technicalities of a hitch in the bottle-stall account as the kettle boiled, she nodding in sympathy at the complexity of it all, understanding nothing. He was such a clever man. He basked in her wonderment and the house relaxed.

This routine would go on for years. There would come the time when D. was allowed to count the coins after the fête and gala had closed, but then only the threepenny pieces — the large twelve-sided ones that could be double-checked. He would be in his twenties then.

At the end of August D. took four days holiday, which was his entitlement for the part year he had worked. He was paid his normal full weekly pay for that week, which surprised him. The boys in the street in Mayhill who were working were not paid during their holidays. Siwni Hughes for instance, who had been working for a full year, had to give up a week of holiday because he could not afford to be away from work. When D. pointed this out to his father, he was told that it was one of the advantages of working in an office. Other benefits were the indoor life in winter and clean clothes. 'They'd all work in offices if they could,' his father said. 'So be grateful for the start in life which you've got.'

He tried his best. He felt utterly lost in the busy life of the office, and when Stanley introduced him to even more offices, which were much bigger and with many more people, he felt despair. These other offices were a short walk away near the docks, and housed the

Finance and Administration departments. It was D.'s job to carry letters and files on a once-a-day trip to these places, and to deliver them to named individuals on various floors. It took him months to learn even the regulars, and he found it a huge task to knock on doors, enquire with painful shyness where a person was to be found, and then to make the delivery. Some of the people were not helpful. There were several office boys, his counterparts, in these offices, and they played tricks on him by sending him to unlikely places. Though D. took it in good part, he didn't make friends with any of them.

On one of his journeys he met G.B. Jones. G.B. Jones had been his father's boss until he had left the private company to join the new National Coal Board.

G.B. Jones was held in great awe by D.'s father, and his name was frequently on his lips at home. D. had imagined him to be large and imposing, and to wear a stiff collar like Neville Chamberlain, but he was none of these. He was a very short man who wore a bright tie and a light-coloured suit. Though his face was pugnacious and tough, D. felt himself at ease for the first time in weeks as G.B. Jones' soft, friendly tones asked him how he was settling in.

'Very well, thank you sir' said D., with respect.

'Oh, you mustn't call me sir,' said G.B. Jones. 'You might have fifty years ago, but not today. You keep that for the army. And that will come soon enough.'

He chatted for a few minutes and then left. As he walked away D. felt positively uplifted by the encounter. How lucky his father had been, thought D., to have had G.B. Jones as his boss for so many years. At the Wind Street office, D.'s ultimate boss was H.B. Davies, referred to as H.B. He took his part seriously, and dressed in a black frock coat and pinstripe trousers. He always carried a briefcase and umbrella.

H.B. spat a lot and had a spittoon hidden behind his desk. His office was enormous, and D. wondered what he did with it. H.B. was old and stooped and was bad tempered. His face sagged, and his lower lip was large, wide, loose and always wet. D. did not like him one little bit and was glad he didn't see much of him.

Some of the men in the office treated him well. Mervyn, who came from Neath, was a cheerful, slightly-built man who always looked very clean. He wore glasses, and listened to the same kind of music programmes on radio as D. He talked to D. in a friendly way, and didn't patronise him like some of the others.

Will Rees came from Llanelli. He was very short and built like a barrel, with no fat on him. As a fellow-lover of good music he often talked to D. about forthcoming events, and the previous evening's Prom concert. Will was placid and easy-going and talked to D. as an equal, and D. felt at ease in his company. There was another side to Will, though. He shared an office with small Stan, a man of permanent scowling features, who was badly shaven, scruffy and untidy. Small Stan was no taller than Will and about half his width all around. Will and small Stan didn't get along. In their shared office at the end of the corridor they quarrelled, shouting and screaming at one another at the tops of their voices, four-letter words and old Army language ringing through the whole building. D. listened nervously, appalled by the crudity and wildness of it.

He supposed that one of the managers would put a stop to it, or that the women would complain, but everyone ignored it. Indeed, when he asked Stanley about it, he was ticked off.

'What do you mean, shouting?'

'Well,' said D., floundering. 'Swearing at each other. Shouting.'

'Imagination,' said Stanley, in a tone that told D. he didn't want to talk about it.

'But Will was threatening to kill Stan,' said D.

'Don't you worry about it then. You just stay clear. It's nothing to do with you — O.K?'

Stanley always ended sentences with '— O.K?' when he was annoyed. D. gave up then, but always tiptoed down the corridor to listen outside Will's door for signs of life after a quarrel was over.

D. began to walk home in the evenings, and saved fourpence a time. He could then buy a sevenpenny cheese sandwich in Cascarini's the following day.

The walk home was about four miles, over a level road with wide pavements. It was pleasant enough at first, despite his mother's complaints when he arrived home late. The walk took well over an hour. Later in the year when the clocks were put back and it got cold, wet and windy, he gave it up and went back on the train.

For a week he went without a midday meal as he had done through most of the summer, but he began to get headaches in the afternoon and his stomach rumbled. One morning before leaving home for work he furtively picked out a tin of sardines from the food cupboard at home and slipped it into his pocket.

At lunchtime he opened the tin and began to eat it in the relative privacy of the postroom. He had forgotten to bring a fork, but he ate with his fingers, confident he would not be disturbed. It was delicious. He could have eaten more. He put the empty tin on the desk and began to lick his fingers clean of oil.

To his mortification Eirlys came into the room, and saw him lick his fingers. Her eye moved to the empty tin. She must thing I'm a savage, thought D., eating from a tin with my fingers. But Eirlys said nothing. She was twenty-four, and came from Llandybie with the Ammanford crowd. She was small and clean and wore thick glasses and no make-up. Her hair was mousy blonde and very long, though sometimes she rolled it into a bun. She always smiled at him.

Now, she pushed a few envelopes into boxes on the wall and smiled at him. 'Would you like a couple of sandwiches, D.?' she asked. She added quickly, 'I've brought too many today and I can't finish them. It would be a pity to waste them.'

Overcome with shyness, D. nodded, silent.

'I'll just go and get them,' she said.

D. quickly wrapped the sardine tin in an old envelope and put it in the wastepaper basket. He wiped his fingers in a grubby handkerchief and waited.

She brought the sandwiches and gave them to him with a smile and left without a word.

When he opened the grease-proof paper he was surprised. There was enough to feed a hungry man. She certainly had brought too many sandwiches that day. He ate them all, and the apple.

He spent the best afternoon at work since he started there. He worked willingly and hard, without the tiredness and headaches he was accustomed to. It was a good experience.

Eirlys brought him sandwiches every day after that. She also tried to teach him arithmetic, so that he could make some progress out of the world of an office boy that he now occupied. D. found her teaching difficult. He perspired, felt hot and uncomfortable at her closeness, and was worried that she might park her breasts on his arm or pat his bum. But she did none of these, and persisted valiantly with him for weeks before she recognised his plight and gave up, tactfully.

'Never mind, D. I know you can do it. If I can, you can. It's just a question of persistence,' she said kindly. But D. knew it was more than that. He just could not 'see the light' as his father often said with a hint of sadness in his voice.

★   ★   ★

When he had been at the job for a year, he had a pay rise, to two pounds three shillings a week. His allowance went up to ten shillings, and he could afford to buy beans on toast three times a week. Eirlys still brought him sandwiches on Fridays, though he had grave misgivings about this sometimes because there was meat in them quite often. Eating meat on Fridays was forbidden by the Pope. D. consoled himself by supposing that the rule applied only to people who had a choice.

The beans on toast three times a week didn't go on for long. He tore a hole in his trouser knee one day as he scrambled over rocks at Mumbles. His mother was not pleased.

'Carelessness,' she snapped. 'Sheer carelessness. I'm not going to mend them. Besides, you need a new pair of trousers for work. Those are looking shabby.'

And they were. He had worn the same pair to school, together with a sports jacket that had once been Uncle Cliff's. They were the only trousers he had, so they never got washed.

'You can buy another pair,' said his mother. 'Now that you're getting ten shillings a week you can afford it.'

D. was aghast. New trousers were three pounds a time. It would take months to save up.

'But Mam ...'

'It will teach you to take care of yourself,' she said. 'Trousers don't grow on trees. I don't know why you have to go running around on rocks by the sea anyway. There are plenty of other useful things you could do.'

'Like what?' asked D. resentfully.

'Well, there's, well ... ' his mother stumbled. 'The garden,' she said. 'Yes. The garden. You could help your father. He's been slaving away out there in all weathers on his own. A growing boy like you should be glad of the exercise. It would do you good.'

He sewed the triangular tear in his trousers very carefully. After he had sponged and pressed it, the mend was undetectable. He felt quite proud of himself.

His mother said nothing, and quickly appeared to forget the whole episode. But he developed an anxiety about his clothes. Sooner or later things would wear out. Already his shoes felt paper-thin under the ball of his foot on stony ground. How on earth was he to pay for a new pair? New shoes cost over a pound when he last looked in a shop window.

★   ★   ★

He asked his father for a patch of garden to look after and grow things of his own.

'What are you going to grow in it?' his father wanted to know.

'I'm not sure,' said D. And he wasn't. It was just a feeling that he would like a bit of garden. After all, there was plenty of it.

'Well, you let me know what you want to grow and I'll give you a bit,' said his father sceptically.

D. finally settled for flowers. He studied gardening books in Oystermouth library, and discussed them with Will at work. He finally worked out a plan that would yield a large oval mound of blooms that would last from May to August. There would be short, very bright red flowers on the outside, rising gradually to tall blue and purple blooms at the centre, creating an upturned bowl effect. To enhance the effect he would sow the seeds in a spiral. This meant that he would need to make up a mound of soil to raise up the shorter blooms as they flowered under the taller ones.

His father approved, and gave over to him a small patch of ground very suitable for his plans.

He dug and raked the soil, combing it and sifting out stones and weeds, building up two mounds carefully. He sowed the seeds with precision and care, watering them in. When he had finished he stood back with satisfaction. Now it was only a matter of wait and see.

The task took all of Saturday and a large part of Sunday, but it was much more satisfying than walking aimlessly around the beach. He had already learned that he had to walk purposefully, as though he was going somewhere, when he encountered groups of females on the sands. They glared at him suspiciously if he walked past slowly.

For two weeks he inspected the mounds carefully, watering and weeding them. Small green shoots began to appear, and with increasing interest he began to consult more gardening books, to see how he could expand his garden. He even considered buying seeds.

At the end of two weeks he came home from work, had his evening meal and went to his patch of garden. It had been a hot day, and the seedlings would want water.

There was nothing there. The mounds were gone. All the tiny seedlings were scattered, shrivelled and beyond saving.

He stood in shock. The mounds had not been stepped on, or kicked accidentally. They had been systematically levelled, and the marks of a rake were plain to see.

When he had convinced himself that what he saw was real, he returned to the house, slowly and in a confused mind.

218

His mother was in the kitchen. 'What happened to my patch?' he asked.

'Oh, I raked it over,' said his mother. 'Those two mounds looked like dogs' graves,' she laughed.

He said nothing. He was stunned. He went outside and looked down the steep garden at his patch, bare and flat, brought to nothing by such ignorance. He felt the same anger of nameless injustice as he had when he was twelve, and his pet rabbit had been stolen by some of the Gwili gang. Then, he had walked down to Gwili gang territory and demanded it back, and to his surprise two sixteen-year-olds had handed it to him.

There was nothing he could do about his patch. It had been thoroughly destroyed.

He didn't try again. The garden, in all its different parts, was not his. None of it would ever be his own to use as he would want.

* * *

Later that year there was activity in the town centre. A new road was being built, it was rumoured. It would be a modern two-lane through roadway and be named The Kingsway. It would cut through a lot of old side streets that were now just pathways through rubbled bomb sites, and be the main shopping focus of the town.

D. went to watch in his lunch hour. He could see the beginning of an outsize roundabout, and the width of the new road was surprising. People watching the works talked about how the town would look when rebuilding was complete, and there was even mention of the wartime bombing as a 'blessing in disguise' that had cleared so much of the old and decaying parts without the need for planning permissions. There was optimism in the air, and a sense of good things about to happen in the town.

* * *

D. nursed his clothing as though he was on a cold desert island. His shoes leaked, his socks had embarrassing holes at the heels so that he didn't like going up the stairs to the top deck of public transport if there were any people climbing behind him, and the collars of his shirts were frayed. Uncle Cliff's jacket stood up well, and the elbows were only slightly greasy, though the inside of the breast pocket and a large part of the lining had rotted away and continued to come away in handfuls unless he was careful. He regretted not having checked on the stopper of the small aspirin bottle of sulphuric acid he had filled in the chemistry laboratory at school. He sometimes wore his father's ties, hoping he wouldn't notice. Luckily his father had been relocated to Grovesend, a steelworks with large offices out Llanelli way, and he left early to catch the steam train at Blackpill, so D. could nip upstairs when he had left and take his pick from the wardrobe.

This arrangement didn't work too well when it came to his father's socks. There were loud complaints about strange holes in them, and D.'s mother was overcome with shame at the thought of her man going to work in an office with holes in his socks.

'But they're new, Frank. I bought these just a few weeks ago.' She held up the pair with the largest hole, a defensive, injured expression on her face. D. watched, silent, apprehensive.

His mother's voice suddenly changed. 'Have you been wearing your father's socks, you cheeky bugger?'

D. was silent. There was no point in denying it.

'Right. You'll pay for these. You walk to work if you have to. And back. They cost three and eleven a pair. You don't know how to look after things, that's your trouble. I'll take it out of your next week's pay.' She folded the socks and laid them aside. 'I'll have to darn these now. I've a good mind to make you do it, you naughty boy.' She turned to D.'s father. 'See what I'm up against, Frank? How can I manage things like this?'

D. thought she was going to cry, as she sat down and put her head in her hands. His father got annoyed with D. as he saw this distress, evidence of the strain of trying to look after a son who had worn holes in his father's new socks.

'Get out. Go on. Out of my sight,' shouted his father with contempt. 'Look at what you're doing to your mother. Go on. Out.'

* * *

Christmas came and went. It was a tense and difficult time. D.'s mother was in a terrible mood, and his sisters fought like cats for days. His father was glum, and D. felt depressed and angry at all the emotional storms tearing apart the festive season.

That year his father set up a drinks table in the lounge. It was a grubby old kitchen table tactfully hung to the floor with a shiny clean table-cloth, and it held a bottle of scotch and half a dozen tiny glasses.

D.'s mother insisted that it be called a 'bar', because she had recently seen a film where the hero had a bar in his lounge and could help himself to a drink whenever he liked.

'The only thing is, we can't shut it away when it's not in use,' she said. 'Otherwise it's just like the one I saw in that film.'

After midnight Mass at Nazareth House and a weary, hair-raising trek over the lonely, cold common road, they all had a drink from the bar. Sometimes a neighbour or two would join them after being pressed embarrassingly hard by D.'s parents, who were convinced that they would be impressed by the display of ready liquor. There would follow an hour of meaningless talk, mainly concerned with the style of the midnight Mass and the priest's sermon. It was invariably critical. But, D. reflected, what is there that is new or refreshing to say about an event that had taken place the better part of two thousand times already? What could any priest say in A.D. 3000, or A.D. 5 million?

They drank whisky from glasses that were meant for cherry brandy or crème de menthe, and which required constant refilling by a gleeful host convinced that the guests were taking things seriously. Perhaps he hoped there would be a sing-song, and he was always disappointed when everyone left stone cold sober after three or even four glasses of scotch.

The early hours of Christmas morning were anticlimactic; tired out of their minds, a slow low glow of expectation for the morning and its tame surprises held in feebly-wrapped parcels whose contents were already well known, they listened wearily to discussion about how long to cook the turkey, was there enough lemonade and would the ice-cream van be around. D. and his sisters went off to bed, leaving their parents arguing in scarcely muted voices above a clattering of pans, to prepare for the ultimate boredom of Christmas lunch.

*   *   *

For his birthday his father suggested that if he bought a bike, D. could repay him over the next twelve months. D. could hardly believe his luck. He couldn't ride a bike, but it seemed easy enough, and just think of the places he could go with it! He might at last ride out to those wonderful black and red cliffs he had spent so much time looking at from his bedroom window in Mayhill, and the glittering water he had seen in the setting sun at Loughor, as well as the Gower beaches he remembered so well.

The bike was the latest roadster model from Raleigh, and cost eighteen pounds. It had dropped handlebars, and a dynamo set into the hub of the front wheel. With its showy cable brakes and brightly coloured logos he felt no shame in cruising the streets. It had six gears, and could be ridden up the steepest hill.

It didn't take him long to master the machine, though he did have quite a few nasty spills. He marvelled at the ease with which he could travel to every corner of the town, and grew more and more adventurous as the weather improved with approaching summer. Life took on extra meaning, and on Saturdays he donned his shorts, cut himself sandwiches, put a shilling in his pocket for a bottle of lemonade, and took off as early as he could.

He bought a mile-counter and fixed it to his bike. He was surprised to find how far he was travelling. On one exhausting trip to Cardiff and around the valleys he clocked 197 miles one fine Saturday.

He cycled to and from work, and the fares he saved were claimed by his father as repayment for the bike. Cycling was fun in the fine weather, but tough going in the rain. He couldn't afford a cyclist's cape, and sometimes arrived in work soaked to the skin. His father suggested that he buy one of the new plastic macs, transparent raincoats that could be folded up and put in a pocket, but even though he reluctantly agreed, he couldn't afford one of these either, at twenty-five shillings a time. So he got wet, but fitter and healthier as the summer drew on.

His thighs grew enormous muscles, and Glenys complimented him on his firm bum, much to his embarrassment. Marion hadn't spoken to him since the pontoon scandal. It would be his first, but certainly not last, experience of being snubbed by a female outside his family. He couldn't understand it at first, and bade her good morning as he had always done, to her and everyone else. After a while he recognised hostility, and gave up. It didn't affect him very much. He had no particular feelings for her, except that she had caused him immeasurable embarrassment since he had joined the office. Will was of the opinion that D. was mad not to take advantage of her, and if D. didn't like her behaviour, he should give her a really sexy hug next time she hung herself around his neck, even give her a pelvic thrust, to frighten her off and she wouldn't do it again. But D. knew if he did that, she would probably conclude he was more worldly wise than he really was, and embarrass him further. As it was, she had taken to following him into the cellar when he was on one of his lonely filing jobs, running her hands all over him while she lingered on the excuse of wanting a light for her cigarette.

And now she wouldn't talk to him. He was thankful, in a way — it was one less problem for him to face each day.

But it began to spread. Several of the girls in the pool ignored him when he greeted them. He found this disconcerting, and when he asked one of them what was wrong she soon put him right, as with a snort and a toss of the head she swept past without a word, leaving him standing in surprise. He pondered this, and began to realise that he was up against something that was all too familiar in his own home — girls indulging in bullying.

'Give a dog a bad name,' said Will. 'That's what they call it.' He looked at D. with some sympathy. 'Do you know that saying?'

D. nodded, only half sure. He had gone to Will to ask him what it all meant.

Will looked at D. carefully and after a long pause he said, 'Stay away from Marion. She's no good.' He patted D.'s arm in encouragement, and turned to leave. 'Look ahead, D. You've still got lots of choices ahead.' He gestured with a wave of his hand. 'This is a small place,' he said. 'There's a big world outside.'

On his way home that evening D. thought about it. Give a dog a bad name. Was Will advising him to leave the office? To go somewhere else? It was October now, many months after the pontoon business, so what had D. done that had offended anyone in the office? It had something to do with Marion of course, though he couldn't think what.

He arrived home depressed and silent. His elder sister was the only one of the family in the house.

She read his morose state of mind, and instead of offering sympathy, she attacked.

'Are you drunk again? Don't think that you can treat me as you like because you've had too much to drink. I'll take you on any time, my boy.'

Drunk? What was she talking about? Treat her like what? He turned and went outside. There was a good view of the sea from the garden. He thought. Last Christmas he did have more beer at the office party than he should have, but then he had had fun with his sister over it until his head had cleared. Now, she had trawled this up for her own reasons.

She followed him outside. 'You just wait. I'm telling Mam when she gets home. Coming home here drunk. Throwing your weight about and me with no protection. You wait.'

She was bullying him, he realised, but he could do nothing about it. He felt more hurt than anger: his elder sister had been a source of comfort in the past. Her goodwill was something he clung to, and had no wish to lose. She was the only one real friend he had. He walked away down the steep garden path, deeply depressed.

Later he returned to the house and quietly took his bike out of the shed. He tucked his trousers into his socks and rode off, turning the front wheel into car-free streets with no clear objective in mind but to work off his frustration.

His mother was waiting for him as he stowed his bike in the dark shed.

'What's this? Your father's waiting for you. Pushing your sister about like that. And let me tell you, my boy, don't you dare come home here into my house drunk. I've seen enough of that kind of thing in my life, drunken men coming home to beat up their wives and children. I'm not having that sort of thing here in my home, you understand?' She wagged a finger at him aggressively. 'Now get in there and face the music, my lad. See what your father has to say.'

His father didn't have a lot to say.

'You been drinking, D.?'

'No, Dad, of course not.'

'Alright.'

He prepared his own meal that evening. His mother refused to do anything for a boy 'who beat up his harmless sister, and it was time he learned to do things for himself anyway'.

* ★ *

In his lunch hour the next day he signed up at the R.A.F. Recruiting Office in town for a five-year term. He couldn't have given a reasoned explanation for his action. But uppermost in his mind would have been the need, the absolute necessity, to get away, the longing to cut himself off and to make a fresh start, to leave behind a world where he didn't belong, where he felt out of place, where everyone else seemed to know exactly where they were going and what had to be done next.

A small triumph lay in telling Stanley that afternoon. Stanley took pride in his claim that he had been a tank driver during the war, but D. was sceptical. Driving tanks in Norway? With all those mountains? D. never voiced his thoughts, but it seemed that all the men in the office had been heroically employed in the war, though none had anything to show for it. Eric, the clerk who looked after the Ynyscedwyn group of mines, seemed the only honest one among

224

them, admitting he had been a clerk, spending all his time in Britain. He was scathing about the other men's claims, terming them as 'shooting the shit' as they boasted of action in famous theatres.

Now D. would be able to understand the background to their claimed lives in uniform.

His mother was very angry. Not because she thought he had done something foolish, but because he had told his grandmother first.

'There was I,' said his mother, 'knowing nothing — my own son. And Nana knew all about it.' Her lips clamped together, forming furrows of meanness. 'My own son,' she repeated. 'And me not knowing. I felt stupid when she told me. Why didn't you tell me first, eh? Wait till I tell your father. He'll have something to say.'

She had nothing to say about his decision to leave home.

His father shrugged. 'Well, if that's what you want to do.'

D. suspected that his father was relieved that at last D. was taking his life into his own hands and moving on. 'You should have told your mother first though. She's quite upset.'

Curiously, D. found himself on the verge of laughter. He didn't care. A week from now he would be free of it all.

He had told his grandmother because he knew she would be the only one in his family who would show interest. Besides, she had always been friendly to him, and since he was excited by what he had done, he saw no harm in sharing the news, and why should there be secrecy, as though he was pregnant or something?

The R.A.F. required him to collect a signature witnessing his own, which should be from a civic stalwart such as a policeman (he didn't know any), a teacher (he wouldn't ask one of them if he could help it) or a minister of religion. The only minister he could think of was the parish priest at St David's, near the Russell Street Mumbles train depot. He went to mass sometimes at St David's, usually when his mother was in a bad mood and threatened to nag all the way to Nazareth House and back. It wasn't so much the nagging and snarling muttered abuse that he minded: it was the shameful change that came over her as she entered Nazareth House to be greeted by the nuns before the mass began. Simpering with self-centred importance she smiled and nodded her way past the nuns, her head high in smug happiness. After all, her husband counted all the money after the fête and gala, didn't he? And the annual flag day, too.

D. found her behaviour profoundly embarrassing. It was not too awful when she was in a good mood, because the contrast in her performance was not as glaring. If only the nuns knew, he thought.

The parish priest was not pleased to see him. D. had cycled to the church in the evening after his evening meal. Seven o'clock was a bad time, apparently. The priest smelled heavily of whisky, and in the dark doorway of the presbytery he moved unsteadily on his feet.

'I don't know you,' he said when D. had explained his mission. 'Where do you usually go to mass?'

'Nazareth House,' said D.

'Why don't you go there?'

'The priest is only a visitor. He's not there during the week,' said D. 'Besides, I often come to St David's.'

'I still don't know you. But you'd better come in.' The priest reluctantly led him inside. He sat down heavily on a faded brocade easy chair and squinted at the form D. had given him.

'It says here you're only seventeen.'

'Yes, Father. I'll be eighteen in March.'

'Bit young to go off fighting, aren't you? You could be killed.'

D. had no intention of fighting, or of being killed. He said so.

'Hm,' said the priest. After a long pause he muttered, 'Well, I suppose you know what you are doing,' and to D.'s relief he signed the form.

'Close the door after you,' said the priest as he poured a drink into a glass.

D. left without a word. There was nothing to stop him now. He didn't need any form of release from his father, even though he was a minor. All he had to do was go to the R.A.F. Recruiting Office, collect his free railway ticket and go.

Chapter Twelve

He set off on a Thursday morning in the first week of December, 1950. The weather was mild, which was just as well, because he didn't have either a raincoat or winter coat. In his pocket he had four shillings, and a packet of ten Player's cigarettes which his father had handed to him with a self-conscious air of generosity before setting off for work. D. had hoped he might give him five shillings, or even half a crown, since he already had two hundred cigarettes and an engraved case presented to him by the office staff at Wind Street last Friday. He had been touched by this farewell presentation: he had no idea that they thought well enough of him for such a generous gift.

Two other young men shared his journey to Paddington.

Owen came from Llanelli and was twenty years old. He was about to start his national service. He was cheerful and friendly, and was seen off by his girlfriend, who was short, fat and had appalling yellow and green teeth. It was the first time D. had ever seen anyone with green teeth, and he found it repulsive. Hadn't anybody told her about it, he wondered? He marvelled that Owen could hug and kiss her as he did on the platform before the train pulled out.

Gwynne lived in Haverfordwest and was already tired of the train journey by the time it arrived in Swansea. He too was friendly, though he talked a lot less than Owen once the journey was under way. Gwynne had signed on for three years, and like D. was therefore a regular. Owen would be paid only four shillings a day, less tax, while regulars got seven shillings a day less tax.

Forty-nine shillings a week was much the same as D. had been getting at his office job, but, Gwynne told him reassuringly, all his clothing would be paid for and his meals would be free. D. thought about the uniform, and wondered if he would like it. The only head cover he had ever worn was his school cap, a showy affair of black with yellow rings that he self-consciously tucked into his blazer pocket once he was out of sight of his mother, who was adamant that he wear it 'proudly, to show everybody that he was in the secondary school'. Soon he would be wearing a beret, with a brass badge which had a crown on it.

Gwynne was twenty-one, even older than Owen, and he quietly took charge when they arrived in London. He had been to London

227

before, he said, and knew the way. D. kept quiet about his own experience of London travel. It had been a long time ago, and he feared they might expect him to lead the way if he said anything.

Their destination was Cardington, in Bedfordshire. They caught a train out of London at King's Cross. It wasn't a long journey, but the carriage was stone cold, draughty and filthy. D. had no idea travel could be so uncomfortable and was very glad when they reached their destination. A short trip by bus and they had their first sight of the R.A.F. station.

D. gazed at the enormous hangars with amazement. It must have shown in his face for Gwynne smiled and said, 'The whole world could say their prayers in that one'. He nodded to the largest building, a monster of featureless steel sheeting out of all human scale, bulging out of the rolling green countryside in faded, vulgar camouflage, as wayward and out of place as a double-decker bus on a bowling green.

The late afternoon was getting colder, and the wind sighed across the miles of flat ground behind the hangars, washing against the huge buildings to continue its way in tumbling, chilling gusts, and D. found it impossible to protect himself from the swirling uncertainty of it. He had never felt so thoroughly uncomfortable in his life. He sincerely hoped things would improve.

They spent an hour being documented and checked, and were joined by thirty or so others, mostly young like himself, others not so young. D. guessed that one or two of them were as old as thirty. That puzzled him, but he didn't ask any questions. He'd find out soon enough, he thought.

It was getting dark now, and D. was very cold, thirsty and hungry. None of the buildings the group trotted through seemed to have anything remotely to do with aircraft or flying. The whole place seemed filled with temporary huts crammed with clerks who sat at shabby desks which were covered with mountains of papers and files. There was no hint of even the smell of cooking to give some hope that there might be just the smallest promise of a break for food and drink. And perhaps a chance to warm frozen hands and feet.

After rebellious mutterings from the older men the group was eventually shown into a small dining room.

'This is the mess,' said the tired but friendly sergeant who had been conducting them around all afternoon. There were some snickers. 'Please don't judge the R.A.F. from your experience this afternoon. There were some mistakes by the admin people. Tomorrow will be different.'

They had a boiled egg, hard as a rock, and a sausage roll with a skin as tough as a football. D. looked around at the the others to see how they were tackling the sausage. One of the older men sat opposite, and D. watched as he took out a clean handkerchief, popped the sausage into it and put it into his jacket pocket.

He smiled at D. 'You can't cut the skin,' he said, nodding at the others as they chased the rubbery goods around their plates with choice language and blunt knives. 'But the meat inside is okay. Take it back to the billet with you. I'll lend you my penknife.'

A pint of hot tea and the boiled egg worked wonders. D. began to warm up and feel less dejected as they wound their way across the station to their billets where they would spend their first night.

The accommodation was freezing cold. The group was split into two, and the man with the penknife was separated from D. as they filed into the wooden hut to spend the evening in shivering discontent. Luckily Owen was still in his billet group, so he had at least someone familiar to talk to.

The hut had only two pale electric lights for the twenty-four beds. There was a stove in the centre, and a small bunker filled with coke, but there was no wood to start the fire.

Nearly everyone was in bed by nine o'clock. The harsh cotton twill bedsheets were icy, the blankets heavy and cold, the mattress hard as wood, and the pillow felt like it had been cut from a lorry tyre. D. slept the sleep of exhaustion, like most of the others.

* * *

They all had medical examinations, and were lined up stripped to the waist and bare-footed to be processed by a tired Medical Officer and a short fat orderly who weighed and measured them and called out his opinion of their build and condition.

'Five feet ten. Fat. Looks O.K.' The orderly waved away the man in front of D. The Medical Officer scribbled the details in a thick file of papers, swung around in his swivel chair to run a stethoscope over his man, glanced quickly at the genitals and returned to his file.

D. stepped on to the height rule and then the scales.

'Six feet. And a bit. Nine stone, dead.'

The M.O. looked up sharply. 'Six feet and only nine stone?' he said. 'Let's have a closer look.'

He examined D. closely. This was a setback to D. He hadn't even thought about medical unfitness. If he was rejected now, he would have to return home. It was a dreadful prospect.

'Ribs,' said the M.O. 'Ever had rickets?'

Rickets, thought D.? Weren't they something that poor children living in city slums had?

'Your legs are O.K. but you've got a very poor build,' said the M.O. 'You need to eat more.'

'Yessir,' D. agreed. But where would he get more, he wondered. For the time being, as far as he could see, he would get only what he was given.

The M.O. returned to his file, waving D. to join the growing number of young men passed as fit. D. sighed with relief.

★   ★   ★

They stayed at Cardington for three days. Mysteriously, Gwynne had disappeared. No one had seen him after the first night, and it was said that his bed had not been slept in. There was a sorting-out process under way, and men were being allocated strange letters and passwords to use at the new stations to which they were shortly to be posted. They were all given small slips of paper, after a swearing-in ceremony, which held their service number. They must remember this number, they were told, on pain of severe punishment. D. never met anyone who had forgotten it.

The promise of better days to follow the first did not materialise. The weather grew bitterly cold, with a severe frost on the first morning. For the first time in his life D. began to worry on his own behalf about his welfare, and on one of the endless treks around the station with the group he stole an empty box file he saw standing unguarded on a desk. He knew there would be thick cardboard and pieces of plywood in the file to break up, and with care and skill it would serve to light a fire in the coke stove that evening.

The box file was enthusiastically torn to pieces by many willing hands that second evening, and there was much praise for D.'s initiative. He was pleased by that.

Only half the file was used, since nobody had any idea how long they would be in frozen Cardington, but it was quite enough to start a roaring fire in the stove, which soon began to glow red and so hot that the blankets on the nearest bed began to steam. The beds were moved, and everyone sat or stood around the fire, where the older men told tales of the wartime R.A.F. Now D. had the answer to his unspoken question: the older men had been unable to settle in civilian life, and had re-enlisted in the service.

The evening passed quickly enough, and the heat of the stove made everyone sleepy so that by ten o'clock they were all in bed. Tonight D. warmed quickly between the cold sheets and his painfully icy feet of the day before were just a memory.

On the third day they were issued with their uniforms. They were badly fitting and uncomfortable, and D. was disappointed, but he did get his first pair of underpants. They felt strange as he pulled up his trousers around them, but he was encouraged by the extra warmth they gave. He would wear them always from now on, he resolved.

They packed their civilian clothes into the suitcases they had brought with them, and the suitcases were taken away into storage. They were told to buy black boot polish, Brasso for their uniform buttons and blanco for the webbing. D. felt the pinch as he forked out what remained of his four shillings. He hadn't had too many cups of tea at the N.A.A.F.I. canteen because he wasn't sure when he would get his first pay, and it was just as well. He had nothing left at all after he had paid for the spit and polish gear. He cadged a cup of tea from Owen that evening.

They were roused at six a.m. on the fourth day. Breakfast was the same as the previous days: two scoops of mashed potato and a sausage with a spoonful of gravy, the gravy congealed long before it completed its journey from hot-plate to table. The mashed potato has strange hard lumps in it and the sausage was knife-proof, small and undercooked. Along with a dozen other men, D. had been putting his sausage in his pocket and reheating it on the sizzling stove top until the skin shrivelled and cracked, and could be peeled off bit by bit. That way, the sausage could last for ten or fifteen minutes, nibbled at like a piece of seaside rock.

This morning was different. They were being posted to a basic training unit, and would not be going back to a toasting fire that evening.

'Typical bloody army,' muttered one of the older men. 'Start getting comfortable and they have to pull you up by the roots. Typical.'

Most of them left the sausage, chiefly because there was no time to eat it. It seemed to D. that they had no sooner sat down than there were shouts of: 'Everybody out. Line up outside'.

They lined up. At a freezing table outside they were handed frozen packets of sandwiches in grease-proof paper and then rushed off to their billets. They collected all their new R.A.F. equipment of large pack, small pack, webbing, kit bag, mess tins and water bottle, clothing and knife, fork and spoon and scrambled on board the buses waiting to take them to the railway station.

231

On the bus they dozed in freezing, silent discomfort. Half an hour of misery brought them to the railway station, where they packed into six-a-side third class carriages which had no corridors. The train also had no heating. As they rumbled along at scarcely thirty miles an hour through the grey, wet, miserable countryside it began to snow, big fat flakes that cut visibility to a few yards beyond the grimy window.

Some of them smoked but nobody dared open a window. It was too cold. The compartment atmosphere grew into a frozen, grey, unbreathable fug which caught at their throats and made them cough. This was awful, thought D. Never had he wished time to pass quickly more fervently. His feet inside his new boots hurt with the cold, and he tried to work his toes to stir up some warmth, but they did not respond. He had literally lost touch with them.

Just after midday the train stopped at a station that nobody could identify, and they changed trains. This one had corridors, and they sat four a side in the dirty compartments, the smart ones avoiding the seats next to the sliding doors, where not only did the draughts slice into already numb ankles, but they were constantly being disturbed as the doors were opened and closed as men took advantage of the toilets at the end of the carriage.

They ate their sandwiches piecemeal. Thin dry white bread with no detectable sign of butter was clamped around slices of spam as thin as a razor blade. There was nothing to drink. As the interminable journey went on and on, some of them got desperate and drank water from the washbasin tap in the toilets, despite warnings that it was not suitable for drinking.

The journey took ten hours. When the train stopped and shouted commands were heard, ordering them to disembark, some of the men could not believe it. They thought that they were doomed forever to travel on this freezing train, like the Flying Dutchman, but this time on a sea of bungling bureaucracy.

In confusing darkness made worse by snow, now falling so thickly that it blinded everyone who took his eyes off his boots, they stumbled their way to a waiting bus that would take them to their final destination. Most of them were so exhausted that even the brightest spirits had become irritable, and courtesies were in short supply. No one talked. Above all they were hungry.

The journey was mercifully short. No one had any idea where they were. There was a rumour that they were not too far from Liverpool: one of the new recruits swore as he stepped off the bus, that he had passed through a certain town on his way south only a few days before, on his way to Cardington. Today he had passed through the same town on his way north. They were all too tired to care.

From the bus they were trudged by shouting N.C.O.s across a vast empty field of snow towards a row of dark single-storey buildings that never seemed to get any closer. D. looked around. There must be more than a hundred men here, he thought. As they tramped along in single file, treading in each other's footsteps through snow over six inches deep, he was reminded of the newsreel films of the war years, showing the prisoners taken by the Russians after the battle of Stalingrad, plodding in an endless stream over a snow-clad ridge into perilous captivity. There were ninety-six thousand of them, the commentary had said. It must have taken days for that column to pass, thought D. He wondered how it must have felt, marching off into the frightening Russian winter, hungry and freezing, not knowing what came next but fearing the worst.

They were marshalled into three groups outside three Nissen huts while their names were called out and checked. They were told which hut they would call their home and then hurried off to collect blankets and sheets at another hut. All the time they were shouted at and harassed by bullying N.C.O.s. One or two of them positively screamed, their voices breaking in anger as the weary recruits, stumbling-drunk with tiredness and cold, failed to perform the miracles of speed and dexterity demanded of them. D. was chosen to dish out two sheets and a pillowcase to each of the men as they filed past a table set up in front of a huge stack of blankets and bed linen. For once he made no errors, nor fumbled, as he passed the items from the stacked pile to the men as they moved past.

'Get your own, stupid man,' snarled a dumpy corporal at D. as the last man stumbled away, and D. followed the rest. They trudged back to their huts, where they dumped their bedclothes on the nearest vacant bed as they were told, then lined up outside to be taken to the mess for a badly needed meal.

Incredibly, the meal was mashed potato and sausage, exactly the same as the Cardington offering: uneatable except by the starving. D. thought of the Stalingrad Germans, and wondered if they had fared as badly as these recruits to the R.A.F. eight years later. Thank heavens for the tea, he thought. At least there was plenty of that, and it was hot.

Bullied back to their huts they prepared for bed. There was no hot water in the washrooms. There was no heating in the huts. Cold became every man's concern as it continued to snow and temperatures fell as the night progressed. They exchanged ideas on how to keep warm, but as one of them put it, 'It's not keeping warm. How the hell do I get warm in the first place?'

The accents ranged from Glasgow to Brighton, and Llanelli to Great Yarmouth. Apart from D. and Owen they were all complete strangers to one another. They would remain so throughout the six weeks of basic training, as self-interested preservation absorbed them: the cold, the new military discipline, drills and kit cleaning and inspections, the cold, the snow, and food. And the pneumonia.

Pneumonia struck the cold damp huts in early January. The men had straggled back to camp after a three-day break for Christmas. They came from every corner of the British Isles, and some had easier journeys than others, but they were all worn out by the effort. Within a week twenty-five of them were in the camp hospital fighting for their lives.

D. was the first in his hut to go down. In the evening when he should have been cleaning his kit, pressing his trousers and polishing his shoes to glittering insanity, he sat on the edge of his bed, unable to move. His head buzzed, he felt cold all over and his limbs felt like lead.

'You all right, D.?' D. looked up. Owen stood over him, query in his face.

D. shook his head, unable to speak.

'Get into bed,' said Owen. 'Swap beds with Jock. He's next to the stove. It's warmer there. I'll ask the corporal what to do.'

Owen moved off. D. still sat, unable to make a move.

'On your feet, lad.' The corporal stood over him, smart in his impeccable uniform, arrogant in his leadership and power.

D. started to rise as he was ordered, and fell.

'Right,' said the corporal. 'You. And you. Get him into bed. Next to the stove. Have him report sick in the morning.'

He stood, hand on hips. 'Come on, come on. Look lively. Get a bloody move on. He may be dead by morning. It'll be too bloody late then.'

They took his boots, trousers and tunic off and put him to bed.

'Keep your shirt on,' advised one of the older men. 'You'll stay warm and you won't have so much to do in the morning. We'll try and keep everyone quiet so you can drop off. Don't worry. You'll be okay.'

He went to sleep immediately. He was thankful for the help the others had given him. Even the corporal had shown a human face.

There were two corporals. They occupied two small rooms at one end of the hut and made everyone's lives miserable. They ran the day-to-day lives of the recruits, and took great delight in inflicting discomfort and unhappiness upon the men in their charge. To most, the corporals seemed devoid of understanding, but as always there was reason in the madness: how else was a group of rebellious young men to be moulded to obedience and unquestioning submission to pure silliness; what other way was there to ensure sacrifice of life, if necessary, for causes beyond understanding. Besides, once they left this place, after six weeks, they could forget most of everything they were forced to learn, and return to a near normal world.

The Medical Officer was in a foul mood.

'I hope you're really suffering, lad. I'm fed up with the string of men through here this morning. Sore throats, coughs and sniffles. They don't make men like they used to.' D. looked at him with glazed eyes. His temperature raged and his rib-cage felt as though it was wrapped tightly in barbed wire. He dare not cough. Speaking was an effort.

'Sir,' he said pointlessly.

'Get your coat off. Let's have a look at you.' The Medical Officer had a cigarette dangling from the corner of his mouth, his eyes screwed up in defence against the stream of biting blue smoke that crept up his cheek.

He couldn't make it. The greatcoat behaved like a steel jacket, completely resistant to his fingers, unyielding even to major muscular efforts of his arms.

'Are you deaf, man? Get it off. How the hell can I tell if you're ill with that bloody coat on?'

D. looked at the chair close by. He wondered whose it was, why it was there. Standing was such an effort. To get here this morning two men had been detailed off to help him from the hut. The Medical Officer's shouting had faded, and the small room he was in receded to the size of an Oxo cube, surrounded by pale yellow lights.

He awoke in a small room washed in a dark blue light. Two men in white coats held him in a sitting position in a bed much wider and softer than the bed he had slept in last night in the hut. He coughed, and instantly regretted it. The pain in his lungs was terrifying. He settled for a wheezing rattling in his throat that alarmed him but at least allowed him to breathe.

The two men wrapped something hot, wet and slimy around his back and lower ribs and gently lowered him back to the pillow.

'This one's bad,' said one of the men. 'He left it a bit late.'

They went away, and D. slept. The poultice was painfully hot and felt awful, but he didn't care.

Four days later he was moved to a larger ward with twelve others, all in bed, comatose, and they didn't move a head as he stumbled to his corner and collapsed into the bed he was shown.

It was another three days before D. summoned the strength to get out of bed to go to the toilet. A man in a white coat noted this, and D. was discharged as fit, albeit with two days' light duties, and ordered to rejoin his unit in the cold damp huts to continue his training.

He was touched by the sympathetic greetings on his return. Men who had been strangers suddenly turned into friends, and they helped him to catch up on a week of missed training, including the mysteries of rifle drill and clearing a jammed Bren gun. He dreaded the thought of being transferred to a new intake of recruits which would mean another two weeks here at the camp.

The snow lay around deeper than ever. None of the original fall had thawed, and it had snowed lightly for most nights that D. had spent in the camp hospital. It was bitterly cold, and every breath hurt as he marched in a daze up and down the parade ground and listened to plummy-voiced officers describe the need for respect of superior ranks.

The day following the expiry of his light duties allowance they were ordered to give blood for the local hospital. There was no question of volunteering: give blood or else.

D. refused. 'I've just come out of hospital,' he said to an incredulous corporal who had asked why he hadn't stepped forward.

'I don't feel very well,' said D.

'You don't look so fucking good either,' said the corporal, and D. quailed. What vengeful retribution could follow, he wondered.

It was a mild punishment. He had to practise his about-turns, solo, on the edge of the parade ground where everyone could see that he was a duffer who couldn't get things right. It didn't last long, and besides, as time went on he was far from being on his own as the exasperated corporals sent one man after the other to the edges of the parade ground to practise their drill movements. By the end of the afternoon there were so many of them out there they they were able to exchange jokes as they jinked and jerked their way through their weaknesses.

The weeks went by until they were in sight of the passing out parade. The food was awful, the cold a constant enemy. Few of them had taken a bath since they had arrived — there were no showers and only two baths far away in a frigid brick hut with no ceiling and no heating. The water was lukewarm too, and misty with concentrated minerals from long storage in a stagnant tank. Many of the men didn't trust the water, believing it to be specially dosed with a medication designed to interfere with their manhood. Most of the men had long since imitated the older hands, and warmed water on the stove in the evenings to shave before going to bed, which saved a lot of time in the morning.

Around this time, D. became aware of his lack of educational qualifications. More than this, he began to realise just how important they appeared to be. For two days the entire intake of new recruits had been given tests, and were now being screened for selection on their future in the R.A.F. D. hadn't given it a thought, he had to admit: thus far he had simply allowed himself to be swept along by the system. Now there were choices to be made, further efforts and disciplines to undertake. He would be required to emerge from the cover of the group, and show himself as an individual, to display initiative, strength of purpose, adaptability, possible leadership and above all, trainability. He must be able to show that it was worthwhile the R.A.F. spending time, effort and money on training and teaching him a useful occupation.

So said the officer who interviewed him. The officer was not all that much older than himself, D. thought. His teeth sparkled and he had a sun tan in the middle of winter, which was curious. He spoke with smooth, rounded vowels like the B.B.C. announcers and was completely self-confident, and talked to D. with the contrived friendliness of master speaking to servant. It was D.'s first encounter with the public school product, and he felt ill at ease with it. He was unwilling to be open and enquiring with the officer, feeling a deep distrust of his motives and the use to which his answers might be put.

'You've been to Grammar school, you say.' The officer moved papers around on his desk and gave D. a glittering smile. D. nodded. 'Yessir.'

'No certificates of any kind.' Perfect eyebrows rose above perfect blue eyes.

D. shrugged in embarrassment. 'No, sir.'

'You didn't do at all well at the R.A.F. tests for maths.'

'It was terribly cold, sir. And I'd just come out of hospital.'

The officer regarded him in feigned sympathy. 'Poor chap. Not too bad now, are you?'

'I'm okay now, sir. But I felt rotten when I sat the tests.'

'Yes, I understand that. But I'm afraid the results must stand, you see. We can't afford to give everybody a second go, can we?' He smiled engagingly at D., made written comments on papers with a gold-banded fountain pen and said, 'Thank you. Please rejoin your unit.'

D. saluted the young officer and left. He felt awkward, saluting. It seemed a silly thing to do, though everybody else did it all the time, and there was no benefit in avoiding it: there was an offence, it was rumoured, of failing to salute an officer, and the punishment was severe.

Back among the rest of the men he listened to the buzz of talk as careers were discussed. 'Aircraft engines,' said one. 'A year on a course, then automatic promotion.' 'Radar,' said another. 'Nine months course. Extra pay.' Owen was to be an airframe fitter, with a six months course. 'If I like it, I can go on and take other courses,' said Owen. 'Though I have to sign on for five years before they let me do that.'

D. felt lonely. There was no reason why he should be offered any of these interesting jobs, of course. He was well aware that they were beyond him, and it was too late to catch up now. He must await the decision of the powers that be.

After the passing out parade, a huge pointless ceremony which consisted of marching up and down a freezing, windswept, snow-covered square of expensively-laid tarmac, presided over by large, fat, elderly men in uniforms quite different to their own, who sat on very large boxes at one end of the square, they were dispatched to the four corners of the Kingdom clutching travel vouchers and reporting documents.

D. was assigned to Henlow in Bedfordshire, where he was required to report after three days' leave, barely enough time to allow him to recover from the journey.

Henlow was agreeable enough. A large sprawling camp with a public road running between the living quarters and the working sites, it had substantial brick-built, modern, centrally-heated accommodation, which was a wonderful relief after D.'s recent experiences.

He spent his first two days tramping every yard of road and pathway in the camp. He carried with him a large blue card which was divided into hundreds of intricate rectangles, each one bearing strange acronyms printed in tiny black print. Someone, somewhere, had to initial a rectangle, transfer his particulars to a register, and then he was free to go on to the next one. Some of the more self-important clerks entered a full-flourish signature instead of initials, and intruded into neighbouring rectangles, much to their owners' chagrin.

'What's this?' A small immaculate sergeant in the equipment store held up D.'s card in horror. Several heads turned. D. was tired, and his response was slow in coming. He should have smiled in a conspiracy of sympathy, but instead he stared blankly.

The sergeant was irritated by his silence and his lack of understanding.

'The signature, lad. In the box next to it. D'you see it? It's all over my box as well. How can I sign it if there's no room, eh?'

He slapped the card on the counter which stood between them. D. was at a loss. He hadn't signed it himself. The orderly at the Dentist's surgery had. He could hardly have told the orderly to write in small letters, even if he had known that his name was Kaposcwinskana.

'You'd better get another card, lad, so that I can have an empty box to sign.' He walked off.

D. stood, silent. He was appalled. He had collected seventeen signatures so far. Would he need to get them again? There must be another way.

A young airman came to the counter.

'Give me your card, quick.' He stole a glance at the nearby office where the sergeant sat, drinking a cup of tea.

D. handed him the card. The airman initialled the card quickly, wrote down D.'s number, rank and name on a piece of scrap paper and pushed the card back to him.

'It'll be okay,' he said. Sarge is fussy. He doesn't like the dentist, either.' He smiled. 'I see you've got the same initials as me — D.F. You got a billet yet?'

D. shook his head. He had spent last night in the transit hut, which was warm enough, but noisy with arrivals and departures of visiting personnel, lorry drivers mainly, staying for one night only.

'Make your way to hut 3B after tea this evening,' said D.F. 'There's a spare bed there. It's comfortable and out of the way.'

They became firm friends after that. D. reflected that D.F.'s words and his action over the card had been the first friendly experience that he had had in many weeks.

D.F. was a national service man. He bitterly resented the enforced two years taken out of his life for no apparent purpose, away from his career as a 'tackler' in a Lancashire cotton mill. As soon as he had finished his apprenticeship, he had been drafted into the R.A.F., and despite his demonstrable aptitude for complicated machines, he had been allocated to the lowly duties of 'Administration Orderly', the catch-all muck-bucket of ineducables and untrainables who shovelled coal for the married quarters on wet winter days and peeled potatoes when the cook wanted extra hands for a change of menu. Don, which was his name, D. learned, was fortunate in having duties in the equipment office, which was at least indoors with a regular cup of tea, though he grudged acknowledgement of his luck.

D. wondered why Henlow was there at all. Very rarely, a Tiger Moth took off from the grass field behind the hangars, and sometimes an articulated airframe transporter was seen grinding along the roads, but little else seemed to be happening. There was some training going on, he would learn, but what it was remained a mystery.

His life was very different now. The heavy weight of his dead and disapproving home town was a distant memory, and his short career at Wind Street was all but forgotten. He certainly never thought about Marion now, and the anguish she had contrived had faded to a detail of his past.

He settled into his new life quickly. Don showed him the ropes, and with few exceptions the young men around him were friendly and without malice. By the summer he began to feel a freedom of spirit that was at the same time strange, and not easy to deal with. He felt a desire to leap in the air, sing loudly at inappropriate times, even, God forbid, the confidence to complain about the food, which he was sometimes invited to do by a bored orderly officer on his rounds of the airmen's hut.

He did none of these things. Instead he played football and cricket on proper grounds, under proper rules, with full teams and stern referees — a goal was a goal and no arguments, and a four was a four when the umpire signalled it to the official scorer.

He discovered the library and his constant presence there was noted one day by no less a personage than the senior Education Officer.

'You spend a good deal of time in here, lad. Can I help you in any way?'

He seemed a kindly man. In his late forties, he sported none of the outward show of seniority designed to intimidate lesser mortals. He had no moustache, his cap was not bashed silly nor was his uniform crumpled. He had a slight northern edge to his accent and D. took to him immediately.

'I didn't do well in school, sir.' D. sought for words, and decided to be honest. 'I regret it now. I'm trying to catch up, as it were.'

'Do you want to go to university, then?'

D. wasn't sure what a university was. He remained silent in hesitation for so long that the Education Officer took up the question again.

'Have you any 'O' levels?'

'No, sir.'

'Hm. That's a different matter. You've been to Grammar school?'

'Yessir.'

The Education Officer thought. 'Tell you what,' he said finally. 'Can you come along tomorrow? Say six o'clock. You can try the standard R.A.F. tests. Much the same as an 'O' level. We'll see how you do, and then we can take it from there. What d'you say?'

D. was eager, and said so. The Education Officer was pleased. If he could save just one lost soul now and again it was worthwhile.

D. found no difficulties with the tests. He did so well that the Education Officer was suspicious.

'Are you sure that you have no certificates from school?' he queried. D. shook his head.

'Have you been talking to someone who has taken the tests recently, then?'

'No, sir. I don't know anyone who has.' The Education Officer nodded. 'You've done very well,' he said. 'What sort of work would you like to do in the R.A.F.?'

'Radar, sir.'

'I see no difficulties there,' said the Education Officer. 'Leave it to me, then. I'll start things moving for you.'

As he left the library D. sighed. For the first time in his life he felt a sense of belonging, an indefinable feeling that he had, or was about to, shake off a burden, to tear off a label hanging around his neck which read 'stupid'. Perhaps now he could join the human race.

A month later he began a nine-month course in radar. He worked hard, and found gaps in his knowledge which amused some of his fellow trainees on the course, but he covered them quickly, and the monthly status reports for the intake of sixty-five on the course showed him consistently third or fourth after tests.

He finished the course in fifth position, a failing he attributed to an impossible question on wave guides. Afterwards he lost no time in finding the answer.

Soon afterwards, he was posted to Germany. It was spring, 1952.

★ ★ ★

Conditions were good in Germany. D. found himself in a large block divided into small four-man rooms. There was central heating, double glazing, curtains, wood-block floors and individual lights. It was an old German Army barracks, and D. found himself reflecting on his early experiences in the R.A.F. It seemed that the Germans had looked after their military much more sensibly.

Discipline at this new station was much more relaxed. Unlike at U.K. establishments, there was a job to do here — the Russians were not so far away. There were very few National Servicemen, too, and this had a positive effect on morale, since most of the airmen thought of the R.A.F. as a career, not as a punishment for being a young man.

He soon found that the R.A.F. depended heavily on the Americans. There was an agreement known as M.D.A.P. — Mutual Defence Aid Program — which meant that the U.S. paid for everything in sight. D. attended several introductory courses in the American equipment, which he at first thought of as the Air Ministry's way of making him useful, but he quickly realised that the whole chain of radar coverage from Trieste to Trondheim was not British but American. Tuition and mastery of the U.S. system was essential, not just advantageous. Only the bulky, weighty and outdated radio equipment was British, presumably because the Air Ministry had been unable to persuade the Americans to pay for it. 'Straight out of the Thirties,' sniggered a U.S. Army Top-Sergeant of whom D. asked an opinion. 'We just shove ours on to a jeep. This stuff — ' he waved a hand over the British equipment, 'You have to build a vehicle around it. And a two-tonner at that.' And it was true. It was also so well-used that it looked like second-hand flea-market offerings.

The U.S. radar equipment was good. It was also very mobile. Known as the A.N.T.P.S. because the Americans called it that, it could be deployed by two small vehicles and set up almost anywhere inside an hour with skill and practice. A strategic ploy was to move a setup every three or four days to fool the Russians, though D. had his doubts about the usefulness of this. Pulse location equipment told them that the potential enemy had found their position within five minutes of starting transmission, and three or four days seemed to stretch things a bit.

Later in the year after he had completed his courses he was attached to the 2 Group Signals Unit that managed these light mobile radars. He went off with eight other men in three trucks, one stuffed with radar and radio gear, another with stores and the third as transport for passengers.

Sometimes they stayed at nearby R.A.F. stations or Army Camps, and tended the A.N.T.P.S. in shifts from comfortable quarters, exempt from the surrounding disciplines of the organised station. More rarely they attached themselves to U.S establishments, which they were reluctant to leave, so sumptuous was the American way of life. And they were friendly, too. Rarely was it possible for the ten p.m. relieving shift to take up their duties sober after an evening at the P.X.

For the next twenty-two months D. travelled most of the N.A.T.O. countries with the radar crews. Promotions came, keeping pace with his own quiet progress in catching up with wasted school years, and he learned to give orders as well as to take them.

At the end of these months, D. was in charge of a crew. His first trip as senior N.C.O. was in late March 1954 on Luneburg Heath, not far from a large R.A.F. flying station. Settling down for the first night after erecting their radar gear, the crew took the normal shift duties in four-hour spells.

At five a.m. next morning D. found himself free of watch. He didn't think it worthwhile sleeping for only an hour or so, when the normal day would resume.

'I'll take the kit wagon,' he said. 'I'll get some bacon and eggs from the cook at the station. We've got enough skillets. And we'll heat it up when I get back.'

He drove off with Jamie, the newest man in the crew, who had to learn the ropes.

It was still dark, and the air was crisp. All the signs of imminent spring were around them, and they trod lightly despite their tiredness.

The cook was sympathetic, and loaded them with enough breakfasts for ten men. They departed in gratitude, pleased at the welcome they had been given, even more pleased by the thought of the welcome the crew would give them at the sight of all this hot food.

They drove quietly along the airfield perimeter. Near the end and close to the exit gate guardhouse, they passed a four-engined Lincoln bomber, engines running, propellers busy. It was getting light, and dawn was only minutes away with a clear green sky showing up a saw-tooth edge of pine tree horizon.

As the truck passed the bomber, a figure stepped out, waving them down. Even in the half light D. and his companion could see the scrambled egg on his cap.

D. stopped. Behind scrambled egg he could see at least a dozen men, most of them in flying gear.

'You the N.C.O. from 2 Group? Radar?'

D. got out of the driver's seat quickly. 'Yessir.'

'Know anything about A.N.T.P.S.?'

'Er yessir.'

'Right. We want you. We're short of a junior flight electronics engineer. We're taking off in ten minutes. You been up before?'

Up? thought D. Up where? He turned to the Lincoln, thundering and trembling on the tarmac a hundred yards away. Scrambled egg was telling him that he was to go on a flight in that machine. What an opportunity! Wait till he got back to base!

'No, sir.'

'Then now's your chance,' said scrambled egg. 'Go off with Warrant Office Leslie there, and get changed. As quick as you can.' He turned to walk back to the aircraft, and the engine noise swallowed him up.

D. turned to Jamie. 'Get the breakfasts off, back to the post. Get back to base by midday. Tell Chiefy what has happened.' As Jamie slid over to the driving seat D. said, 'I only hope there's enough documentation to cover this'.

Fifteen minutes later they were airborne, climbing slowly into a rising sun that washed the chilly March landscape in a yellow sheet of clean light.

His duties were simple: keep the three small sets of ground-scanning radar working. He sat on a small swivelling stool alongside the two radar operators, feeling utterly out of his depth, hoping to hell that nothing went wrong. The adrenalin flowed as the old bomber lurched in the occasional turbulence, and he began to wonder about parachutes. He glanced around furtively. No one was wearing a parachute. Everywhere he looked there were men, self-confident, competent, sure of themselves and what they were doing.

The plane thundered on. There were no windows in the fuselage, and D. had no idea where they were or where they were going.

After twenty minutes or so he began to relax. He took his eyes off the radars, and began to examine the plane. He was looking down the fuselage, wondering what all the electronic gear was for, when the missile struck. He didn't hear a sound. Nothing. But he saw the muddy yellow flash and the barrelling cloud of dust and fragments, the flailing wires and pipes, as the belly of the aircraft exploded.

★ ★ ★

The Court of Inquiry was held at his bedside. To be exact, all around it. Screens were drawn, chairs were hustled up, and men in

244

immaculate uniforms seated themselves around him. The only sounds were creaking knee joints and stretching trouser cloth. All the men were Senior officers, wearing scrambled egg on their caps and thick bands of pale blue edged in black on their sleeve cuffs.

They can't touch me, thought D. Not in my present state. I don't even have to salute them, lying here in plaster and bandages. And I'm not aircrew, so I can't be held responsible for my answers to any questions they ask. Besides, if things get embarrassing I can just fall asleep.

'Can you answer questions?' The Air Commander sitting closest on D.'s right spoke in the soft, plummy resonance of a man used to being listened to. Of course I can answer bloody questions thought D. resentfully. Did he think he was illiterate, or dumb?

'Yessir.'

'Good.' There was a stir amongst the assembled Court.

'Tell me. In your own words. What do you remember of the crash?'

In my own words, thought D.? Who the hell else's words would I use?

'Nothing, sir.'

'Nothing?' The Air Commander seemed disappointed. 'Nothing at all?'

'No, sir. Nothing.'

'Think, man.' His voice held an edge of impatience. 'No radar trace, no warning? No evasive move by the aircraft?'

'No, sir. Nothing.'

At a signal, all five rose, threw aside the screening curtains and disappeared.

Nurse Catch appeared. She smiled as she drew aside the chairs and clipped back the curtains.

'You sent them packing, didn't you? I doubt that they'll be back.' She looked at him slyly. 'What have you been up to?' she said quietly as she fiddled with his bedclothes.

D. was nonplussed. He said so. Sister Catch nodded and went away, slightly miffed.

★   ★   ★

Later that day a young man shuffled up to his bed in hospital slippers. He wore the blue shirt and red tie of the rehabilitation ward.

'Hello. I'm Steve. Next ward.'

245

D. nodded and told him his name.

'You had the brass here this morning.' It was not a question. Just an introduction for what was to follow.

'I knew they'd come to grief sooner or later.' There was a long pause. D. absorbed it in silence.

Steve looked out through the open window to the sunshine outside.

'You're the only one,' he said finally. 'Did they tell you?'

D. shook his head slowly. What was he talking about?

'No. They wouldn't, I suppose.' He turned to face D. 'They'll put you back at a desk. Keep you quiet. They won't let you out. How long you in for?'

'Five years. Eighteen months to go.'

Another long pause.

'The R.A.F. won't want you when you've finished here. When you're up and about again. But they'll make sure you don't tell anyone about that Lincoln.'

D. regarded him with surprise.

'Flying off-course, you see. Testing the enemy's reaction times, their chain of command, calibrating and locating the radar, where the signals go, who gives orders to scramble fighters, where they come from, and so on. They've been doing it for years.'

He smiled sympathetically at D.

'You were unlucky. Or lucky. Depends how you look at it. They didn't bother with air traffic this time. Just sent a S.A.M. — six up. You're the only survivor.'

There was silence.

'You'll be pretty crook after this lot.' Steve waved a hand over his bandages. 'Even in eighteen month's time. What'll you do when you leave the R.A.F.?'

D. hadn't thought about that. Now quickly looking forward he realised with a sinking feeling of massive failure what his course must be.

'Go home, I expect,' he said. 'To my parents.'